PRAISE FOR DEBORA[illegible] DRAGONFIRE NOVELS

EMBER'S KISS

"The Dragonfire series continues to delight its fans with the dragon shifters finding their destined mates and the danger they face as they complete their trials. If you love dragons, this series is sure to please."

—Romance Reader's Connection

"*Ember's Kiss* is another well-written, fascinating and amazing storyline in Deborah Cooke's Dragonfire series. Deborah creates a world of beautiful dragons and timeless love. I have loved Deborah's dragons since the very beginning and I was immensely pleased that she brought together the *Pyr* in this amazing tale."

—The Reading Cafe

FLASHFIRE

"Deborah Cooke is a dragonmaster of a storyteller...Lorenzo fills the pages with enigmatic glory only rivaled by his mate, Cassie, and I did not stop turning pages until the firestorm was ended."

—The Reading Frenzy

"Cooke's long-running series continues to be a sexy and thrilling winner!"

—Romantic Times

"Thrilling and unpredictable...*Flashfire* is another great addition on one of my favorite paranormal romance series."

—Paranormal Haven

Darkfire Kiss

"Deborah Cooke's Dragonfire novels are impossible to put down. *Darkfire Kiss* is no exception. I dare any reader to skim any part of this terrific story!"

—Romance Reviews Today

"Quick action, engaging prose, and hot sex."

—Publishers Weekly

"Another book not to be missed!"

—Fresh Fiction

"An action-packed, fast-paced romantic read."

—TwoLips Reviews

Whisper Kiss

"This is a terrific Kiss urban romantic fantasy...The author has 'Cooked' another winner with the tattoo artist and the dragon shape-shifter."

—Alternate Worlds

"Cooke introduces her most unconventional and inspiring heroine to date with tattoo artist Rox...Cooke aces another one!"

—Romantic Times (four and a half stars)

"*Whisper Kiss* by Deborah Cooke is now my unofficial official favorite!...Bursting with emotions, passion and even a real fire or four, I count myself lucky not to have spontaneously combusted! Don't miss this sizzling addition to Deborah Cooke's Dragonfire series—it is marvelous!"

—Romance Junkies

"Deborah Cooke has again given readers a truly dynamic

story in her Dragonfire chronicles."

—Fresh Fiction

Winter Kiss

"A beautiful and emotionally gripping fourth novel, *Winter Kiss* is compelling and will keep readers riveted in their seats and breathing a happy sigh at the love shared between Delaney and Ginger...Sizzling-hot love scenes and explosive emotions make *Winter Kiss* a must read!"

—Romance Junkies

"A terrific novel!"

—Romance Reviews Today

"All the *Pyr* and their mates from the previous three books in this exciting series are included in this final confrontation with Magnus and his evil Dragon's Blood Elixir. It's another stellar addition to this dynamic paranormal saga with the promise of more to come."

—Fresh Fiction

Kiss of Fate

"Second chances are a key theme in this latest Dragonfire adventure. Cooke keeps the pace intense and the emotions raging in this powerful new read. She's top-notch, as always!"

—Romantic Times

"An intense ride. Ms. Cooke has a great talent...If you love paranormal romance in any way, this is a series you should be following."

—Night Owl Reviews (reviewer top pick)

KISS OF FURY

"Those sexy dragons are back in the second chapter of Cooke's exciting paranormal series...The intriguing characters continue to grow and offer terrific opportunities for story expansion. Balancing a hormone-drive romance with high-stakes action can be difficult, but Cooke manages with ease. Visiting this world is a pleasure."

—Romantic Times

"The second book in Deborah Cooke's phenomenal Dragonfire series expertly sets the stage for the next thrilling episode."

—Fresh Fiction

"Entertaining and imaginative...a must-read for paranormal fans."

—BookLoons

"Riveting...Deborah Cooke delivers a fiery tale of love and passion...She manages to leave us with just enough new questions to have us awaiting book three with bated breath!"

—Wild on Books

"Epic battles, suspense, ecological concerns, humor, and romance are highlights that readers can expect in this tale. Excellent writing, a smart story, and exceptional characters earn this novel the RRT Perfect 10 Rating. Don't miss the very highly recommended *Kiss of Fury*."

—Romance Reviews Today

"Deborah Cooke has only touched the surface about these wonderful men called the *Pyr* and their battle with the evil dragons...I am dying for more."

—Romance Junkies

Kiss of Fire

"Cooke, a.k.a. bestseller Claire Delacroix, dips into the paranormal realm with her sizzling new Dragonfire series...Efficient plotting moves the story at a brisk pace and paves the way for more exciting battles to come."

—Romantic Times

"Paranormal fans with a soft spot for shape-shifting dragons will definitely enjoy *Kiss of Fire*, a story brimming with sexy heroes, evil villains threatening mayhem, death and world domination, ancient prophesies, and an engaging love story...An intriguing mythology and various unanswered plot threads set the stage for plenty more adventure to come in future Dragonfire stories."

—BookLoons

"Deborah Cooke has definitely made me a fan. I am now lying in wait for the second book in this extremely exciting series."

—Romance Junkies

"Wow, what an innovative and dazzling world Ms. Cooke has built with this new Dragonfire series. Her smooth and precise writing quickly draws the reader in and has you believing it could almost be real...I can't wait for the next two books."

—Fresh Fiction

Don't miss Deborah's paranormal young adult spin-off series:

The Dragon Diaries

Blazing the Trail

"There are so many twists in this book, I loved it. I could not put it down, and read it in a day. If you have read Deborah's adult books, with the adult dragons, then you will love this series with the kids!"

—Books Complete Me

"I have been a huge fan of Deborah Cooke for many years. When a new release comes across my path, I truly do a happy dance. Cooke has lived up to her previous work with *Blazing the Trail*. I loved how Zöe deals with the everyday issues in front of her while trying to save the world with the *Pyr* and fellow shifters."

—Fresh Fiction

Winging It

"[Cooke's] clever ability to convey what it means to be going on sixteen while being faced with dark, world-altering dilemmas has created a unique and compelling young-adult series bursting with magic, mayhem, and danger."

–Fresh Fiction

"Zöe is as kick-butt as ever...another fast-paced, well-thought-out novel in [Cooke's] Dragonfire universe. Teen readers will love that Zöe and her friends get to be the stars."

—Romantic Times

Flying Blind

"Whether you're young or just young at heart, you will equally enjoy this brand-new series by Ms. Cooke...It's entertaining, it's exciting and it's adventurous...a wonderful new series."

—The Reading Frenzy

"The first of a new dragon series sure to become a classic...Cooke has written a fantastic offshoot of her *Pyr* universe...After turning the final page, I sat for a moment with a sense of excitement I haven't felt since I finished my first of Anne McCaffrey's Pern books."

—Fresh Fiction

"This story crosses the boundaries. It will appeal to both teens and adults across the board. The story is engaging and fun. It's bringing to life a world of dragons and magic that appeals to all."

—Night Owl Reviews (5 stars, top pick)

"The writing is swift and fun, just like I'd imagine flying on the back of a dragon...If you're looking for a break from vampires and werewolves or you're a fan of Cooke's adult Dragonfire series, you won't be disappointed."

—All Things Urban Fantasy

"This. Book. Rocks."

—One a Day YA

"Zöe is a wonderful heroine—smart, strong and sympathetic."

—#1 New York Times Bestselling Author
Kelley Armstrong

Dear Reader;

I've always had a soft spot for Thorolf, the big passionate dragon of the *Pyr*. It's true that he'll do pretty much anything for a couple of steaks grilled rare or the attention of a cute waitress, but when it comes down to it, Thorolf always comes through for his fellow *Pyr*. I had a lot of questions about Thorolf that had to be resolved in his firestorm, including the reasons why he was so easy to underestimate. I knew that Erik, the leader of the *Pyr*, knew more about Thorolf's past or heritage (remember that Erik recognized Thorolf on sight and challenged him immediately) and had to figure out what it was. I had to wonder whether Thorolf was really as irresponsible as he tried to appear, or whether there was more to his story. (You can guess the answer to that.)

I was also intrigued by Chandra, the woman who pretended not only to be a boy but a thief, and who was tracking Viv Jason. She definitely had a secret, if not more than one, and I was as determined as Thorolf to find out more. I really enjoyed how the firestorm—and Thorolf—awakened new feelings in Chandra and showed her a side to living that she hadn't experienced in her many years of life. In my mind, these two balance each other very well: Chandra bringing Thorolf's innate responsibility to the fore, and Thorolf teaching his destined mate the benefits of play and pleasure.

When we last left Thorolf, he was enthralled with Viv Jason, unaware that she was deliberately distracting him from his quest to destroy the *Slayer* Chen. In the Dragon Legion Collection of novellas, the root of Viv's quest for vengeance was revealed and the final restriction against it was removed. Having Viv in action and Chen seeking domination meant it was time for Thorolf to show his stuff. I ensured that the happy resolution of his firestorm didn't come easily to him, because I knew that he'd need a big push to move beyond his past. I loved the fact that his loyalty would be misdirected, potentially in the most dangerous way. It's not a spoiler to tell you here that during his firestorm and the challenges that result, Thorolf comes through again, and does so with flying colors.

He's just the kind of *Pyr* you really might want to have defending your back.

There is some bonus content in this edition, including a guide to the next generation of the *Pyr*. Many firestorms mean a lot of sons, so this list includes all the ones born to date. The same list is on my website and will be amended there as the series continues.

There's also an excerpt here from Sloane's book, which will be called **Firestorm Forever** and will be published later this year. Sloane's is the last title in the Dragonfire series, and takes place at the end of the Dragon's Tail Wars. There will be more dragon shifters from me, though, and we'll probably revisit our favorite *Pyr* in other linked series, but this cycle will come to its resolution with Sloane's book. I'm looking forward to going back into the past with my dragon shifters and also to move into the future with the younger generation. Stay tuned for more *Pyr* adventures!

And now I'll step aside and let you get to the firestorm. I hope you enjoy reading Chandra and Thorolf's story as much as I enjoyed writing it.

Until next time!
All my best—
Deborah
also writing as Claire

More Books by the Author

Writing as Deborah Cooke

Paranormal Romances:
The Dragonfire Series
KISS OF FIRE
KISS OF FURY
KISS OF FATE
Harmonia's Kiss
WINTER KISS
WHISPER KISS
DARKFIRE KISS
FLASHFIRE
EMBER'S KISS
THE DRAGON LEGION COLLECTION
(including Kiss of Danger, Kiss of Darkness, Kiss of Destiny)
SERPENT'S KISS

Paranormal Young Adult:
The Dragon Diaries
FLYING BLIND
WINGING IT
BLAZING THE TRAIL

Contemporary Romance:
The Coxwells
THIRD TIME LUCKY
DOUBLE TROUBLE
ONE MORE TIME
ALL OR NOTHING

Writing as Claire Delacroix

Time Travel Romances
ONCE UPON A KISS
THE LAST HIGHLANDER
THE MOONSTONE
LOVE POTION #9

Historical Romances
THE ROMANCE OF THE ROSE
HONEYED LIES
UNICORN BRIDE

THE SORCERESS
ROARKE'S FOLLY
PEARL BEYOND PRICE
THE MAGICIAN'S QUEST
UNICORN VENGEANCE
MY LADY'S CHAMPION
ENCHANTED
MY LADY'S DESIRE

The Bride Quest
THE PRINCESS
THE DAMSEL
THE HEIRESS
THE COUNTESS
THE BEAUTY
THE TEMPTRESS

The Rogues of Ravensmuir
THE ROGUE
THE SCOUNDREL
THE WARRIOR

The Jewels of Kinfairlie
THE BEAUTY BRIDE
THE ROSE RED BRIDE
THE SNOW WHITE BRIDE
The Ballad of Rosamunde

The True Love Brides
THE RENEGADE'S HEART
THE HIGHLANDER'S CURSE

Urban Fantasy Romance
The Prometheus Project
FALLEN
GUARDIAN
REBEL
ABYSS

Serpent's Kiss

A DRAGONFIRE NOVEL

BY

DEBORAH COOKE

Serpent's Kiss
By Deborah Cooke

Cover by Frauke Spanuth of CrocoDesigns

Serpent's Kiss

A Dragonfire Novel

For Angela Wegert and Stephanie Gradel.
With many thanks.

PROLOGUE

Chicago—June 15, 2012

Erik checked the perimeter of his lair, ensuring that his dragonsmoke barrier was woven thick and deep. It was late at night, or early in the morning, depending upon how he looked at it. Zöe had been put to bed hours before and even Eileen had fallen asleep. Drake had departed with the new *Pyr* a week before, revitalized by the opportunity to train a new company of dragon shifters.

Erik had spent the week trying to avoid a sense of pending doom. He couldn't scry the future or see anything beyond the present moment, but he'd had a persistent sense of trouble brewing.

Maybe it was that footage of Jorge appearing, then disappearing, in Seattle. What had the *Slayer* been carrying? It had looked like a severed arm, one that was still bleeding. Erik hadn't thought much of Jorge shaking blood over the gathering crowd, not then, but today's news had changed that.

People were becoming sick in Seattle. Very sick. There was a hum of panic building as doctors and hospitals noticed the connections between sudden illnesses and deaths. They hadn't used the word epidemic yet, but the first hospital had put itself into quarantine. They'd already realized that most of the victims had been at the scene of Jorge's appearance.

It was only a matter of time before dragons were blamed.

Erik shivered, remembering the old hunts that had driven his kind into hiding and claimed so many *Pyr* he'd known and loved. Surely it couldn't happen again.

Surely his suspicions were unfounded.

The loft was still, despite Erik's restlessness. He stood at the window and watched the moon ride high overhead, listening to the pulses and breathing of his partner and child. He heard the resonance of his dragonsmoke and felt its icy glitter. The blaze in his mind had quieted, perhaps because he no longer feared it.

The numbers of the *Pyr* had swollen, virtually overnight, thanks to the darkfire crystal and its ability to make reality out of possibilities. The stone itself remained dark—he had checked it again after Drake's departure—and he sensed that it would always be so. Its task was completed.

His, unfortunately, was not.

Erik knew he should feel optimistic instead of worried. What could he do? If Jorge had a plan, was it possible that the other *Slayers* knew of it? He'd never been able to determine how much they communicated with each other, and their alliances shifted like the wind.

Confident that his barriers were robust and his family safe, Erik left the loft and went to the apartment he'd acquired directly below. There the *Slayer* JP was imprisoned, confined by a barrier of dragonsmoke breathed by Erik and buttressed by every *Pyr* who had come to visit since JP's capture.

Erik felt a little bit sorry for the other dragon shifter. JP had been branded by Chen, claimed by that old *Slayer* and held captive by his more ancient magic. JP had raved and fought when he'd first been captured by the *Pyr*, venting about injustice and plots. Erik had hoped to learn something about Chen from JP, but the *Slayer* was too incoherent to provide any information of use. Then he'd collapsed into a deep slumber, dozing in his dragon form and seldom awakening.

Chen's sorcery seemed to be killing him. JP's scales were thinner each time Erik visited him. He wasn't sure when the other dragon shifter ate, but he didn't consume much. JP's breathing was becoming shallower and his pulse slower. Worse, the fight had gone out of him. It was such an unnatural state for a dragon shifter that Erik assumed JP would soon die.

It was such a waste. He could never understand why a *Pyr*

would turn *Slayer* in the first place, never mind why Chen would enchant another *Slayer* just to let him fade away.

Erik unlocked the door to the apartment where JP was captive, fearing as he did each time that he would make a gruesome discovery. He passed through the cold shimmer of the dragonsmoke, only to find the apartment in darkness. The drapes were drawn but the apartment was unnaturally dark, given the brightness of the full moon. The light should have crept into the room somehow, as well as the illumination from the city itself.

Erik smelled brimstone.

It was a warning.

He slammed the door and shifted shape immediately, but even at his fastest speed, he was too slow. A plume of flame lit the middle of the main room. It was breathed by a young Asian man dressed in leather, a man with malice and violence in his eyes.

Chen, in one of his human guises. He could breathe fire in human form. It was remarkable how easily Chen seemed to do it, but Erik would save his admiration for another time.

Erik leapt at Chen, talons bared, but the *Slayer* laughed. He grabbed the inert JP by the scruff of his neck, waved to Erik, then they both disappeared before Erik reached them.

Erik landed hard on the bare floor, but his prey was gone. Chen had used his power to spontaneously manifest in another location to bypass the dragonsmoke barrier and collect his prey.

Why did he want JP?

What would he do to him?

What else had the darkfire changed? Erik closed his eyes and checked the connections in his mind, following each conduit to one of the *Pyr*. It took him longer, with the influx of new dragon shifters, but he soon realized that one was missing.

Thorolf.

Erik had been angry with Thorolf for revealing himself to humans. There was even a YouTube video of Thorolf shifting shape in Washington, one that was impressive in its popularity. Thorolf was all impulse and powerful energy, but he spent himself in indulgence. That he made such foolish choices was in direct contrast to his impressive lineage. If Thorolf focused, or even tried to hone his skills, he could have become one of Erik's most reliable *Pyr*. He could have replaced Erik as leader. But he didn't try and he didn't seem to care, and when he had vowed to go to Asia to hunt down Chen, Erik had let him go in disgust. He'd been sure that it would be good for Thorolf—maybe a rude awakening—to be ostracized by his fellow *Pyr*. He'd been sure nothing would come of the entire quest, that Thorolf would find a woman somewhere and spend a few months exploring her charms.

That had been exactly what had happened. Erik had checked and checked again just the day before.

But now Thorolf was gone. There was no glowing conduit to him from Erik's mind. There was no link to his spirit, either. He wasn't dead, just missing.

Erik shifted back to human form, impatient with his own failing in this. He should have kept a closer eye upon Thorolf, and he knew it. His frustration with Thorolf had driven his choices, and that had been a mistake.

He turned on the lights, intent upon checking the apartment, on the outside chance that Chen or JP had left some clue.

Chen had. There was a spiral burned into the hardwood floor, a spiral exactly like the mark branded on JP's neck. It was about fifteen feet across and had been the source of that smell. Erik stepped into it and knew too late that he shouldn't have done so. The spiral drew him forward with relentless force. He was pulled against his will to the very core of the spiral, fighting it even as he saw it begin to burn again. First the mark glowed, like embers, then it was coaxed to a small fire by a wind Erik couldn't feel. In a heartbeat, the flames were burning as high as his knees. He couldn't stop himself from moving closer, even when he heard Chen's laughter echo through the empty apartment.

"I could take you now," Chen whispered in old-speak. His claim echoed in Erik's mind and fed his fear. It was terrifying because it was true. Erik couldn't break free of the spiral. *"All I need, after all, is the element of air."*

Erik had an affinity to the element of air, which wasn't the most reassuring realization he could have had in that moment. The last thing he wanted to do was provide the final key to Chen's spell, giving that *Slayer* the ability to triumph over the *Pyr* and destroy the *Pyr* forever.

It didn't seem he had a lot of choice, though. Erik fought hard against the invisible force that was pulling him closer to the center of the burning spiral, but his efforts made no difference. He refused to summon anyone to help him, because he wouldn't lead another *Pyr* into such danger.

"I could snatch you from your own lair and make my spell complete," Chen continued, a trace of amusement in his voice.

There was a sudden crack like lightning.

The fire disappeared. The spiral on the floor was black for a heartbeat, and then it disappeared completely.

Erik was standing in an empty apartment, one tinged with the frost of his own dragonsmoke barrier. His heart was pounding and there was a trickle of sweat running down the middle of his back. He blinked and looked around, startled by the change.

There was a red salamander in the farthest corner, its tongue flicking.

Chen, in another guise.

Erik didn't know what he could do to stop the *Slayer*, but he had to do something.

As soon as he took a step, the salamander began to shimmer with a pale blue light.

"But I'd rather let you watch," Chen murmured in old-speak, the darkness of his threat making Erik shiver. The blue light brightened, then the salamander disappeared.

Erik was completely alone.

He stood for a moment and listened, knowing in his heart that the *Slayer* wouldn't be back. Chen's plans had been defeated several times by the *Pyr*, yet he was so confident this time of his success that he'd let Erik go.

That couldn't be a good sign.

But without knowing Chen's plan, Erik didn't know what he could do to stop him. Thorolf was gone. JP had been collected. Pieces were moving into place.

Chen needed the element of air to complete his spell. Unfortunately, Erik and Thorolf shared the same affinity. Would Thorolf's disappearance make Chen's spell complete?

Erik felt sick at his own unwitting involvement. There had to be something he could do to save Thorolf.

Erik owed Thorolf's father no less.

Thorolf awakened with a familiar sense of having over-indulged the night before. His head was pounding and his tongue was thick. Although he knew he'd been sleeping hard, he was as exhausted as if he'd run a marathon.

Never mind how sore he was. His entire body ached. In fact, he hurt in places he hadn't felt in years. What had he done the night before?

What exactly had he drunk?

He had a vague memory of taking a dare from Viv to drink some combination of the bartender's own devising. It was the kind of dare he always took, laughing, when he was drunk enough. His constitution was sufficiently strong that he could sleep off pretty much anything.

But that drink had been fierce. He knew he'd only had a sip, and he didn't remember one thing after that. Maybe he was getting old. After nine and a half centuries, he supposed it was reasonable to expect some loss of vigor. He was starving, too, hungry enough to eat at least three big steaks.

Or pie. He'd kill for an apple pie.

Not a slice: the whole damn thing.

With ice cream.

He really hoped he didn't have any new tattoos. The ones he chose when he was wasted were never the right ones, and he didn't have Rox protecting him from his impulsiveness with ink anymore.

Thorolf wondered when he'd see Rox and Niall, and all the other *Pyr* again, and felt even worse. He'd never succeeded in his self-appointed quest to destroy Chen, because he'd never done more than get to Bangkok. He hadn't hunted Chen down and fought the old *Slayer* to the death, because he'd gotten involved with Viv.

How had Viv gotten him back to their apartment? For a small woman, she really got things done. He was impressed by her resourcefulness all over again.

It was more reason to make a fresh start on this day. He owed her better than what he'd been, and he owed more to the *Pyr* than he'd delivered. If he wasn't going to be a fuck-up forever, the time to change was now.

Thorolf braced himself for the worst and opened one eye warily.

Evidently he wasn't really ready for the worst, because the sight shocked him wide awake. There was a huge green snake curled up on the bed beside him, its eyes glittering and its tail flicking. It seemed to be waiting for him to show signs of wakefulness because as soon as his eyes opened, it reared up and bared its fangs.

It was huge, the biggest snake he'd ever seen. It might have weighed as much as Thorolf did, which was impressive. As its eyes glinted with malice, he knew he'd seen a snake this big only once before.

In this very apartment.

When Chen had attacked him.

He'd never been able to find it later, much less ensure it was evicted or dead. Viv had said that Thailand's jungles were thick with snakes and told him not to worry about it. Thorolf hadn't liked that reasoning one bit, and now he liked it less. The snake was back, or maybe it had never left.

And it was after him.

He cast a quick glance over the apartment and was somewhat relieved. There was no sign of Viv, which was good. Thorolf would have a hard enough time defending himself in his current state.

He scrambled backward, only realizing then that the snake had already wrapped itself around his leg. The snake's coils tightened, squeezing his calf and holding him captive. It opened its mouth, as if to laugh at him.

Thorolf tumbled out of the bed and fell on his butt, knocking over Viv's cute little nightstand from the flea market. The table and lamp crashed to the floor, and he dreaded that she'd cry. He hated when she cried. The snake dove for him even as Thorolf tried to crawl away and its weight landed on his chest.

It was incredibly heavy, heavy enough to knock the breath out of him. Thorolf grabbed it and flung its head against the wall. The snake hit the plaster and hissed in fury. Thorolf reached to free himself from the snake's coils with both hands, blood running from one. He caught one coil and ripped it away, but the snake launched itself toward him again.

Its weight knocked him off balance, but Thorolf kept fighting against its grip on his leg. Looking away was his mistake: the snake struck in that instant. He winced as its fangs sank deeply into his arm. He saw the cold glitter of its eyes but reached for its head again, determined to get it off him.

No sooner had his hand closed over its cold skin than he felt a strange languor steal through his body. A chill was emanating from the bite, spreading over his skin, so he knew the serpent's toxin was paralyzing him. Even the bite looked wrong, because it was turning his skin dark. Thorolf had time to open his mouth, but he never made a scream. Numbness claimed his body and began to seep into his thoughts. He only managed to make a choking sound before he couldn't make any noise at all. His eyes closed despite his efforts and he felt himself fall limply to the floor. The snake's weight left him, its coils releasing his leg, but it was impossible to escape.

Chen's familiar laugh echoed in Thorolf's ears, a sound of triumph that didn't bode well. It would have been bad enough if the old *Slayer* had killed him, but Thorolf knew Chen would have more devious plans for him than that. He remembered the brand that Chen had burned against the neck of the shadow dragons he'd enslaved, remembered how the old *Slayer* had tried to brand him, too, and felt sick with dread. It wasn't as if he could defend himself, not like the last time, not when he was like this. The brand had been shattered, but Thorolf wouldn't have put it past Chen to have forged it new.

He was in very deep trouble, and outcast from his fellow *Pyr*, the only ones who could have helped him.

It appeared that Thorolf had made his last mistake.

That night, Niall Talbot, the Dreamwalker of the *Pyr*, dreamed. He was in the dream of another *Pyr*, he had to be, because the scene was completely unfamiliar to him. Niall glimpsed pine trees and mountains, an icy length of water—and a village consumed by flames. He was flying toward the devastation, seeing what another *Pyr* had once seen. He felt the *Pyr*'s horror and his fear of what he'd discover. His heart was thundering, and he flew with reckless power. He descended toward the flames and caught a scent that he knew better than his own heart.

Astrid was alive.

That was his thought, filled with relief and hope. The *Pyr* followed the scent and found her, outside the village, bound to a large rock like an offering to the gods. Niall was shocked but the *Pyr* was not. He'd expected worse.

Worse? The woman was burned badly, bruised and muddy. Niall saw that she'd had stones thrown at her, because they were around her feet, stained with her blood. Her body had been broken before the attack that had left her burned.

Niall wondered where he was, and what this woman had done. The *Pyr* whose dream he shared saw only the woman's beauty and kindness, his heart aching that she had paid this price. Niall could glimpse how pretty she had been, even though the mud, blood and the burns. She caught her breath at the *Pyr*'s arrival, her fear tangible, but he shifted shape in a shimmer of brilliant blue.

Why did the scene smell like *Pyr* as well as *Slayer*? Niall had a bad feeling. What was left of the village and the woman's clothing looked primitive, maybe medieval, and there was certainly no industry in the valley. In what era was he? Before the late middle ages, there had been no *Slayers*, per se, Niall knew that, but he didn't doubt his keen sense of smell.

He supposed there had always been those of his kind with darkness in their blood, even if they hadn't been given a name yet.

The *Pyr* fell to his knees before the woman, pushed her hair back from her ravaged face with a shaking hand, and bowed his head, overwhelmed to find her like this.

My Astrid.

"All I did was love you," she whispered, the words barely audible. Her lips were cracked and it had to be painful for her to speak. She coughed then, blood leaking from the corner of her mouth. "Who would have guessed that would cost so much," she murmured before her eyes closed. A tear leaked from her eye and meandered down her cheek, even as she stilled forever.

She was dead. A fury filled the other *Pyr* as he realized as much, then he tipped back his head to roar. He shifted shape at the same time, taking flight with power. Niall felt his pain and his betrayal, and his conviction that his own kind had done this, to teach him a lesson.

It was one he would never forget.

Niall awakened with a start, shaking, horrified and sickened by the stench of burned flesh. He could have been in that village still, the air filled with smoke, the dead woman bound and burned before him. "Astrid," he whispered, his voice hoarse with another *Pyr*'s pain.

"Who?" his partner Rox demanded, bracing herself on her elbow to look down at him in the darkness. She spoke softly, probably not wanting to awaken their twin sons. Kyle and Nolan were just over a year old and finally sleeping with some predictability.

Niall realized that he was in New York, safe in bed with Rox in their apartment over her tattoo shop. The familiar lights and sounds of the city outside the window reassured him. He could hear his sons sleeping in the next room, but couldn't keep from pulling Rox close. His heart was racing and his mouth dry.

Astrid.

"Who's Astrid?" Rox murmured into his ear.

"I don't know," Niall admitted, even as the shards of the dream faded from his mind. The pain of betrayal lingered though, like a bitter taste on his tongue. "I don't remember."

"Whose dream was it?"

"I don't know." Niall shook his head. "I couldn't see. I could only feel." He shuddered again and tried to think. "No one has ever talked about an Astrid." He frowned, fighting to recall details, even as Rox reached for the notepad she kept by the bed for exactly this purpose. "'*All I did was love you.*' That's what she said before she died. He was furious at what she'd endured."

"Because he hadn't defended her?"

Niall shook his head. "Because he believed the *Pyr* were responsible for her death. That they were teaching him a lesson."

Rox made a note then shook her head. "That doesn't sound very much like the *Pyr* defending humans as one of the treasures of the earth."

"No," Niall admitted with frustration. "It doesn't. But it's gone already. I can't remember more."

"Maybe he wasn't *Pyr*," Rox suggested, nestling beside him again.

"If he was *Slayer*, he wouldn't have loved anyone other than himself," Niall murmured. "And even if he was *Slayer*, the *Pyr* wouldn't have murdered a woman because of him."

"Other *Slayers* then?" Rox suggested.

"I don't think that's what he meant." Niall shook his head. "Even if it happened before we used the term *Slayer*, we still would have been aware of wickedness in our own kind. He thought it was the good *Pyr*. I felt his conviction!" He shoved his hand through his hair. "It doesn't make sense."

"Maybe more of it will come to you later."

Niall didn't sleep, though. He knew in his heart that it had been the dream of a *Pyr* and that the experience had influenced his fellow dragon shifter for good. He also knew that he had to be experiencing the dream for a reason.

Astrid. Niall breathed her name and saw her in his mind's eye for the barest moment. She was fair with blue eyes, tall and slender. Those trees and mountains could have been Scandinavia. Maybe it was one of Erik's relations. He'd come from that part of the world. Niall would ask the leader of the *Pyr* about it the next day.

He wished he could remember more detail, but he had to make do with what the dream brought to him. He rolled over and caught Rox close, breathing deeply of her scent and fiercely glad that she was safe beside him. The dream made him feel vulnerable and made him fear for those he loved.

What would he do, if he found Rox in such a state and believed his fellows were responsible? Niall didn't even want to think about that. It wouldn't be a friendly discussion, that was for sure. He slowed his breathing and exhaled a steady stream of dragonsmoke, strengthening the protective barrier that already encircled his lair and the precious treasures that were his partner and sons.

On this night, he couldn't have too many defenses.

Niall didn't realize then that Rox would fill a notebook with his recurring dreams of the other *Pyr*'s last moments with Astrid.

He would have that same nightmare every single night for the next twenty-two months, except that it became more violent and the *Pyr*'s reaction more vehement each and every time. It was as if the *Pyr*'s fury was being steadily fed to become greater and more consuming.

And yet, over those same months, he didn't manage to find a single *Pyr* who had been loved by an Astrid.

Much less understand why the dream was so persistent.

CHAPTER ONE

Bangkok—April 15, 2014

It wasn't right.

The city Thorolf knew as home didn't look right. It made no sense that it had changed so much in just one night. The evening before he'd drunk some vile concoction, nearly killing himself on a dare from Viv, and by morning, the world had changed drastically. He couldn't understand it.

He was also feeling jumpy. Maybe it was the hangover, but he'd never had one like this. A single phrase repeated itself incessantly in his thoughts: *it could happen again*. It terrified him, even though he refused to explore his memory of whatever had happened. The past was over and done. He'd made his choices.

No matter how many times he told himself as much, his conviction continued to grow. Thorolf couldn't let the same thing happen again. He felt a strange need to find Viv so he could defend her. He should never have left her, even though he didn't remember doing so. She wasn't his destined mate, but she was his lover and companion. He'd never been anxious when they were apart—Viv was good at taking care of herself—but that had suddenly changed.

Maybe it was the pain. He ached all over, his skin burning from head to toe. The torment grew with every step he took and he was sure his skin was inflamed. It was as if he'd gotten a new tattoo while he was drunk—which wasn't out of the question—but this one burned as a new tattoo never should. Had he gone to some hole where they didn't change the needles? Did he have an infection?

How could *all* of his skin be affected?

Thorolf didn't know, but the pain was driving him crazy. He checked out his forearms as he walked and didn't like the look of the spirals that were traced all over them. The moron had even tattooed over top of the blue dragon tattoo that Rox had put on the back of his left hand. What kind of loser would obliterate a masterpiece like that dragon, obscuring it with this kind of meaningless scribble? The spirals were all over his arms and hands, and from the burning sensation of his skin, all over the rest of his body, too.

Just how drunk had he been for some jerk to take advantage of him this much?

Thorolf felt a new anger against losers who called themselves tattoo artists but were incompetent idiots, a rage that surprised him with its intensity. All the same, he couldn't deny its persuasive power. The pain and anger melted with the fury, as well as that fear that something bad could happen again. He blamed his fellow *Pyr*.

The *Pyr* had cheated him.

The *Pyr* had stolen from him.

He couldn't work it through, but he had to find Viv.

Thorolf walked a street that should have been familiar, unable to account for how much had suddenly changed. The signs were different. The businesses were different. The bikes darting through the foot traffic were louder and faster. More people had cellphones than he remembered, as if some technological genie had showered the city with expensive new devices. The phones were bigger, too, with more elaborate displays. Maybe it was a market test. He was starving, but his favorite chicken place was closed and boarded up, an injustice that unsettled him even more.

Maybe he wasn't in Bangkok, after all.

The sky was dark and becoming darker, even though it was mid-afternoon. Thorolf crossed an alley, which gave him a sudden view of the sky, and he saw that the sun was being obscured. An eclipse! Thorolf didn't remember that there was going to be one: in fact, he'd been sure that the next total eclipse was years away. He stopped to stare for a long moment, breaking every sensible rule by looking straight at the sun, but there was no mistaking the eclipse for what it was. That shadow crept steadily across the sun, blocking it and turning the light to a strange orange color.

A total eclipse, and he hadn't known it was coming.

Yet he was *Pyr*, and a total eclipse often sparked a firestorm. Eclipses were important to dragon shape shifters, and he wasn't that lax about his responsibility to his fellows. Firestorms could require the help of all the *Pyr*, to ensure that the dragon shifter in question successfully defended and courted his destined mate.

Thorolf always knew when there was going to be an eclipse, but not this one. He had a very bad feeling about that. He strode quickly toward the apartment he shared with Viv.

As the sun was plunged into darkness, he felt the spark of the firestorm ignite somewhere in the world. He closed his eyes as its heat sent a welcome surge through his body, driving a chill from his bones. It even eased the pain of that stupid new tattoo, and soothed his concern about evil repeating itself. He breathed deeply of it, wishing it could be his own.

The firestorm was close. Could it be Sloane's? Was the Apothecary in Bangkok? What other *Pyr* were in Bangkok?

The heat of firestorm grew with every step he took. The firestorm was really close, a tangible golden heat in his vicinity. The fact that there was a firestorm, though, meant that *Pyr* and *Slayers* would gather.

And Viv could pay the price.

It could happen again. Thorolf remembered the smell of Astrid's burned flesh all too clearly and the sight of her body damaged beyond healing. He saw the betrayal and disappointment in her eyes once more and heard her whispered last words. The worst part was that his fellow *Pyr* had been responsible.

It could only happen again over his dead body.

Thorolf broke into a run. He had to find Viv!

Smart people took one look at him and scurried out of his path, casting fearful glances backward. He was comparatively tall in this city, and his fair hair made him stand out. Thorolf felt his body hovering on the cusp of change and wondered if his eyes had shifted to dragon eyes as yet. There probably was a glow of pale blue around his body, a mark of his intent to shift. He forcibly calmed himself, pushing back the insistent urge to change shape, trying to corral his growing fear.

It only pissed Erik off when Thorolf changed to dragon form in public. He could do with not pissing off the leader of the *Pyr* any more than he already had.

Thorolf arrived in the street where the apartment was located and narrowed his eyes against the changes he noticed there. Did it matter if the used bookstore had become an internet cafe? Did it matter if the old noodle shop was gone, or that the beggar who was always on the corner had disappeared? No! The only thing that mattered was Viv. He inhaled deeply, but even his keen *Pyr* senses couldn't discern Viv's presence.

Had they taken her away?

Was he too late?

Fear had him taking the stairs three at a time. Thorolf kicked in the door and shouted for Viv, hearing his own fear. The door swung back hard enough to slam into the wall behind and the wooden frame shattered. He frowned as he surveyed the apartment.

It looked so different that he checked the number on the door.

This was the apartment but where was Viv?

Had he failed his lover?

Again?

A nude man who emerged from the bathroom, brushing his teeth, his expression astonished.

"Where's Viv?" Thorolf demanded.

"Who?"

This human had to know where she was. She'd lived in this very apartment with Thorolf until the day before. That this man should lie only meant he was one of those wicked humans, like the one who had cursed him with this tattoo. He must be in league with the *Pyr*.

Just like the humans who had tied Astrid down and stoned her.

Anger flooded through Thorolf. Viv couldn't die because of his failure. He took one step and seized the man by the throat. He lifted him off the floor and slammed the man back into the wall. The toothbrush fell to the floor as the man's eyes widened in terror and his legs flailed as he gasped for air.

Thorolf pressed his thumbs against the man's windpipe, watching as his victim began to choke. His skin hummed with the steady pain of that new tattoo, filling him with a need to do violence. He felt a chilly determination to see justice done.

No matter what the price.

"Where is she?" he demanded.

The man kicked and struggled as he tried to escape, his fingers grasping at Thorolf's hands. "I don't know who you're talking about!"

"Don't lie!" he snarled. "I'm talking about Viv Jason. She lives here."

"No. No! *I* live here. I've lived here for almost two years..."

"Liar!" Thorolf lifted the man closer, then summoned the change to his dragon form, ensuring that his eyes changed first. He controlled the change, mindful of Erik's injunctions against revealing his powers to humans, but desperately wanting to terrify this guy. Thorolf knew when his eyes changed to dragon eyes with vertical slits for pupils, because the man freaked out. Did he think Thorolf was stupid? Did this moron think he could just lie about something so obvious and Thorolf would believe him?

"Tell me where she is," Thorolf repeated. He wished he was good at beguiling, so he could convince this guy to spill the truth.

He'd have to make do with brute force, as usual.

The halo of blue light that surrounded Thorolf's body before he shifted shape was already glowing, the change sliding through Thorolf's body. He wouldn't be able to stop it in a second, but his rage was overcoming his desire to hover on the cusp of change.

He felt powerful as the dragon began to claim his body, and once he acknowledged how good the change felt, it accelerated. He'd shred this deceptive human if necessary and cast him aside, then follow the heat of the firestorm to the *Pyr*. He'd fight every one of them to defend Viv, fight them to the death if necessary.

No one would take what—or who—was his.

The man made incoherent noises in his terror. His eyes were just about popping out of his head. Thorolf pressed a little harder on his throat and smiled as the man gasped.

"Where?" he whispered.

"I don't know!" the man squeaked.

"Lies won't help you now." Thorolf lifted his victim higher and tightened his grip, determined to squeeze the life out of him slowly. He deserved no less if he were in league with the *Pyr*.

The man struggled and flailed, but Thorolf was relentless. When this liar was gone, he'd find the *Pyr*. He'd get the truth out of them. He'd find Viv in time.

He'd do what was right. He bared his teeth, feeling the change rocket through his veins. The man's eyes widened and he tried to scream...

Suddenly, Thorolf became aware of an inferno burning near his side. The firestorm was closer and hotter, close enough that he'd be able to see the lucky *Pyr*. Sparks danced over his flesh, the orange flames piercing the blue shimmer around his body. It was as if the hairs on his forearm were on fire. The fury that had filled him was pushed back, and the raging pain on his skin faded. He felt heat on the side of his face and a strange seductive warmth flooding through his body.

The heat of desire. He was abruptly aroused, as he never was when fighting. He was amazed that the proximity of this firestorm had the power to affect him so strongly. He couldn't imagine what it would be like to experience one himself. The dragon retreated as Thorolf turned to look to his left, unable to stop himself. He fully expected to a see a *Pyr* come to fight with him over Viv, a *Pyr* experiencing a firestorm.

But no. A young boy was climbing through the window, a boy dressed all in black. One sniff told Thorolf that the boy wasn't *Pyr*. His intense dark gaze was locked on Thorolf, commanding his attention as much as the strange heat. The fire seemed to emanate from the boy, dancing between him and Thorolf in a way that defied everything Thorolf knew to be true.

Something tickled in Thorolf's mind, a vague memory of a boy who wasn't a boy.

The new arrival smiled, as if reading his thoughts, and the smile was so feminine that Thorolf realized his mistake. It was a slender woman who approached him, a woman with dark hair and dark eyes. She was just dressed as a boy. She walked closer and the golden radiance of the firestorm burned so brightly that he had to narrow his eyes against it. His mouth went dry and the need within him was strong enough to make his grip loosen.

She was having a firestorm?

With who?

"The thief," Thorolf said, remembering the night he'd found Viv in Bangkok. Her wallet had been stolen by a hungry young boy and he'd pursued the thief to retrieve it.

This thief.

Who hadn't been a hungry young boy after all.

What was she doing here? Intending to rob Viv again? His anger took new force from that idea.

But the woman didn't answer. She neither looked left nor right. She kept her gaze locked with Thorolf's and walked steadily toward him. She didn't appear to be armed, and her hands were empty. She held them up as if to let him see that she meant him no harm.

It was a ridiculous idea that this small woman could ever do him, a dragon shifter, injury, but Thorolf let her keep her illusions. The orange flames grew brighter and hotter with every step she took, filling the room with a brilliance that heated him to his core.

And made him forget everything but how much he *wanted*. Desire pounded through his body, making him keenly aware of this woman, of the slender curves beneath her boyish clothes and the sweet allure of her smile. He could seduce her, right here and right now, make her moan and beg for more.

When she was two steps away, she lifted her hand toward him. A spark of flame leapt from her fingertips to Thorolf and he staggered when it struck him in the forehead, right between his eyes.

His own firestorm.

Thorolf stared at the woman who must be his destined mate, even as the firestorm crackled between them. The heat of its spark slid lower, rendering him speechless as it left him burning with hunger. He could almost taste the kiss she would surrender to him, the fire it would light within him, the way it would warm him for all eternity.

He'd waited so long for this. He both wanted to savor the firestorm's burn and satisfy it immediately. He would take her, and it would be a seduction worth remembering, one that would destroy all the wounds of the past and light the way for their new future together.

"He doesn't know where she is," his mate said and Thorolf liked the sultry sound of her voice. It was a bit husky, deeper than he might have expected. "Let him go."

Thorolf glanced at the man whose neck he still held, the man he'd nearly forgotten about, the man who was still watching him in terror. He set the man on his feet with care. Thorolf was dazed and overwhelmed by the firestorm's power, even as the man backed away warily.

His mate put her hand on his arm, and he inhaled, savoring the surge of passion that emanated from her touch. He felt so much better than he had, settled and soothed and passionate. When she stood right beside him, he wondered how he could have doubted her gender. A thousand secrets shone in her eyes, filling him with a desire beyond anything he'd ever experienced before. She was Asian and slender, her dark hair cut short, her eyes darkest brown. She smiled up at him and slid her hand up to his shoulder. The flames burned hot at the point of contact, sending lust through Thorolf that eliminated every thought from his mind.

Except one. He closed his eyes, reveling in spark's touch, and knew there was nothing more important than this.

Than her.

"The firestorm," he whispered. This was his mate, his destined lover, the woman who could bear his son. Thorolf was awed and humbled to experience the firestorm himself. He really didn't want to screw this up.

It was the one thing in his life that he had to get right.

Thorolf turned to face her. He would be gentle and tender, as well as passionate. He'd be sure he didn't frighten her with his desire. She was so much smaller than him, so fragile, so delicate. His mate. Thorolf cupped her head in his hands, bent and touched his lips to hers.

Her mouth was warm and soft, enticing and perfect. Her sigh of pleasure was ideal, but far less than what he wanted. He slanted his mouth across hers, encouraging her to join in his embrace, and was delighted when she touched her tongue to his.

Thorolf kept his eyes open and was glad he did. Before his eyes, his mate shifted through a hundred feminine forms, each melting into the other in rapid succession. She had long hair, short hair, blonde hair, black hair, auburn hair, blue eyes, green eyes, brown eyes. She was tall, then short, then curvy, then not. She changed from one form to another seamlessly and with astonishing speed, becoming a kaleidoscope of different women in turn. Throughout it all, her knowing gaze remained locked upon him, telling him that all these women were the same one.

This one. Thorolf couldn't believe his eyes. It was some kind of magic, not just to have a firestorm but to have a mate like this. Thorolf had always worried a little bit about the firestorm's promise, particularly the conviction of his friend Rafferty that a *Pyr* should make a permanent commitment to his mate. Creating a son and satisfying the firestorm was something Thorolf knew he could handle, but long term plans weren't in his repertoire. He liked variety. He liked exploration. He liked mystery, and he liked women. He couldn't see himself being happy with just one woman, no matter how much he didn't want to disappoint Rafferty.

But his mate was incredible. He wasn't even sure what she was, but she clearly was some kind of magical being. She was a hundred women, maybe even a thousand, all wrapped into one gorgeous package. Were these past lives he glimpsed? Other forms? Was she some kind of shape shifter who could take any guise she chose? Thorolf didn't know and for the moment, he didn't care.

She was his destiny and he was glad.

What he'd just witnessed convinced him that Rafferty was right about the firestorm, and that the Great Wyvern had chosen the perfect mate for him. Thorolf wasn't going to mess it up.

He locked one arm around her waist and tugged her closer, spearing one hand into her short hair. A searing heat surged through him, making his heart pound and his body demand satisfaction. He lifted her to her toes, then deepened his kiss, letting her taste the vigor of his response. To his satisfaction, she kissed him back with equal fervor, a promise of what they'd experience together.

Thorolf had just one more moment to savor the sweet intoxicating heat of the firestorm, before he was struck hard on the back of the head.

Thorolf was a good reminder of why Chandra always worked alone.

She had a quest. She had a perfect plan to fulfill it. Everything should have been neatly resolved by now.

Instead, her plan had been very nearly trashed by the *Pyr* who needed only to provide one small detail for her success. After centuries of planning, Thorolf had vanished for close to two years, right when his presence might have been useful. The creature who called herself Viv Jason had also disappeared without a trace. The only thing Chandra knew for sure was that Viv had been with Thorolf.

He should have been easy to find. From him, she'd learn the location of Viv Jason, and proceed with the completion of her quest.

But no. Thorolf had vanished without warning. Chandra had spent twenty-two months checking and rechecking every single lead and contact she'd ever had, without success. She'd had plenty of time to panic.

Then on this day she'd finally found the missing dragons shifter. He'd appeared out of the blue, which she didn't trust one bit. He didn't have the ability to spontaneously manifest elsewhere, unless something had changed. Even worse, by the time she reached his side, he'd been trying to kill an innocent human.

Worse again, there was a firestorm sparking between them, probably some stupid trick of her brother's just to add to his own amusement. A firestorm and an amorous *Pyr*—never mind one with a talent for making trouble—was a challenge she could have done without. These complications might have been enough to make another goddess walk away from the whole quest.

But no. Chandra always finished what she started.

She always kept her word.

Even with complications.

And Thorolf was more of a complication than she'd ever expected to encounter.

Chandra knew all about the *Pyr*, she'd studied every resource she could find about their nature and abilities in preparation for undertaking this quest. She had to study because the *Pyr* were passionate creatures, as different from her as any being could be. She did her homework when she undertook a task. She knew about the firestorm and its promise, the respect the *Pyr* gave it.

She also knew that no mortal woman managed to resist the power of the firestorm once it sparked. She wasn't a mortal woman, so she'd never expected it to undermine everything she knew to be true.

But with one kiss, Thorolf had shaken the foundations of Chandra's universe. She stared down at him sprawled on the floor, touched her lips and took a deep breath. Thorolf's kiss had awakened a desire in her body unlike anything Chandra had ever experienced. And it had worked fast. In seconds, she'd practically forgotten not just her quest but her ancient vow of chastity. Incredibly, the longer his kiss lasted, the more she wanted it to continue. Pleasure had filled her body in a new and wonderful way. She'd wanted to explore the firestorm's promise. She'd wanted to learn the truth of the pleasure she understood a man and woman could share.

She'd even revealed herself, her barriers dissolving before the firestorm's sensory assault. It was frightening to have been so impetuous.

It was *dangerous*.

Thank the gods and goddesses that the mortal had hit Thorolf in the back of the head. He'd saved Chandra from the firestorm—or maybe from herself. He'd proven to be more useful than mortals generally were.

Even with Thorolf out cold, she couldn't keep herself from admiring his physique. Tall and muscular, with long blond hair and eyes of vivid blue, Thorolf was a veritable Viking and a force to be reckoned with. Passionate, loyal, powerful. In human form, he was enough of a sight to make her heart skip. In dragon form, she could imagine that he'd always taken her breath away.

But now she needed to get herself and Thorolf into hiding, quietly and quickly, and revise the plan as necessary. She needed to keep him from attacking humans in order to find out what he knew about Viv, which meant she had to take him to her sanctuary.

The very idea troubled her. It smacked of complication. But Chandra had to repair the damage that was done, or everything could be lost.

The apartment's resident had disappeared into the bathroom. Chandra hoped he'd lock the door and ignore them.

She knew enough about this *Pyr*'s nature to understand that so long as Thorolf was within a talon's length of urban temptations, she'd never get his attention, let alone convince him to tell her what he knew. She'd have to touch him to move him, then the firestorm would spark, desire would overwhelm her and they might end up somewhere completely different due to her inability to focus. She needed to deal with the existing complications before inviting more.

The easiest and fastest way of moving Thorolf was to have him shift shape and fly them both to her sanctuary.

Which meant she had to wake him up.

In that moment, the apartment resident reappeared with a towel wrapped around his waist. Worse, he was reaching for his cell phone. She'd already missed the chance to ensure they didn't attract more notice, thanks to the distraction of Thorolf.

Quick and quiet, that's how Chandra preferred to work. Humans didn't really need to know what was going on beneath their noses.

That was another good reason to work alone.

What would a mortal woman do?

Beg for mercy. Try to persuade the guy to help her.

"Please don't call the police!" Chandra stood up and put out her hand in appeal. The firestorm's glow diminished to a faint radiance.

The guy still looked at it, his lips thinning in suspicion. Chandra wished she had the *Pyr* ability to beguile humans, even though she didn't approve of it. In this moment, though, she could appreciate its usefulness.

"He's crazy! I don't have a choice," the man protested, but his hand stilled before the number was completely entered. "You saw what he did to me!"

Chandra tried to sound persuasive. "But he didn't know what he was doing..."

"It sure felt like he did." His hand rose to this throat. "It already hurts to swallow."

"He's just confused. He didn't take his medication." Chandra patted her empty pocket as she lied. She wished she was better at this. "I have it. I've been looking for him all morning."

The guy's eyes narrowed. "You know him?"

"I work at the hospital," Chandra continued with her fabricated story, trying to invoke the man's sympathy. "He's a good guy. He just gets confused and angry. He doesn't have anybody, really, and

I feel so sorry for him." She smiled down at Thorolf with apparent affection, hoping he wouldn't wake up and reveal her lie for what it was. "The doctors say he has trust issues."

"He's sharing that joy around."

"Well, I can't blame him. Especially after what she did to him," she continued. "Some people are so unkind." Chandra shivered but didn't have to fake it. It was easy to be appalled by the choices made by the viper who called herself Viv Jason.

"She?"

"He lived here before with some woman. A redhead. That's why he came back here. He doesn't remember that he doesn't live here anymore, that *she* doesn't live here anymore. She wanted to ditch him but he wanted to stay together." She sighed. "He thought love could conquer all."

"So, that's who he was talking about." The guy lowered his phone. "You mean that bitch with the pet snake?"

Chandra nodded.

"He doesn't know she moved," he guessed.

"He does, but he forgets. The doctors say the mind is a delicate instrument. It's like he's trying to remember what happened that night, because the betrayal makes him so angry, but his mind is trying to save him the pain of the precise memory."

The guy winced in sympathy. "You said he loved her." His words were quietly uttered, as if that explained everything.

She should have given that detail more emphasis earlier. Humans had a strange respect for love.

Just as the *Pyr* did for their firestorms. It was irrational, but endearing in a way. She glanced down at Thorolf, not having to pretend to find him attractive, and the guy misinterpreted her expression. "You like him a lot," he said softly. "That's why you're looking for him."

It was as good an excuse as any. Chandra nodded as if it were true. "But he keeps thinking about *her*."

"Okay," the man said abruptly. "Okay, you take him back to the hospital and make sure he gets his meds and I won't call the cops. It sounds like he's got enough trouble as it is." He gave her a smile. "I'd like to think that if I needed a second chance one day, someone would give it to me."

"I'm sure they will." Chandra didn't have to pretend to be

relieved. "Thank you!"

The guy fingered his throat. "Not much harm done, anyway. Just make sure he doesn't come back here. Ever."

"I promise."

Thorolf stirred just then, his eyes opening slowly. His gaze darted over the apartment in confusion, then he spotted Chandra and smiled. That smile was like a dart to her heart. To have his attention focused solely on her, to see such admiration and desire in his eyes, was strangely affecting. She could almost understand the appeal of the firestorm. Chandra found herself smiling back at him, as if inviting his attention. It wasn't like she could reveal the truth, not with the apartment guy watching so closely.

The weird thing was that she found herself standing taller, feeling beautiful, wanting his caress again. She felt the firestorm's heat grow with dizzying speed and crouched beside Thorolf, putting her hand in his before she even thought twice. The jolt of raw lust made her catch her breath. She heard Thorolf do the same, then his thumb slid across the back of her hand. He was warm and strong and powerful. The firestorm glowed brilliantly between them, making her narrow her eyes against its brightness.

Thorolf grinned, a gleam of sexual intent lighting his eyes and making her mouth go dry. He had a dimple below one corner of his mouth, a dimple that made him look like a whole lot of trouble. Which he was, but that didn't seem to diminish his appeal. Chandra had never felt anything like this before, and she didn't want the feeling to stop.

She thought of his kiss and her heart fluttered in an uncharacteristic way. It was easy to believe Thorolf was a dragon shifter when his eyes glinted as they were doing now, never mind that he had passion and appetites. The firestorm made her wonder why her vow of chastity had ever seemed like a good idea.

It made her hunger for another kiss, no matter what the price.

Thorolf planted a kiss against her palm, his warm lips smooth against her skin. His expression turned sultry and a little bit wicked as a very definite surge of desire took Chandra's breath away.

And he knew it. Thorolf's eyes gleamed, his gaze fell to her lips, he braced his weight on his elbow and reached for her again—yet even knowing what he meant to do, Chandra was powerless to move away. She found herself leaning closer, meeting him halfway. She was fascinated by him, by his intent, by her own desire to taste his kiss again. She could have been someone else, someone passionate and impulsive, someone with no ability to think rationally at all.

Someone a lot more like Thorolf.

The scary thing was that Chandra didn't care. The firestorm burned, capturing them in a golden haze of desire that drove everything sane from her mind. Her heart raced in anticipation of what would happen after that kiss. Right here, right now, they could satisfy its demand. Chandra licked her lips and Thorolf chuckled, just as the warmth of his fingers brushed her cheek. A flurry of orange sparks exploded from the point of contact, a delicious heat racing through Chandra, and she closed her eyes in surrender just as the apartment resident swore.

"What the hell is that light anyway?" the guy demanded, sounding fearful.

His exclamation recalled Chandra to her senses. She pulled her hand from Thorolf's grip and the firestorm's heat faded enough that she could think straight. She leapt to her feet, turning her back on Thorolf, but still felt strangely unsettled. "What light?" she demanded, as if she had no idea what he meant.

"*That* light. It, like, sparks between you. It's weird."

"There's no light," she insisted, sensing a losing battle. She heard her voice rise. "It must be your imagination."

"No, there's *light*. What's really going on here? Who are you both?" He backed away as he punched numbers into his cell phone.

No matter what the emergency code was here, it would be short. Chandra couldn't risk him making that call.

So much for negotiation and subtlety. She leapt across the room and seized his phone, flinging it so it shattered the window and fell to the street below.

Problem solved.

If not in her usual discrete manner.

"Great shot," Thorolf said with admiration as he got to his feet. He shoved his hand through his hair and grinned at her, the sight of his stupid dimple making her pulse go crazy again. "We're going to get along just fine," he declared as he seized her hand.

And she was looking at his mouth, like a besotted idiot.

What was the firestorm doing to her?

"Hey!" the guy protested. "That's a new phone! Do you know what it cost me..."

Chandra responded quickly and instinctively once again. She pulled her hand from Thorolf's, backed the man into a corner and grabbed his chin, compelling him to meet her gaze. She felt him swallow as he fell silent, saw his shock that her grip was so strong.

"You saw *nothing*," she whispered with force. "There was no light."

"I know what I saw..."

"Sparks flying between people would be illogical." Chandra dropped her voice to a hiss. "Only crazy people see lights where there aren't any. That's what they'll say if you tell anyone." She smiled as fear lit his eyes. "Maybe we'll meet again at the hospital. I could make sure you two share a room."

His terror was tangible, then he nodded quick agreement. "No light," he said, holding up his hands. "I saw no light. Just get out of here!"

"Done." When Chandra released him, the guy fled into the bathroom again and locked the door.

Thorolf was rubbing the back of his head. He smiled at Chandra with obvious admiration, any concussion evidently not interfering with his plans for satisfying the firestorm. If he laid another sizzling kiss on her, there was no telling what she'd do. She already felt that she was out of control. "You could teach me about beguiling," he said easily then reached for her hand again.

Chandra panicked as desire melted her knees. *Nothing* was going right.

When Thorolf looked at her like that and the firestorm's radiance glowed between them, Chandra could easily forget her quest.

But there was too much at stake for that.

"We have to go," she said. "Right now."

"Anywhere specific?"

She spoke firmly and loudly, ensuring that the guy in the bathroom could overhear. "I'll take you somewhere safe."

"I'm all yours." Thorolf squeezed her hand and smiled down at her, his expression so proprietary that Chandra felt a rare thrill. "How about we get something to eat first? Build up our stamina?"

He lifted a brow, looking like trouble in spades, and Chandra couldn't take a breath. She was keenly aware of her gender, as she seldom was, and her mind was filled with the prospect of pleasures she'd never explored before.

One thing was for sure: this would be the last time she *didn't* work alone.

CHAPTER TWO

Chandra and Thorolf left the apartment quickly, darting down the stairs to the street. A group of people were gathered around the cell phone, several pointing up at the broken window as they compared what they'd seen.

Chandra bit back the urge to swear. She shouldn't have revealed her strength by chucking the phone hard enough to break window glass.

She indicated the direction away from the crowd, then released Thorolf's hand. She couldn't think clearly with the warmth of his fingers closed around hers, with the firestorm feeding her awareness of him. She liked tall men and strong ones, she liked muscle and she liked blue eyes. A lot. Never mind dimples. The thing was that her choices had been historically about eye candy, not about satisfying any desires. Hunks made for better views, that was it. Her vow of chastity was resolute. With the firestorm on Thorolf's side, raw lust was making it impossible to strategize.

And that could ruin everything.

Already a voice in her mind was whispering about new experiences and stones left unturned. Chandra refused to listen. She felt a rising edge of panic. Everything was spinning out of control, the carefully constructed plan shredding before her eyes, and she had to *think*.

"Where are we going?" Thorolf asked, amiable and amorous. He was completely at ease, his mood so at odds with her own that Chandra was incredulous. "There used to be a great chicken place a couple of blocks away..."

"No. We're going somewhere private," she said flatly. As an

afterthought, she offered him a smile that she hoped was enticing. She didn't have a lot of practice with seduction. She didn't want any, but she needed to get Thorolf to move. She couldn't just convince him to shift shape in the middle of a busy street so they could disappear.

She'd manage some subtlety on this day, if it was the last thing she did. Questions would attract attention, and the firestorm was enough of a liability in that way. She'd need the element of surprise on her side to triumph. She had to get him to her sanctuary and find out what he knew.

Fast.

Was it true that the *Pyr* could all feel the heat of the firestorm? That *Slayers* were drawn to it, like moths to the flame? She couldn't even imagine the complication of a gathering of dragon shifters—more enemies to battle and more consensus to build.

Chandra felt her anxiety increase even more.

They ducked into an alley, the firestorm's radiance lighting its dingy shadows like a beacon. It was about as subtle as a nuclear blast. Chandra could practically sense curious mortals looking out windows for the source of the light. She walked faster. The alley was narrow, lined with doorways to cheap apartments. Crockery was stacked outside the nearest door, a pile of metal pails just behind them. Laundry was strung back and forth overhead, although it wouldn't dry in this damp darkness. The pavement was wet underfoot and smelled of fish. She could hear a market at the other end of the alley.

The light between them shone like the golden glow of forgotten treasure.

"Aren't *Slayers* attracted to the firestorm's heat?" Chandra asked before she could stop herself.

Thorolf caught her shoulders in his hands, sending a jolt of desire through her body that weakened her knees. He spun her to face him as if he couldn't resist her, a wonderful sensation. The stupid thing was that she couldn't step away, even knowing she should. His hands were strong on her, but his touch was gentle. Possessive. She was tempted to lean into his embrace and surrender to the firestorm's heat.

Just one more kiss. That's what the voice in her mind suggested.

This *Pyr* was trouble.

"I can think of a better reason to satisfy it," Thorolf murmured, his voice pitched so low that it made something hum deep inside her. Chandra felt as compliant as a kitten, unable to resist his allure or even step away. His blue eyes sparkled and his smile was mesmerizing.

That treacherous voice in her mind was quick with a tantalizing suggestion. After the firestorm was satisfied, she could resume her quest. It sounded so sensible—even if the sensations kindled by the firestorm felt far from it.

She had to pull it together. "We need to get to my sanctuary," she said, amazed by the breathless sound of her own voice.

"We can spare a minute or two," Thorolf whispered. He pushed his fingers into her hair again and drew her closer, the possessive gesture just about killing her. Who had ever defended her? Who had ever thought of doing it? Thorolf tugged her against his rock-hard chest and lifted her to her toes. Chandra felt small, fragile, feminine and desired, all alien qualities to her life. Maybe that was part of Thorolf's allure.

"What's your name?" he whispered.

"Chandra," she admitted, the word falling from her lips with ridiculous speed.

"Chandra," he repeated and she liked how he said it. His gaze darkened. "My mate."

The word sent a shock through Chandra. She was independent and free, beholden to no man or *Pyr*. She had to remember that the firestorm was about making more *Pyr*, about the mate conceiving a son...

Her gaze fell to Thorolf's mouth. He had a great mouth, firm lips that curved readily to a enticing smile. She found her fingertips on his face, sliding over that dimple and leaving a burning trail of sparks. His smile broadened, both knowing and wicked. He had no shortage of confidence, that was for sure. But then, maybe they had that in common.

It was a smile filled with promise and intent.

A smile that made her mouth go dry and her heart thunder.

Thorolf whispered Chandra's name again, folded her into his embrace and bent his head to claim a kiss. He certainly knew how to go about a seduction, and his mix of tenderness and power drove everything else from her mind. She could feel that he wanted her with the same vigor as she wanted him. She was sizzling from head to toe, hot and compliant and burning for a satisfaction that only he could give her. She was blind and deaf to the rest of the world. It was irrelevant. There was only Thorolf and the incredible feeling of the firestorm.

According the *Pyr* lore, their partnership was destined. She knew better than to doubt the power of destiny. A long chain of events had brought them both to this point, a chain that culminated in the fiery heat of the firestorm. Chandra found her head falling back, her lips parting, her eyes closing, her body melting with the need to be claimed.

She was his for the taking.

For better or for worse.

"There!" shouted the familiar voice of the apartment's current resident. "There's the guy who attacked me and the woman who broke my phone!"

Thorolf swore. He shoved Chandra behind him and spun to confront the speaker. There was a police officer with the guy from the apartment, who was now wearing jeans, flip flops and an open shirt, as well as a small crowd of onlookers in pursuit. Chandra recognized several who had been gathered below the broken window.

So much for a covert escape.

The police officer stepped into the dark alley in pursuit and Thorolf blocked its width with his body. There was something very pleasing about his determination to protect her. The police officer pulled his gun warily.

"Run," Thorolf advised in a low tone as he visibly braced for a fight. "I'll find you."

Chandra shook her head. "Not in this city." The place was a warren. If she left him now, they might never find each other again. She'd just spent close to two years looking for him and wasn't going to let him out of her sight until she learned what she needed to know.

Thorolf leveled a look at her. "Didn't I find you before?"

He had, on the night she'd stolen Viv's purse to learn what name the viper was using. Chandra knew theoretically about the keen senses of the *Pyr*, but even better, Thorolf reminded her that she'd seen them at work. Thorolf *had* tracked her down, once upon a time, following her through the maze of the city at night, when it shouldn't have been possible for him to track her.

Plus now there was the firestorm's heat to guide him.

It had to be good for something.

And a little distance might clear her thoughts.

"I'm right behind you," he commanded. "Go!"

Chandra retreated down the alley. She wasn't used to running from a fight, but she wasn't used to having a partner either.

She told herself not to get used to it. To her relief, the firestorm cooled with distance, letting her mind settle so she could make a plan. If this was the market she suspected it was, it would be crowded and busy. They could cross it to...

She heard sounds of a fight behind her, followed by a yelp and a crash of pottery. She glanced back to see that Thorolf had tossed the police officer into the stacked crockery and that the others were backing away from him. The cop wasn't hurt but he was surprised.

A little old lady emerged from behind the broken pots and began to berate Thorolf in rapid Thai. At another time, it would have been amusing that her indignation made her so fearless, while the others were frightened, but Chandra wanted only to get away.

The faint glow of pale blue that surrounded Thorolf's body wasn't a good sign. She knew the *Pyr* weren't supposed to let humans see them shift shape, but that blue light could only mean that he was on the cusp of change.

Trust her luck to be trying to save a passionate and impulsive dragon.

Maybe *the* most passionate and impulsive of the *Pyr*.

Subtle might be completely out of the question.

"Thorolf!" Chandra whispered his name urgently, counting on his keen hearing. Thorolf jolted slightly, a sign that he'd heard her. The blue light dimmed as he reached into his pocket. He flung some cash at the old lady before backing away. He hauled down a load of laundry into the alley, kicked over the metal pails to slow pursuit, then pivoted to charge toward Chandra.

His triumphant grin nearly stopped her heart. It ought to be illegal for a man to have such an effect on her.

No, the firestorm ought to be illegal.

She raced onward at full speed, confident that they'd escape together.

As for how she'd deny the firestorm after they were secured and alone in her sanctuary—after he *carried* her there in his dragon form—Chandra would worry about that detail later.

Thorolf bolted after Chandra, well aware that those behind him were climbing over the scattered pails. He'd chased her like this once before, though it had been at night and the streets had been quieter. Once again, he was impressed by her agility and speed, never mind the nice tight curve of her butt. She was fast and nimble. He liked that a lot. He liked that she was strong enough to break a window with a phone. That was impressive. He'd chase her even without the firestorm to urge him on and feed his desire.

Especially after being denied another sizzling kiss. He couldn't wait to find out what else they had in common. He had the definite sense that his life was finally beginning.

Plus he wanted to know more about that weird shape shifting she'd done while he kissed her. How could she do that? Which one of those women was really her? What else could she do? Thorolf had a thousand questions and wanted answers to them all.

As Chandra put distance between them, fear began to resonate in his heart. How would he defend her when they were far apart? *It could happen again.* His breath caught with a strange panic, even as his skin started to burn again.

It *couldn't* happen again, not with his mate.

No *Pyr* could consider a firestorm to be a distraction.

But Thorolf couldn't convince himself of that. The terror filled his mind, a panic that he couldn't stop. He ran faster, intent on getting to Chandra's side, fighting a fear that couldn't be checked. His skin hurt again, but it wasn't the exhilarating glow of the firestorm.

He'd feel better when she was pressed up against him, when he could scoop her up and take flight to protect her, when he could hold her close and breathe fire over her head at anyone who dared to threaten her.

Just then, Chandra ducked around the corner at the end of the alley and disappeared into a busy square. The firestorm's heat faded to a mere glimmer. White fear shot through Thorolf that she was out of his sight and his skin burned so that he nearly screamed aloud. His paranoia felt new for all its vigor. If he couldn't see her, the *Pyr* could target her and set her up, work with humans to see her eliminated for his own good.

Just like before.

It could happen again.

No! Thorolf lunged after Chandra. He raced around the corner and was startled by the bright sunlight in the square beyond. The eclipse was over, the sun so bright that the shadow might never have been. The square was filled with a busy and bustling market, crowded with people shopping and negotiating. The firestorm's radiance touched him, its golden light surprisingly reassuring, and he caught his breath as his terror faded.

Thorolf noted bright piles of vegetables, smelled fresh fish and heard the babble of half a dozen languages. His gut growled at the smell of hot dumplings being sold from a cart. He was starving. When had he last eaten? He saw Chandra leap an array of baskets before a stall selling dried legumes, her athletic ease filling him with pride. The vendor complained loudly, but Chandra raced away.

She must know the area. Thorolf followed her lead, trusting in her choice. They'd be a great team. He heard the police officer shout behind him, but didn't slow down. He had to catch Chandra. He saw her duck into a lane on the far side, then leap onto a corrugated metal roof. She raced up to the roof's pinnacle, then disappeared over the top.

When he lost sight of her, the heat of the firestorm diminished to the point of invisibility.

That strange fury possessed him again, as well as a need to retaliate against the *Pyr* for what they'd stolen from him before. The only way to ensure Chandra's safety was to eliminate all of the *Pyr*, one at a time, and make the world safe for his mate.

It was a compelling notion, one that resonated with conviction.

It also filled him with anger and resolve.

Thorolf glanced back at the people pursuing him and his anger multiplied. He had the sudden urge to shred them all, these miserable humans who dared to obstruct his firestorm. For all he knew, this new painful tattoo had been a plot, a plot hatched by miserable humans working with the *Pyr*, a plan to weaken him so he couldn't defend his mate. And now, hundreds of humans were separating him from Chandra so she could be stolen from him, too. *It could happen again.* Who cared about a cell phone, when a firestorm was at stake? He should turn and fight. He could shift shape and breathe dragonfire, fry them all to cinders in their tracks.

The fury roiled and multiplied, making him see red.

When he smelled *Pyr*, he was sure the trap was closing.

A heartbeat later, Thorolf caught the scent of *Slayer*, the putrid and distinctive stench of a dragon shifter gone bad, it was the last straw. The villain had been drawn to the firestorm, whoever he was, attracted to the spark with the hope of killing Thorolf's mate. *Pyr* and *Slayer* were present, at least one of each, drawn to the firestorm. The *Slayer*'s scent was stronger because he was closer. It didn't matter which of them tried to sacrifice Chandra, no one was going to touch her while Thorolf drew breath.

Thorolf shifted shape with a roar, right in the middle of the market. The change shot through his body so swiftly that it nearly left him dizzy. He was briefly surrounded by a pale blue glow, then became a massive moonstone and silver dragon. He knocked over a table of vegetables during the shift and didn't care.

Even Erik couldn't take issue with Thorolf's need to defend his mate.

It felt so good to take his dragon form that Thorolf roared, spewing a long stream of dragonfire into the sky. People screamed and he loved their terror. They should all see him like this. They should know that dragons lived among them, that their pathetic lives could be erased if he so chose.

Thorolf pivoted in flight and breathed more dragonfire, sending them scattering. He scanned the crowd, seeking some sign of the *Slayer*. He exhaled fire at the closest stall, one hung with hundreds of silk textiles, and felt a wicked jolt of delight when the lengths of cloth lit and burned like tongues of fire.

He'd turn it all to fire and leave it all burning. That would teach them.

The other dragon appeared suddenly then, on the far side of the square. He might have been conjured from nothing at all.

Thorolf had drawn the *Slayer* out of hiding!

Now that new arrival would die for his audacity.

If only his skin wasn't burning, as if he were on fire from head to tail. He hoped the pain wouldn't affect his ability to fight.

Thorolf's opponent was enormous, as muscular as Thorolf himself. They'd be evenly matched, Thorolf thought with satisfaction. The other dragon's scales were opal and gold, glittering in the sunlight like pale jewels. His black blood would flow over those scales, revealing the truth of his nature and marring his deceptive beauty. Thorolf would be vindicated when his opponent died in excruciating pain.

He'd be an example to all the others.

Then Thorolf would hunt the *Pyr* who dared to draw near his firestorm. He'd track down every last one of them to ensure his mate's safety forever. Chandra's defense required no less.

Thorolf bellowed and flung his challenge coin at his opponent. Let there be no misunderstanding between them! The silver *thaler* was a thick and heavy coin with a lion rampant on the one side, one so much better than the silver penny he'd used when still allied with his father.

His father. The first and worst of the *Pyr* against him. Bitterness curdled in his gut at the memory. The coin caught the sunlight as it spun through the air. The *thaler* tinkled as it landed in the marketplace, but the other dragon didn't rush to pick it up.

In fact, he seemed to be surprised. He stared at it, blinking, as if he wasn't sure what it was or what it meant.

But that was impossible. All *Pyr* understood the ritual of the challenge coin. It was a fighting tradition older than Thorolf.

"Pick it up, coward!" Thorolf roared in old-speak. He launched himself at the seemingly frozen intruder, determined to defend his mate from harm.

The other dragon leapt into the air at the same time and they collided with a clash over the awestruck crowd. His opponent hadn't picked up the coin, but it didn't matter. They'd still fight to the death, whether the coward agreed to the challenge or not.

Thorolf wasn't going to lose. They locked claws in mid-air in the traditional fighting pose, even as Thorolf buried his teeth at his assailant's chest. He ripped flesh with satisfaction, shredding the muscle beneath the opal scales.

The other dragon cried out, then thrashed, pulling himself

away. *"What's happened to you?"* he demanded in old-speak. When Thorolf roared and snapped at him again, the other dragon decked him. Thorolf fell back dizzy, but undeterred, blood running from his snout. The opal dragon gave him a thump with his tail.

"Thorolf!" he shouted aloud. "What are you doing?" His voice was familiar, but Thorolf knew it had to be a trick.

Some dirty *Slayer* trick.

He heard blood fall on the pavement below and sizzle, which meant it was *Slayer* blood. So, he'd injured his opponent already. It would be a short fight.

Thorolf didn't pause for conversation. He breathed fire at his opponent and that dragon fell back as his scales were singed. Thorolf then drove him down toward the ground with a relentless plume of flame.

The opal dragon fell, gasping, his scales smoking. He reached for the challenge coin and Thorolf laughed that his wager was accepted. No sooner had his opponent's talons closed over the *thaler*, than Thorolf seized the opal dragon by the tail and hefted him into the air. He spun him around, then flung him across the roofs of the city. The other dragon stopped his fall by beating his wings hard, then turned his course.

He didn't come back to fight, the loser.

To Thorolf's horror, the opal dragon flew in the direction Chandra had taken, as sure a sign of his malicious intent as there could be. Thorolf could smell his mate, the intoxicating scent of her desire and faint whiff of her perspiration. He could hear that she was running hard, her breath coming quickly, her fear rising. She knew it wasn't good for them to be apart. She was afraid. She'd expected him to be right behind her. He'd promised to follow and protect her.

He wasn't going to let her down. Thorolf flew after her with purpose, as swift as an arrow shot through the sky, determined to reach her before his opponent.

To defend her, then claim her forever.

The opal dragon seemed to be using his own keen sense of smell to hone in on Chandra. He was ahead of Thorolf, but not by much. The possibility that Chandra could be injured only made Thorolf more furious. Didn't *Slayers* target mates as the easiest way to stop a firestorm? No *Slayer* would stop his! He was angry enough to ignore the burning pain beneath his scales, even though he felt as if he were being jabbed by a thousand tiny needles.

Thorolf flew hard in pursuit of the other dragon, breathing a long plume of dragonfire when he was close enough to singe his opponent's tail. The other dragon turned and ducked, flying an evasive route but one that led directly to Chandra. Thorolf lunged forward, reached out his claws to seize the enemy's wings and rip them from his back, just as the pair soared over a roofline to fly over a quiet canal.

The golden light of the firestorm rose from the wharf to touch the tips of Thorolf's talons. Its heat slid through his body, dismissing the fury that had filled him. The burning sensation in his skin faded abruptly, as if Rox had spread one of her aloe balms over a new tattoo.

He realized suddenly that the other dragon was familiar, even as the scent of *Slayer* faded.

No, his opponent was *Pyr*.

What was going on? Where was the *Slayer*? Thorolf looked around himself in confusion, even as the firestorm's heat kindled his desire. His grip loosed on the other dragon, who hovered in the air to watch him. The opal dragon held Thorolf's gaze and offered him the silver challenge coin, clutched in his outstretched claw.

It was Rafferty. Thorolf blinked, looking between the coin and the *Pyr* he'd be most likely to call his mentor and friend.

What the fuck?

"You dropped this," Rafferty said in old-speak. *"Take it before someone misunderstands your intent."*

Thorolf was stunned. Not only had he attacked his old friend, he hadn't even recognized him. How could that be? Had the firestorm and his fear for Chandra's safety overwhelmed everything?

And where was the *Slayer*?

Thorolf looked around, then took a deep breath. He could smell only the two of them, but a definite scent of *Slayer* lingered. Had a *Slayer* like Jorge materialized and disappeared?

No. Thorolf had thought Rafferty a *Slayer* and had challenged him to fight to the death. He wouldn't have believed it if the other *Pyr*'s chest hadn't been bleeding. He felt sick as he eyed the wound he'd given his friend, then wondered where the black *Slayer* blood had come from. Rafferty's expression was wary, but he waited patiently for Thorolf to take back his own challenge coin.

Thorolf did so, not knowing where to begin to apologize. "I'm sorry..."

"You didn't know who I was."

Thorolf shook his head, hoping the other *Pyr* would have an explanation for that. Rafferty was older, after all, and paid a lot more attention to *Pyr* lore.

Rafferty gave Thorolf a hard look, then turned gracefully in the air and descended behind a derelict warehouse. Chandra was standing behind a pile of wooden crates, her expression as uncertain as Rafferty's had been.

Thorolf didn't understand what was going on, but he followed Rafferty. The golden glow of the firestorm brightened as he drew closer to Chandra, the heat of it searing his doubts and filling him with both desire and optimism. He felt more like his old self, if more hungry than usual. The destructive passion was burned away by Chandra's presence, although he couldn't make any sense of it. Thorolf landed beside her and shifted shape.

He looked down, not happy to see that the swirling new tattoo was darker than it had been, as if the ink were changing color with time. He didn't like that one bit.

The other *Pyr* watched him, then shifted shape and landed a few paces away. Rafferty winced as he walked, and Thorolf saw that his friend's skin was badly burned on the one shoulder where Thorolf had breathed dragonfire at him. His chest was bleeding, as well. But why had Thorolf felt compelled to attack him? Why had he thought him a *Slayer*? It made no sense.

"Truce?" Rafferty asked, as if uncertain.

"I'm sorry," Thorolf said, horrified by what he had tried to do. "I smelled *Slayer*."

"*So did I,*" Rafferty replied in old-speak, his gaze unwavering.

Thorolf glanced around worriedly, wondering where the other dragon shifter had hidden himself. "We have to find him! He's come for the firestorm..."

"Yes, in a way he has," Rafferty said quietly. He folded his arms across his chest, looking disinclined to begin a search.

Thorolf eyed him in confusion. Rafferty wasn't a *Slayer*.

Chandra flicked a handkerchief from her pocket, then reached to wipe the blood from his nose. Thorolf gasped when he saw its dark color on the white cloth. His blood wasn't quite black, but it was darker than it should have been, a burgundy instead of a brilliant red. It was rotting the cloth as he watched, burning a hole through the handkerchief and emitting a plume of steam. At the look in Chandra's eyes, he lifted his own forearm and sniffed it, taking a deep breath of his body's scent.

And it was there, faint but unmistakable: the scent of *Slayer*.

He was the *Slayer*.

"How can that be?" he asked aloud, but neither of them seemed to have the answer.

Chandra was reassured by Thorolf's surprise. It had frightened her to see him attack the other *Pyr* with such power and made her fear him as she hadn't before. His dragon nature wasn't frightening to her when he tempered it, but he'd looked out of control. When he'd attacked the guy at the apartment, he'd had the same livid expression.

But the *Pyr* were supposed to defend the treasure that was the human race.

And they didn't attack each other.

At least Thorolf couldn't explain his own reactions either. Chandra wondered what exactly had happened to him in the past twenty-two months.

Where had he been?

Not that it mattered, really. She had her quest to fulfill. All she needed from him was one little piece of information, not complications and distractions.

"I don't understand," Thorolf said to Rafferty. "How can this be? What happened to me?"

"That's what I'm wondering," Rafferty replied. The other *Pyr* was almost as big and broad as Thorolf, but with dark hair and dark eyes. He seemed to be older, too, or maybe just wiser, and he spoke with deliberation. As she worried about this, the older *Pyr* smiled and offered his hand to her. "I'm Rafferty."

She smiled politely and shook his hand. No sparks. Of course. "Chandra."

"I'm honored to meet you."

That amused Chandra. If he'd known who she really was, he might not have been so gracious. "But you don't know anything about me."

"The firestorm has chosen you to be Thorolf's mate. That's all I need to know to be honored to meet you." He turned to Thorolf again. "Do you know where you've been?"

Thorolf shook his head, glancing at Chandra in confusion.

"You've been missing for almost two years," she said, thinking all the while about what she'd seen. It was strange that whatever had enraged him had been dispelled, twice, in her presence.

Did the firestorm help?

Or was it the reason for his change in the first place? She doubted the *Pyr* would conclude that, but she had no irrational expectations of the firestorm and its so-called promise.

Maybe her nature was the issue.

"Twenty-two months," Rafferty said. "You disappeared the same day that JP vanished from Erik's captivity."

Thorolf shook his head. "Twenty-two months? No way. It was just yesterday that..." His voice faded as he obviously became uncertain.

"That what?" Rafferty prompted. "What's the last thing you remember?"

"Viv and I went to a new bar. It was fun. The music was good and the women were hot." Chandra caught her breath at the mention of her target, but Thorolf didn't seem to notice. "She dared me to drink some mix the bartender had made up." He smiled in recollection and affection. The expression softened his features, making him look appealing, but Chandra knew any affection for Viv Jason was misplaced. "She always does that. This one, though, it was wicked shit."

"And then?" Rafferty prompted, his disapproval clear.

Chandra wondered if he disapproved of Viv or of Thorolf's taking the dare. She didn't doubt that Thorolf was inclined to indulge, given his robust metabolism.

"That's it." Thorolf shrugged, mystified.

So, he didn't know where Viv Jason was.

Chandra could have bailed and gone on to search for her prey alone. But Thorolf had a bond with her. Chandra decided to wait and see if Viv Jason turned up.

Besides, Thorolf might know more about her location than he realized. She'd still take him to her sanctuary, then, just to be sure.

Chandra might have considered all of this a rationalization to linger in the glow of the firestorm, but Rafferty frowned, distracting her from her thoughts. The older *Pyr* reached out and touched a fingertip to a dark mark on Thorolf's forearm. There were two round holes in the middle of what looked like a large bruise. "Where'd you get this?"

Thorolf frowned, looking so vulnerable that Chandra wanted to help him. "I don't know."

"And a new tattoo," Rafferty said, indicating the rows of spirals on Thorolf's arms. The repetitive design covered all the skin that was visible, even the blue dragon on the back of his left hand. That dragon was blue and its tail wound around his wrist. It was very well done.

The spirals looked amateur. Like doodles on his skin.

Thorolf frowned at his forearms. "I don't remember these swirls," he said. "But they must have taken a while. And I hurt all over." He peeled off his T-shirt abruptly, baring his muscled chest to view.

The way Rafferty caught his breath told Chandra that the spiraling tattoo covering his torso and throat was new, too. She found herself catching her breath for an entirely different reason. Thorolf was magnificent.

"How can you not remember getting such an extensive tattoo?" Rafferty asked quietly.

"It burns, too," Thorolf said with a wince. "Like I went to some dirty hole to get it. Rox would kill me."

"And your legs?" Rafferty asked.

"It's everywhere," Thorolf said. "Like a nasty burn." He looked at Rafferty with fear, clearly expecting the other *Pyr* to know the answers to everything. "How can that be? How could I be drunk long enough for someone to do all this?"

Chandra decided to try an experiment. How helpful was the firestorm?

"You must remember more," she said, deliberately putting her hand on Thorolf's arm. The firestorm burned hot and golden, the flurry of sparks from the point of contact taking her breath away. Even though she'd braced herself for its power, it shook her.

And aroused her.

It felt so good that she wanted to explore it more.

Thorolf smiled and drew her closer. "You're right. I remember I woke up in the apartment, alone." He inhaled sharply and looked agitated. "And then something happened." He shoved his hand through his hair, looking so troubled and vulnerable that Chandra wanted to fix everything for him. "Something bad, but I don't know what it was." He glanced between the two of them with concern. "Almost two years? Seriously?"

"We've been looking for you," Rafferty said with affection. "But you vanished without a trace." His gaze trailed over the tattoo and he frowned.

Since Thorolf was looking at her, Chandra nodded agreement. She declined to mention that no one could hide from her without a trace, not unless more powerful forces were involved. She'd assumed that the creature who had become Viv Jason was responsible, but now she wondered.

Who else might have targeted Thorolf?

Did his disappearance have something to do with his attacking Rafferty?

And why had he reappeared now?

Had the firestorm revealed him, or was that enemy using the firestorm against them both? Given the firestorm's influence on Chandra and the havoc already wreaked on her carefully laid plans, it was easy to believe the latter. She could almost have blamed her brother.

She lifted her hand and the ink of the new tattoo seemed to have faded. Thorolf followed her glance. "It hurts less," he said with surprise.

"Then it's not a normal tattoo," Rafferty murmured. "Not if it's affected by the firestorm."

Then both *Pyr* looked at Chandra, their expectation clear.

CHAPTER THREE

Chandra changed the subject quickly, not wanting either of them to make the suggestion that she could or should heal Thorolf by consummating the firestorm. She reminded herself of the merit of working alone.

"Who or what can hide a *Pyr* from other *Pyr*?" she asked instead. "You all have such sharp senses." That wasn't all of the truth—her abilities were considerable, too, but Chandra didn't want to reveal too much too soon.

Rafferty cast her a quick glance, one filled with assessment. "You know about us?"

She simply nodded.

Rafferty waited for a long moment, long enough to make her wonder what he saw. He then glanced back toward the city. "We'll be pursued. Have you anywhere safe to go?"

"I have a sanctuary," Chandra admitted.

Rafferty's eyes narrowed at her choice of word. "How safe is it?"

"Safe enough."

Again, Rafferty gave her a long steady perusal. Chandra didn't tell him more.

Thorolf spoke up. "But I can't be *Slayer*, Rafferty. That's crazy."

"Your blood was dark," Rafferty observed.

"It's like you spontaneously manifested today," Chandra added and Rafferty gave her a hard look. "I know some *Slayers* can do that."

"Some *Pyr*, too," Rafferty said tightly.

Thorolf flung out his hands. "But I'm having a firestorm! *Slayers* don't have firestorms."

"That must mean that there's still hope," Rafferty said with confidence. "You must not be completely lost as yet."

"But *Slayers* are made," Thorolf protested. "I would never choose to be *Slayer*. I'd never sacrifice the chance of a firestorm." He took Chandra's hand in his. The flurry of brilliant sparks that erupted from the point of contact made Chandra hot and bothered. She could taste that kiss again, feel his hand in her hair, and wanted him to stroke her from head to toe. "See?"

Chandra pulled her hand from his and stepped back, putting distance between them. Rafferty watched, his expression inscrutable. "I thought the *Pyr* were supposed to defend humans, as one of the treasures of the earth," she said.

The two *Pyr* nodded agreement. "Of course," Thorolf said.

"So, you weren't trying to kill that guy in the apartment?"

Thorolf frowned.

"What's this?" Rafferty looked between them.

"I found him, choking the life out of a man who had apparently moved into his former apartment. Isn't that *Slayer* stuff?"

"I guess if it's been two years, then Viv must have left the place." Thorolf pushed his hand through his hair again, then paced a few steps. He spun to stride back to them. "I was so pissed. I came looking for Viv, to protect her, but he was hiding her."

"Protect her from who or what?" Rafferty asked.

"From the *Pyr*." Thorolf seemed dazed by the admission, and it certainly shocked both of his companions. "I was going to squeeze the life out of him because I thought he was helping the *Pyr*. I thought he'd given Viv to them."

Chandra should have been so lucky.

Then she realized that something—or someone—had turned Thorolf against his own kind.

How could that even be? It didn't sound like one of her brother's pranks. He adored the *Pyr* and considered them his favorites of all creation.

What *was* going on?

It was probably a bad sign that she was curious enough to be tempted to put her own quest aside.

Rafferty and Thorolf seemed to be just as mystified as Chandra.

"Your wanting to injure the *Pyr* and humans is consistent with you turning *Slayer*," Rafferty mused. "But why aren't you violent now?"

Thorolf shook his head, then appealed to Rafferty. "How could I be made even partly *Slayer* without my agreement?"

Chandra didn't know nearly enough about this kind of transition, despite her research, so she just listened.

"Chen," Rafferty said with quiet heat. "I had wondered."

"Chen?" Chandra echoed, unfamiliar with this name.

"An ancient and powerful *Slayer*, possessed of lost dragon magic," Rafferty said. "He's targeted Thorolf before and his lair is hidden in the Himalayas. In this part of the world, damage can be easily attributed to him."

"He likes enslaving *Pyr* and has made *Slayers* and shadow dragons with the Elixir," Thorolf said.

"I thought the Dragon's Blood Elixir was gone," Chandra said, inadvertently drawing Rafferty's attention again. "Or at least its source."

"You're well informed," Rafferty said softly.

"Yes," she said simply. He waited, but she didn't elaborate.

Chandra would have to see what she could learn about Chen once they got back to her sanctuary. She supposed it only made sense that the *Pyr*'s traditional opponents might be involved, although it was yet another complication. She folded her arms across her chest, unable to dismiss the sense that life would only get more complicated the longer she remained with Thorolf.

She had to find Viv Jason and she believed Thorolf would lead her to her prey, one way or the other. She wasn't leaving yet.

"But it can't be Chen this time," Thorolf argued with Rafferty. "He almost got me once, but he failed."

"Why couldn't he come after you again?" Chandra asked.

"He did say he needed a *Pyr* with an affinity for air," Rafferty said. "That's why he targeted you, and Lorenzo, and Brandon."

"If he didn't get any of them, what makes you assume he got

me?"

"Where else could you have been all this time?" Rafferty demanded and Thorolf looked bewildered again. "And this tattoo took time. Remember that Chen uses spirals in his dark magic."

Thorolf stared at his skin in horror.

Rafferty tapped him on the shoulder. "Remember: it was the firestorm that led me to you."

Purpose lit in Thorolf's blue eyes. "You think it can save me."

Rafferty smiled. "I think that's what firestorms do. The firestorm saved Delaney from a plan to turn him *Slayer*."

"So, I'm having a firestorm at the perfect moment," Thorolf said with satisfaction. He reached for Chandra but she backed away.

This was all getting too complicated too fast.

"I thought firestorms were about the creation of more *Pyr*," she felt obliged to note. She wasn't going to be anyone's sexual toy or destined mate, much less the mother of his son. She was in this realm to complete a quest and had already lingered longer than she'd planned.

This was an expectation she had to stop in its tracks.

"They are," Rafferty agreed. "But sometimes they're about more than that. Sometimes they're about partnership and alliance."

"Sometimes they're about second chances," Thorolf agreed. "New beginnings and all that."

That was exactly what Chandra didn't want to hear. She didn't do commitment and long term and partnership. "No. That's out of the question. I work alone," she said. "Always have and always will. I complete the task at hand, then take on another."

Thorolf stared at her, his astonishment making her feel mean for stating the truth. "You'd just carry on, as if the firestorm had never happened, as if you'd never had a son? My son?"

"I'm not going to have your son."

"Of course you are! When we consummate the firestorm, you'll conceive my son."

Chandra folded her arms across her chest and glared at Thorolf, wishing the firestorm would stop making the *Pyr* plan sound so desirable. "Just because there's a firestorm doesn't mean it has to be consummated."

Thorolf's eyes gleamed and his hand landed on her elbow. The heat made Chandra swallow, but she didn't back down.

In a way, she liked that he didn't admit defeat easily.

In another way, she was afraid he could succeed.

"Maybe I'll change your mind," he said with an intent that made her swallow. The heat that emanated from his touch melted Chandra's protest from her lips and had her leaning toward him, yearning for another sweet kiss. She was losing her mind but when the firestorm burned so hot, she didn't care.

If she let him kiss her again, there was no telling where this would stop.

She shook off Thorolf's touch. "There's too much at stake," she said flatly, and he studied her. She felt herself blushing, as she never did, and wishing he didn't agitate her so much.

"Maybe the firestorm will change your mind," Rafferty said with a smile. He lifted a finger and a moment later Chandra heard the distant sound of police sirens. "You need to leave."

"We'll go to my sanctuary," Chandra said, her words coming quickly. It wasn't an ideal plan, but she didn't have a better one—and she couldn't think with him standing so close to her. "We can argue about the details there."

"We can consummate the firestorm there," Thorolf countered, that pale blue shimmer appearing around his body as he prepared to shift shape. "Is it far?"

Chandra nodded, not at all confident that she'd be able to resist the firestorm's call when he held her against his chest. Even having a small increment of space between them helped her to remember everything she had to do, every detail she'd put in place for this last battle.

No doubt about it: the firestorm was every bit as much trouble as Thorolf.

"Let me give you a firestorm gift," Rafferty suggested. "Confide the sanctuary's location to me and I'll take you there."

Chandra shook her head at the very possibility. "I won't tell anyone..."

"Then think of it," Rafferty commanded, his manner terse. "Fill your mind with the vision of it, the scent and sound of it, your every memory of it. We haven't much time and Thorolf is tired."

"Rafferty can spontaneously manifest elsewhere," Thorolf contributed when Chandra hesitated. "He can take us anywhere pronto."

Chandra could do the same trick, but didn't trust herself to stay focused while in contact with Thorolf and distracted by the firestorm's burn. She remembered only now that Rafferty was the *Pyr* who had been so changed by the darkfire. That must be why he could spontaneously manifest as some *Slayers* did. "Thank you. That would be best."

Thorolf eyed the other *Pyr* with concern. "If it's not too much for you."

Rafferty didn't even nod, much less leave more time for protest, before a shimmer of pale blue outlined his body. He shifted shape, becoming an opal and gold dragon again, then offered one claw to Chandra. She gripped one of his talons.

Thorolf shifted shape in turn, and Chandra averted her gaze as Thorolf caught her around the waist. She didn't want to look at how magnificent he was, in the form of a moonstone and silver dragon. It was bad enough being held in the crook of his powerful arm, feeling the firestorm's burn dissolve every conviction she held to be true.

She'd been right about the firestorm. Its light was brilliant yellow, almost white, and the heated desire it sent surging through her body made her wonder how anyone could resist it. Thorolf crushed her against his chest, and she leaned her forehead against him.

He felt so good.

She was never going to be able to keep her vow of chastity if this temptation kept up.

She shivered, realizing that she didn't even know the price of breaking it.

She'd never find out because she couldn't risk failing in her mission.

Rafferty took a deep breath, and then another. Chandra felt a weird quiver slide through her body, even as the scene around them began to waver. It was like the reflection on the surface of a lake, rippling slightly, revealing that it wasn't real.

How interesting that his ability to move through space and time felt so different from her own. When Chandra moved, she felt nothing. The transition was instant and without sensation.

As the scene around them vibrated with greater force, Chandra heard police motorcycles pulling around the corner of the warehouse. An unwelcome nausea suddenly ripped through her body. She held tightly to Thorolf as a wind swirled around them, one as ferocious as a tempest.

Her mouth went dry, even as her desire doubled and doubled again. She was trapped against Thorolf, held captive by one great claw, and consumed with memories of his scorching kisses. These *Pyr* felt such powerful sensations and passions that she was awed. She'd never felt so vehemently or been so keenly aware of another person. Her tendency to keep everything and everyone at arm's length was incinerated by the firestorm, making her feel vulnerable and emotional.

Alive.

And burning with desire for more.

Did she have the fortitude to deny the temptation that was Thorolf?

Chandra hoped for the sake of both of them that she did.

The sensation of manifesting elsewhere was a strange one. Thorolf felt himself flung off his feet and cast through the air, something that didn't happen often when he was in dragon form. After a long interval, his back suddenly collided with stone. He landed so hard that the breath was knocked out of him, but he shifted shape. He cradled Chandra close, determined to protect her.

Would the firestorm really save him from turning *Slayer*?

Why couldn't he remember almost two years?

And how the hell had he gotten this tattoo? The possibility that it was Chen's work seriously creeped Thorolf out, never mind wondering what had been put in the ink. That had to be why it burned so much.

Was Chandra really determined to deny the firestorm? Or had she just been surprised enough to protest?

Thorolf took a steadying breath and the smell of wet vegetation filled his nostrils. He couldn't discern Rafferty at all, which meant that *Pyr* had continued on to another destination. Thorolf let the firestorm's radiant heat slide through his body, reassuring him even as it fed his desire. The firestorm had to save him. Chandra would save him. He wasn't lost yet and he wasn't going to be lost so long as he had anything to say about it.

The firestorm was the key.

Which meant he needed to convince Chandra.

With the firestorm on his side, he was confident that could be done.

Thorolf was lying on his back in human form, with Chandra sprawled over him. The light of the firestorm had changed, turning to an ethereal silver, although it still fed that simmering desire within him. The silver radiance touched Chandra's features, making her look so alluring that she was irresistible.

Thorolf pulled her closer, intending to claim a kiss but she braced her hands against his chest and pushed back.

"No way," she said with a steely resolve that surprised him. "We have to work out a lot of things first."

He didn't believe for one minute that they could resist the firestorm, but he was prepared to give her a bit of time to get used to the idea. After all, she was his destined mate. She'd kissed him back. She was attracted to him. If she was feeling anything like he was, she might be arguing because she knew she'd lose the battle. If she wanted to try to deny the firestorm, it would only burn hotter and be better when they did sate it.

Thorolf decided he could live with that.

Chandra got to her feet and put distance between them so deliberately that he understood it was on purpose. He also knew it wouldn't make any difference. He noticed the way she caught her breath, and how she couldn't keep herself from taking a good look at him. He listened and heard the rapidity of her pulse, which was all the confirmation he needed.

The firestorm was on his side.

He wasn't the most patient *Pyr* on the planet but for the sake of his firestorm, he'd give patience a try.

Thorolf braced his weight on his elbow and smiled as he took a long slow look at her. His perusal agitated Chandra, more proof that the firestorm was undermining her self-control and destined to win. "You're right," he mused. "The view is better at a distance." He was gratified by the way she blushed. There was a sweetness, almost an innocence, about her when she was flustered that he found very attractive. Maybe that was because it was in such contrast to her air of command. She seemed to be so confident and strong, but was shaken by the firestorm's effect.

Thorolf figured they had at least that much in common.

And he liked the idea that he might be able to teach this competent and powerful woman a few new tricks. He lifted a brow and grinned at her. "If you think you can resist the firestorm forever, you're made of tougher stuff than me."

"It's got to burn out and fade away," she said, her words a little rushed. She might have been trying to convince herself. "Everything does."

"Not this."

"Nothing lasts forever."

"True. We'll succumb to it sooner or later."

"I don't believe it," she insisted. "It can't be true. There's too much at stake."

He glimpsed fear in her eyes, then she pivoted and leapt to a stone outcropping. He wondered what she was worried about and wanted to know. If it was something obstructing the firestorm, he needed to eliminate it.

He also guessed that asking her point-blank wouldn't get him an answer. With this space between them, she looked defiant and cool, as unlike the woman who had kissed him as possible.

Never mind the thousands of women she'd been during that kiss.

She sat down and watched him as the firestorm burned slowly and steadily. Even with the change in hue, it was more commanding than a bonfire. He found himself admiring her hands, the line of her chin, the intelligence in her eyes. Every bit of her seemed to feed his desire to possess her completely.

It was funny that he'd always had hopes for his firestorm, but he'd never truly believed how it could shake his world, not until it lit. He felt that everything was different—and so much was possible.

"How long do you think we can last?" Thorolf asked.

"Forever," Chandra said with a resolve he didn't share.

"Why? What's at stake?"

Her eyes flashed. "Everything!"

It wouldn't solve anything to be frustrated with her. Thorolf averted his gaze from his enticing mate and let the firestorm pick up the slack, simmering and burning while they were together.

On the upside, that weird tattoo seemed to have faded. The marks were so faint that it might have been done with temporary ink. It didn't hurt anymore, either. He caught Chandra looking and was glad he'd peeled off his shirt. He wasn't broken-hearted that he'd forgotten to tuck it beneath his scales, either. He made a show of checking out the tattoo, ensuring that he flexed his muscles as he did so.

She caught her breath and he smiled.

It was only a matter of time.

"It's better," he said, purportedly examining the tattoo. Really, he was watching her from the periphery of his vision. "You're healing it."

"Not me," she said quickly.

"The firestorm then."

She shook a finger at him. "Don't go there."

"Well, it's true."

She regarded him skeptically. "You've got to have a better line than that."

Thorolf laughed and she smiled, another flush stealing over her cheeks. When she lightened up and her eyes sparkled, he had to stop himself from moving closer.

Patience was the key.

Thorolf looked around and was surprised by their surroundings. They seemed to be in some kind of large stone temple, or maybe a lost city, one being steadily devoured by the jungle. The buildings had crumbled to ruins, no doubt with the help of the thick vines that wrapped around the stones. The pillar Chandra sat on was cracked, leaves erupting from the gap. He was startled to realize that an eye was carved from the stone beneath her, a huge eye that seemed to be watching him.

In fact, the whole pillar depicted a face, one with a serene smile and a thousand-mile stare. Far from making Thorolf feel a similar serenity, it gave him the creeps. He sat up warily, realizing that the jungle stretched endlessly in every direction. He felt a moment's panic that there were no bars, coffee shops, restaurants or other people. If he'd had his cell phone, he probably couldn't have gotten a signal here.

They could have stepped off the edge of the world. The very idea was troubling.

There wasn't a damn thing to eat.

The vegetation was thick and fleshy, of a green so dark that it disappeared into shadows. Mist gathered along the ground and huddled around the stone pillars. He had a vague sense that it was night, although the sky was hidden from view by the growth of the jungle.

The realization that this would be the perfect habitat for snakes filled him with fear and loathing, although he wasn't sure why his thoughts had turned in that direction.

Snakes. He shuddered involuntarily. He didn't remember disliking snakes before.

His gaze dropped to those two holes on his arm, and the dark skin around them. The sight revolted him, although he couldn't remember where he'd gotten the scars.

"Where's Viv Jason?" Chandra asked, her blunt question startling Thorolf.

"I don't know. Why?"

"I assumed she'd still be with you." She tilted her head to watch him, unreadable again. "Or that you might know where she was."

"I thought she'd be at the apartment." That reminded him of the missing period of his life and made him sit up straighter. Was it just the firestorm, or was something else going on? "What difference does it make to you?"

Chandra smiled, looking a lot like the face carved on the pillar.

Was she jealous of Viv? It would just figure that a woman would think another woman was a threat, even when she was in the midst of a firestorm. Thorolf heaved a sigh and gestured to the jungle around them. "I thought we were going to a sanctuary."

"We were."

"Did Rafferty mess up?"

Chandra shook her head, amusement in her expression.

"But this is jungle. Where are all the modern conveniences? The bars? The restaurants? The *bed*?"

She laughed, which completely surprised him. "I thought we just agreed we weren't going to need a bed."

"We didn't agree on anything. Besides, a firestorm doesn't

have to be satisfied in a bed." Thorolf rose to his feet. "I was thinking more about sleeping."

Her eyes danced with mischief. "Do *Pyr* sleep before their firestorms are satisfied?"

He regarded her warily. "Why are you so happy all of a sudden?"

"I feel better, being here. Safer." She blew out her breath. "Not having to worry so much about who sees what."

Thorolf smiled and took a step closer. "Sounds promising to me."

Chandra held up her hand. "Stay back. I need to think. The distance between us is part of what's working for me."

He folded his arms across his chest even as he did as she asked. "I'm probably supposed to be discouraged by that, but it sounds promising that the firestorm is messing with you, too." She blushed crimson and looked away, catching her breath quickly. Thorolf smiled. "There are other things we need to do, more important things than *thinking*."

"You ducked my question," she reminded him.

"Maybe I learned that trick from you."

Her smile was quick and playful, its unexpectedness making it feel like a gift.

"Is there any steak in this place? Cheeseburgers with fries?" He looked around. "There was pie at the diner near Delaney's firestorm," he said, yearning a bit as he remembered.

"Do the *Pyr* sleep before their firestorms are satisfied?" Chandra repeated.

He leveled a look at her, because she'd ducked a question again. "They sleep afterward, with satisfaction. Does that count?"

Chandra tilted her head to study him. "Do the *Pyr* ever really sleep? I thought you just slowed your metabolic rate, so you look like you're sleeping." She arched a brow. "Maybe breathe a protective dragonsmoke barrier at the same time."

Her words stopped Thorolf cold. "How do you know so much about the *Pyr*?"

Was he supposed to be so suspicious of his destined mate? But how could he avoid it? Every other firestorm he'd witnessed had required the *Pyr* in question to explain his nature to his mate, but Chandra seemed to know as much about being a dragon shifter than Thorolf did.

Was that why she'd already decided to deny the firestorm? She had to have a good reason not to want to try the most potent pleasure imaginable.

Although he couldn't think of a single one.

Instead of answering him, she whistled. Thorolf looked around with trepidation, wondering what she was doing.

Or who she was calling.

There was a hoot then a rustle, a rustle that made him look for snakes in the undergrowth. He didn't see any, but that didn't reassure him much. A bird sailed out of the foliage, swooping down to land on a tree near Chandra. It turned to consider him with solemn eyes and was strangely still. It even blinked slowly.

It was a silver falcon.

Where the hell were they? "I never knew there were falcons in the jungle," Thorolf said, feeling way out of his depth.

"You study flora and fauna?" Chandra smiled at the bird. "That's unexpected."

He felt insulted by her tone and folded his arms across his chest. "What would you expect me to study?"

"Women. Intoxicating substances. Jujitsu." She looked him right in the eye. "Pleasure."

Well, she'd nailed him without even trying. Thorolf couldn't bite back his smile. "Want a personal tutor?"

She caught her breath and Thorolf chuckled. The firestorm heated just a bit, its light becoming more radiant between them. He eyed his mate, deciding just where his lesson would start.

She rose abruptly to her feet, her cheeks burning. "Don't get any ideas."

"I've got plenty already," Thorolf admitted. She was so uncertain of herself that he eased up a bit. "It just seems odd for there to be a falcon here." He gestured to the bird. "I mean, it's light grey in a place that's all green. How will it hide from predators?"

"Falcons *are* predators."

"But still, even predators can be prey to something bigger."

She gave him a slow thoughtful look. "What hunts *Pyr*?"

"*Slayer*," he responded instantly. "Humans, once upon a time."

She nodded once. "It's not indigenous," she continued,

indicating the bird. "It came here with me."

So it *was* tame. She offered her hand to the falcon as Thorolf watched. The bird flew down immediately to land on her fingers, then she passed it to her shoulder. It wasn't as big as he'd originally thought, maybe fifteen inches high with its wings folded. It settled itself on Chandra's shoulder as if it sat there all the time, then regarded Thorolf again.

As if sizing him up. The way it surveyed him without blinking was spooky.

Maybe it was the yellow of its eyes that were spooky.

Thorolf thought about the way Chandra had changed when he kissed her, and wondered exactly what kind of trouble he'd gotten himself into this time. Maybe she was right to want to take it slow.

Not that he ever bothered with caution.

He looked around himself pointedly. "You said this is your sanctuary, right?" Chandra nodded. "So, where exactly are we?"

"I don't know." She mimicked his move, looking around as if seeing their surroundings for the first time. "I know how to find this place, but I'm not really sure what or where it is." She met his gaze with a confidence he didn't share. "All I know is that it's safe."

"That's nuts. You can't know it's safe if you don't know where it is..."

"But I know I'm safe whenever Snow meets me."

"Your pet," Thorolf guessed, knowing she meant the bird.

"She's much more than that." Before Thorolf could ask, Chandra continued firmly. "As for this place, I think it might be Myth."

Thorolf was so surprised that his mouth fell open.

Chandra smiled at him, then got to her feet and strode away. She liked surprising him, he realized, and he hated looking like a dope in front of his mate. She was moving quickly again, the falcon at complete ease with her stride, and Thorolf realized that she might disappear and leave him alone.

At least, he'd be alone if the snakes didn't find him.

Why couldn't he stop thinking about snakes? Every vine looked to him like it could come alive, and every leaf appeared to be a viper's head. He'd never thought much about snakes before, so maybe it was the jungle that made him fear them and their bites.

Those wounds in his arm should teach him something about drinking too much.

Something moved in the undergrowth, he was sure of it, and Thorolf jumped. He shuddered as he realized that the firestorm's light had faded. That it was silvery in this place instead of gold made it seem more insubstantial and ethereal.

As if Chandra could deny it.

As if it might fade to nothing and disappear.

Which would apparently suit his reluctant mate just fine.

Thorolf didn't like the sound of that at all. He was going to have to change her mind and soon. "Hey!" he shouted and ran after Chandra before she disappeared completely. "Wait up!"

The mist was gathering along the ground and Chandra could feel the air becoming colder. She spared a glance at what she could see of the sky. It had been twilight here for a long time, no longer day but not quite night. The consistency relieved her, and reinforced her sense that being in her sanctuary was best. They didn't have to worry about attracting human attention, not here where there were no humans.

As had been the case recently, one edge of the sky was darker, when she could discern it, and there were a few stars glistening there. She'd often wondered if it really was east or not. Once upon a time, it had always been midday in this sanctuary, but steadily the sky had darkened. Chandra understood that an era was coming to an end. She wondered what she'd do when the sky darkened completely to black.

What would be the fate of them all?

Still, something felt different since she'd last visited. Was it colder—or was she just more keenly aware of her surroundings?

Had the firestorm changed *her*? That was a terrifying prospect. She hadn't changed in several thousand years and wasn't about to start now.

And why had the firestorm's light changed color? Instead of having the radiance of the sun, it reminded her of the moon's luminescence. Chandra didn't trust that change one bit.

Her lips thinned that she was even experiencing a firestorm. She'd assumed it was a joke of her brother's, one with more serious potential for his beloved *Pyr*, but her experiment made her wonder. What *had* happened to Thorolf? Could she really leave him, knowing that her presence—or the consummation of the firestorm—might heal him?

What had seemed simple was becoming more complicated by the moment.

Chandra had to work quickly, before things got worse.

She had to find Viv.

She heard Thorolf running behind her, his footsteps getting louder, and smiled at the realization that he'd never sneak up on anybody. He could have been in his larger dragon form for all the noise he made. She could teach him so many things: maybe her brother had planned for that to be part of Thorolf's allure.

Whatever her brother's plan had been, the firestorm was making Thorolf—and what he could teach Chandra—nearly irresistible.

"Myth is a place?" Thorolf demanded.

Snow hooted, as if the bird was laughing at him.

Chandra wondered how much information Thorolf really wanted. "That's what the ghosts say," she admitted.

"Ghosts?"

She turned to find him frozen in his steps, his expression alarmed. "What's wrong with ghosts?" she asked, struck by his concern. That a dragon should be afraid of anything wasn't an idea she'd considered.

"Besides the fact that they're dead and they haunt people?" Thorolf shuddered. "I do better with living people."

"I noticed that in the market. And the apartment." Chandra failed to keep the humor from her tone.

Thorolf gave her a look, then braced his hands on his hips. Mmm. He was seriously good to look at. Chandra wasn't disappointed that there were no T-shirts to be had in the sanctuary.

He glared at her. "Okay, something or someone is messing with me. Rafferty said I'm turning *Slayer*, but here's the thing. Most of the *Slayers* I know are dead, and some of them are dead because I killed them. Never mind the shadow dragons, who are also evil and also dead, and have the distinction of having been controlled by the *Slayer* Chen, who might be responsible for this missing chunk of my life. So, meeting up with ghosts, with or without strong links to Chen, isn't exactly a high priority item for me right now."

"You sound like a kid who's scared of the dark."

"I'm no kid."

"Compared to what?"

"I'm old enough to have kicked some butt over the centuries." He eyed her. "How old are you exactly?"

"Why do you ask?"

"Because you did that shifting thing when we met, as if you were a hundred different women. Were those past lives, or are you a shape shifter, too?"

Chandra felt a jolt of fear at the reminder of how much she'd revealed to him. "It's complicated." She turned away and marched to the structure that housed her library.

"So, you know a lot about me and I know nothing about you," Thorolf complained. "That doesn't sound right."

"Maybe it's a test of the firestorm."

"Maybe you like to be the one who has the answers," he retorted, sounding disgruntled. "Maybe you just like being in charge."

His comment stung, mostly because it was true, so Chandra pivoted to face him and ended up admitting more than she'd intended. "The portals tend to be where there are a lot of ghosts gathered. I'm not sure why that is." At his stern look, she shrugged. "I'm not holding out on you. I don't know. Maybe they're the ones who remember the stories."

"The myths, you mean."

She nodded.

"So where are the ghosts?" He looked away, staring into the shadows of the vegetation.

"Everywhere." Chandra could feel their presence, even when she couldn't see them. It was like being watched by a million silent observers.

None of whom blinked.

"I can't see them," Thorolf admitted, but he kept looking.

"It's more like a feeling of being watched."

"I can't feel them," he said, but his eyes narrowed. She saw him take a long slow breath and his eyes glittered as he scanned the area. When he was avid like this, focused totally on something, Chandra found him even more appealing. He looked invincible and brilliant, committed.

A hero.

And all dragon. She thought of the loyalty of dragons, their power and their protectiveness, their ability to keep secrets and solve riddles, and yearned to feel his bare skin against hers. Would he overwhelm her? Claim her? Seduce her? Entice her? Chandra found herself tingling with the possibilities.

Which only meant that she had to get this mission back on track.

CHAPTER FOUR

"Where's Viv?" Chandra demanded and Thorolf eyed her with consideration. She supposed she should have worked up to the question or been less blunt, but those weren't her best skills.

"I'll trade you," Thorolf offered unexpectedly, impaling her with an intent look. "Answer for answer. And those half-answers of yours aren't going to cut it, so don't even try."

Chandra folded her arms over her chest. She instinctively kept her knowledge to herself and had done so for a long time. She disliked that he'd seen so much of her nature already, but there was some merit in the notion of working together. She wondered whether he knew just what or who was against them. "Okay," she said, pretty sure he noticed her lack of enthusiasm. "Ask."

"What are you?" Thorolf asked, going right for the big question. Chandra wasn't going to answer him and he must have guessed as much because he laughed. "Not that one?"

She shook her head.

"You do enough beating around the bush for both of us." He leaned closer, his gaze bright. His fingertip landed on her shoulder and began to ease toward her throat. Heat seared Chandra's skin and her arousal made her mouth go dry. He knew exactly what he was doing, and she was determined not to let him know how much his touch excited her. It would have helped if he hadn't ditched his shirt. All that bare flesh was seriously distracting. "I told you half answers weren't enough."

"So I went with no answer instead."

He laughed again. Despite herself, Chandra found her resistance melting and her mouth curving in an answering smile.

They stood and eyed each other, the firestorm's light heating between them in a most distracting way.

His fingertip reached her chin and she caught her breath, unable to stop herself. Thorolf's confident grin widened and that dimple, that tempting dimple, appeared once more. She was looking at his mouth again, remembering...

"That's complicated," she said in a hurry and stepped back. "It's too much too soon."

To her surprise, Thorolf let her break the contact between them, although he now echoed her pose. The stance made him look formidable and determined, as well as very male. They stood toe to toe and Chandra felt that low quiver of awareness continue to become more vehement.

She wanted another kiss. A longer and slower one, one that ended with them naked together.

Her curiosity was, of course, just to find out whether kisses had a diminishing appeal. It might just be novelty that had made the first two so hot.

It was a purely logical consideration.

Even she knew that was a rationalization.

He smiled as if he could read her thoughts. His eyes glittered as he leaned down toward her. This time, Chandra felt so mesmerized that she couldn't move away. "Okay, let's try something simple." he murmured, even his voice feeding her lust. "How do you know so much about the *Pyr*?"

"Research." Her tone was resolute.

"But that's just the thing. How could you research us? Unless you are *Pyr* and know from personal experience, or hang out with *Pyr*, how would you know?"

Her gaze danced over him, his muscular build showed to advantage by his pose, and lingered on his good tattoos. The blue dragon on his left hand had a tail that wrapped around his forearm. The other dragon wrapped its tail around his right upper arm. The weird spirals were fainter. "And if I hung out with *Pyr*, you'd know about it?"

"Absolutely."

Chandra was intrigued. "But there are so many of you. Do you share memories?"

"There weren't so many of us until the darkfire crystal took

Drake and his men back into the past." He answered her easily and honestly, his trust in her so complete that she was amazed. Was it possible that he had no secrets? She couldn't imagine that. "Those of us who were here before they created generations of sons are pretty tight."

Chandra nodded, knowing that strange revision of world history created by the Dragon Legion. The darkfire crystal had changed both the past and the present, maybe even the future, which was impressive magic.

It had also created the problem that she had vowed to solve.

Thorolf held her gaze steadily, waiting for her answer. Fortunately, this was one thing she was prepared to share with him. "I have a library."

In fact, Thorolf might be able to trigger the library to tell them exactly what they needed to know. The ghosts in the library were reliable like that.

They were also reliable in that they usually left out some key detail that Chandra always wished later that she'd known sooner.

She'd have to take the chance.

"A library?" he echoed. "We're not in any books, not really."

"But you're in this library. Come on, I'll show you." The falcon took flight as Chandra spun with purpose. She strode toward the stone building that had once been a temple of some kind. Thorolf matched his steps to hers and caught her elbow in one hand. It was a gentlemanly gesture, one that surprised her, and maybe that was why the firestorm flared to incandescent brilliance.

She pulled her arm from his grasp, uncertain what would happen if she was this distracted when she did any sorcery. "Just keep your distance," she warned, hearing the strain in her own words. "I have to think straight to complete this quest."

Thorolf grinned in a way that both excited her and warned her. "Keep my distance during our firestorm?" he asked. "Not a chance." He caught her hand in his and gave her fingers a squeeze. "The burn is part of the reward."

When his palm collided with hers, Chandra felt a vehement thrum of desire, one that slid through her body and filled her with need. She could have turned and surrendered everything to him in that moment, without a second's hesitation. The feeling was completely seductive and exactly the wrong response if she intended to keep Thorolf at bay.

"What quest?" he demanded, bending to whisper in her ear. That he could think straight during the firestorm was like salt in the wound.

Chandra shivered with pleasure even as she forced herself to answer. "My quest to save the *Pyr*, of course," she said, realizing that once again, she'd revealed more than she'd intended to.

And Thorolf, his gaze bright, hadn't missed it.

The *Pyr* didn't need saving, as far as Thorolf was concerned, so Chandra's answer made no sense. Sure, there were obstacles before them, and Chen was still out there, making trouble, but that wasn't anything the *Pyr* couldn't handle on their own.

Saving the *Pyr* in the final battle against the *Slayers* wasn't the job of a mate.

He decided that she was just being evasive again, giving him a half answer instead of the truth.

Thorolf decided to let it go, for the moment. If he could win her trust, she'd tell him more. If Chandra always worked alone, as she said, then she wasn't used to exchanging confidences. He'd win her over. Gradually.

No problem.

In fact, with the firestorm on his side, his success was a given.

She seemed relieved that he let it go.

Chandra led Thorolf to a small stone building that was less derelict than the rest. It was built like a fat column, but with a rounded top. It was maybe twenty feet wide and twice as tall, and the stone exterior was heavily carved. There was one of those big serene smiling faces carved over the low opening. This time, Thorolf was reminded of a midway ride, the kind that you entered through some demon's mouth.

Maybe that was why he had such a bad feeling about going inside.

There were some gaps in the stone and some pieces missing, as well as those vines growing all over it, but this structure was clearly in better shape than the others.

Was that because she'd maintained it?

He looked at Chandra, only to find her watching him with a challenge in her smile. He'd come to expect her to push him, but the change in her appearance startled him. He blinked, but she stayed in this new form.

And watched for his reaction.

Her hair had grown longer and hung in ebony waves to her hips. She was Caucasian now, her features pretty and her breasts more full. She was still tall and athletic, but now her eyes were clear blue and thickly lashed. Her lips were lush and rosy, offering an invitation he was inclined to accept. She had a blue tattoo that wound around her arms, a network of Celtic knots that looked like chain mail.

Not snakes, thank the Great Wyvern.

His body responded with enthusiasm to the change. She could have been a new mate, a new conquest to be made, a whole new firestorm. The silver flame that danced between them burned with the same vigor and brilliance, turning her features to silver.

"Surely dragons aren't afraid of temples," she said as he took a step toward her, and he realized that her voice was lower, too.

Sultry.

Almost familiar. Thorolf frowned, trying to grasp an elusive memory. Did he know her already?

"Which is the real you?" He had to ask. "This form or the other?"

The question seemed to amuse her. "Which is the real you? The dragon or the man?"

"Do you always answer questions with more questions?" he demanded in frustration and she laughed. He smiled in return, liking how laughter made her look carefree.

He'd make her laugh when they satisfied the firestorm.

He smiled, knowing just how he'd do it.

She blushed in a most satisfactory way, as if she'd guessed his thoughts.

"Sometimes there are no easy answers." She glanced at the doorway. "Unless you look in the shadows." Again there was a dare in her expression and her tone. "Sure you're not claustrophobic? Or afraid of the dark?" She didn't wait for his denial, but stepped inside, disappearing so completely into the shadowed interior that it could have been a portal to another realm.

Thorolf shivered, not liking that thought one bit.

While he hesitated, eyeing that face and the vines that looked so much like snakes, the falcon flew over his head and into the darkness.

That decided it. He wasn't going to look like a chicken beside a falcon.

Not in front of his mate.

Thorolf ducked his head and stepped through the doorway. To his relief, he found a small space inside, not a yawning portal to another realm. Chandra was standing to one side. She'd put on a quiver that was full of arrows and held a loaded crossbow. She must keep her weapon in this place, which hinted to Thorolf of its importance.

The interior was far creepier than the smiling face over the door.

There were skulls stacked in rows all around the walls. They gleamed white, as if bleached, their teeth bared in empty smiles and their eye sockets dark. They lined the entire structure, row after row of skulls, grinning back at Thorolf like a silent audience of thousands. They were stacked all the way to the top of the circular structure, and he wondered how many rows deep they were. Then he wondered what had happened to the rest of the bones from each body. Had she found this place or created it by gathering the skulls and arranging them? Thorolf shivered, not sure which answer was worse.

He was pretty sure that if he asked, she wouldn't tell him.

There was a small hole at the top of the dome overhead, showing a tiny speck of the sky overhead. The interior of the building was illuminated by the silvery light of the firestorm, which only made the skulls look cold. Dead. The falcon had landed on a skull opposite the doorway, its claws clutching the cracked crown as it watched him.

"This would be where the ghosts come from?" he asked, trying to sound as if he weren't freaked out. His voice caught, though, giving him away.

"I don't know." Chandra was calm and composed, exactly as he wasn't. "Maybe."

"For someone who likes to know the answers, you could know

a few more," Thorolf said and Chandra laughed again.

"Wouldn't that be wonderful?" she mused. "But the world is full of more questions than answers." She looked him up and down. "Is that what you're afraid of? Dying?"

"Isn't everybody?"

Chandra shook her head. "Some of us are afraid of living." Her confession seemed to startle her as much as it did him.

"Excuse me?"

"Comes with the territory," she said quickly, as enigmatic as ever, then gestured to the skulls. "Trust me. They'll tell us something."

"How?"

Her eyes shone, as if she could read his thoughts. Certainly she had to sense his trepidation. His heart was racing, as if he'd run a couple of miles, and he felt it was practically echoing in this small space. It wasn't just because of the firestorm, either. He could have done without the reminder that death comes as the end. He could almost taste death on his tongue, taste the ash of burning and the smell, that smell...

"Choose one and see," Chandra invited, interrupting his thoughts.

She might have been suggesting he pick a sandwich from a tray. She must do this all the time. What was she and where was she from?

What exactly *was* her territory?

The last thing Thorolf wanted to do was touch a skull, no matter how long it had been without flesh. Still he sensed that Chandra didn't think he'd do it. He wanted to surprise her.

"Bones don't talk," he protested.

"Ghosts do," she retorted, so quickly he imagined someone had made that argument before.

So the ghosts and the skulls had a connection, and that had something to do with how she knew about the *Pyr*. Thorolf didn't get it, but it was clear that Chandra intended to demonstrate rather than explain.

"Okay." Thorolf looked around, trying to discern a difference between the skulls or at least something that would invite his choice. They all looked pretty much the same.

The falcon was sitting on one. If the bird was some kind of

familiar for Chandra, or even if it just understood the rules of this sanctuary, its selection might matter. Maybe it wasn't arbitrary.

It was as good a choice as any other.

Thorolf reached impulsively for the skull the falcon sat upon and the bird fluttered its wings, only taking flight enough to move to another skull. Thorolf lifted the skull in one hand, surprised to find it a little smaller than he'd expected and certainly lighter. He turned to offer it to Chandra, without knowing what she'd do with it, but she was gone.

In fact, the whole temple was gone. He was standing alone, a skull cradled in his hand, and it was raining blood.

He was impressed.

And more than a little spooked.

Rafferty didn't expect Erik to be pleased that he'd been defiant. He was prepared for the annoyance of the leader of the *Pyr* when he returned to Chicago. Rafferty deliberately traveled in the form of a salamander, because he found the nausea less debilitating that way. His back hurt where Thorolf had burned his dragon scales and his chest was torn in a way that wouldn't heal quickly. Worse, he was troubled by what he'd learned. He manifested in the middle of the glass coffee table, not really caring who saw him.

He was among friends, after all.

He immediately realized that he was among more friends than he had anticipated. Erik was pacing the floor of the loft, the strain of the past two years still clear on his features. It smelled as if his partner, Eileen, was making yet another pot of strong coffee in the kitchen. Rafferty's mate, Melissa, was perched on the edge of one of the black leather sofas and gave a little gasp of relief when he appeared. He shifted shape and moved to sit wearily beside her on the couch. She took his hand in hers and squeezed his fingers tightly as he closed his eyes for a moment. Then she pressed a glass of water into his hands, knowing what he needed after such a journey.

"You're hurt!" Sloane said with dismay. The Apothecary of the *Pyr* had arrived during Rafferty's absence.

Melissa swore and pushed open his shirt.

Sloane knelt before Rafferty to examine the wound. He looked careworn and older than he had before, but then the plague in Seattle showed no signs of abating. It was spreading slowly, thanks to the efforts of medical authorities and the help of the Dragon's Tooth Warriors, but Seattle had been devastated by the illness, and it was still spreading.

Worse, the *Pyr* knew the infection had been the result of the darkfire crystal sending the Dragon Legion into the past. Sloane had been working day and night to isolate the contagion and its source, but had only determined that it was both a resistant virus.

An antidote was elusive.

"I'll heal," Rafferty said. "You have more important riddles to solve."

"You'll heal faster if I tend the wound," Sloane replied. "Take off that shirt and let me see the whole thing."

Rafferty did as instructed, knowing there was no point in arguing, especially as Sloane was right. He heard the other *Pyr*'s sharp intake of breath when his wounds were revealed and could practically smell Erik's disapproval. Melissa's grip tightened on his hand, and she helped Sloane apply one of his salves.

"Thorolf did this to you?" Erik demanded tightly.

"He didn't recognize me."

Erik swore and began to pace again.

"It wasn't his fault." Rafferty expected argument, but instead there was only silence. Maybe Erik was giving him time to collect himself. Rafferty could almost feel his skin healing in real time, thanks to Sloane's concoction, and he sighed in relief. He closed his eyes as the Apothecary and his mate rubbed the cream over his skin, glad to be safely within the dragonsmoke perimeter boundary of Erik's lair. He smelled the cup of coffee Eileen brought him, as well as the pair of shortbread she'd put alongside.

"Thank you," he said with a smile, knowing the combination would revive him as much as the healing unguent. He thanked Sloane and tugged on his shirt again, then sat on the couch beside Melissa. He felt better already.

If still troubled.

"You need to rest," Melissa scolded gently.

"Not before I tell everyone what I've seen." It was dark

outside the windows, as it had been when he'd left. The eclipse had occurred just before two in the morning Chicago time and in the mid-afternoon in Bangkok. It appeared that Rafferty hadn't been gone very much time at all, although he was exhausted. It was still snowing in Chicago, the relentless constant snow that had plagued the northern hemisphere for three winters now, and he could feel the cold pressing against the window. He was aware of the girls still sleeping soundly in Zoë's bedroom. Zöe was Erik and Eileen's daughter and should be the new Wyvern. Isabelle, the girl he and Melissa had adopted, was slightly older than Zöe but the girls got along well.

Rafferty turned the black and white glass ring on his finger, needing the reassurance of touching it, as he so often did after such an ordeal. He supposed it was because the ring was the last thing remaining of Sophie, the former Wyvern, and Nikolas, the Dragon's Tooth Warrior who had loved her. The ring had been made of a white dragon and a black one, twisted together for all eternity after they made the supreme sacrifice for their kind. Whenever he spontaneously manifested, Rafferty was reminded that this skill was usually reserved for the Wyvern among the *Pyr* and hoped he used the gift as responsibly as Sophie had used hers.

Slayers like Chen had stolen this power of the Wyverns, with the Dragon's Blood Elixir.

Rafferty took a restorative sip of coffee then cleared his throat, intending to report. Erik was still glaring at him, which wasn't a surprise. He respected that Erik had a heavy burden of responsibility, but also had learned more of the challenge before them while in Thorolf's presence—even if he had been there in direct defiance of the leader of the *Pyr*'s command. He prepared to explain, but Erik gave him no chance to speak.

"Save your breath," Erik said sharply, then bent over his laptop computer. He tapped the keys and the widescreen television on the wall came to life. "We've seen it all already."

Rafferty's heart sank to see that, once again, Thorolf had been captured on video while shifting shape. Yet again, the other *Pyr* was the star of a YouTube video that was gaining likes and views with record speed. He winced as Thorolf breathed a volley of dragonfire at him in the video and felt again his dismay when Thorolf threw the challenge coin. It was strange to see himself recorded, but that, too, had happened before.

No wonder Erik looked so grim. Rafferty knew that the leader of the *Pyr* was haunted by the memory of their kind being hunted to near-extinction in the Middle Ages and always was troubled when humans saw any of the *Pyr* in dragon form. It was proof that they existed.

That Thorolf had been filmed in the act of shifting the first time was the main reason Erik had been so disgusted with him. Rafferty remembered only too well that incident had been during his own firestorm, which only strengthened his determination to support Thorolf during his.

"A challenge coin," Sloane said, shaking his head. "An invitation to fight to the death."

"I thought my eyes were deceiving me the first time I saw it," Eileen said.

"He didn't know what he was doing," Rafferty protested again.

"But he injured you all the same," Erik pointed out.

"He could have *killed* you all the same," Melissa added.

"It's not his fault!" Rafferty insisted again, but Erik was launching on a tirade.

"Even knowing the danger, you had to go to him," the leader of the *Pyr* said. "I commanded you to stay here. I *forbade* you to go to Thorolf's firestorm, but you went anyway."

"He came to my firestorm, even with the darkfire burning," Rafferty felt obliged to remind him. "He stood by me."

"This isn't the same!" Erik was pacing even more quickly than he usually did. "He's been missing for almost two years, and it wasn't just because he was indulging himself." Erik flung out his hands. "Thorolf was *completely* gone."

"Even you couldn't sense him?" Sloane asked in surprise and Erik shook his head.

"Gone." He snapped his fingers. "Like a snuffed candle."

"Hidden," Sloane guessed, his manner thoughtful.

"Captured," Rafferty ventured.

"By whom?" Erik demanded before Rafferty could continue. "I see all of you, no matter where you are."

"Can you sense Thorolf now?" Rafferty asked, curious.

Erik started to say something, probably to reply in the affirmative, but he stopped. "No. What happened to him?"

Interesting. "He's with his mate," Rafferty mused, trying to make sense of it.

That did put a new spin on the problem. Who exactly was Chandra—or what was she?

"Do you know where he was?" Erik demanded.

"He must have been abducted and enchanted," Rafferty said. The others stared at him. "He doesn't remember, but something has been done to him. He has a new tattoo, one that's all over his body and burns."

"If he doesn't remember, it was done against his will," Sloane said.

"Chen," Melissa said with heat. "He's after Thorolf again."

"He said he still needed a *Pyr* with an affinity for air," Erik said.

"He can disguise his scent," Sloane agreed. "Maybe he can veil the scent of others in his captivity."

Rafferty shuddered at that prospect.

"Look at Thorolf's scales," Sloane said as Erik started the video again. Thorolf's scales in his dragon form, which were usually the color of moonstones mounted in silver, looked tarnished. Rafferty was reminded of clouded old mirrors, their silver peeling from behind the glass. He'd noticed it at the time, but appreciated being able to have a better look while not defending himself.

"Chen's turned him *Slayer*." Sloane sounded defeated.

Rafferty heaved a sigh. "He was fighting me because he smelled *Slayer*."

"He thought you were the *Slayer*?" Eileen demanded, her tone incredulous.

Rafferty nodded.

"Yet the *Pyr* are particularly perceptive. That's really dark magic at work," Melissa said softly.

Erik sat down hard, sparing Eileen a thin smile for the cup of coffee she offered him.

"It's not your fault," she said, placing a hand on his shoulder.

"You're wrong," Erik said with some gentleness. "It's completely my fault. I was frustrated with Thorolf and despaired of ever getting him to assume his legacy. I tried to push him by taking a hard stance and that was the wrong choice. In the end, I failed

Thorolf and now he's lost to us."

"Are you sure he's lost?" Melissa asked. "Can't we help him?"

Erik fixed her with a glare and bit off his words. "He's bait." Rafferty winced at the term. "Chen has released him to lure the rest of us into a trap. He expects us to go to Thorolf, to try to help him, which was why I forbade Rafferty to go." His eyes flashed. "You saw what came of that."

"Because Chen would only have released Thorolf if he couldn't be saved," Sloane concluded softly. "It *is* a trap."

"And we're supposed to watch him be destroyed, without being able to do anything about it, unless we sacrifice ourselves," Erik said. "It's brilliant, if evil." Their leader's discouraged mood settled over all of them, the room falling into silence as the video looped again.

Rafferty finished his coffee and put the cup aside. "But what about the firestorm?" he asked. "Thorolf can't be *Slayer* if he's having a firestorm."

"It could be a feint or a spell," Sloane suggested.

Rafferty shook his head. "I felt the heat and saw the sparks. I found him because of it. It's as real as any firestorm."

"Maybe Chen wasn't counting on the firestorm and its healing power," Eileen said, looking hopeful. "Maybe he miscalculated."

"I'd like to believe that." Erik got up to stare out the window. Rafferty thought he heard him mutter something but he didn't understand it.

What was "*Fimbulvetr*"? Or had he heard wrong?

"But he's with her and is lost to Erik again," Rafferty said, unable to understand that.

Erik sighed. "There will be four total eclipses over the next year and a half. The one in September 2015 marks the end of the Dragon's Tail. You understand what that means, don't you? Either the *Slayers* will finally and irrevocably be defeated and destroyed..."

"Or we will be," Sloane concluded.

"In a year and a half," Eileen said softly.

"We've been winning!" Melissa insisted, but Erik shook his head.

"Which is why Chen would make such a bold play. Capture a *Pyr*, enchant him, turn him *Slayer* and release him to draw us close in a futile effort to save him. For all we know, he faked the firestorm."

Rafferty winced.

Erik's disgust was clear. "Chen knows we'll support a firestorm at any cost." He shook his head. "I can't let this tactic succeed. I failed Thorolf, but failing the rest of you won't fix anything."

"Is he really *Slayer*?" Sloane demanded of Rafferty. "Has his scent changed?"

"It's not consistent," Rafferty replied. "It was darker when I arrived, more necrotic, but it changed while I was with him."

"If Chen had Thorolf, could he have escaped?" Melissa asked.

Rafferty was dismayed to find himself wondering if Erik was right about Thorolf being deliberately released by Chen. "Maybe he needs us to be healed," he suggested.

"Maybe we can't risk that." Erik shook his head wearily. "We're besieged on every front," he continued with quiet force. "These past two years, we have battled earthquakes, tsunamis, tornadoes and flooding. We have tried to avert disaster all over the planet as Gaia avenges herself on mankind."

"With the encouragement of Chen's spells," Eileen added.

"Yet we can't find him because his scent is hidden," Erik continued. "We certainly can't rout him from his sanctuary, and that means we can't defeat him." He frowned. "We don't know the old magic Chen has mastered, and even in their diminished numbers, the *Slayers* are doing much to imperil the survival of humans. Even with the addition of the Dragon Legion and the power of the elemental witches, we can't be everywhere and solve everything."

"I've got to find a way to stop that plague," Sloane murmured. "If it's the last thing I do and the only legacy of the *Pyr*."

Rafferty was startled to find any *Pyr* talking as if their demise was near.

Melissa leaned forward. "Look, I've told you before that the door is open for another television special. That show with Rafferty had phenomenal ratings, so we'd have carte blanche. We could explain the *Pyr*'s role in society..."

"We will not reveal ourselves any more than we have!" Erik said, interrupting her. "I refuse to repeat the past!"

Rafferty cleared his throat and took Melissa's hand in his own. "I think there's merit in the idea."

Erik looked at each of them, his eyes snapping with irritation. "I don't want to risk any more *Pyr*."

"Then what do we do for Thorolf?" Sloane asked.

"We stay away," Erik said.

"We go to him," Rafferty said simultaneously.

"It's a trap," Erik snapped. "I won't risk it."

"I will!" Rafferty retorted.

A pale blue light began to shimmer around Erik's body. "You won't defy me again!"

Rafferty wasn't daunted. He was just as determined as Erik, and he, too, stood up. "I will serve the firestorm, as I always have served the firestorm." He saw the blue shimmering light surrounding his own body, a hint that he was also hovering on the cusp of change. He knew this could devolve to a dragon fight but he didn't care. He would even battle the leader of the *Pyr* over this, an issue he saw as fundamental, not only to Thorolf's survival but to that of all the *Pyr*.

If they divided forces now, it could only lead to disaster. The air crackled between the two old dragons, each as convinced of his view as the other—and equally determined to hold his ground.

"It's Thorolf's only chance," Rafferty insisted. "It might be ours."

Erik shook his head, his eyes snapping. "No firestorm could destroy magic like this. No mortal woman could bring enough power..."

"She's not a mortal woman," Rafferty said, interrupting Erik in a breach of *Pyr* protocol. The others fell silent in astonishment. "I don't know what she is, but she's not human."

"She could be a trick," Erik said.

"She could be his salvation," Rafferty replied, choosing to believe.

The two older *Pyr* eyed each other, then Erik's lips tightened. Rafferty didn't know whether to expect a command or a concession. Erik turned away and marched to the window, bracing his hands on the frame as he stared out into the flying snow.

"So, we vote," the leader of the *Pyr* declared.

"No. It can't be a binding vote," Rafferty protested to the

obvious surprise of the others. "I'll go either way, even if I go to him alone."

Erik turned to consider him coolly, dragon in his gaze. "You would defy me again," he said softly.

"I believe that if we lose Thorolf, we will lose the Dragon's Tail War," Rafferty declared, his heart in his words. "And I'm not prepared to surrender everything as easily as that."

Erik bowed his head for a moment and Rafferty saw there was more silver mingled in his dark hair than ever before. He felt a bit sorry for his old friend, given this unwelcome burden of responsibility, but that didn't change his mind.

"So be it," Erik said. "There will be no vote. The leadership is simply yours, Rafferty. Since my counsel and experience is not of interest, do as you will."

Then the former leader of the *Pyr* strode from the room, leaving them all in astonished silence as he retreated to the sanctuary of his hoard.

Rafferty took a deep breath and squeezed Melissa's hand. "Make the deal for the show," he said softly. "We're going public. I have a feeling we're going to need all the positive publicity we can get."

Chapter Five

Thorolf was surrounded by blood, bathing in blood, swimming in blood. He feared he would drown in blood. The scent of it filled his nostrils and blurred his vision. It was warm and wet, pulsing around him. He heard a sound like the beating of a drum, echoing all around him, pounding into his own body. He felt safe, which made no sense.

He'd been flung off his feet and onto his back. His grip loosened on the skull and it rolled away, disappearing into the heaving red that surrounded him. He might have been in a satin bag or some kind of red-walled funhouse, one that shifted and changed constantly. He tried to stand up again even as his bloody world heaved. A ripple slid through the surface beneath him and he was shoved forward.

He saw a light, a bright spot in the blood, and instinctively tried to swim toward it. He wasn't sure his efforts made any difference, but the rippling walls pushed him closer to the light. The beating became faster and he realized it was a pulse, a heartbeat but not his own. His surroundings convulsed again, forcing him into the light.

Understanding dawned as the baby Thorolf had once been was shoved into the cold light of the world.

He could hear his mother panting, although he couldn't feel her heartbeat anymore. The midwife cleaned off his face and he took his first choking breath. She blew into his mouth to make the second breath easier, and he saw her triumphant smile when he took another breath and hollered at the indignity of being shoved into a cold world. Then she laid him on his mother's belly. He felt a hand cradle his head, his mother's hand, and closed his eyes as the glorious familiar sound of her pulse resonated beneath his ear. It was too far away, but hearing it and feeling it reassured him.

His mother. Tears pricked Thorolf's eyes.

She'd died too soon.

"A boy," the midwife announced, in a language Thorolf hadn't heard in many centuries.

It was a language he'd never wanted to hear again. He stifled his resentment and his anger, knowing that this vision must have a purpose. He should just go with it.

For now.

It was strange that he was both observer and participant in this vision: his own distant memories were mingled with what he had learned since that day. The infant couldn't have seen his surroundings as well as Thorolf did now. He recognized the hut, his mother, the midwife who had died when he was ten, the smell of the peat fire, the trunk against the wall where his mother had kept all of her treasures. He knew without looking that it was snowing outside. The feel inside the hut had always changed in the winter. He knew all of this, even as he felt the wonder of his own self in these first moments. He smelled the dead deer just before the door opened to admit his father.

His breath caught, his emotional reaction shaking him. He felt the old anger, and could have expected that and the burn of betrayal, but was surprised by the warm presence of love.

That was a lie. His father had never loved him. Thorolf had loved his father and believed himself loved, but he'd learned the truth of that when it counted. He'd gotten over it.

Still, it wasn't all bad to see his father again.

Thorolf remembered his father as being large and powerful in both forms, a giant of a man with a resounding laugh and ferocious loyalty to those he called his own. He'd been a *Pyr* who didn't mind making different choices from others: in his day, few dragon shifters had remained with their mates after the firestorm, but Thorvald had.

Thorvald had been a fierce and decisive judge, too.

Thorolf remembered that detail a bit too well.

His father was dressed in furs and leather, his shoulders covered with snow, his beard long and fair, his eyes as bright a blue as a summer sky. A deer was flung over his shoulder, his hunting knife jammed into his belt. He looked vital and male, a man providing for his family in the midst of winter. He also looked younger than Thorolf remembered him, but then, the day father and son parted was the memory that haunted him. That was decades away from this moment, and he wished with sudden force that they hadn't disagreed.

That he hadn't been judged and found wanting.

Thorolf felt his mother's pulse skip at his father's appearance and recognized that the firestorm had continued to light the days and nights of these two.

"A boy, Thorvald," she whispered and Thorolf's father grinned. He shut the door behind himself and slid the deer to another table.

The midwife stood and bowed deeply, even as Thorvald came to his wife's side. He bent and kissed her cheek, pushing the damp hair back from her face. His smile was filled with such tenderness and affection that Thorolf's heart clenched. He'd seldom seen this side of his father's nature. "I knew it would be a son, Solveig," he said with a confidence Thorolf recalled. "And I knew he would be strong. My fear was all for you."

He bent and kissed her, and Thorolf watched as she closed her eyes in relief. A tear slid from the corner of one eye and Thorvald captured it with one roughened finger, lifting it to his own mouth as he watched her. "Nectar of the gods," he said, as he always had when he'd removed Solveig's tears.

As Thorolf remembered, it made her smile.

It was remarkable to witness this moment, this emotion in a man who had usually hidden all of his emotions from view.

Solveig smiled, then exhaled. Her features softened, her gaze locked upon her *Pyr* until her eyes closed. She slept and Thorvald watched her avidly, even as the midwife cut the cord, cleaned and wrapped the new baby.

"She will survive?" he asked, his fear clear.

"It was hard for her," the midwife said softly. "He's big, like his father. He was not easily brought to light."

Concern lit Thorvald's eyes and Thorolf saw his grip tighten on his mother's hand. "She will be well, though?"

"Tomorrow I will tell you for sure. If she is well, you should wait a while before another," she cautioned and Thorvald nodded, still watching his mate.

The midwife bit her lip, then decided to speak outright. "Maybe you should not have another, but be content with one."

Thorvald smiled. "Who is ever content with one?" he joked and the midwife smiled. "The choice is Odin's, in the end."

The midwife's lips tightened a little. "So all the men say," she muttered.

Thorolf knew it would be the second son who killed Solveig, both infant and mother dying in childbirth. His mother would live five years after Thorolf's birth, long enough for him to remember her and mourn her loss.

But these people didn't know that. Not yet.

He suspected the midwife saw many women die in labor, for the only way to completely prevent more pregnancies was to abstain. The passion between his parents was such that Thorolf knew that unlikely to happen.

And it hadn't.

Once he had blamed his father for his mother's death. Once he had flung that crime in the old *Pyr*'s face, believing that his passion had been selfish and out of control. Now he saw his father's fear for his mate's survival and realized the truth his father had hidden from him.

It was startling to think he hadn't known everything about Thorvald. How much else had his father hidden from him?

The midwife lifted Thorolf into her arms, clearly intending to focus on the good news. "A fine boy you have, Thorvald. I can tell you today that he will be well."

"Indeed. I heard his robust cry. He is big and strong." Thorolf's father smiled, and reached a hand to gently touch his son in wonder. "We will feast for three days and nights to celebrate his birth. His name will be Thorolf, son of Thorvald, son of Thorkel." His eyes burned with a pride that tightened Thorolf's throat. "He will be the first of my sons and the greatest, the one who carries the power of my lineage, the son who wields the Avenger of the Aesir."

Inevitably, there it was. Thorolf wasn't surprised but he was disappointed. His father was glad of his birth because he had a task for him. Barely out of the womb and there were expectations, measurements, duties and obligations.

Thorolf remembered all too well how that task had gone. He hadn't forgotten about his father's blade, but he'd never wielded it and he hadn't worried about it once he'd ditched it. He could see the sword in his mind's eye, the Helm of Awe carved into its pommel, the vicious blade flashing like lightning as his father trained him to use it.

Seeing it again, he remembered what a majestic weapon it was.

But it had nothing to do with him. The price had been too high.

"He will be more than that," a woman said in a sultry voice.

Thorvald and the midwife spun to confront the woman who had silently entered the hut. Thorolf felt his father's alarm, for the door hadn't opened again, and she hadn't been there before.

It was Chandra, in the form she'd taken in this temple. She looked incongruous in this place, modern and purposeful, as well as being of different coloring than the others. Her tattoos looked right though, although they seemed to glow, as if she were lit from within. She possessed a sense of command that seemed to startle the midwife and Thorvald's father as much as her clothing and coloring.

Thorolf blinked and stared, but it *was* Chandra.

How could that be?

Was she older even than him?

What was she?

Chandra strode closer as they stared at her, the crossbow in her left hand. She glanced at the child, then her gaze locked on Thorvald. At her expectant expression, he fell to his knees before her. "You are one of them," he whispered, bowing his head and holding his son protectively against his chest. "The Vanir, walking in our midst."

The Vanir? Whoa! Chandra was a *goddess*?

If so, that explained a lot.

And, incidentally, left Thorolf with a million questions.

The midwife fell to her knees and bowed her head as well. She began to murmur a prayer.

"I've been sent to choose a hero," Chandra said crisply. She was perfectly at ease with their reactions and seemed to have expected as much. "I choose your son."

Thorvald caught his breath.

Thorolf felt a chill slide through his body as Chandra planted a kiss on the baby's head. Quicksilver raced through his veins from the point of contact, a sensation not unlike the firestorm's touch but cold instead of hot. Her lips were cool and firm, not soft and warm as they'd been when he'd kissed her. It was a dutiful kiss.

A blessing.

She stared into the baby's eyes, and Thorolf saw the thousand shades of blue, grey and silver snared in her eyes. When she spoke, her tone so authoritative that no one dared defy her. "You have the blade and he has the mark of my blessing. Together, they will make it right. He will be the salvation of the *Pyr* and of the world."

Defiance rose in Thorolf at her words. She had no right to claim him and command him without his consent. She had no business assigning him a job.

Was that what her refusal to sate the firestorm was about? Did he have to pass some kind of test first? Besides, the *Pyr* didn't need saving.

"But the *Pyr* don't need saving," Thorvald protested. Thorolf was startled to hear his unspoken reply on his father's lips.

Chandra smiled. "Not yet." She nodded at Thorvald. "I give you my pledge that he will survive until they do."

Thorolf shivered, fighting a major case of the goosebumps.

Chandra held Thorvald's gaze, her air of command a palpable force. "You will pledge to me that you will bestow the Avenger of the Aesir upon him."

Thorvald bowed deeply. "I can do nothing else, my lady."

Did anyone ever say no to her? Thorolf thought it unlikely.

Chandra spun on her heel, as if to leave, but never reached the door. She disappeared instead, her form replaced by a flurry of what looked like falling snowflakes. The flakes twinkled, then disappeared in a heartbeat.

She might never have been there at all.

Thorolf was aware of his father's astonishment and the midwife's uncertainty, even as the vision was obscured by swirling snow. He had a good bit of uncertainty of his own and more than a little irritation. How could his mate be a goddess? How could she be the one who had set him on the path to failure?

How could his firestorm not be about love and partnership? Thorolf had spent centuries yearning for his firestorm, for a woman and mate who would love him for what he was, and not for what she could do for him.

Yet the firestorm was simply bringing him back to his father's unfinished business, back to what had been called his destiny, back to an obligation that he'd never wanted and had refused to fulfill.

It was wrong.

It was unfair.

And it was Chandra's fault.

Thorolf opened his eyes to find himself back in the temple of skulls, with Chandra before him. She was watching him with dismay, as if she were shocked.

Well, that made two of them.

"*You* started it," he said, shoving the skull back into her hands. Her fingers shook and he thought she might drop it. He was too pissed off to care. "You!"

Her mouth opened and closed, and she stammered as if lost for words. It wasn't like her, but Thorolf didn't care. For all he knew, her apparent surprise was another trick. He'd been betrayed in every possible way, and his mate was at the root of it.

His *mate*.

A memory he would have preferred to avoid was filling his mind and his senses. He smelled ash. He smelled burning skin. He saw destruction and felt the weight of his own failure to defend what he loved. He felt ripped apart all over again, furious and devastated.

And Chandra had launched the whole thing, by choosing him at birth for a task he didn't want.

"This is why you don't want to satisfy the firestorm," he charged and she flushed scarlet. She didn't deny his accusation, though, which stung. "Because I haven't done what you wanted me to do. You're just like my father: everything is an exchange."

"It's not like that," she said, stammering a little in a way that was both uncharacteristic and endearing. Thorolf gritted his teeth, not wanting to cut her any slack at all. "You don't understand."

"The problem is that I *do* understand." Thorolf flung out his hand. "Everything, all of it, was *your* fault!"

Chandra lifted a hand, maybe to beg for his understanding, but Thorolf didn't care. He refused to be affected by her show of vulnerability. He'd manage to hang tough as long as she didn't cry.

He couldn't imagine Chandra crying, which gave him a chance.

"You weren't supposed to see that..." she began but Thorolf interrupted her.

"Not part of your plan? I'm guessing that everything always goes the way you want, seeing that you're a goddess. I'm guessing that no one ever says no to you."

"That's not how it is!"

She looked angry, which worked for Thorolf in a big way. He'd make her just as mad as he was, then she'd never cry.

Then he'd never cave, just to make the tears stop.

"No? Well, maybe you're right about the firestorm," he said, tossing it like a taunt. "Maybe we shouldn't satisfy it. Maybe it would just be another mistake."

Chandra bristled and her eyes flashed. Her displeasure was making sparks fly between them. The firestorm shimmered around her, caressing her hair, her lips, and making her look touched by moonlight. It was easy to believe in this moment that she was a goddess.

A goddess and his mate.

Thorolf felt awed by the firestorm's gift, but fought against it. Chandra wasn't telling him all of the truth. He shouldn't trust her.

But he couldn't look away either. "So, it's fine for you to decide against the firestorm and say you don't want me, but quite another for me to agree with you?" Thorolf scoffed deliberately. "Is everyone supposed to want you?"

"That's not the point," she retorted. "What about your responsibility to your kind?"

Responsibility was just about the worst argument she could have made, if she'd been hoping to change his mind.

He shrugged, as if he didn't care. "They're probably better off without me. Last thing they need is another one from my bloodline."

Chandra's eyes snapped with fury. "That's not what you just saw," she scolded. She jabbed a finger through the air at Thorolf.

"You're destined to wield the blade that saves them forever. You can't turn your back on that!"

Thorolf folded his arms across his chest, kept his tone indifferent, and watched the show that was his mate. She had to be the most gorgeous woman he'd ever seen—and there were dozens of versions of her. He couldn't wait to meet them all. "I didn't volunteer."

"Destiny isn't that picky!" She straightened. "You were *chosen*." She inhaled, pride in her stance. "I chose you and I'm never wrong about champions."

"But I'm choosing not to play."

"You can't do that..."

"Of course I can. I don't have the sword, and I'm not going to look for it." He leaned down so that their noses were almost touching to let her see his resolve. The firestorm was a brilliant silver orb of light, snapping and crackling between them. "Your assignment isn't my problem anymore."

Chandra drew herself up to her full height and braced her hands on her hips to lecture him. Thorolf was starting to hope she'd smite him. Otherwise, the desire fed by the firestorm might make him spontaneously combust. Even knowing what he did of her—and how conflicted it all was—he wanted her with every fiber of his being. "You have a duty and a responsibility," she said through gritted teeth. "You can't just walk away..."

"Watch me."

"You were chosen," she argued, her voice rising. "You have an *obligation*. Your father vowed..."

Thorolf couldn't resist her any longer. He caught her by the nape, lifting her to the tips of her toes. The mention of his father made him feel volatile and angry, and he saw the pale blue glow that heralded his shift to dragon form. "Now you're the one who doesn't understand." She felt small and precious in his grip, and the firestorm once again turning his anger to desire. He couldn't decide whether to kiss her or wrestle with her.

"Then explain it to me," she whispered.

The words could have been a challenge, but her voice had gone all soft and breathy. Her gaze was flicking over him, her awareness almost tangible. Thorolf could smell her arousal, which didn't help him think straight at all. The firestorm was sparking and glittering between them, brilliant white and silver, its touch turning his blood to fire.

His gaze fell to her lips and Chandra licked them without meaning to do so. The sight fed that burn of desire, the lust of the firestorm that made it impossible to think straight.

A single thought shot through Thorolf's mind: she was just trying to manipulate him.

Again.

And that was enough to make him step away.

She'd chosen him for a task, but he hadn't done it. She was just like his father but worse, a goddess who was never denied. He had to guess that she'd do anything to make him fulfill the destiny she'd selected for him.

Even pretend to be tempted by the firestorm, the one she'd said flatly she wouldn't satisfy.

Maybe Rafferty was wrong about the firestorm.

Maybe if the firestorm could be twisted like this, it wasn't worth having one. Thorolf dropped Chandra and charged out of her so-called library. He headed for the thickest part of the jungle. Maybe he'd find a poisonous snake. Maybe he'd be lost in Myth forever.

Maybe none of it mattered anymore.

In his lair, far beneath the mountains of Tibet, the *Slayer* Chen dozed in his dragon form. He was perfectly still in his cave, the light from the sconces on the walls caressing his lacquer red and gold scales. He breathed slowly and deeply, fortifying the dragonsmoke barrier around his lair with every exhalation.

And he dreamed. He dreamed the dreams of Thorolf, his chosen prey. He'd already cursed the untimely spark of that *Pyr*'s firestorm. Just a few days in the world would have been enough to let the tattoo ink leach into Thorolf's body and darken his blood. Just a few days would have been enough for him to destroy at least a few of his fellow Pyr. But the firestorm had complicated things.

The mate was an enigma until Thorolf dreamed.

Chen's eyes opened suddenly when Thorolf slammed the skull

back into Chandra's hand.

"So that's it," he whispered, his pulse quickening as he considered the implications of what he'd just learned. "It explains so much."

Challenges so often came back to the curse of family.

Chen's gaze flicked to the large egg-shaped rock in one corner of his lair. He smiled, liking that the last member of his family and the only one who had ever spoken against him had been so perfectly contained. He was glad that he hadn't killed Lee.

At least not quite.

He liked to think that on some level, Lee was aware of his older brother's doings. The *Pyr* Lorenzo was right in that there was little point in a brilliant performance without an audience.

Too bad Lorenzo had gotten away. Chen thought they might have agreed on many things.

But Thorolf wouldn't escape this time. The magic was too strong. Chen narrowed his eyes and reviewed his scheme, certain it would succeed.

The ghosts shouldn't have shown Thorolf that.

Chandra had deliberately kept her truth to herself, just because she'd doubted he was ready to hear it. The ghosts, though, had outed her and now Thorolf's support was lost.

But then, Chandra was coming to realize that nothing about this particular quest was going according to plan. The firestorm was changing everything, making her doubt her past choices, even eroding her own conviction that she would succeed.

It wasn't the firestorm: it was Thorolf. She had to wonder now why she'd chosen him, why she'd felt even before his birth that he would be so special.

She'd been right, of course, but she was starting to wonder what had guided her choice. Instinct? Destiny? An awareness that one day she would have a firestorm with him? Either way, Chandra was quickly becoming convinced that her *Pyr* was remarkable. He was far more dangerous than she'd imagined.

She'd let Thorolf choose a skull to learn what he knew about the creature who now called herself Viv Jason. That was all. He had to know something of use, even if he didn't realize its importance. She'd assumed his choice of skull would reveal some part of his truth.

Instead, he'd learned part of *her* story.

Worse, he knew what she was—if not specifically who she was—and more about the connection between them. He knew she'd been the one who'd chosen him for his destiny, which wasn't going to help convince him to confide in her.

She was never going to complete this quest.

Miserable ghosts! They always played games with the truth, hiding what she most needed to know, pretending to offer wisdom but really only giving partial data. She wouldn't have trusted them at all if she'd had any other resource, but this went beyond any previous deception.

The worst part was that she felt such compassion for Thorolf. He felt used and manipulated, and the truth was that he had been. It wasn't an unfair reaction, but Chandra couldn't change the past.

She couldn't undo what she'd done.

She'd never considered over the centuries what it was like for some individual, some mortal, to be chosen to play a particular role. If a job needed doing, she found a way to do it. Chandra thought about results, but results from her perspective. She'd never before considered the price paid by the one she'd chosen.

Chandra changed lives and never gave it a second thought.

She'd changed Thorolf's life by choosing him, and now, that could be the reason she failed.

That sounded like a lesson her brother would engineer.

Somehow she had to make this right.

The heat of the firestorm faded to a faint glow with distance. She knew Thorolf was furious: in fact, she could feel his anger more clearly than the firestorm's invitation to passion. Despite that, she felt disheveled and disturbed. If ever she could have hoped for her usual clear thinking, this would be the moment.

Instead, she felt guilty.

It was a new sensation and Chandra didn't like it at all.

But the change in her perspective didn't change that she *had* chosen Thorolf. Centuries of preparation couldn't be discarded now that the battle was upon them. The creature who called herself

Viv Jason was out in the world, seeking the destruction of the *Pyr*. Chandra had chosen Thorolf as the champion who could save the *Pyr*. Thorolf was the lynch pin, whether he wanted to be or not.

Even her short bit of time in Thorolf's company, even that one kiss had given Chandra a new conviction that the world could not be without the *Pyr*.

She didn't want the world to be without Thorolf.

Which meant she had to succeed. Somehow.

She lifted a hand and a pale spark of the firestorm danced on the tip of her finger. Maybe she could use the firestorm. Maybe it wouldn't be so bad to surrender *something* to get Thorolf on her side. Sometimes destiny needed a helping hand, and this time, it had to be Chandra's.

She would have to use pleasure and sensation and the firestorm's seductive power to change Thorolf's mind. It was the only tool she had, the only thing powerful enough to affect a stubborn *Pyr*. She didn't have to actually satisfy the firestorm, but a few more kisses wouldn't be all bad—especially if they helped her to achieve her goal.

Could she offer more without surrendering everything to him?

There was only one way to find out.

Thorolf ran.

He bolted though jungle, jumping over roots and vines and ducking through the lush vegetation. He didn't know where he was going, or how far this place extended. In a way, he didn't care. He wanted the heat of the firestorm to fade. He didn't want to feel torn and betrayed and disappointed. He wanted to exhaust himself and sleep.

Preferably for a long time.

Maybe in Myth, he could sleep forever.

Actually, he could have used a Texas buffet. They'd lose money on him, that was for sure. He thought about chicken fried steak and deep fried okra, mashed potatoes and gravy. Biscuits, definitely. Maybe some huevos rancheros to start things off, because he hadn't had breakfast in a while. He couldn't remember when he'd last eaten and his gut was empty enough to ache.

It said something for his state of mind that he wasn't going to ask Chandra, the only person in this place, for help with that.

He'd rather starve.

He leapt more than one river, and eventually the jungle thinned. The ground became more rocky and the vegetation more sparse. The air cooled and was less humid, the sky turned a midday blue. Pine trees grew on either side of him, springing out of the earth as he ran. It was as if the landscape was changing to suit him, or to frame him.

No. To remind him.

Thorolf saw the mountain grow out of the ground on either side of him, stretching into the sky and looming over him. He saw the snow on their peaks, the sparkling streams crashing down their sides, the eagles soaring near their precipices. He ran, knowing full well what land he'd entered and wanting only to emerge on the other side of it. He saw the brilliant blue water in the fjords, felt the sting of cold air in his lungs, saw the alpine meadows beneath his feet turn to snow. He saw the smoke rising from the village, felt his heart shred, but couldn't stop.

He shifted shape instead.

He was flying then, soaring in his dragon form, swooping over the land in his haste to reach Astrid. He knew what he would find, and he realized that he'd known it even then, even before he'd seen her. He swooped low over the burning village, knowing where she was by the weak beat of her heart. He'd have known the sound of her anywhere, the smell of her, the sound of her.

Her pulse was so weak. Her breath was so thin. Her pain was beyond belief.

He hadn't believed it until he'd seen her, until he'd touched her, until she'd seared him with her accusation.

Until he'd watched her die. The last words passed her lips and she was gone.

He could have torn out his own heart then in his despair. The one person who had loved him for himself was gone.

He roared into the sky, bellowing with anguish. The world was quieter because she had breathed her last. It was empty. A void. A prison. He flew long and hard, journeying far before he returned home, aching and weary. He sought refuge and sanctuary.

Instead he found an answer he'd never wanted.

His father was waiting for him, his gaze steely. He surveyed Thorolf, nodding once when he saw his son's devastation. *"It was for the best,"* he said in old-speak. *"She was a distraction from your purpose."*

Thorolf had stared at his father, shocked to stillness by his words.

"She was not your destined mate," his father said, as if explaining something simple to a child. *"You will see in time that mine was the right decision."* And he offered the Avenger of the Aesir to Thorolf, the blade forged with the Helm of Awe, the blade that was both his destiny and his condemnation.

A distraction.

Thorolf seized the weapon without a word and took flight again. Fury gave him new strength and he knew where he had to go. He strained himself to fly to the edge of the world, the place where the cliffs fell sharply down to a bottomless chasm. He shifted shape and stood on the peak in his human form, then flung the blade out into the void. It caught the sunlight as it spun through the air, then plummeted to the depths where it could never trouble him again.

He spat after it.

He was done with destiny, with obligation, with those who cared for him only because he could fulfill their dreams. He was done with love, although he wasn't done with sex by a long shot. If his father wanted to judge him by his deeds, Thorolf would give his father plenty. He would enjoy every pleasure of the flesh that could be had. He would drink and eat and fight and fuck and never care about any of it. He would indulge himself and only himself.

Until one day, his firestorm gave him the mate no one could ever call a distraction.

And now, centuries later, Thorolf stood on the lip of that chasm again, his mind filled with the anger and the passion of the past. "Astrid," he whispered, his wound as raw as when it had been newly inflicted. "Astrid, I'm so sorry."

He stood on that precipice and was sorry to be what he was.

Because that was the root of it. Because he was *Pyr*, he couldn't give a son to a woman who wasn't his destined mate. Because he was *Pyr*, he was chosen for a quest he didn't want, and that woman had been called a distraction. Because he was *Pyr*, his kind were responsible for the razing of her village. He didn't know the dragons who attacked human settlements, but he knew of them. His father knew them, clearly, and had directed their most recent attack. Eventually, such destructive dragons would be called *Slayers*. When Astrid died, there had been no formal division in the ranks of the *Pyr*.

His own kind, no matter how Thorolf looked at it, were responsible for Astrid's death.

And she was right: all she had done was love him for himself.

Thorolf kicked a stone and watched it fall, knowing he'd never hear it splash in the water far below. He'd cast aside everything for the sake of principle. He'd surrendered everything he could have done, just to deny those who demanded he deliver on an obligation he hadn't made himself. He'd bet everything on the promise of the firestorm.

But his firestorm had proven to be the biggest betrayal of all.

CHAPTER SIX

Niall sat bolt upright in bed, his fists clenched in the sheets and his body taut. The recurring dream was crisp in his mind, so vivid that he could taste the cold wind. There was blue light all around his body and he recognized that he was poised to shift shape and fight. He breathed deeply, but his lair was safe, as were Rox and the boys. He forced himself to relax and remember what he could of his nightmare. He felt the devastation of the *Pyr* whose nightmare he'd shared repeatedly and finally knew who it was.

Rox rolled over at his motion, and her eyes widened in surprise. "Okay?"

"It's Thorolf," he said tightly, then swung out of bed. "The dream is Thorolf's."

"What?" Rox turned on the light. "T never loved anyone except himself..."

"He did. Long before we knew him. And he chose not to ever love again because of what happened." Niall was pulling on his jeans, Thorolf's bitterness affecting his own mood. "I don't blame him."

"Because she died?"

"Because his father somehow made that happen. He thought she was a distraction."

"What? What about defending humans?"

"I guess his dad thought something else was more important." Niall tugged on a T-shirt then grabbed a hoodie. "I have to go to Erik. I can't tell him this in old-speak or over the phone. He'll know what to do next. He might even remember something related to it."

"You think you're going alone?"

Niall turned to see that Rox had crossed her arms over her chest. She looked disheveled, annoyed and sexy as hell. He sat on the edge of the bed beside her, controlling his impatience with an effort. She had to know the rest of it. "I felt a firestorm ignite today. It was Thorolf's."

"So he isn't missing."

"Not any more."

"Then this will all tie together," Rox said, then rolled her eyes. "And knowing T, he's going to need all the help he can get."

There was that. Niall pulled out his phone to see how soon they could get a flight to Chicago, while Rox went to awaken the boys and pack

Booking a flight proved to be harder than he expected. The relentless snow had become yet another blizzard, and O'Hare was closed. In fact, most of the airports in the Midwest were closed, with the eastern seaboard already canceling flights. Getting seats for a party of four was almost impossible, even with his connections at the airlines. The boys were three and tall for their age, too big to sit in laps.

If they moved fast, though, he could get them on a flight to Los Angeles, then a connection to Bangkok.

"What?" Rox said as she grabbed a backpack for carry-on.

He summarized the situation for her, then shrugged. "So, either I fly us to Chicago, or we take commercial flights straight through to Bangkok."

"You can't fly us all the way to Bangkok," Rox said, as decisive as usual. "You're going to need your strength to fight and bad weather will hamper you as much as a commercial airline." She straightened to smile at him. "And really, I'd rather go right to T, where the action is."

"With the storm, this might be our only chance to get a flight."

"Two minutes," Rox said, holding up her fingers. "And we are out of here."

"You can be packed that fast?"

"I can be ready that fast." She grinned at him. "There's this tour operator who taught me that they sell toothpaste and underwear all over the world. I'll grab my favorite tattoo guns and we'll just go. We'll buy whatever else we need after we arrive."

Niall grinned and booked the flight, assured one more time that his mate was the perfect woman for him. Then he went to get the boys dressed.

They had to make that flight.

In Traverse City, Sara Keegan was updating the online inventory for her bookstore. There were days when being the partner of a dragon shape shifter wasn't any different from being any other mother of three small boys.

She had one eye on the clock, because six-year-old Garrett had to be picked up after school to be taken to his Little League game. It would be the first game of his first season and he was so excited that he hadn't slept the night before. Three-year-old Ewan had a play date this afternoon with the son of one of Sara's part-time employees, so she'd pick him up first.

She rocked a cradle with one foot as she worked, ensuring that two-year-old Thierry kept sleeping until she was done. She'd perfected the art of rocking this cradle with her foot, regardless of what she was doing, sleep having become a precious resource in her life in the past few years. He'd be awake later, but she'd take what she could get.

Her partner, Quinn—the Smith of the *Pyr* and an artisan blacksmith—was working longer hours than usual, preparing for a busy season of art shows. He was trying to build his online business, since it was becoming increasingly complicated to travel to shows with their growing family. He was going to pick her up at four and gather them all for Garrett's game. There would be another set of hands for the evening, much to Sara's relief. There was a container of homemade spaghetti sauce thawing in the fridge at home, because pasta and tomato sauce was a reliable hit with her boys.

It was quick, too. She just had one more box of new titles to add to the inventory, then she'd get Thierry ready to go.

She admired the cover on the next book, then opened it to the copyright page. Instead of typing in the title, author and publication date, though, she found herself typing something else.

"A union of five will tip the scale
When the moon aligns in Dragon's Tail;
This Pyr *alliance can defeat the scheme*
And cheat the Slayer *of his dream.*
Fulfilling a pledge long been made
Will put darkness in its grave.
Know Pyr *and* Slayer *can share one curse:*
A vulnerability wrought of their birth.
Keep the pledge and defeat the foe,
So the Dragon's Tail brings triumph not woe."

Sara stared at the words on the screen, knowing they hadn't come from her mind. Once again, she was being a conduit for messages to the *Pyr*. It was a bit spooky how her role as Seer manifested itself, but she knew well enough to take notes when she could. She copied the text and pasted it into another empty document, then printed it out. When she looked back at the screen, the field on her inventory form was as blank as if she hadn't typed anything.

She shivered, then glanced around the bookstore, knowing her Aunt Magda would have no troubles believing in the turn Sara's life had taken after inheriting her New Age book shop. Her stomach twisted with the nausea that was increasingly familiar.

Trust her to get morning sickness in the afternoon.

Sara was lifting the sheet out of the printer when Quinn came into the shop. He was early and she knew that combined with the message could only mean one thing.

Another firestorm.

"Whose?" she asked, handing him the printed sheet of paper.

"I'm not sure. It's far away." He frowned at the prophecy, then met her gaze. Quinn was quiet and intense, fiercely protective of her and their sons. She'd learned to read the varying levels of his silence and sensed that he was agitated.

Probably about this firestorm.

Probably about them going to it. He was always torn between helping his fellow *Pyr* and exposing his own family to danger. A firestorm attracted *Slayers* and the *Pyr* in question often needed assistance in defending his mate, but taking his loved ones into the proximity of *Slayers* and dragonfights never appealed to Quinn

If he didn't know already, she'd have to tell him.

"It was like automatic writing." Sara flexed her fingers, trying to coax his smile. "Kind of interesting, actually. It's never been like that before."

Quinn flicked her a very intent look, then sat on the edge of her desk. Thierry was stirring, but not quite awake yet.

They had about thirty seconds, in Sara's view. She opened her mouth to tell Quinn that she was a few weeks along, but Quinn beat her to it.

"Are you pregnant?" he asked softly.

She smiled, wanting him to know that she was pleased. "I can't figure out how it keeps happening," she teased. His eyes turned a deeper hue of sapphire, his gaze locking on her in the way that made her shiver with desire.

"Maybe because I find you irresistible," he murmured, giving her a kiss that would have been more satisfying if it had been longer.

"Maybe the problem is that the feeling's mutual," she replied. "Maybe we should do something about that."

"Maybe not." His eyes glittered and he kissed her again, more slowly this time. Sara felt that old heat begin to simmer, the one that been lit by the firestorm and never extinguished. When he lifted his head, Quinn surveyed her with a lazy satisfaction that always made her think of his dragon powers. "Unless you think otherwise."

Sara shook her head, then found herself as breathless and shaken as she always was after Quinn's kisses. "No, this suits me just fine, actually." She smiled at him. "Although I might draw the line after five sons."

"Fair enough," Quinn agreed. "It's up to you." He perched on the edge of her desk to read the message once more. Sara put her hand on his thigh, liking both its muscled strength and how he covered her hand with the warmth of his own. He frowned slightly, then shook his head. "We're not going to this firestorm then," he said. "I'll tell Erik about this prophecy right away, though."

"Old-speak?" Sara asked.

"I'm thinking email," Quinn replied, giving her a wink as he pulled out his phone. There was a shimmer of blue-green light between the bookshelves at the back of the store.

Sara caught her breath, but Quinn had already moved to stand between the light and his family. She saw the telltale shimmer of blue that indicated he was on the cusp of change.

Then Marco, the Sleeper of the *Pyr* and the one with the greatest connection to darkfire, stepped out of the shadow. "I'll take care of it," he said quietly as he plucked the sheet of paper from Quinn's hand.

Before either of them could reply, Marco smiled, the darkfire glittered, and they were alone in the shop again.

They had time to exchange a glance before Thierry awakened.

Chandra followed the light of the firestorm, amazed by how far Thorolf had traveled. At least he was safe in this place. She'd never seen anyone else within Myth, other than the ghosts and the visions they summoned. It had always been a place of solitude for her, just her and Snow, until she'd brought Thorolf along.

Which was strange, now that she thought about it. There were so many mythical entities. This space should have been crowded. Maybe they each had their own personal sphere, the layers of the realm of Myth divided from each other with a neatness that wasn't echoed in the world of men.

Chandra shouldn't have been surprised at Thorolf's destination, that he'd found his way back into the stories of his boyhood. She'd never been to this part of Myth, although she'd visited the real place, and wondered if she was venturing into his corner of the realm.

If so, she was glad she was being permitted to do so.

Maybe the firestorm was responsible for that.

The wind was icy and the mountains high in the world he had once known. She'd always liked the pine forests of the north and the clear blue of the lakes and fjords. Snow flew behind her, silent and watchful. Chandra walked with one hand held out before herself, the firestorm's sparks brightening with every step. The shape of the land reminded her of the old stories, of Thor and his hammer, of Loki the wolf, of the Jormungand lurking for the end days. She remembered that the Vanir had been defeated by the

Aesir, that she and Freyr and Njord were only hostages in Asgard.

She wondered how the loyalties would fall when it all ended.

It was snowing higher in the mountains, their peaks obscured by flying white, and she thought of the three endless winters that were to come before the end of the world.

Fimbulvetr.

When the silver sparks were leaping from her fingertips with blinding light, Chandra knew she was close to Thorolf. She was in the midst of a cedar grove, one so sheltered and silent that it felt outside of time. There was no wind, the stillness of the space feeling expectant.

As if all of Myth knew she was going to take a chance.

As if the world held its breath in anticipation.

It wasn't uncertainty that made Chandra's own heart pound, or even a fear of the unknown. She realized she was filled with an excitement and anticipation herself, and one that wasn't tinged with any fear at all.

She wanted to know more about being with a man.

No, she wanted to know more about being with Thorolf.

When the lake appeared in a clearing ahead of her, Chandra smiled in recognition of the perfect spot. The lake was round and dark, as if it had no bottom at all. Steam rose from its surface and she knew without touching the water that it would be warm. There were volcanic vents in these mountains, vents that heated water in certain pools. The snow fell thickly all around her, melting on contact with the surface of the water. She straightened and turned at the sound of approaching footsteps, her pulse fluttering.

The firestorm's radiance told her who it had to be. Snow flew into the cedar forest and seated herself on a limb, silent and watchful as always.

Chandra watched until she saw a man's silhouette in the trees, her mouth dry. Thorolf strode toward her, that first glimpse of him making her heart skip. In either dragon or human form, he stole her breath away. He marched through the forest, a muscled man without a shirt, and Chandra's mouth went dry. Thorolf moved with purpose and frustration, and she feared in that moment that he might never be persuaded to fulfill his destiny.

She wouldn't even think of a world without the *Pyr*.

Never mind a world without Thorolf.

That woman who had died, she'd been no one in particular. She hadn't been his mate. She hadn't been his destiny. She might have been a pleasant girl, but it had been unthinkable that she should distract Thorolf from his training for the task ahead. His father had thought it expedient to draw the attention of marauding dragons to her village, and Chandra had played a role in that as well. She'd been convinced of Thorvald's logic once and the merit of his choice. Now, she watched Thorolf, tasted his anguish, and wondered if his father had been wrong.

She'd never understood the power of love before.

She knew she still didn't fully understand it, but she knew that she would destroy anyone who took Thorolf from her.

Never mind one who called him a distraction.

Even though, Chandra knew he was. She should have been hunting Viv Jason, that was her primary mission in this moment. If she were honest with herself, she would have to admit that it wasn't even that old choice of him as champion that had her pursuing him through Myth.

She'd hurt his feelings. She'd destroyed his trust. She'd infuriated him. And against all odds, Chandra had wanted to make amends.

She hoped that Thorolf never learned the part she'd played in that girl's death.

Maybe she could make everything up to Thorolf with this firestorm. He had such hopes for the firestorm's promise. She never would have expected him to be idealistic or romantic, but he was, and that side of him made her want to see his dreams fulfilled.

With every step he took toward her, the firestorm heated her skin an increment more. She took a deep breath and savored the rare and wondrous desire that filled her, a sensation she'd never experienced before the firestorm's spark had lit. Chandra straightened as Thorolf walked closer and tried to memorize this feeling. She understood with painful certainty that there was a whole realm of experience that she'd avoided, and for the first time, she wanted to sample it all. She knew in that instant that there was an easy way to tempt Thorolf, and it wasn't with words. She made her decision with an impulsiveness that would have shocked her just days earlier.

Chandra dropped her quiver and unfastened her belt with

shaking hands. She pulled her tunic over her head and tossed it onto a cedar branch, well aware that she knew nothing about seducing a man. She chose to remain in this form, the dark-haired and tattooed huntress. She liked it and thought Thorolf had, as well. She also liked that she'd first seen him in this guise.

No sooner had she stripped off her shirt than Thorolf stepped into the glade. She caught her breath as the cold beaded her nipples, as the firestorm touched her with its silvery heat.

Thorolf stopped and stared. His eyes brightened in a way that she found gratifying.

She paused in the act of unfastening her breeches and swallowed. "I thought you liked this form," she said, hearing her own uncertainty.

"I thought you refused to fulfill the firestorm," he said, and his words were hard. "Is this just a tease?"

"I don't tease. I don't know how. I thought the firestorm was a force that couldn't be denied." Chandra tugged off her boots, then wriggled out of her breeches, baring herself completely to his view. "Maybe I'm surrendering."

"But maybe you're not." He was understandably wary. "Maybe it's a game."

Chandra shook her head. "No game."

"Maybe you're trying to kill me."

She smiled despite herself. "Don't tempt me."

"You couldn't."

"Sure about that?"

An answering smile tugged the corner of his mouth as their gazes locked and held. Thorolf's eyes blazed blue, then he surveyed her. His gaze fell to her bare breasts, her tight nipples, her bare thighs and his eyes glittered. The firestorm seemed to heat, warming Chandra so that a trickle of perspiration ran down her back.

She saw the snow melting away from them as he took another step closer. Once she had been insulted whenever a man was so bold as to look upon her, but she liked the admiration in Thorolf's gaze. She'd chosen to show herself to him, and she was proud of how thoroughly he surveyed her. When he came closer again, almost stalking her, as if he expected her to disappear, she stayed put. Her heart began to race with trepidation of what would happen next, how it would feel, whether it would be enough to win him over.

It was only when Chandra heard the drip of water that she noticed how quickly winter was driven back by the heat of the firestorm. The cedar boughs and branches underfoot had been revealed and were steaming slightly. The fine mist that resulted only made the encounter more magical. The light of the firestorm was refracted, turning each drop of airborne water into a crystal. They could have been surrounded by glittering stars.

Thorolf paused right before her, so powerful and masculine that Chandra couldn't take a breath. If she was going to be touched by a man, let it be one like him, a dragon shifter, an honorable man, a loyal man, a champion and a fighter. A man who knew what he wanted and reached for it.

A man well aware of the enticement of pleasure.

Who better to introduce her to it? She didn't have to surrender everything. She could sample.

Chandra's gaze dropped to his mouth and the memory of his kiss made the heat inside her redouble. She felt hot and cold at the same time, simmering with desire but shivery, too. She felt an unfamiliar dampness between her thighs, indicating that her body knew what to expect even more than she did.

She knew the theory. It was the experience that was a mystery to her. She'd never felt the omission until now.

It was a bit late to realize that she didn't know the price of breaking her vow.

The amazing thing was that in this moment, faced with Thorolf and the awe in his gaze, Chandra didn't care what toll the firestorm took from her.

That was what made the firestorm so dangerous. She had to keep her objective in mind, and be sure she didn't offer too much.

Funny that it didn't seem so easy anymore.

"In the vision, they said you were Vanir, a goddess," Thorolf said, holding her gaze steadily. "Is it true?"

"Don't you trust in dreams and visions?"

He shrugged. "I don't know. I don't usually have them. I'm black-and-white, believe-in-what-I-can-hold-in-my-talons kind of guy." His crooked smile showed his ease with his own nature and tempted her to be charmed in her turn. That dimple invited her caress.

Chandra *was* charmed, her fingertips rising to his chin seemingly of their own volition. He had a little bit of stubble and she liked its rough masculinity. "Then you must not believe in me."

He chuckled in a way that sent a shiver through her. "But I've held you in my talons." He caught her around the waist and drew her close, his move making the firestorm burn so hot that Chandra thought she'd burst into flames. Her breasts were crushed against his chest, his height such that she was drawn up to her toes. She had to tip her head back to hold his gaze. "And you're definitely real," he murmured, and she could feel the rumble of his words against her own chest.

Thorolf's hand rose to cup her bare breast, his expression both hungry and awed. His touch was gentle, a slow caress that left Chandra tingling. She found her back arching as he teased the nipple to an aching tight peak. His hands were large and strong, a bit rough. The dragon tattooed on the back of his left hand seemed darker and more alive.

As if she would ever forget what he was.

Thorolf smiled down into her eyes, then bent to take her nipple in his mouth.

Chandra gasped at the sweet heat of his mouth on her breast. White fire seemed to emanate from that point and race through her body, filling her with a yearning that she knew only Thorolf could satisfy.

"Go on," he murmured against her skin. "Tell me what you can do."

Chandra stared at him, so overwhelmed with pleasure that she didn't even understand the question. Her hands were on his shoulders, her fingers digging into his muscled strength.

"You're Vanir. You have powers," Thorolf reminded her. His teeth grazed her taut nipple and she moaned as she had never moaned before. She felt the breath of his laughter before his mouth closed over her again.

When he lifted his head this time, her nipple was tight and hard. His eyes were darkest blue, his gaze intent. She was wet and filled with a need beyond her experience. He surveyed her with satisfaction, then ran his hand over her other breast. His touch made her shiver.

"Maybe an easier question," he teased. "Which one of them are you?"

"Freya," she managed to admit before he worked his magic on her other breast. Who could have believed that such pleasure could come from one small erogenous zone? Who could have believed she'd spill the truth so readily? Thorolf closed the warmth of his hand over her other breast, working that nipple with his finger and tongue at the same time. Chandra wasn't sure her knees could continue to support her.

But she didn't want him to stop.

And it wasn't just because she hadn't won his cooperation yet.

"Depending who you ask, of course." Her words fell quickly, as they seldom did. "Gerd, Godiva, Selena, Demeter, Diana, Isis; all facets of the same divine truth."

"Which do you prefer?"

"Chandra," she admitted. "For the moon."

Thorolf nodded, smiled and glanced over her. "And this guise?"

"Freya." She felt her cheeks heat. "I like Scandinavia."

His eyes gleamed. "Since when?"

"About nine hundred and fifty years ago," she admitted, referring to the date she'd chosen him as her champion.

He was pleased, but ducked his head to hide it. She gasped when he kissed her nipple again. "The huntress," he murmured against her skin. "Fertility, death, magic, beauty and war." He flicked her a glance and his eyes were a vivid blue. "You should know that seriously works for me."

Chandra found her mouth opening and closing, but no sound came out. Had anyone ever looked at her with such admiration and desire? Respect, yes, she was used to that and maybe fear, but not this kind of sensual awe. He pushed his fingers into her hair, doing that thing of making her feel fragile and treasured as he drew her against his chest, and kissed her deeply.

"What exactly can you do?" he whispered into her ear, his breath making her shiver.

"Shift shape," she admitted, noting that she sounded uncharacteristically breathless.

"Seen that. Talk to the dead?"

"Gather them," Chandra admitted with a nod, letting her head fall back as he nuzzled her throat.

"Leader of the Valkyries," he mused, clearly remembering. "Mistress of Cats." Chandra breathed agreement to both. Thorolf returned to her breasts again, cupping them with his hands as he kissed first one and then the other.

"Summon visions," she whispered. "Cast spells."

"Move between Myth and the mortal realm," Thorolf suggested, but she shook her head.

"That's what Snow does." Her breath caught as his teeth grazed one tight peak. "Snow takes me between realms."

She lost the thread of the conversation as Thorolf's touch became proprietary and more demanding. His thigh eased between her own and his erection pressed against her hip. They were surrounded by the blazing white heat of the firestorm, a brilliance that filled Chandra with insatiable need. She couldn't imagine how or why she'd avoided this pleasure for so many eons, and couldn't think of a single reason to continue to do so. She forgot her plan to surrender just a kiss or two. She rolled her hips against Thorolf without even knowing what she did, welcoming him and inviting him with one caress.

She was on her back on the fallen cedar boughs in a moment, Thorolf on top of her. He held her captive beneath him, suspending his weight so she wasn't crushed. That he thought she was fragile was both flattering and amusing. Chandra had never been treated like a delicate flower before. Thorolf's elbows were braced beside her shoulders, her breasts crushed beneath his chest, his pelvis over hers and his thighs outside of her own. She was surrounded by him, protected by him, wrapped securely beneath him. It was a strange sensation, but even more strange was the pleasure she found in it.

Chandra realized how many centuries she'd fought alone. Once she'd been glad to be solitary and self-sufficient: now she saw how lonely she'd been. The firestorm's brilliant silver light seemed to shine into every corner of her mind and illuminate every doubt she'd ever had, showing her that making love with Thorolf could make her complete in a way she'd never been before.

She couldn't care about the cost when she glimpsed the reward.

Thorolf smiled down at her before he kissed her again with deliberate intent. His kiss was persuasive and tender, even as his mouth locked over hers and he coaxed her response. Chandra's fingers eased into his hair, framing his head and drawing him closer as she opened her mouth to him. He was patient and persuasive, and she echoed his moves, wanting to give as much pleasure as she received. She must have succeeded because Thorolf groaned and deepened his kiss, the fire in his touch kindling her own. Their kiss became hungry and feverish, as if they would devour each other and be consumed with pleasure. There was nothing in Chandra's world but the heat of the firestorm and Thorolf's commanding caress.

He abruptly broke their embrace, his eyes bright as he studied her. Chandra knew she didn't look like herself. She was disheveled and flushed, her lips swollen from his kisses and her body burning for more. She watched his mouth, wanting to taste his kiss again, but Thorolf's eyes narrowed.

"Why did you change your mind?" he demanded in a low murmur. She could feel the vibration of his voice against her own skin.

"About what?"

"About the firestorm." He was studying her intently and she guessed that the answer mattered. She supposed it should, given that he'd been determined to change her mind, but couldn't admit that sensation had overwhelmed her. It sounded weak.

It sounded mortal.

His eyes narrowed when she remained silent. "What do you want from me?"

She told him the truth. "Just an answer."

"Where's Viv?" Thorolf repeated her question, then rolled his eyes. "Why's that so important?"

"I told you, I have a quest..."

"And what happens when you fulfill it?"

Chandra blinked. "I go back and take another mission."

He drew back to study her. "You're going to leave? That's why you said you wouldn't fulfill the firestorm? Because you're going back to Asgard or wherever?"

"It's what I do."

"And you do it alone. Got it." Thorolf rolled away from her, his disgust clear. "So this *is* just a tease."

"You don't understand..."

"I think I do. How much were you planning to trade for my cooperation?"

It sounded very callous when he explained her actions like that. Chandra found herself blushing. "I'm trying to complete my quest. You should understand that—I gave my word!"

"And you'll do whatever is necessary to fulfill your pledge," he concluded, his tone hard. "Even play with the firestorm."

"No!" She felt her cheeks heat even more. "Well, maybe."

"You're just like my father!" Thorolf leapt to his feet, and flung out one hand, his anger clear. "Everything is conditional! Everything is about duty and responsibility!" He turned on her, his eyes flashing. "Here's a newsflash for you: for me, the firestorm is about *love*."

"Love?" Chandra echoed, without meaning to do so.

Thorolf's eyes blazed and she knew she'd said the wrong thing. "Love. It's a mutual respect thing. Maybe you've heard of it. It's about being more together than is possible alone. It's about partnership and affection and even *destiny*." He glared at her. "I thought you'd know about that bit, or is destiny just something that applies to mortals?"

Chandra couldn't think of a thing to say that would improve his mood.

No matter how she looked at it, she had to admit that her quest wasn't going well.

And she had no clue how to save it.

This was not good.

CHAPTER SEVEN

Thorolf would have turned to march away, but Chandra seized his elbow. To his surprise, she admitted something. "I planned to surrender something to win you over, that's right. Because there are two things that need to be done to save the *Pyr* and you're the key to both of them."

He glared at her, the pale blue shimmer of change tingeing the light of the firestorm. "You're shitting me."

Chandra shook her head. "No. I took a vow to help to ensure the survival of the *Pyr*."

He folded his arms across his chest, letting his skepticism show. "Don't talk to me about the Avenger of the Aesir."

"But I have to. It's part of it all. You have to listen to me!" Chandra's words spilled out quickly, which Thorolf knew wasn't characteristic. Was she trying to manipulate him, or was this really important to her? He knew which answer he liked best, but that didn't make it the truth.

The possibility of his mate deceiving him was infuriating, and he felt the change build in his body. Thorolf knew his eyes changed first, the pupil becoming a vertical slit. To his surprise, Chandra didn't back away or falter. It seemed almost that she found him even more enticing in dragon form, and she certainly wasn't afraid of him. She stayed right by his side.

In fact, her fingers dug into his arm, and her gaze bored into his, as if she could convince him by sheer will. "You are the one, the one who will wield the blade that was forged for your hand before you were born. You are the one who will save the *Pyr* and the treasures they defend." She caressed his arm, sending fire through his veins, and an answering heat lit in her eyes. "I chose you. I know what I'm doing."

"What if I don't want to be the one?" he demanded.

"You'll just condemn your fellows." He made to turn away at that, but Chandra stepped toward him and put her hands on his shoulders. He caught his breath at the powerful of the firestorm's heat. Her next words caught him by surprise. "What if the firestorm is giving us both the chance to have what we want?"

He glanced over his shoulder, regarding her with skepticism. "What do you want? Tell me the truth this time. All of it."

Chandra smiled a little, then actually did as he asked. "To keep my vow to my brother, the one that will ensure you save the *Pyr*." Her voice dropped low and her eyes sparkled a little. Thorolf's heart clenched at the sight. She was incredibly hot. Tantalizing. Challenging. Irritating, but sexy, too.

"Why?"

She smiled. "I like dragons." He could tell by the warmth in her voice that she was telling him the truth. "I like a world with dragons in it."

That was promising.

"How *much* do you like dragons?" he asked, letting his voice drop low.

She blushed a little, her gaze darting over him in that unexpectedly innocent way, and she granted him a look that could have been playful. "A lot." That confession made her turn even more red.

The problem then, wasn't his nature. He knew the attraction was mutual, so it wasn't that either. Thorolf confronted Chandra, then, curious and intrigued. "So if the problem's not me, what's your issue with satisfying the firestorm?"

He expected her to say something about love and affection, or about getting to know each other better, so her confession surprised him.

"I took a vow," she said, averting her gaze. Her cheeks were burning.

"A vow to never satisfy a firestorm?"

"A vow of chastity," she replied quickly.

Thorolf blinked. "Are you kidding me?"

She straightened as if insulted and her tone was prickly. "Why would I joke about something so important? Celibacy gives focus and improves athletic performance..."

"I've never found that," he said with resolve. She shot a look at him and he thought he'd hurt her feelings. "Okay, it's a noble idea," he acknowledged, slowly closing the distance between them. She watched him, her arms folded over her chest, and held her ground. Warily, but she didn't run. "And you've kept the pledge for a while. That's good, right? How long has it been?" He thought she'd admit to a month at the outside, which would have impressed the hell out of him.

"I stopped counting after two thousand years."

Thorolf felt his mouth drop open in shock. Chandra held his gaze steadily. He was going to protest that it was impossible, then had a thought. "Have you ever...?"

She shook her head, blushing again.

"Then you could only do it because you don't know what you're missing." Thorolf grinned but before he could make a suggestion, Chandra backed away, shaking a finger at him.

"You're not going to offer to tutor me."

"It's the only decent thing to do," he said and was pleased to see that she couldn't hide her reaction.

"I'll bet you've indulged enough for both of us," she charged, but there was no heat in the accusation.

More of a fluttering awareness.

Thorolf could work with that. He stopped right in front of her, hearing the rapid pulse of her heart. His own heart started to synchronize with hers, a powerful and incredible sensation. Her eyes were wide, her lips parted.

Oh, he'd make a feast of consummating this firestorm.

"Practice," he murmured, bending to touch his lips to her temple. "Practice is the key to good performance." He let his mouth graze her skin, then kissed her earlobe. He felt her exhale, was aware of how she quivered, and was completely certain he could change her mind.

Then she abruptly stepped back, holding her hand up between them.

"Turnabout is fair play," she said. "What do *you* really want?"

Thorolf didn't even have to think about it. His reply was immediate and resolute. "To be loved for who I am, not for what I can do for someone."

"Don't be ridiculous," Chandra chided, her tone dismissive. "Everything is an exchange. Do you think anyone ever loved me for who I am?" Her mood had changed completely, and Thorolf watched, guessing this was important. "They're afraid of me. They pray for me to fix things in the mortal realm. The other gods negotiate with me." Her eyes lit with impatience. "Nothing is ever without an exchange."

It was important. Thorolf understood why Chandra didn't believe in love and partnership. She'd never experienced it. People always wanted something from gods and goddesses. If sex was just an exchange, he might not have wanted it either.

Um no, he'd still have wanted it.

Maybe the firestorm was about changing her perspective.

Maybe his task in this *was* to change her mind.

"Maybe that's why you don't believe..." he began, but Chandra didn't let him finish.

Instead, she reached up and kissed him. Even though he guessed that she was using the firestorm to shut him up for a moment, her ploy worked. The heat seared his mouth, feeding that desire deep within him. The amazing thing was that the firestorm affected her, as well. She became soft, seductive and completely perfect in his embrace. As she kissed him, Thorolf felt like he could do anything.

Even win the heart of a reluctant goddess.

He had to believe a treasure like that wouldn't be easily captured.

When he lifted his head, Chandra was nestled against his chest, flushed and pleased and clearly overwhelmed. He pushed back a strand of hair from her temple, then touched the same point with his lips. "Maybe you're right about just tempting the firestorm," he murmured and she glanced up with surprise. "Feeling like this for a long time could be kind of fun."

She smiled as if she didn't want to but couldn't help it. She gestured to herself. "You just like this form."

Thorolf shook his head. "I like all the ones I've seen so far." He surveyed her with a smile. "Mostly I like how fast you are."

She frowned. "I don't understand."

"You run fast, you think fast, you act fast." Thorolf nodded with approval. "It makes sense that you're one of the Vanir, because you're a warrior. Like me."

"Not exactly like you."

"Not exactly, no," he agreed, but he didn't mean the dragon part. "You strategize. You plan." He smiled ruefully. "I'm more of a brute-force, get-shit-done type."

Chandra laughed and he liked how her eyes danced. "It works for you."

"It has." He drew her a little closer and whispered in her ear. "But I'm starting to imagine what kind of team we could be." Her lips parted, as if to invite his kiss, and that was an offer Thorolf had no intention of refusing.

Chandra could have lost herself in Thorolf's kiss. She wasn't supposed to be charmed by anyone mortal, much less by one of her brother's beloved *Pyr*. Thorolf was supposed to be a tool or a means to an end, and the firestorm should have been more of the same. But every time he coaxed her smile, every time he kissed her, Chandra felt her determination to keep her vow of chastity erode a little more. Thorolf was potent stuff. She had just slid her hand into his hair to pull him closer when a bird screamed a warning.

Snow!

Something had happened.

Chandra broke their kiss and pushed Thorolf away. She saw his surprise at her strength, then looked up as the silver falcon swooped low over them. Snow turned, then flew with remarkable speed away over the trees, guiding the way. Thorolf reached for her, but Chandra was on her feet and beyond his reach. She hauled on her clothes, hoping she could catch up to Snow.

"You can't follow me!" she insisted, but Thorolf was right behind her.

"Bullshit. We're a team," he insisted, as she should have expected he would. "Wherever you go, I'm going, too. This is the *firestorm*, Chandra. That's the deal." He was glowering at her, hovering on the cusp of change.

It didn't matter. He couldn't intimidate her.

"Not here it's not. This is my realm and I know the rules. You will *not* follow me." She tugged on her boots and seized her quiver. Her crossbow was on the ground, a few feet away. She was inwardly amazed that she'd been distracted enough to let it be so far away, but then Thorolf had that effect on her. "It's not safe."

"Bull. I'll fight beside you." He was already dressed and waiting for her, arms folded across his chest. "Back to back. Let's do it." Thorolf looked formidable, unpredictable, pissed off and very appealing. He lifted one brow, daring her. "A team," he said with emphasis, which was exactly what Chandra didn't want to hear. "You should try it before you knock it."

"You don't understand. It's dangerous!"

His eyes blazed at that, and Chandra realized she shouldn't have suggested he couldn't protect her. "I don't care! This is the firestorm."

"The firestorm is just sex." Which was plenty as far as Chandra was concerned, but Thorolf didn't need to know that. "It's not got anything to do with anything else."

"It's not just sex!" Thorolf argued and reached for her.

Chandra evaded him, but only just. There was no telling what had sparked Snow's warning or what kind of battle might result. She didn't need the distraction of the firestorm, or Thorolf's presence. Her foe could easily use her concern for Thorolf against her.

She knew how hard the divine could play.

"You can't follow me," she insisted, backing toward the surrounding trees.

"Watch me." Thorolf came after her anyway, purpose in his every move.

"You are infuriating."

His sudden grin took her off guard, making her heart skip. "It's part of my charm."

Chandra swore, then struck him between the eyes with the heel of her hand. The blow sent Thorolf stumbling backward and he tripped over a root. He tried to recover his balance, but failed. He fell hard and didn't get up again.

Chandra checked on him, although the firestorm's shimmer told her that he was okay. He was out cold, and there was no telling for how long.

He'd certainly come after her when he awakened, and the firestorm's light would help him as much as his keen senses. She eyed him for a moment, debating her choice, then Snow screamed insistently again. Chandra had to take her chances on Thorolf staying safe while she dealt with whatever Snow had discovered.

The lacquer red salamander was the only warning Viv Jason had.

She was touring a luxurious house with a real estate agent. She had plenty of money now, thanks to Chen's gratitude, but she'd discovered that she liked the idea of spending it more than actually letting any of it go. While she still had the money, she had freedom and opportunity. Once she bought a house, the capital would be tied up and she'd be bound to one location.

It was fun to savor material comfort and pleasure. Plus, being an immortal meant she couldn't be adversely affected by any indulgence. She could drink as much champagne as she wanted and feel fine the next day. She wouldn't age or sicken—she could only die if someone killed her, and there didn't seem to be anyone left to do that. She'd done a favor for Chen, which really was had been a fulfillment of her own oath to avenge herself against the *Pyr*, and now she was rich. The best part was that Chen was doing the dirty work of completing her vengeance and eliminating the *Pyr*.

The worst part was that he was using Thorolf to do it. As a defender of justice herself, Viv wasn't entirely happy to see Thorolf used like that—never mind that she'd been key to getting him into Chen's clutches. While he was one of the *Pyr*, and she was sworn to destroy them, he'd never personally done anything to her.

In fact, he'd been good to her.

He'd been a passionate lover.

He'd been game for any pleasure or indulgence and had defended her more than once. He had a loyalty and sense of honor that reminded her of her relationship with her sisters. It hadn't been all bad having a pet dragon, and she sure hadn't rushed to keep her bargain with Chen. In the end, though, she hadn't had a choice. Chen's spell had to be worked before these four total eclipses, and the old *Slayer* had insisted it required time to be effective.

She still felt guilty about that bite.

Maybe Viv was shopping because she didn't want to watch the end of the *Pyr*, or the end of Thorolf.

She wasn't quite sure what would happen to her after the *Pyr* were gone. She had a pervasive sense that there was a change afoot in the world, but without any contact with her own kind, she wasn't sure what it was. She supposed she could be returned to Hades and her sisters at any time. It hadn't happened yet, but so maybe it was keyed to the complete elimination of the *Pyr*. Given Chen's determination, that had to happen soon. If so, there was all the more reason to enjoy the pleasures of this sphere so long as she had the ability to do so.

Shopping for the perfect house seemed like the ideal choice to fill her days and nights. As long as Viv had so much money, there were people willing to pay for her to see properties, to fly her to private locations, as well as buy her meals and drinks, to court her business. Viv saw no reason to make a decision quickly. She'd been "indecisive" for nearly two years and was wondering how much longer she could make it last.

Although she did like this house. A lot. It had everything she needed, which mostly meant complete privacy. Against all expectation, it was also close to the city, offering the best of both worlds on its large, perfectly landscaped lot. There was, after all, a possibility that Chen might fail, and that she might have to re-assume her own quest to destroy the *Pyr*. She'd need a place to live. To hide. To build her strength and plan her campaigns.

Why not this place? She could envision herself living in it so easily. She even liked the decor, which was eclectic—she guessed from the real estate agent's reaction that he expected the bold color scheme in the main rooms to be an issue with finding a buyer.

Maybe she could even get a deal on it.

Viv loved the blood red walls in the living room, especially against the gilded gold of the dining room. The furniture was black lacquered wood with upholstery in bright striped silks. It was bold, modern yet traditional. It might not be to everyone's taste, but it perfectly suited her own.

The house would look fantastic at night. Viv could see it lit by a thousand burning candles. The living room had one long glass wall that opened to a patio and pool with an infinity edge. Steps led down to the extensive gardens, all of the property surrounded by a high impenetrable hedge. The relaxing sound of falling water carried into the house as the real estate agent opened the glass wall. The glass panels folded back to disappear completely into receptacles in the wall on either side, letting the house and the garden meld into one living space.

It reminded Viv of someplace she'd been a long time ago, someplace she really didn't want to think about anymore but that she had admired. She smiled at the realization that there could be a serpent in this garden, too. She stepped out into the sunlight, seeking fault but finding none.

When she saw the red salamander dart across the garden path, she started. Did it have gold edging on its lacquer red scales?

But it disappeared into the undergrowth, in exactly the way Chen wouldn't have done. Viv exhaled with care, telling herself that she was jumping at shadows.

The agent excused himself when his cell phone rang, but Viv was glad to be alone. She wouldn't have been surprised if he'd faked the call, because he'd sensed that she needed a few moments to agree that this was the house. Viv strolled the garden, enchanted. It might be worth it to surrender the power of having money in exchange for having *this* house.

It might even be worth letting one or two *Pyr* survive to ensure that her task carried on after Chen. She knew which *Pyr* she'd choose.

She'd missed Thorolf.

Imagine that.

Viv saw a blue shimmer of light in the periphery of her vision and spun to face it.

She was too slow. She caught a glimpse of Chen in his female form, then he snatched her up in his fierce grip. "The job's only half done," he whispered in her ear, even as a cold wind began to spin around her. She tried to shift shape but couldn't. His grip on her was like a vise, one she couldn't escape.

What was going on?

"Hey!" Viv shouted and struggled but it made no difference. "I kept our deal!"

"But I let him go. Collect him again," Chen insisted.

"That's your mistake."

"It was part of the plan!"

Viv smiled, glad that Thorolf had changed the rules of play. She didn't care how he'd done it, but she liked that Chen wasn't getting his way easily. "That's your problem. I did what I promised!"

"You'll do more."

"You can't force me. I kept my promise..."

But Chen only laughed and held her tightly. Sparkling dust, like snowflakes, suddenly appeared on all sides of her. The garden and the house were gone, that snow swirling around her as if she'd been plunged into the middle of a blizzard. Chen's grip disappeared but Viv still couldn't control what was happening. She fell onto a hard stone platform as if it had risen out of the depths to collide with her body.

The snow cleared.

A woman with a long blond braid smiled down at her, her confidence a sure sign that she wasn't human. She was dressed in black, pants and boots and a leather jacket, and she carried a crossbow in one hand. She had tattoos all over her arms, blue Celtic knots that seemed to writhe when she moved. Viv could have admired that, but the woman also had a collection of human skulls hanging from her belt. She could have been vengeance personified. She lifted an arrow from a quiver on her back with casual ease and fitted it into the crossbow.

Then she lifted the weapon to aim at Viv.

It was close enough range that Viv could see the scratches on the side of the arrow point. It looked kind of like a lightning bolt cut into the stone.

"*Sowulo*," the woman said, her voice pitched low and filled with a humor Viv didn't find appropriate. "Another perfect choice."

"I don't understand," Viv said, stalling for time.

"The rune on the arrow head. It means the triumph of light over darkness. Exactly right." The woman's eyes narrowed as she chose exactly where the blow would strike, and Viv tried again to shift shape.

This time it worked.

Viv slithered away in her serpent form, moving rapidly across the stone. She'd take cover, then strike at her assailant by surprise.

Light over darkness. Who was this warrior and what did she know?

Viv never reached the undergrowth. She screamed as pain shot through her. The woman had shot the arrow into Viv's tail, securing it to the ground. Viv spun, coiling upon herself, and saw the head of the arrow wedged into a moss-filled chink between the stones. It was buried deep. She tugged, felt excruciating pain as her tail tore and saw her own blood flow. The arrow didn't budge.

The woman smiled. "It wasn't a lucky shot," she said calmly, and loaded the crossbow again. "The vengeance of the sun is upon you, Tisiphone."

Viv's eyes widened.

No one could know that name without having followed her from Hades.

And no one could have done that who wasn't immortal.

Which explained a lot.

It also meant that all bets were off.

Viv lunged at her assailant, baring her fangs to bite. The woman kicked her in the face, spinning smartly, then landed a trio of fast kicks that sent Viv reeling backward. Viv had a moment of fear that she might have met her match. She tore her tail free, nearly fainting at the pain, then shifted fast. She was on her feet in the blink of an eye, aiming a kick at the woman's face.

The woman ducked, caught Viv's ankle and twisted it hard. Viv spun down to one knee, unable to help herself. Who was her opponent? If she knew her name, she might know her weakness. The woman jerked Viv's ankle then sent her sprawling on her stomach. Before Viv could rise, her assailant landed on her back, her weight pinning Viv to the stone and her knees locked around Viv's waist.

Viv thrashed and kicked, but couldn't dislodge her. She couldn't shift shape. She couldn't do anything, and the powerlessness terrified her.

"Who are you? What do you want?" Viv stilled and swallowed

when she felt the point of an arrow at the base of her skull. Her heart was galloping in terror. If the woman shot the crossbow from such close range, there was no chance Viv would survive.

"I'm the huntress," the woman admitted easily. "I've been looking for you, Tisiphone." She paused and Viv heard that damn smile in her voice. "Or should I call you Viv Jason? Do you still remember your old name or not?"

"I don't have to tell you anything." Viv writhed and struggled, but it made no difference. The woman's knees were tightly locked around her and that arrow point was drawing a trickle of blood. Viv tried to roll over, but her head was abruptly slammed down into the rock by that loaded crossbow.

"We can make a deal," she began, hearing the desperation in her voice.

The woman scoffed. "Is that what you said to Thorolf?" She leaned down, her voice dropping to a whisper. "How did you overcome him? Where did you take him?"

"I'll tell you if you release me."

Her captor laughed. "Not a chance. It's too late for you to negotiate."

"But I know what happened to him," Viv said, using her most enticing tone of voice. "I know how to break the spell that was laid upon him..."

"Your price is too high if it means you get to live." The woman dropped her voice to a whisper. "Don't worry. I'll find the truth another way."

Viv felt a trickle of sweat on her temple as the crossbow clicked. It must have a safety guard, which the woman had removed.

"Think of it this way: you won't have to face his anger," the woman said. "At least not in this life."

"I'll find you," Viv said with heat. "I'll find you and I'll make you pay for this..."

"If you pray to anything or anyone, say your prayer now," the woman said coolly, interrupting Viv's tirade, and the crossbow moved slightly. She had to be depressing the trigger.

It was over.

A furious Viv closed her eyes tightly.

Which was why she didn't see Thorolf coming.

What the hell was going on?

Thorolf awakened alone, the light of the firestorm faded to a glimmer. Chandra had left him. Even worse, she'd insisted that he couldn't follow her. She'd been protecting him, a dragon shape shifter, and had decked him when he'd refused to agree to her crazy plan. He had the lump on the back of his head to prove it.

He *could* defend her. Even if they were arguing, he'd protect her with everything he had. That's what the firestorm was about.

It occurred to him that his mate wasn't much used to relying on anyone else.

But then, she'd admitted early that she always worked alone.

Was that why she couldn't trust in the firestorm's promise? Every possibility just made Thorolf more determined to change her mind.

What *had* the falcon been screaming about? Could she understand what the bird said? Either way, something was going down and Thorolf was going to follow his mate. He shifted shape and flew hard, following the silver gleam of the firestorm. When it brightened, he knew he was close to her.

But the sight before him couldn't be true.

It *was* Chandra, it had to be, even though she'd changed form again. She was blond now, dressed in the same black hunting gear, her hair braided into a thick plait that hung down her back. He thought she looked like a Valkyrie, especially with the skulls hanging from her belt, but the firestorm revealed that it was his mate. But then, Freya was the leader of the Valkyries. A bird was circling around her, silent and watchful, but it was a black raven instead of a silver falcon.

He rubbed his eyes, looked again, but nothing important changed.

Chandra was going to shoot Viv in the back of the head.

Not if he had anything to say about it.

"What the *fuck*?" Thorolf roared. He fell on his mate in his dragon form, his claws locking around her shoulders. He groaned as the seductive heat of the firestorm surged through him, reminding him of what they hadn't finished.

His weight forced Chandra from Viv's back, and they tumbled together across the stone. He would have gathered Chandra close, but she elbowed him hard, then kicked him, fighting with amazing strength.

She'd been strong before, but in this guise, she was nearly as tall as him in his human form, and powerful.

Maybe more powerful than him.

It was a bit late to remember that she was, after all, Vanir.

"Run!" he shouted to Viv and she did.

"Idiot!" Chandra roared and Thorolf knew he'd invited the wrath of the goddess. She bit him, then rolled to her feet in one fluid movement. She fired the arrow loaded into the crossbow after Viv before he could stop her. Thorolf did manage to smack the weapon with his tail as she fired, disrupting her aim.

She swore thoroughly, turning on him with blazing eyes. She cracked the crossbow across his snout in retaliation, making him blink at the pain, then jabbed one fist into his gut. No normal person could have driven the wind from him with that punch, but Chandra did. At least, Viv was running into the jungle, the sound of her passage loud to Thorolf.

"She'll get away!" Chandra fumed.

"Exactly!" Thorolf had to give Viv time to escape. He owed her that much.

Meanwhile, the firestorm burned with distracting power. Thorolf found its heat more compelling in his dragon form. He wanted Chandra, this goddess who might just be able to kick his butt, more than he'd ever wanted a woman before. He wanted to defend her and gather her close, maybe take flight and find some place they could be alone to consummate the firestorm. He wanted to wrestle, winner take all, and he'd be glad to lose so she could take advantage of him.

He could install her as the prize gem in his hoard, secure her in his well-defended lair. It could take the rest of his life to understand her, to figure out all of her powers and to convince her to confide in him fully. The firestorm urged him to go for it. That she'd changed form again only increased his interest. He could discover her all over again, which was a tantalizing possibility.

The problem was that Chandra was furious with him. He didn't want to hurt her, but she didn't seem to be worried about injuring him. She fought him with remarkable strength, biting and striking so ferociously that Thorolf knew he'd be bruised. He roared and seized her, holding her in a tight grip. He even wrapped his tail around her, although her struggles turned his thoughts in a predictable direction.

"Let me go," she demanded. "There's no telling what trouble she'll make in this place."

"I can't let you hunt her," Thorolf insisted.

"I'll explain later!"

"I'm not letting you go."

Chandra swore, muttered an apology that made no sense, then drove her boot heel into the place where it hurt the most. Thorolf fell back, stunned by the pain, and shifted involuntarily back to human form. He cupped his hands over his groin and moaned a little. Chandra stood over him, looking like a warrior queen.

A disgusted warrior queen.

The firestorm burned brightly as she loomed over him, filling the space between them with its silvery light. He was sure he'd never seen a more beautiful woman in all his life, and despite his pain, his body responded to the vision of her. Her eyes were shining, her feet braced against the ground. She could have been an action hero, or his favorite fantasy.

For a moment, Thorolf forgot that she was pissed at him.

Chandra didn't. She hauled off and decked him. Thorolf couldn't believe it until he saw the blood spurt from his nose.

To his delight, it was red.

Because of his firestorm.

He laughed and reached for Chandra. She kicked his feet out from underneath him and he fell to the ground, seizing her on the way down. "I like wrestling," he warned her as he rolled on top of her. "Don't start what you can't finish."

"Nothing said you're going to win," Chandra said through gritted teeth and drove her elbow into his chest. "I can't believe you stopped me."

"I can't believe you were going to kill her," Thorolf muttered, as the pair of them grappled together.

"It was my quest to kill her."

Thorolf was startled. "The one that has you going to Asgard once you finish."

She cast him a look, as if he were a particularly slow child.

"All the more reason to interfere," Thorolf said. Chandra glared at him. "You're my mate. This is our firestorm. Clearly, I need more time to convince you that surrendering to it is a great idea."

"I work alone!" Chandra shouted as she rolled him to his back. She wriggled free, but this time, Thorolf tackled her, sweeping her feet out from beneath her.

They tumbled together across the ground and Thorolf had to admit he was having the time of his life. It was incredibly hot to be wrestling with his mate, and he found himself aroused by how vigorous a fighter she was.

He was starting to feel that a celebration would be in order.

No matter who won.

He caught her wrists in one hand and moved quickly, grinning when he trapped her beneath his weight. "Green eyes this time," he noted. "I like it."

She twisted and bit, tried to kick him, then glared at him. "You like this," she accused.

Thorolf couldn't pretend otherwise. "Oh yeah. Big fantasy. I always wanted a woman who would wrestle with me."

"Only because you want to win."

"Only because I want to lose, so you can have your way with me." Thorolf chuckled and rolled his hips against her, letting her feel his reaction to their fight.

"My way with you is to leave you," she said, but her lips had parted in an inviting way. She was still talking tough, but the firestorm was provoking her response. Thorolf could tell by the way her eyes had started to sparkle.

"Hasn't happened so far," he felt obliged to point out.

"It would have happened right now, if you hadn't interfered."

"Then you can't expect me to have any regrets," he murmured, then bent and stole a kiss. The firestorm was crackling silver between them, and the sparks that exploded from their kiss nearly blew his mind.

"Centuries of preparation," Chandra said through her teeth, her eyes narrowing again. "And you don't even care that you screwed it up."

Thorolf braced himself on his elbows to look down at her.

"Aren't you taking female jealousy a bit far?" He made a joke, hoping she'd smile. "There's enough of me to share."

"I should smite you," she said through gritted teeth.

"Go for it," he invited. "I'm ready."

Chandra's eyes flashed. Her knee moved so fast that he almost wasn't prepared for it. His weight shifted through as he protected his jewels, and he realized too late that she'd expected him to do just that.

"Idiot dragon!" she charged, and Thorolf was shocked to find himself sprawled on his back, her boot planted on his chest. "This isn't about jealousy," she informed him, a disgusted and triumphant warrior queen once more. "This is about keeping my word."

"Your promise to your brother?" Thorolf guessed.

"That's the one, the vow that saves his precious *Pyr* from extinction."

"We aren't becoming extinct..."

"Where have I heard that before?"

"Who exactly *is* your brother?" he asked, but Chandra was striding away. She pulled another arrow out of her quiver, her gaze scanning the jungle.

She flicked a look at the arrow before loading it into the bow. "Jera," she muttered. "It'll have to do."

Thorolf leapt to his feet. "Don't hurt her!" He reached out a hand in appeal. A spark leapt from his fingertip to Chandra's chest, as if to soften her heart, and she caught her breath at the impact. At least she paused before shooting. He felt he was making progress and tried to make more. "Okay, she was my girlfriend, but we broke up. No matter what your deal with your brother is, you don't have to *kill* her..."

"She is your *enemy*." Chandra pivoted to face him, her eyes bright. "She nearly killed you and you don't even get it. I'm hoping that's because you're loyal, not stupid."

Thorolf shook his head. "No, you've got it wrong. Viv's not my enemy." The raven descended suddenly and landed on his shoulder, making him jump. It made a cry and Chandra strode back to his side. She grabbed his arm and turned it hard to the right, stared at the dark mark, then nodded thoughtfully.

"Of course. Snakes," she said, hissing out the word.

"What about snakes?"

She pressed her fingertips against two spots in the middle of the bruise. "You were bitten. Those are fang holes."

Thorolf's gut churned at the very idea. "No way. No snake could be that big."

"Not a normal snake."

"Forget it. I've never been bitten by a snake..." But as Chandra pressed his skin, Thorolf remembered a large green snake. He remembered fighting with it, back in that apartment, then he remembered it biting him, the feel of its fangs sinking into his arm and the toxin of its venom immobilizing him.

Right there.

CHAPTER EIGHT

"I should have realized earlier what they meant, but then—" Chandra's lashes fluttered and she blushed. She licked her lips, flicking at glance at him, then frowned "—but then, I was distracted."

The firestorm's silvery heat surged through Thorolf, reminding him all too well what could have distracted Chandra when she'd been close enough to check out his skin. "I can help with that," he offered, but she rolled her eyes and marched away.

The firestorm dimmed with distance, reminding Thorolf of their argument. "But what does that have to do with Viv?" Even if she'd kept the snake in the apartment without telling him, it wasn't her fault that it had bitten him. "Just let her go."

"In this place? I don't dare risk it." Chandra was raising her crossbow to aim it at him, her expression grim. "You can help or you can continue to hinder. Choose."

Thorolf understood that she'd fire at him without a moment's hesitation.

He reached for her but she backed away. She aimed the weapon and Thorolf held up his hands in surrender. "You wouldn't fire at me," he said, hearing the uncertainty in his own voice. "We have a firestorm. We could be good together."

"Maybe that's why it's *Jera*," she mused.

"What? The rune?"

"There's one on every arrow," she told him. "Or there is when I choose it. It's always the perfect rune."

"I forget what *Jera* means," he said and felt like a loser.

She clicked her tongue and shook her head, but her gaze

wasn't as condemning as it could have been. "Good thing you're cute," she said, then her voice turned stern. "Change toward completion," she said and lifted the crossbow. "It might be right."

Thorolf raised his hand. "That's not a good way to end the firestorm," he said. He dared to smile and saw her eyes narrow. "Just let Viv go and I'll try to help in your quest. How's that for change?"

"You are infuriating," she murmured again, then exhaled with obvious exasperation. "Even for a dragon."

Thorolf smiled, hoping to charm her. "I do my best."

Chandra shook her head, a gesture of affection and resignation. "You would have a dimple," she muttered then lowered the crossbow.

A dimple clearly was a good thing.

That concession was enough encouragement for Thorolf.

He leapt in pursuit of his mate, not wanting to lose the advantage of the moment. To his shock, he ran smack into a wall of glass that had somehow been erected between them. It cracked from his point of impact, shattering the image of Chandra. He wondered if it also broke his nose.

It might have been a mirror and it certainly was a barrier. As the pieces fell away, he thought he saw images of Viv in the shards. She looked really angry, but then there was only snow where Chandra had been.

No, where the image of Chandra had been.

Thorolf spun to look behind himself, but her sanctuary disappeared and he was surrounded by that swirling snow again. He was caught up in a wind that spun around him. It might have been a tornado or a maelstrom, spinning more and more quickly and lifting him off the ground. He had to close his eyes against the wind and the pellets of ice that struck his face.

She'd tricked him. He should have resented it, but he admired how artfully it had been done. She had incredible powers. She probably didn't need his protection.

That was a deflating thought, especially as she was so fascinating.

If manipulative.

Thorolf hadn't felt so turned inside out by a woman in a long, long time.

No, not ever.

No sooner had he had the realization then suddenly the wind stopped.

He almost didn't want to look.

But he did.

"Meet me."

The old-speak slid into Lorenzo's thoughts, licking his mind in a way that he found both revolting and inappropriate.

He didn't reply, but continued to review his plans for a new show in Las Vegas. He missed performing in a way he hadn't expected, and he knew that his mate, Cassie, missed the States. Venice was elegant and beautiful, but three winters of dreary cold and endless acqua alta had been enough to diminish even his love of the city. They were never going to finish the renovations on the palazzo, not with the flooding each winter creating new damage, and he was starting to think the tourists outnumbered the pigeons.

The incessant dampness wasn't much good for little lungs, either—now that Lorenzo was a father, he worried about Antonio's health, too. Cassie's current pregnancy had tipped the balance. With another son due in May, it was time to return.

Some good dry desert heat would be just the thing for all of them.

Of course, his final show had culminated with his apparent death, which made for a great disappearance but complicated a comeback. There was good promotion to be had in returning from the dead, but the niggling detail of the *Slayer*'s corpse that had been found in his car and mistakenly identified as Lorenzo was an issue. He had a feeling he'd be pushing his talent for beguiling to its ultimate limit to convince many people that they hadn't seen what they thought they'd witnessed.

In a way, he was looking forward to the challenge.

Lorenzo was sitting at his desk before a blazing fire in the large room overlooking the Grand Canal on the third floor of their palace, reviewing a midnight inspiration that had promise, when the old-speak slithered into his thoughts.

He couldn't smell the speaker, or sense his presence, which meant either that he was far away or very good.

Or *Slayer*.

Lorenzo prickled at that possibility. Of course, a firestorm had sparked concurrent with this lunar eclipse. That invariably brought the *Slayers* out of the woodwork, so to speak.

The blue-green light of darkfire glittered, then the chair opposite was filled with Marco, the Sleeper of the *Pyr*. He was watching Lorenzo closely, his thoughts no easier to read than Lorenzo's probably were.

So, he'd heard the old-speak, too.

Lorenzo thought of Cassie, sleeping in the next room, exhausted after another night of Antonio's teething. She was feeling good in her final trimester, but had difficulties finding a comfortable posture to sleep. In a way, Antonio's teething was a mixed blessing, because he would only take comfort from Cassie, which left her so tired that her posture didn't matter. He'd suggested that he could beguile their son, but Cassie had—predictably—forbidden it.

"Not her," came the old-speak, the words underscored with humor. *"I prefer to fight in my own class these days."*

Lorenzo was jolted that the other dragon had followed his thoughts. He was losing his touch. Or his legendary control. It was time to get back in the game.

Lorenzo met Marco's gaze. The Sleeper mouthed the word *Jorge*, and Lorenzo nodded. A *Slayer* approaching him. Interesting.

He flicked his fingertips, trying to emulate the spark of the firestorm, and Marco smiled. *Thorolf*, he mouthed, which surprised Lorenzo. Hadn't that *Pyr* been missing?

Marco nodded, evidently following the line of his thoughts.

Very interesting.

"Should I be flattered?" Lorenzo replied in old-speak after letting Jorge wait for it, and Marco bit back a smile.

"Probably. I have a proposition for you."

"The proverbial offer I can't refuse?" Though Lorenzo made a joke of it, he was intrigued. *Slayers* didn't come to *Pyr* and they didn't offer anything. Ever.

Was it a trick?

"I'm hoping so." Jorge named a coffee shop that was in the same block, revealing that he knew the location of Lorenzo's lair. That wasn't reassuring at all, but Marco settled into his chair and nodded once.

He'd guard Cassie and Antonio. As irritating as Lorenzo had found Marco during his firestorm with Cassie, the Sleeper had grown on him with longer acquaintance. He quite liked Marco and trusted him.

Cassie liked him, too, and wouldn't be dismayed if she awakened to find him standing guard.

"Five minutes," Lorenzo replied, disliking that he was unable to resist temptation and knowing that Jorge had probably relied upon that.

Marco unfolded a piece of paper and laid it on Lorenzo's desk, pushing it across the leather blotter with a fingertip. Lorenzo quickly realized it was a prophecy of the kind that characteristically came to the *Pyr* during a firestorm. It was printed out on a plain sheet of computer paper.

"A union of five will tip the scale
When the moon aligns in Dragon's Tail;
This Pyr *alliance can defeat the scheme*
And cheat the Slayer *of his dream.*
Fulfilling a pledge long been made
Will put darkness in its grave.
Know Pyr *and* Slayer *can share one curse:*
A vulnerability wrought of their birth.
Keep the pledge and defeat the foe,
So the Dragon's Tail brings triumph not woe."

Marco took a pen and underlined *This* Pyr *alliance.*

He gave Lorenzo an enquiring glance.

Lorenzo thought for a moment, then beckoned for the pen. He wrote his own name, volunteering for the alliance since he'd been targeted by Chen during his own firestorm. He paused for only a moment before adding that of *Erik*, because he couldn't imagine the leader of the *Pyr* not taking a role. He added *Thorolf*, who had been targeted by Chen before, then glanced up at Marco.

Marco added *Brandon* to the list. Lorenzo nodded, recalling that Brandon had also been targeted by Chen. Then Marco wrote his own name.

Five *Pyr* volunteers. According to the prophecy, if they banded together, they could defeat Chen.

The question was how.

Lorenzo nodded understanding, then rose to his feet. He had to wonder what Jorge wanted, and how it tied in. He exchanged a glance with Marco, flicking a look toward his sleeping family. Marco nodded and settled back in his chair, evidently intent upon remaining to defend Cassie and Antonio.

That was an offer Lorenzo couldn't refuse.

Jorge was waiting in his human form, as Lorenzo might have anticipated. The tall blond *Slayer* was incapable of blending into any group of humans, with the exception of trained mercenaries. He looked almost ridiculous with a small cup of espresso before himself, but no one would have dared to laugh at him. He flicked a look at Lorenzo, who ignored him deliberately.

Jorge was anxious, although he disguised it well.

Lorenzo found himself even more intrigued.

Lorenzo chatted with the proprietor, whom he knew well, admired the pastries, ordered an espresso, and read the headlines on the newspaper while he waited. He gave every impression of having all the time in the world, knowing it would annoy Jorge.

He'd come, but Jorge wasn't going to have it all his way.

He turned finally with his espresso in hand, the paper in the other, and cast a glance over the cafe in search of a table. He feigned surprise at the sight of Jorge, and headed toward him. "I didn't know you were in town!" he declared, ensuring that all attention was drawn to them.

Jorge glowered at him. *"So much for subtlety,"* he complained in old-speak.

Lorenzo smiled as he took the seat opposite the *Slayer*. *"They were all watching you already. Instinctive reaction, maybe."*

Jorge exhaled and looked out the window.

"You're supposed to be meeting an old acquaintance,"

Lorenzo reminded him.

Jorge's eyes narrowed, just a fraction, then he turned a tight smile on Lorenzo. "I didn't know you were here, either," he said, forcing out the words.

"Gives us a chance to catch up," Lorenzo said. "How's that beautiful wife of yours?"

"As beautiful as ever," Jorge replied, his eyes glittering. "Yours?"

Lorenzo met the *Slayer's* gaze steadily. *"Touch her and die,"* he murmured in old-speak, then spoke aloud. "Wonderful. The light of my life."

"I told you already. That's not what this is about."

"What then?" Lorenzo opened his paper, as if their conversation had been exhausted already. They exchanged a few more comments aloud, clearly not very close friends or those very glad to see each other. The proprietor peered out the window, scanning the overcast skies for signs of a thunderstorm, as the two dragon shifters spoke in old-speak.

"You're the one who finished Balthasar," Jorge said.

Lorenzo glanced up. *"And so?"*

The *Slayer* leaned closer. *"By beguiling him."*

Lorenzo lifted a brow, inviting more.

"They say you're the best at it."

Lorenzo turned the page of his paper. There was no need to confirm the obvious.

"To beguile a Slayer *is no small accomplishment, much less to send him willingly to his death."*

"I assume you have a point."

"I fight in my own class, but I fight to win."

Lorenzo glanced up.

"I want you to beguile Chen."

Lorenzo shrugged. *"I'd have to find him first."*

"I can take you there."

"So he can fry me on sight? I think not."

"I can get you into his lair," Jorge insisted, showing an insistence that Lorenzo found fascinating. He knew that both *Slayers* had consumed the Dragon's Blood Elixir, which meant that they healed quickly from their wounds and possessed a kind of immortality. He also knew that the source for the Elixir had been

destroyed, that the substance was highly addictive, and that Jorge had eaten other fallen *Slayers* to get more of the Elixir in the only way possible. *"You won't have long, but if you're as good as they say, you won't need it."*

So, Jorge wanted Chen out of the way, likely to assume his role among the *Slayers*. That likely meant Jorge couldn't beat Chen in combat. Lorenzo didn't know if the *Slayers* still had a hierarchy like the *Pyr*, but it wasn't a battle that interested him much. Getting rid of Chen, especially if that only gave Jorge more power, wasn't an improvement in any way. Jorge was merciless in a rare and evil way.

The alliance had to offer more upside to be worth the risk.

"*Pass*," Lorenzo said and folded up his newspaper. He drained his espresso and set the cup down in the saucer before speaking aloud. "How pleasant to see you again," he said in a tone that conveyed the opposite. "I hope the weather improves for the rest of your visit." He rose to his feet, intending to leave.

"You never asked what I could give you in return."

Lorenzo stifled the urge to scoff. He did, however, smile in his most disparaging manner before turning away.

Jorge sat back, his eyes gleaming with confidence.

If he hadn't been so good at bluffing, Lorenzo would have paused.

As it was, he knew he had something Jorge wanted badly, and the only way to find out more was to make the *Slayer* work for it. He inclined his head and left the cafe.

He had just moved past the window when the old-speak echoed in his thoughts.

"You can save one of your own," Jorge said. *"Otherwise, Chen will suck him dry."*

And that made Lorenzo's footsteps falter. He pretended his shoe lace had come undone and bent to retie it. *"Who?"*

"Thorolf."

The grandson of one of his grandfather's best friends.

It always had to be that way, didn't it? The ghosts never did abandon the living completely. Lorenzo knew he hadn't done nearly enough for the *Pyr* since his firestorm—and he'd done even less before that. He knew that Erik was giving him time and space, showing more patience than Lorenzo had expected.

And Thorolf would be the son of a good friend of Erik's father, too.

"It's already happening," Jorge continued lightly. *"Chen's had him for almost two years."*

There had to be something to the prophecy.

Lorenzo could do the beguiling. Not easily, but it could be done. Of course, he'd need Jorge's help to get to Chen in the first place. On the one hand, he'd be making a deal with the proverbial devil. He couldn't count on Jorge to be honest or truthful or keep the terms of their deal. He could expect a trick. On the other hand, if he could outmaneuver Jorge, he'd be saving a *Pyr*. The prophecy had to be right.

It wasn't just ego that made him sure of which wager he'd take.

Lorenzo gave every sign of checking the lace on his other shoe, taking his time before he replied just as Jorge had anticipated he would. *"Let's talk terms,"* he said and felt Jorge's triumphant smile.

Marco watched the darkfire crackle. It danced amidst the fire burning in the fireplace in Lorenzo's office, its blue-green light making the fire look unworldly.

It summoned him. It spoke to him. It drove him, as it always did, and he only knew to obey its whispered commands.

He watched its light and knew he had to collect the last darkfire crystal to finish what had begun. Marco didn't know how it would all play out and had no ability to see the future. He simply trusted the darkfire.

He'd given away the last surviving crystal that still nursed a darkfire flame deep inside it. He'd done that because the darkfire commanded it. Now he knew that it had only been a loan.

And he had to collect the crystal as soon as possible.

He couldn't leave Cassie and Antonio, not with Jorge close at hand. But he had to go. Marco felt an uncharacteristic prickle of urgency. He reached for Lorenzo's phone, hoping that Drake or some of his Dragon Legion were near at hand.

Time was of the essence.

Thorolf found himself lying on the ground in an urban street. People chattered around him, apparently astonished to find him in their midst.

He was back in Bangkok, he was sure of it.

No, he knew *exactly* where he was. That smell couldn't have been anywhere but the Ko Ratanakosin amulet market. He opened one eye warily to find himself on the pavement between vendors, their tables loaded with carvings and their yellow umbrellas arched overhead, brilliant in the sunshine. He could see the wall of a shop hung with Muntjac antlers for protection against evil forces, a row of *Kuman Thong* golden boy sculptures, waiting to be adopted in exchange for warnings of future mishaps, and *Palad Khik* wooden penis sculptures hung from the lip of the nearest table. No one ever had to ask what that charm was supposed to bring. Thorolf could smell the dust and the distinctive scent of old bones and relics, as well as his favorite noodle vendor around the corner. He could have kissed the ground—and sucked back the noodle vendor's entire inventory.

It was hot, hot the way it was in late April.

He hoped he had some cash in his pocket. Noodles wouldn't fill him up, but they'd be a decent start. He was starving.

He also felt bruised and battered, as well as strangely elated. His mate was gorgeous, and she was a thousand women in one. She was literally a goddess. She'd kicked his ass, and all Thorolf wanted was more. She'd said she wouldn't fulfill the firestorm, it was true, but he'd been making progress on that front.

The firestorm was on his side. It had to be. It hadn't seem like it at first, but there had to be an explanation. The firestorm had to be right.

He just had to believe.

And maybe talk to Rafferty.

Plus ask Chandra more questions. Too bad Thorolf knew he was alone. There was no spark of the firestorm, no hint of Chandra's presence.

She must have tossed him out of her sanctuary.

That was a sobering thought.

It certainly was overwhelming for Thorolf to think back on his firestorm so far. A mate who was a goddess. A fury that made him attack the stranger living in his apartment and try to kill Rafferty. Chandra's insistence that Viv was his enemy. The contradictions and complications were enough to make his head hurt.

On the other hand, kissing Chandra had been incredible. He wanted his firestorm to be real. And the vision she'd given him of his birth had been both consistent with everything he knew, and a revelation. He recalled the falcon and the skulls and the mirror on the threshold of the place she called Myth and was amazed.

"They should make drugs this good," he muttered to no one in particular. "I'd buy a lifetime's supply."

Chandra was trying to keep her word. He could understand that. She was a kick-ass fighter and a shape shifter, two more things they had in common. He knew the sex would be really great, even after the firestorm was satisfied. It had been a while since Thorolf had wanted anything enough to fight for it, but this firestorm was a contender.

He was going to satisfy it, if it was the last thing he did.

Chandra would be worth any battle.

The voices around him grew louder then and he felt someone draw close. He was nudged in the knee, probably to determine whether he was dead or not. The nudge annoyed him in an unexpected way.

Thorolf sat up, which made people move back warily. He rubbed his head and guessed that he didn't look his best. His jeans were rumpled and a bit dirty, no surprise given his adventures, and his jaw hurt where Chandra had decked him. He was probably getting a bruise. He had a few other new aches, too.

In a way, though, the fact that she'd come so close to kicking his butt was really sexy. Thorolf got up slowly, testing his steadiness on his feet. He figured he felt better than he should.

His T-shirt was gone and to his horror, that swirling tattoo was becoming darker again.

And it burned like acid.

In fact, his skin could have been lit by inner fire, and he stared in disgust at the incompetent ink all over his body. He could almost watch his skin inflame. Where had he gotten this tattoo? What kind of moron had done this to him? Who would remove it?

Thorolf suddenly smelled *Slayer*. He spun in place, seeking some sign of his opponent, hovering on the cusp of change and ready to fight. All rational thought abandoned him, that cold fury filling him with violence.

And a need to slaughter.

That was probably why he didn't even notice the moonstone and silver dragon scale that had fallen on the pavement.

It could happen again.

Thorolf looked around, seeking his foe. An opal salamander was considering him from six or eight feet away. The lizard was hidden in the shadows between baskets of *Phra Kreuang*. These amulets with the face of the Buddha were made by the millions and had been plentiful for a long time. Vendors bought lots of them for resale and optimists spent hours with jeweler's loupes, sifting through them in search of rare versions.

The salamander's hide shone opal and gold in the darkness. It shouldn't have been there. Thorolf felt an overwhelming sense of rage billow though him. It was outrageous that some vermin should invade the market like this! Red fury filled him like a cloud, obliterating everything else in his mind. He wanted to kill the salamander, to smash it with his fist, to smear it to nothing on the stone.

That fate was no less than it deserved.

Thorolf lunged toward it with a snarl, sending the crowd scattering in dismay. People gasped as the blue light of the shift brightened around his body, but he couldn't have stopped the shift to save his life. He changed to his dragon form with a roar of triumph, intent upon making the world right. People screamed and ran. Thorolf didn't care. He seized the salamander in one claw, filling his nostrils with the creature's abhorrent scent.

Instead of being frightened, the salamander held its ground. "*See what happens when you abandon your mate?*" it said in old-speak, the words echoing in Thorolf's mind. The creature had a deep voice, one that seemed familiar somehow, and it spoke with a measured calm that seemed inappropriate under the circumstances. "*She is your salvation, Thorolf, and a gift from the Great Wyvern. Cast her aside at your own peril.*"

That this lizard should dare to tell him about his life only made Thorolf more livid. He began to squeeze the small creature in his claw, so intent upon crushing the life out of it that he didn't immediately notice the tendrils of dragonsmoke circling around his legs. The salamander made a little squeak of pain, then some of its blood ran red between his talons. Thorolf grinned and squeezed harder.

The dragonsmoke barrier rose thick and fast, the tendrils weaving with alarming speed. It came out of nowhere, conjured so quickly that he couldn't evade it. It was up to his hips in a heartbeat, frosty cold and burning when he tried to kick his way through it. It snared him like a net, one that scalded him on contact, then tightened around him like a shroud. Thorolf screamed as the dragonsmoke enclosed him completely and trapped him. He tried to thrash his way free, without success.

"*Take a deep breath,*" the salamander advised in old-speak, then they were engulfed in pale blue light.

Thorolf tipped back his head and bellowed in frustration, sending a fiery plume of dragonfire shooting into the air. It didn't destroy the dragonsmoke barrier, either. The permissions were set against him, and that realization did nothing to diminish his anger.

He would destroy whoever was responsible for this.

He would make them hurt before he killed them.

Then he would hunt down everyone they had ever loved or known, and kill them, too. He glared at the salamander in his hand, but the creature shifted shape and he lost his grip. It slithered between his fingers as if it had no bones at all. He snatched at it, only to have his talon burned by the dragonsmoke as the salamander slipped through it.

Instead of being trapped in dragonsmoke with a small opal salamander, he was trapped in the same space alone. The salamander shimmered blue, then became a gold and opal dragon, one that watched him with care from the other side of the dragonsmoke barrier.

It was the same dragon he'd fought before, the one who had

picked up his challenge coin.

This was *his* dragonsmoke.

He'd imprisoned Thorolf to stack the odds in his own favor, to win with an unfair advantage. It was exactly the kind of trick a *Slayer* would play.

A thought struggled to be heard in Thorolf's mind, a protest that he didn't want to consider, but he let his anger obliterate it. The pain in his skin was driving him out of his mind. As furious as he was, there wasn't anything he could do to the other dragon. He raged and breathed dragonfire, he roared and shouted, but the dragonsmoke held him perfectly captive.

"We exchanged challenge coins!" Thorolf bellowed, beating at the dragonsmoke barrier with his tails and claw. "How dare you walk away? Coward!"

The opal dragon shifted shape again, becoming a man with long dark hair and dark eyes. He shook his head at Thorolf in disappointment, even as he lifted his T-shirt to consider the blood running from his side. "You don't know what you're doing, Thorolf," he said wearily. He poked the wound and winced. "We're old friends, you and me, even though you've forgotten."

"Liar!" Thorolf railed against the dragonsmoke barrier, but only succeeded in burning his own scales. "Sorceror!"

"Let me see that." Two other men joined the one who had been the salamander, one with dark hair and one with fair hair. They were *Pyr*, as well, Thorolf could smell as much, even though they were strangers, too. He realized that they were all in a luxurious hotel room, its quiet opulence as different from the amulet market as was possible. The blond *Pyr* took a long look at the first one's wound, then considered Thorolf with apparent concern.

"You don't look so good, T," he said with some sympathy.

Thorolf didn't want sympathy. He bared his teeth and snarled at the other *Pyr*, which seemed to startle him. The only thing Thorolf wanted to do was shred them all.

They deserved no less for abducting him like this.

He would make them pay.

Especially if anything happened to Chandra.

In Chicago, Erik Sorensson sighed and turned off his laptop. His partner Eileen watched him from the other side of the room.

"That bad?" she asked, but he could only shake his head.

"I need to think," he said, hearing the strain in his own voice. Erik felt the absence of Sloane and Rafferty keenly, although he didn't know what else he could have said to convince them to stay away from Thorolf. They'd departed immediately in a blue glimmer of light, Rafferty carrying the two *Pyr* and his own mate to Bangkok.

He'd spoken to Niall and knew that Niall had taken Rox and the boys directly to Bangkok instead of coming to Chicago. Quinn said Sara had a prophecy, but Marco had claimed it and they didn't remember it all. Something about a *Pyr* union destroying Chen.

Erik was out of the loop. Given that the situation was of his own choosing, he was surprised by how vehemently he disliked it. It wasn't natural for a *Pyr* to stand back or step aside.

Even if he had been trying to protect his own kind.

Erik supposed he should be honored that Rafferty and Melissa had left Isabelle in his care and under his protection.

Instead he felt the weight of his many years.

It had been painfully quiet and now there was this new video of Thorolf.

Eileen watched him, then nodded in understanding. "You should sleep," she said softly. "Everything always looks worse when we're tired." Her acceptance of his responsibilities and his nature made his heart swell with love.

He stopped to kiss her, drawing strength from her touch, then pushed back the hair from her cheek. "I'll be with my hoard."

Eileen pursed her lips, her gaze assessing. She knew him too well. "You already quit. You don't have to plan any more."

"I still have responsibilities."

"How about taking care of yourself?"

Erik nodded, letting his fingers trail down her throat. "You're right. But I do need to apologize to an old friend first."

Her expression turned questioning.

"I let him down. I didn't keep my promise."

Eileen smiled and laid her hand against his face. "If you didn't keep your promise, that was because you couldn't. And if you couldn't do it, it couldn't be done."

Erik smiled, appreciating her faith in him. "But still, it should have been done." He planted a kiss in her palm, then retreated to their bedroom.

In the back of the walk-in closet was a hidden door, one that opened into a secret room. Here Erik stored the treasures he'd gathered over the centuries of his life. The room was defended with locks and dragonsmoke, secured against both men and curious *Pyr*, even though the most precious prizes were not to be found in this small room.

Erik knew that Eileen and his daughter Zöe were the true gems in his hoard.

Still, there was enough in the small space to make him feel his life hadn't been wasted. There were piles of gold and silver coins, most old enough to be worth more as relics than for the weight of precious metal in them. There were gems and jewels, swords and blades, armor for both men and dragons. The room wasn't small, but it was so packed with riches that there was only a small place to stand in the middle.

He considered the broken Dragon's Egg, the large obsidian scrying stone that had been destroyed in the loss of the Wyvern, Sophie. He ran a fingertip along one jagged edge, remembering its discovery and knowing this loss had been another of his failures as leader of the *Pyr*. To lose both the stone and the Wyvern had been a serious blow to his kind.

But on this day, he'd come to apologize, not to brood. He moved coins and small chests aside, revealing a long box that had been hidden at the back of the hoard. He could almost feel the presence of Thorvald as he opened the case to reveal the gleaming sword within.

The Avenger of the Aesir.

Lost, broken, found and repaired.

But still not where it should be.

CHAPTER NINE

The Avenger of the Aesir was a long and heavy sword, so massive that only a man of Thorolf's large stature could wield it. The blade was forged true and etched with runes to bless and protect whoever carried it. The hilt was bronze, simply designed, for it stole no attention from the pommel. That disk had been impressed with the most powerful rune known to Erik and his kind, the Helm of Awe.

The Helm of Awe was an insigil, a composite of individual runes resulting in an amulet. The Helm of Awe was a circle, with eight lines inside it, two intersecting crosses. In that, it looked like the points of a compass. Each arm terminated in a fork, and each had three crossbars halfway down its length. Erik found his fingertip tracing the incised line of the insigil, as if to draw protection and strength from it himself.

There was a dent in the pommel and several deep scratches in the hilt. They were all the evidence that remained of Thorolf's rejection of this duty. They'd been buffed out by a master swordsmith but had been impossible to completely remove. Erik supposed the blade had to carry the mark of Thorolf's refusal to be his father's son. He hadn't been surprised that after Thorolf and Thorvald parted, Thorvald had hunted the world for the missing blade.

He certainly wasn't surprised that Thorvald had found it.

Although Erik had taken the blade in trust, and though he'd known the location of Thorolf for centuries, he'd never thought Thorolf ready for the responsibility of this blade and its burden. In a way it made sense that Thorolf had refused the task: he seemed incapable of fulfilling it, and no *Pyr* courted failure. Even when Thorolf had reappeared during Erik's own firestorm, Erik had been disappointed by the other *Pyr*'s state. In fact, he'd been annoyed that Thorolf could have wasted so many centuries so frivolously, but Thorolf had shown little sign of changing his ways.

Or learning much of anything. Niall had tried and made some progress, but there was always another party—or another woman—to distract Thorolf from any serious study.

Finally, Erik had hoped to provoke the other *Pyr* into becoming the dragon his father would have wanted him to be. He'd rejected Thorolf and dismissed him. He'd hoped that the other *Pyr*'s newfound connection with his fellows and his hatred of Chen would have motivated him to work for a reconciliation. He had hoped that if nothing else, Thorolf's firestorm would have prepared him for this duty.

Instead, Erik's tough love had made the other *Pyr* vulnerable. Thorolf had been trapped and enchanted by Chen, turned against his kind when the *Pyr* hadn't been there to defend him. Now, Erik's promise to Thorvald could never be fulfilled.

Worse, the prophecy would never be fulfilled.

And the *Pyr* would be exterminated.

Erik had failed spectacularly.

"You never showed me that one before," Eileen murmured from behind him. Erik barely glanced over his shoulder. She shouldn't have entered his hoard without express invitation, but he supposed none of those old rules mattered much any more.

He lifted the sword from the case, struck again by its incredible weight. He had to support the blade on his palm to hold it horizontally when he turned to face Eileen. At his gesture, she stepped into the hoard, glancing about herself before bending over the blade. She lifted a finger as if to touch it, but her hand hovered over it. "These are runes carved into the blade." She glanced up. "Can you read them?"

"Blessings and protection spells," he said with a shrug, his gaze falling upon the Helm of Awe.

Eileen followed his glance. "But this one in the pommel is important."

"The *Aegishjalmur* is the old name for it," Erik said. "The Helm of Awe."

Eileen looked at him, hard. "That's in a story."

Erik watched her with a smile, loving to see her mind at work. Eileen's specialty was comparative mythology and she knew thousands of stories. He waited while she sought the right one.

It didn't take long. She shook a finger at him. "Sigurd," she said with satisfaction. "The dragon slayer."

"He killed the dragon Fafnir to claim the Helm of Awe," Erik said. He nodded. "Fafnir, the first dragon shifter."

"A man turned to dragon to defend the golden treasure that was more important to him than anything else in the world," Eileen said. She touched the pommel. "And Sigurd fought for this sigil because it gives power in battle, making the bearer invincible."

"Giving the bearer the power to conquer with both physical and psychic force," Erik agreed, eyeing the sword.

"And you have this, why?" Eileen asked. "Because you *Pyr* took it back?"

"A *Pyr* had this blade forged and used this ancient symbol to imbue it with power."

"Who?"

"Thorkel."

"Father of Thorolf?" Eileen guessed.

"Father of Thorvald, father of Thorolf," Erik corrected. "At Thorolf's birth, Thorvald was told that the *Pyr* would need to be saved, and that his son would be the one to save us, with this blade."

"I'm guessing there's a reason why you have it and not Thorolf." Eileen's fingertips fell to the dent in the pommel, and Erik wasn't surprised that she'd noticed it, much less that she'd guessed the blade and its burden had been rejected.

"The story is not mine to tell," Erik admitted.

"Thorolf must have had a good reason to turn his back on all of you," Eileen mused.

"Thorvald died estranged from Thorolf," Erik said, not really answering her. "I think it broke his old warrior's heart to lose his only son. He entrusted the blade to me on his deathbed."

Eileen folded her arms across her chest and studied him. "And now that you think Thorolf is lost, you figure you've failed to keep some promise to his dad."

"Clearly."

"Maybe he's not completely lost yet," Eileen suggested. Erik shook his head, but she continued. "Maybe this is his test, and your faith in his survival is necessary to his triumph."

Erik stared at her in dismay as he realized her implication. "I can't take the blade to him! I can't imperil it!" Eileen held his gaze, untroubled. "If I refuse to put the *Pyr* in danger, why would you imagine I would sacrifice this blade, too? It's our last hope."

Eileen watched him with care. "But if the final battle is lost, you'll all be exterminated right? And if Thorolf is the one who's supposed to avenge you, that seems unlikely to happen with the blade locked away here. You could end up being the reason he fails."

Erik didn't like the sound of that. He turned to put the sword back in its case. "I don't think you understand," he protested. "We could lose everything."

"No." Eileen interrupted him firmly. "I don't think you're seeing the situation clearly. It looks to me like you've got nothing left to lose."

It was shocking to hear his worst fear given voice, and given voice by his mate. Erik looked at the blade, his gaze lingering on the Helm of Awe, then at his love and partner. "Losing it could make things worse."

"Nothing could be worse than losing the *Pyr*," Eileen argued with conviction. "You're the basis for a thousand human stories. You're the truth that our myths have their toes in. We are human because of our stories. If we lose our stories and their roots, the human race you've vowed to defend will be lost, as well."

Erik had never thought of it that way before.

"If you act as if you believe you'll win, then you will triumph." Eileen reached up and touched her lips to his, her gaze searching his. "It's a case of making the future you want. Think of this as the darkness before the dawn."

"You think we'll survive."

"I have complete faith," she said, smiling so that Erik believed her. "Every good story includes a test, and a moment when it looks as if good can't possibly prevail."

"Unless those in the story believe in their success."

"Exactly." She smiled as she unfolded a sheet of paper, then turned it for him to read the text. "This fax came for you earlier, from Lorenzo."

"I thought the fax was for you."

Eileen shrugged. "Oops. I guess I thought the moment wasn't right."

"A union of five will tip the scale
When the moon aligns in Dragon's Tail;
This Pyr *alliance can defeat the scheme*
And cheat the Slayer *of his dream.*
Fulfilling a pledge long been made
Will put darkness in its grave.
Know Pyr *and* Slayer *can share one curse:*
A vulnerability wrought of their birth.
Keep the pledge and defeat the foe,
So the Dragon's Tail brings triumph not woe."

This Pyr *alliance* was underlined, then in Lorenzo's writing, there were the names of four *Pyr*, including his own. Lorenzo. Erik. Thorolf. Brandon. It looked as if another hand had added Brandon's name as well as Marco to the list. There were check marks beside Lorenzo and Marco's names and a question mark beside his own.

Erik recognized that three of the others had been targeted by Chen. It was personal.

"Looks like there's hope after all," Eileen murmured.

Erik looked at the sword, determined to see it as an opportunity and not a failure. To his surprise, he was able to do it. He felt lighter and younger, energized by a new optimism. He had to join the others in Bangkok as soon as possible, and he had to take Thorolf the means to triumph. "How am I going to get this sword through airport security?"

Eileen only laughed. "You'll find a way. You always do."

There were more details than that to be arranged before Erik could leave. He knew he couldn't take Eileen and the children with him, as carrying them into what would surely become a battle would only make them vulnerable. His departure, however, might leave them vulnerable here. He marched out into the living room with the sword in its case, planning quickly.

Eileen clearly anticipated his concern. "I'll stay behind the dragonsmoke barrier with the children," she said. "We'll be fine."

"No." Erik shook his head. Jorge and Chen couldn't cross his dragonsmoke barrier without permission, but they both had the ability to spontaneously manifest elsewhere. They could manifest inside the protective barrier of dragonsmoke. "That's not good enough." He closed his eyes and summoned Donovan, Quinn, and Delaney in old-speak. It wasn't a command, but a request for their counsel, for they were the three *Pyr* closest to Chicago. He would have liked to have commanded all the *Pyr* to defend his mate and lair, but he had surrendered authority to Rafferty.

"The sound of subway trains when there aren't any," Eileen said, her hand on his arm. "What did you say in old-speak?"

By the time Erik sat down in front of his laptop, Donovan had already set up a Skype conference call and Delaney was signed in. Quinn joined them a moment later.

"Counsel about what?" Donovan asked, his manner wary.

"I've been trying to call you," Quinn said. "But Eileen said you couldn't be disturbed. Sara and I remembered part of the prophecy."

Erik interrupted him. "I have it," he said. "Lorenzo sent it to me."

"Lorenzo?" Donovan echoed.

"I felt the firestorm," Delaney said. "Whose is it?"

"First, I no longer lead the *Pyr*," Erik admitted, noting their surprise. "I surrendered command to Rafferty, who has taken Sloane to Thorolf's firestorm. Niall's also on his way there. He's probably already arrived."

"Then Thorolf's turned up again," Donovan said with excitement. "That's good news."

"Not really. Something's very wrong with him. He's turning *Slayer* right before our eyes."

"Sloane wants to heal him," Quinn guessed.

"I fear it's a trap, set by Chen," Erik admitted.

"The firestorm could be his chance," Delaney said immediately. "That's why Rafferty wanted to help him, I'm sure."

The firestorm had healed Delaney, destroying the Dragon's Blood Elixir in his body. He'd been forced to consume it and it had begun to turn him *Slayer*, but Ginger and the firestorm—and Delaney's own will—had allowed him to push back its darkness.

Erik realized that his concern was based upon uncertainty as to Thorolf's will. He'd never seen that *Pyr* really try to achieve anything. In contrast, Delaney had struggled mightily against the Elixir and only just defeated it.

"Chen has to have a weakness," Delaney said. "There has to be something we can use against him."

"That's what the prophecy indicates," Erik said and read it to them. "I think an alliance of those with an affinity to air can defeat him."

"What about the second part, about each of us having weakness in our past?" Donovan asked. "That has to be important, too."

There was a beat of silence, because none of them knew much about Chen's past.

"He has a brother," a fifth voice contributed. It was a familiar voice but not one Erik expected.

Delaney's expression turned to one of shock. "Marco! When did you get here?"

"It doesn't matter," the Sleeper of the *Pyr* said in his characteristically calm tones. He always sounded on the verge of sleep. "The brother is his weakness."

Erik wasn't convinced. "But I can sense us all, whether *Pyr* or *Slayer*..." he began.

Marco shook his head and smiled. "There are enchantments that take dragons out of your sight. Chen did the same to Thorolf."

"But where is he?" Donovan demanded, just as Delaney jumped.

"Gone again," Delaney said, then shook his head.

"We have to trust that it will become clear," Quinn said.

"I have to take his father's sword to Thorolf, to give him a chance," Erik agreed. "But I have the children here as well as Eileen."

"We're on our way," Quinn and Donovan said in unison.

"We are, as well," Delaney agreed. "But I'll leave Ginger and the boys at your place. I'm going to Thorolf, to help him any way I can."

"Don't imagine you're going anywhere without me," Ginger said, appearing behind Delaney. "Thorolf's mate might need some help, too."

Thorolf's mate didn't think she needed help.

She certainly wasn't happy, though.

On the upside, Thorolf was gone from the sanctuary. Chandra's thoughts cleared immediately with the absence of him and the heat of the firestorm. She'd been angry with Thorolf and the firestorm hadn't helped her to decide how best to proceed. She supposed that thumping him and chucking him out of her sanctuary hadn't been the best choice, but to finally be so close to completing her quest, after centuries of preparation, and to be cheated of victory in that last instant had infuriated her.

She shouldn't have talked to Viv.

She should have executed her immediately.

She considered that she'd been impulsive and passionate again, acting more like a dragon than a goddess. She refused to think that the firestorm was changing her. She was immortal. She didn't change. Ever. And she wouldn't for an annoying dragon shifter—even if his kisses made her forget everything she knew to be true.

She wouldn't even consider that satisfying the firestorm might be worth it.

On the downside, Thorolf was gone. Chandra wasn't entirely sure where he would have ended up after her forced eviction, because she'd hurled him out while distracted by the firestorm. Now that she could think straight, she feared that she'd put him in more danger again. She felt badly about that. That was the problem with trying to do two things at once. Without perfect concentration, complications happened.

She was never going to have perfect concentration so long as the firestorm burned. Even now, it tingled at the edge of her consciousness, as if it would guide her directly to Thorolf. Satisfying the firestorm would solve that, but at the same time would be breaking her oath.

Chandra had a feeling she was going to be choosing between better and worse instead of right and wrong for the foreseeable future. She didn't have to like it. Compromise wasn't one of her skills, but the firestorm might teach her to do it better.

She was standing in the familiar jungle of Myth, not far from the temple filled with skulls and ghosts. All around her on the ground were shards of the mirror she'd created to trap Tisiphone. The mirror was broken to thwart her victim's escape from it, and the force of that magic had been easily put to work to expel Thorolf. Piggybacking the magic had seemed like a good idea at the time—when the firestorm had been addling her thoughts—like killing two birds with one stone. She liked that Thorolf's collision with the mirror had broken it.

The mirror spell was a double-edged one: Tisiphone was trapped in the mirror in Viv Jason's form, but she was also protected from Chandra while snared within it. She couldn't shift or escape, which was good, but Chandra couldn't deal a death blow, either, which was less than ideal. Chandra sighed, acknowledging once again how distracting the firestorm was. She just couldn't think straight with Thorolf by her side.

She wasn't doing too well with him gone, either, come to think of it.

She saw there was another downside to her solution. She watched two shards of mirror ease closer to each other, seemingly of their own volition, and watched with concern. Before her eyes, two pieces touched, aligned, then merged into a larger piece of mirror. It wouldn't take long for the mirror to be reassembled, and then her prey could be freed by someone gazing into the mirror.

This banishment should have lasted for years, not moments.

Was Tisiphone's sorcery this strong? Chandra didn't want to think about the implications of that.

She didn't want to think about Thorolf either, but she couldn't seem to control her thoughts. In a way, she respected his loyalty. He clearly didn't know the truth of Viv's nature, much less what she'd done to him. Chandra had to appreciate that he wasn't afraid to put himself at risk to do what he thought was right.

It was pure *Pyr* to defend a damsel in distress and to be loyal to the end.

It was pure Thorolf to defend someone who didn't deserve his protection.

Two more pieces of mirror joined with the others, creating a larger seamless whole.

Chandra was afraid to leave the mirror unsupervised, uncertain as she was of what Tisiphone might manage to do in this place. Because it was of Myth, she couldn't take a shard with her when she left the sanctuary either.

At least there was no one to look into the mirror. The thing was that Thorolf shouldn't be loose in any world without protection. Chandra had seen that the firestorm's spark seemed to help Thorolf. So, all the other *Pyr*, and maybe a number of other people, were in danger when she wasn't with Thorolf.

The firestorm was a responsibility she hadn't expected, but then her brother did like to complicate things.

"Not a bad save," said a man close behind her. Chandra spun to find her brother, looking confident as ever. He was in his guise as Apollo, the eternal golden boy, his gold armor shining with particular brightness in this realm. Snow gave a cry of joy and circled out of the sky, coming to land on his outstretched hand.

He surveyed the mirror shards, then lifted a brow. "But most unlike you to miss. Losing your edge?" They'd always been competitive siblings, always prepared to challenge and goad each other.

He'd also routinely undermined her efforts, making a situation worse just to test her abilities more. And the *Pyr* were his favorite creatures.

Chandra glared at him. "Did you spark the firestorm?"

Apollo grinned, caught at his own mischief. "I thought you deserved a last chance to break that vow of chastity and try the pleasures of the flesh."

Last chance?

Before she could ask, he flicked a glance upward. Chandra noticed that the sky was darker than it had been and that the air was cooler. "It's time to go, sister. The portal's closing."

The end of an era. It had been foretold for as long as she could remember, but she had a hard time believing that all the deities she knew were going to pass into some corner of Myth forever.

On the other hand, many of them had abandoned interaction

with mortals centuries before. They were essentially already gone.

"No, I can't leave yet. I haven't fulfilled my quest..."

"You had your chance." He looked suddenly sad. "Maybe it doesn't really matter anyway. Maybe our time has been over for a long while."

Chandra couldn't stand to see him like this. He was always bold and confident, always filled with laughter and power. "What about your precious *Pyr*? I thought they were your favorites..."

"They're doomed."

"No, it can't be..."

Apollo spun his hand, conjuring a sphere that nestled in his palm. Inside it, a red lacquer dragon breathed fire on an enormous crowd of people, setting them aflame with the help of a dark dragon.

One with black spirals etched on his scales.

Thorolf.

"You picked the wrong champion, sister, and now it's too late."

"It doesn't have to be that way. Just because it looks dark now doesn't mean the future can't be changed..."

"Face facts." His voice hardened as more pieces of the mirror joined. "You missed. You *failed*."

"I don't fail!"

"You never used to," he acknowledged, his voice softening as he studied her. "Maybe that's just another sign of the end of an era. Maybe it's just a reminder that it's time for us to go." He turned his hand, eliminating the sphere and the glimpse of the future. "Maybe the point is that it's time to just leave the mortals to themselves."

"I can't leave this half done," Chandra protested, gesturing to the mirror. "What about Tisiphone?"

He shrugged. "She's already in Myth."

"What about Thorolf? What about all the people in that vision of the future?" Chandra demanded. "I can't just walk away and leave mortals to deal with the consequences of my task being incomplete."

He gave her a shrewd look. "You never used to worry about mortals."

It was true, but she was worried about them now.

"I'm not going yet," Chandra said firmly, knowing that her decision surprised her brother. "I need more time to get this done."

He considered her. He eyed the sky. "Most are going now," he acknowledged and she sensed his reluctance to cede to her. "But I'll be last. I'll send Snow to you when the portal is closing forever." He fixed her with a look. "I can't control it, sister. I won't be able to do anything for you if you're trapped on the wrong side."

Chandra swallowed. "I understand."

She couldn't just ignore her duty, regardless of the risk to herself.

"You can't save him," Apollo said gently.

"But the firestorm can," Chandra replied.

To her surprise, he came to her side, took her hand and kissed her cheek. "Good hunting," he whispered in her ear and then he was gone, Snow with him.

A third of the mirror was reassembled. Chandra had to move.

"He's really got it bad," Niall said, watching the snarling Thorolf with dismay. "He actually wants to kill us."

He never would have believed this if he hadn't seen it himself.

He'd never seen Thorolf so angry. Sure, they'd fought together before, but that had been against *Slayers*. To have Thorolf as an opponent was a fearsome thing.

Especially as he didn't seem to be himself. Thorolf was livid, violent, and beyond reason.

And he wanted to kill *Pyr*.

He'd fought Rafferty, twice, and hurt him badly both times.

It made no sense.

Niall walked around the confined and furious *Pyr*, studying him as he tried to understand. Sloane was assessing Rafferty's injuries on the other side of the room. Thorolf turned within the dragonsmoke barrier, still in his dragon form, a cold assessment in his eyes as he kept Niall in his sights. He looked like a predator, a hungry and unpredictable one, less like the easygoing Thorolf who Niall knew so well than he could have imagined.

But it *was* Thorolf. His scent was clearly his own, even if it was developing that undertone of dark rot characteristic of *Slayers*. The signs were all there, as much as Niall didn't want to see them. A few places where the dragonsmoke had burned Thorolf were bleeding, and his blood was dark. It wasn't quite black but it sure wasn't red anymore.

That worried Niall. He remembered Delaney's battle with the Elixir and how narrowly it had been won. Niall thought of the shadow dragons that he'd fought during his firestorm, and his twin brother Phelan, too. Thorolf didn't appear to be in a trance, like the shadow dragons enslaved by the Elixir. He was still Thorolf, just had his allies and enemies mixed up. His scales had changed color, as well, the moonstone and silver armor that was usually so magnificent now looking tarnished and decayed.

How far gone was Thorolf?

Could they even bring him back?

Or was he lost already? He hadn't wanted to agree with Erik that it would be smarter to just stay away from Thorolf and deal with his loss, but now, seeing what had happened to the *Pyr*, he wondered.

Was it too late?

Niall was glad that Rox and Melissa were secured in the next room, and that Rox wasn't seeing Thorolf like this. Rafferty had insisted that the mates barricade themselves and get some sleep, maybe because he'd had the best idea of Thorolf's state. Niall knew the women had been surprised that they had slept.

He and Rox had gotten to LAX with the boys before they discovered that there was a storm over the Pacific, interfering with flights there. Rafferty had intervened, spontaneously manifesting there to collect them all. Rafferty had been determined to have as many *Pyr* with him as possible, and the boys had been thrilled by the adventure. Niall had found the transport unsettling, but Rafferty looked dead on his feet.

He admired that the older *Pyr* wasn't going to let Thorolf go to the *Slayer* side without a fight. Niall had to worry, though, just how much Rafferty would give to support Thorolf's firestorm. The sad truth was that Niall was starting to doubt their chances of success. Erik could be right.

Niall dared to use his Dreamwalker abilities to peek into

Thorolf's mind, but only found a yawning chasm of darkness and fury.

Thorolf seemed to feel even that minute intrusion. The other dragon roared in anger, then breathed a long plume of dragonfire at Niall in response. Niall moved out of range, worried.

He was so concerned that he didn't hear Rox coming out of the bedroom.

"T, you look like shit," she said, making Niall jump and Thorolf snarl.

"His scales look like they're tarnished," Sloane said, shaking his head.

"No," Rox said, peering at the trapped *Pyr*. "They look tattooed."

To Niall's astonishment, she was right.

Rox straightened and put her hands on her hips, looking determined as she surveyed the dragon shifter who had once been her pet project. "What kind of trouble have you gotten yourself into now?" she asked sternly and Thorolf roared with incoherent rage.

The trapped *Pyr* thrashed against the dragonsmoke like a caged animal, beating his tail against the misty barrier that held him captive and tearing at it with his claws, even though it burned his hide. The suite filled with the sickening smell of burning scales, but that didn't stop Thorolf's struggles.

Niall remembered how the shadow dragons had felt no pain, how they'd kept fighting even as they were dismembered.

He feared then that Thorolf's firestorm wasn't going to end well.

"Two broken ribs," the Apothecary of the *Pyr* pronounced to Rafferty. "You got off lucky."

"I feel so lucky right now," Rafferty said wryly, then shook his head before turning to Niall. "Chen has snared him well."

"He had a lot of time to get it right," Niall said. He watched as Rox peered at Thorolf's scales.

"I wish I could see it better," she murmured, and would have taken a step closer but Niall drew her further away. He didn't trust Thorolf to remember that Rox was his friend.

Not when he was like this.

"We don't know that he was captive the whole time," Rafferty said.

"We don't know much of anything!" Sloane protested. He cast a considering glance at Thorolf. He began to apply a salve to Rafferty's chest and side, one that obviously was giving the older *Pyr* some relief. Niall didn't even want to think about how it would feel to be crushed by Thorolf. "I've no idea how to heal him. I don't even know where to start."

"The firestorm can heal him," Rafferty said with conviction. "When he was with her and the sparks were flying, he was himself."

"But where is she?" Niall asked. "Why aren't they together?"

The *Pyr* exchanged glances, because none of them knew the answer to that.

"If she abandons him, he's lost," Rafferty said softly, and Niall knew it had to be true.

"But how can she even stay away from him?" Sloane asked, as if thinking aloud. "The firestorm is an irresistible force. It draws *Pyr* and mate together, and only becomes stronger when it's denied."

"You said she wasn't human," Niall said to Rafferty. That *Pyr* nodded, then winced as Sloane applied pressure to one side. "Is that how she stays away?"

"Maybe."

"But what is she?" Niall asked. "An elemental witch, like Liz?" He referred to Brandon's mate, who was a Firedaughter and had the ability to command the element of fire.

Rafferty shook his head. "I don't think so. It's not that her scent is different: she doesn't have one."

That wasn't a good thing. Niall folded his arms across his chest, knowing he had to say his worst fear aloud. "The only beings we know who have no scent or can disguise it completely are *Slayers* who've drunk the Elixir."

"Jorge and Chen," Sloane said. "Maybe JP."

"What if she's not real?" Niall asked. Rox looked at him in horror.

"That's what Erik thought," Sloane said.

Niall paced the room. "Erik sensed that Thorolf's firestorm was a trap, a plan to draw us close. How could anyone plan that, unless the firestorm was faked?" Sloane frowned and Rafferty made to speak but Niall continued. "How many forms can Chen take?"

Rafferty sighed and rubbed his forehead, looking uncharacteristically weary.

Niall counted off Chen's known forms. "Chen can be a dragon, a man, an old man, a young man, a beautiful young woman."

"A salamander," Rox reminded him grimly.

"That's a lot. What if there are more?"

Sloane caught his breath. "You mean what if the mate is Chen in another guise?"

The *Pyr* exchanged dark looks.

"I'd like to think that's impossible," Rafferty said, but his uncertainty was clear.

"But Chen did take a female form and try to seduce Thorolf before," Niall reminded them all. "During our firestorm. Maybe he's trying the same strategy again."

"If so, the firestorm isn't going to save him," Sloane said quietly, turning to look at Thorolf. "Nothing will save him."

"Especially as he's lost a scale," Rafferty said. Niall looked and caught his breath to see that the older *Pyr* was right. There was a gap in Thorolf's silvery armor, a scale missing in the middle of his chest. "It was there the last time we fought," Rafferty said and Niall sat down hard.

They sat in silence for a long moment, Thorolf fuming at the four of them.

"I choose to see hope in the missing scale," Rafferty said abruptly, pushing to his feet. Trust Rafferty to have faith as a force of will.

Before anyone else could speak, there was a sudden shimmer of pale blue. They turned as one to see Thorolf shift shape, taking his human form. The dragonsmoke contained him all the same. He tried to kick his way through it and threw his weight against it, which made no difference at all. Then he swore as the dragonsmoke burned his skin. He sounded more pissed off than furious, and Niall watched him warily.

"What's wrong with you guys?" Thorolf demanded in obvious irritation. "What kind of stupid trick is this?"

"He knows us now," Niall said. He took a step closer to Thorolf and saw recognition in his old friend's eyes.

Thorolf glared at him, as if he were the one who had lost it. "Of course, I know you! You better be taking good care of Rox, Niall Talbot, or I'll do worse than this to you." He kicked at the dragonsmoke, then winced at its burn. "Friends like this, who the hell needs enemies?"

Thorolf was wearing only his jeans, and Rox wasn't the only one who caught her breath at the state of his skin. It was red and angry all over, like he'd been burned, and there was a huge tattoo covering all of his skin that Niall could see. The contrast in quality between its swirls and the dragons Rox had given Thorolf was striking.

"Where'd you get this crappy ink?" Rox demanded, marching toward Thorolf so boldly that Niall snatched after her to hold her back. He couldn't stop her from telling off the other *Pyr*, though. "Didn't I forbid you to get tattoos when you were drunk? Where did you go? Down to some seamy hole where they use the same needles until they break in half?" Her expression revealed her disgust.

"Easy, Rox!" Thorolf protested. "I don't remember."

"You loser," she scolded, launching into a lecture. "It looks like the whole damn thing is infected. I bet it hurts like hell and that serves you right..."

"Why is he better?" Sloane murmured, edging closer to Thorolf.

"Because the spark of the firestorm heals," a woman said with resolve.

Niall and the others spun in surprise, because they hadn't heard her approach at all. She hadn't knocked at the door to the suite, but she was standing in the room with them all the same. It shook Niall that he hadn't heard her, because he trusted in his keen senses, and he saw that the other *Pyr* were similarly startled.

She was tall and athletic in build, dressed all in dark clothes, with long dark hair hanging down her back. There was a quiver on her back and she held a crossbow in one hand. There was a bruise rising on her cheek.

She had no scent.

But the golden light of the firestorm lit the room with its unmistakable glow, a bright fire that Niall could feel right to his marrow. The firestorm filled him with more than heat: it made him feel strong and optimistic.

Thorolf's mate.

She spared them no more than a glance before striding to Thorolf with purpose. "The fury dims, the closer I am to him," she said to no one in particular, her voice husky and her tone firm. The *Pyr* exchanged a glance. The light of the firestorm brightened to brilliant yellow, illuminating the room with its radiance.

Thorolf smiled at her, a predicable gleam in his eyes. "Hey, Chandra. Come to bust me free or to kick my butt again?"

"Still deciding," she said, a thread of humor in her tone.

"You *are* going to kill me."

"I warned you not to tempt me."

Thorolf looked embarrassed. "I'm guessing maybe I did last time."

"Maybe." She gave him a second to worry about that, then stepped right through the dragonsmoke, framed Thorolf's face in her hands and kissed him.

The firestorm became as blinding as the sun and sparks shot from the point of contact. Thorolf moaned in pleasure, then reached to grab Chandra's butt and lift her against him as he deepened their kiss. The heat of the firestorm turned incendiary, so white and hot that Niall had to take a step back and shield his eyes.

"If that firestorm is faked, there's more magic in the world than I've ever seen before," Rafferty said in old-speak.

Niall could only nod agreement.

Which still left the question of what or who this Chandra was.

CHAPTER TEN

Thorolf had felt Chandra's approach.

He'd been trapped in a night of deepest darkness, a realm of shadows and death. He'd been more angry than he could ever remember being and wanted only to destroy everything and everyone around him. His skin had burned as if he'd been flayed alive, and he knew that the *Pyr* were responsible for everything wrong in the world.

He had to slaughter them all.

Then a spark lit in the distance, a spark that burned gold and beckoned him closer. He couldn't move toward it, not when he was surrounded by the icy burn of dragonsmoke, but he could yearn for it to brighten. He could blame the *Pyr* for imprisoning him, too.

To his relief, he saw the light grow larger and brighter, felt its heat as it came closer. He felt his anger burn away and breathed deeply of what might have been a new day. The darkness faded, illuminated by the golden spark, and he could clearly see the hotel room around him. He saw Chandra appear in a swirl of snow, the firestorm's light as brilliant as the sun, and his heart thundered in anticipation.

Had she chosen her huntress form because she thought he liked it? Or was it her favorite guise? Thorolf didn't know. He didn't really care.

He was just glad to see her, not just because of the restorative heat of the firestorm. Desire burned within him, instead of rage. Even better, this desire was more than physical. He wanted to satisfy the firestorm, but he also wanted to partner with Chandra.

Life with her would be an adventure and a half, and he was ready for it.

He wanted to be cast into her visions and even the world of Myth, to learn what she knew, to see her eyes sparkle with rare humor. He wanted to know everything about her. He knew he could lose himself in this woman, that he could spend centuries with her and never know all of her secrets.

And he was more than intrigued by that. She might have been made for him, except that she'd existed first. He wanted to know why she'd chosen him at birth and was starting to wonder if it was like the firestorm in reverse.

He was even thinking she might be right about his father's sword, but he wasn't going to tell her that just yet.

He liked it too much when she tried to convince him to fulfill his destiny.

When she'd appeared in the room, Thorolf had been the only one unsurprised. She'd walked toward him, smiling like that stone carving, looking as if she could read his thoughts. She had to be able to read his body's reaction as she closed the distance between them, because her hips had started to swing with promise. He didn't care about the other *Pyr* being there, didn't care what they saw.

He'd been born for this firestorm.

He wasn't entirely kidding when he asked about her plans for him, but he liked how her eyes twinkled when she teased him.

And he felt like the luckiest dragon in the world when she caught his face in her strong hands and kissed him. She tasted like heaven and heat, honey and power. Their heartbeats matched rhythm again, as did their breathing, and Thorolf closed his eyes, surrendering to the perfection of the firestorm. The sensation of his body matching its rhythms to hers left him both dizzy and thrilled. It was better than any high he'd ever had, better than anything he'd ever experienced. He caught Chandra close and deepened his kiss, halfway surprised that she let him.

When she placed the flat of her hand on his chest long moments later, his heart was thundering. Her eyes were filled with stars and her cheeks were flushed. Her heart was racing, as well, but she somehow managed to take a deep breath and step back. Thorolf reached for her, then winced and withdrew as the dragonsmoke burned his hand.

"Better," she said, her gaze watchful.

Thorolf smiled at her and pretended he misunderstood. "Come back here and we'll try to improve on even that one."

Her smile was fleeting and she blushed a bit. "I mean *you're* better. The firestorm burns away whatever has been done to you." Thorolf didn't really understand, but she turned to Rafferty.

"His skin looks better," Rox said. "And that horrible tattoo is fading. What kind of ink is it?" She gasped, her fingers rising to her mouth as she stared at Thorolf.

"What?" Niall, Rafferty and Sloane asked in unison.

"He's turning *Slayer*," Rox reminded them. Before Thorolf could argue, she continued. "And those are little spirals."

"Just like Chen's brand," Sloane said, rising to his feet to stare at Thorolf, too.

"It's not ink," Niall whispered. "It's *Slayer* blood."

"From a *Slayer* who has drunk the Elixir," Rafferty concluded. They were all staring at him, even as Thorolf surveyed himself.

"Well, how do we get rid of it?" he demanded, his panic rising. "I don't want to turn *Slayer*!"

Chandra spoke to Rafferty. "Can the firestorm completely heal him, and if so, can it do so by burning steadily for a long time or does it have to be consummated?"

"Wait a minute," Thorolf protested. "Sating the firestorm isn't optional. We have to consummate it!" Especially now. Especially when he had this crap on his skin.

Chandra spared him a look. "I told you..."

"And what a perfect time to break a vow of chastity," Thorolf said, trying to convince. "The firestorm is a rare and wonderful thing, a force of nature..."

Rafferty smiled and nodded at that.

"And as a bonus, you might heal me."

Chandra's lips tightened. "But I don't break my vows."

Thorolf wanted to argue with her, but he could see that she was digging in her heels. This had to be a test. He had to seduce Chandra and win her over, maybe to deserve having her as his mate. He wouldn't have been given a firestorm that couldn't be consummated. It didn't happen. Didn't Erik say that the Great Wyvern gave no one a challenge that he couldn't accomplish?

Thorolf was thinking this had to be worth any effort involved.

He eyed Chandra, thinking. "But, it's not personal?" he said, looking for the bright side. Any bright side would do.

"Personal?"

"I thought maybe I wasn't your type."

She smiled quickly, her gaze sliding over him, and blushed more. "No. It's about keeping my word."

Thorolf would take progress where he found it.

But why would Chandra make such a vow? Had someone broken her heart? Treated her badly? Hurt her? If so, he'd rip the offender apart. Then he'd show her that it didn't have to be that way.

But Chandra had no trouble defending herself. She'd have taken care of any vengeance that was due.

Thorolf remembered her assertion that she'd never done it and found himself intrigued all over again. Was that why she blushed so easily? Because this was all new? He quite liked the idea of being his mate's tutor in the pleasures of the flesh. It could take years to teach her everything he knew.

And she'd chosen him. That had to matter.

Chandra cleared her throat pointedly, reminding the *Pyr* of her question.

Rafferty indicated Sloane. "Our Apothecary would know better than me."

Sloane frowned. "I can't know how to heal him without knowing what exactly has been done to him."

Chandra frowned. "I was afraid of that." She eyed Thorolf. "But he doesn't remember."

"Why do I have the feeling that you know more about this than we do?" Rafferty asked.

"Maybe because it's true," Thorolf said. "You should show them some of your eye candy, bring them up to speed." He grimaced. "Just maybe not the ghosts."

"It's all ghosts." Chandra reminded him, pretending to be stern. "Ghosts make everything possible. But you're right. You need proof of what I was trying to tell you earlier." She turned her hand in the air. Thorolf braced himself when he saw snow spinning like a small maelstrom, snow lit by the gold of the firestorm. He could have been looking into one of those souvenir snowballs, one that captured a snowy day.

But the scene that appeared inside the spinning snow wasn't of Santa's wonderland or a modern city with its name written below. He saw a black dragon and a pregnant woman standing before what looked like an ancient king.

The figures moved.

Chandra threw the spinning vision into the middle of the hotel room, as if it were a strange snowball. It struck the floor with a flash of lightning, and then they were in the scene that had been in the snowball.

"Welcome to the Underworld," Chandra said, sounding like a bored tour guide reciting a warning for legal purposes. "Our first stop. This is a record of past events. No one can see you and you cannot influence what happens." Her tone hardened. "Don't try. I can't be responsible for whatever happens if you do."

One more time, Thorolf wasn't just witnessing the scene; he was part of it.

Damn. Chandra was some kind of awesome.

The king before them was dressed in long dark robes. If this was the Underworld, he had to be Hades. His beard and brow were silvered and his expression was grim. His courtiers were arrayed behind him and there was a corpse at his feet.

It was some kind of ugly creature that had died. It could have been an old woman, if not for the leathery bat wings sprouting from her shoulders. She was naked, her breasts wrinkled and stretched low. Thorolf stifled a shudder.

"Who dares to slaughter one of my own?" Hades cried.

Two similar creatures came screaming out of the sky. They could have been sisters of the one on the ground, but were even more horrible alive. Blood ran from their eyes, like streams of red tears, and their hair looked like it was made of writhing black snakes. Thorolf couldn't have blamed anyone who killed a creature like this.

The two landed on either side of a warrior who Thorolf recognized to be *Pyr*. He looked more closely at the woman beside that *Pyr*, guessing it to be his mate. She was very pregnant. There was something familiar about the *Pyr*, and Thorolf realized that he was one of the Dragon's Tooth Warriors. They had that stillness about them and an air of mystery. They were also hard for him to tell apart. He took a deep breath, and sure enough, Chandra's vision was a full sensory experience: he could smell the scent common to the Dragon's Tooth Warriors.

When had this happened? He was out of touch when it came to news about the *Pyr*.

The two hags seized the *Pyr*'s arms and shoved him forward, so that he fell on his knees before the ruler of the underworld. Okay, he'd killed the dead one.

"Did you do this deed?" the king demanded.

"She attacked me," the *Pyr* said, his tone bold and unapologetic. "I had no choice."

"No choice but to die," Hades said. "And you were already in the realm of the dead." He bent to touch the face of the horrible creature. "She was always a loyal servant."

The other two winged hags began to wail, and the blood flowed from their eyes more copiously. They really were creepy old babes.

Hades glared at the *Pyr* standing before him. "You will pay a price for this."

The *Pyr* spoke formally, as Drake's men tended to do. "I apologize for killing one of your own."

The god of the Underworld smiled. "The price will be higher than that." He reached out one hand and was given a chalice brimming with some dark liquid. He sniffed it, nodded approval, then poured it over the corpse. "Tisiphone, the face of retaliation and the avenger of murder, take life again and exact your own vengeance upon your murderer and his kind. Pursue them through all eternity, until your thirst for revenge is sated."

Whoa. Wait. She was allowed to avenge herself on the *Pyr*? When *had* this happened? Thorolf couldn't imagine that her thirst for revenge would be easily satisfied.

To Thorolf's horror, the corpse began to change. It shifted shape from a winged harridan to a large green snake. Thorolf looked away from the snake, more agitated than he knew he should be. His entire body seemed to itch and those two fang holes burned.

Meanwhile, the snake became a harridan again, then the scene began to dim before them. A violent swirl of snow hid it completely from view.

In the hotel room, Chandra snapped her fingers.

In the blink of an eye, they were on a dusty mountain road, one with little vegetation on either side. The sky seemed larger here, and the sweep of the land almost endless. A man lay in the road, like he'd fallen there, and a woman knelt beside him. Thorolf guessed that she wanted to help, but couldn't do much for the man. Maybe he was sick, or maybe just old. The pair were cloaked and bent over, and they moved as if they were tired.

But then, the location was pretty brutal. A ribbon of road wound up the side of the mountain to this point, and it was the only path. Thorolf couldn't see any shelter anywhere on its length before it disappeared. They must have walked up it, and he could feel that it was hot as well as dry. One tree with strange shimmering bark cast a thread of shade upon the ground. Thorolf felt thirsty, and he wasn't even really there.

"The road outside the Garden of the Hesperides," Chandra announced and Thorolf was awed again by her abilities. How could she do this vision thing?

He hoped she never stopped. It was awesome eye candy, and an amazing way to experience stories. He'd never been much of a reader.

This must be another glimpse into Myth. The Garden of the Hesperides sounded like it should be in Myth.

Best of all, they'd arrived in time for a dragon fight. A *Pyr* in his dragon form fought with one of those winged hags. The *Pyr*'s scales were so dark that Thorolf knew he was one of the Dragon's Tooth Warriors. He looked closely at the dragon and decided it wasn't the same warrior. The woman with the bleeding eyes was battling against him with surprising strength, clearly prepared to fight to the death.

She was one creepy chick.

Thorolf took a step forward to help his fellow *Pyr* before he remembered that he couldn't make any difference. Then the dragonsmoke stung him all over again. The hag ripped at the *Pyr* and Thorolf willed the other dragon to win. The *Pyr* cast aside the harridan with sudden force, backhanding her so that she fell away, then his eyes glittered as he scanned the ground.

Seeking something.

"What does he smell?" Niall demanded of no one in particular.

Thorolf caught the scent of *Slayer* just before the *Pyr* in the vision did.

"*Slayer*," muttered the dark *Pyr*, then snatched for a yellow salamander that abruptly appeared.

"Jorge!" Rafferty and Sloane cried in unison.

"Shh!" Chandra advised.

Thorolf hoped the *Pyr* smashed that old *Slayer* to oblivion. It wouldn't be all bad to be rid of Jorge. The salamander shimmered blue, then shifted shape to become a yellow dragon. Oh yeah, it was Jorge all right.

Slayer and *Pyr* locked talons as they began to fight. They spun end over end in a bid for supremacy, biting and slashing at each other, their tails entangled. They exhaled brilliant dragonfire at each other, then the *Pyr* sank his teeth deep into his opponent's flesh. The *Slayer* cried out as his blood ran black from the wound. It dripped to the ground and hissed on impact, emitting a plume of steam.

Jorge tore himself free, slashing at the *Pyr* in retaliation. The *Pyr*'s blood ran brilliant red from his cut shoulder and wing. Jorge laughed, then began to breathe dragonsmoke. The plume of dragonsmoke glittered like a snake of frost as it wound toward the *Pyr*, then it stabbed into his open wound.

Thorolf winced in sympathy.

The *Pyr* fell toward the ground, fighting against the dragonsmoke but losing steadily. He was weakening by the time Jorge grabbed the hag and tossed her at the *Pyr*. She landed on his chest, and Jorge touched the tip of his talon to a spot on the fallen *Pyr*'s chest.

"He's missing a scale," Rafferty whispered. "He loves his mate."

"No!" a woman screamed, appearing out of nothing beside the fallen dragon. Thorolf blinked. Where had she come from?

"Ah, the mate," Jorge said with satisfaction.

But there were no sparks. The firestorm must be satisfied. It wasn't right that the mate could be left to raise a young *Pyr* alone!

"Take me instead." She offered her bared arm to the snakes

that twined around the hag's head. "It's my fault he's vulnerable."

"Take them both," Jorge suggested.

The hag took one snake in her hand and offered its hissing head to the mate. "Kiss this one," she commanded, and her voice was somehow familiar. Thorolf felt sick at her suggestion. "Show me that you mean what you say."

"And you'll let him go," the mate tried to negotiate.

"I'll take him if you don't. See if you can satisfy my hungry vipers."

The mate leaned forward, her devotion to her dragon making Thorolf's heart swell. He wanted that from Chandra. He wanted the partnership that Rafferty always said was possible.

Which meant he had to win her over.

"I forbid this!" a woman shouted, just before the snake made contact.

There was a flash of brilliant blue-green light, like a crack of lightning out of a clear sky.

"Darkfire," Rafferty murmured. "Drake said the darkfire crystal plunged them into the past. This must be part of what it did."

Everything happened very quickly and Thorolf didn't know who to watch. Jorge pounced on the man fallen by the side of the road. He snatched at that man's arm, tearing it away from his body with savage force. The man's body was dragged across the ground as Jorge tore the arm free, and blood flowed copiously when it did. The man moaned in agony but Jorge suddenly disappeared.

"So, that's where it came from," Sloane breathed. "That's the source of the virus in Seattle! I wonder what the man had."

"Quiet!" Chandra snapped.

Meanwhile, the woman who had been huddled beside the fallen man had leapt to her feet. Her cloak had fallen away, revealing that she was young and beautiful. She pointed at the hag with the snakes for hair. "Your battle was your own until you dared to threaten a child of mine. I banish you from this age and this realm!"

"You can't banish me!" the hag replied. In the strange blue-green light, she looked even more like a nightmare come to life.

The beautiful woman stalked toward her as she spoke.

"Across the centuries and the years,
You will wait and shed your tears..."

She kept talking but the vision sputtered.

Snow appeared around the perimeter of the scene, gradually encroaching on the middle. The sound became static, the beautiful woman's words obscured even as her mouth kept moving.

The hag screamed in protest. She took the form of a snake again, a large green snake that made Thorolf take a step backward. This had to be who—or what—had attacked him.

In that moment, thunder boomed loud enough to make the earth shake. The light of the darkfire disappeared, along with the vision.

There was only the hotel room, and Chandra looking about herself with dismay.

She hadn't ended the vision on purpose.

Something had gone wrong.

Thorolf had to think that if Chandra lost her powers, that would be a very bad thing. He had to reassure her, somehow.

They had to become a team. And the only way to do that was to work together to help her fulfill her pledge to her brother.

It was only if they joined forces that they could save the *Pyr* and satisfy the firestorm.

Chandra felt the fizzle. She knew the vision was slipping away, although she couldn't make sense of why. She fed it new strength, buttressing it, but it faded all the same.

What was going on?

This had never happened to her before.

Despite that, the vision disappeared before it was done, and there was nothing she could have done to stop it. Chandra stared at the space, shocked by her own failure.

"Excellent," Thorolf said. "I'm glad to see we have things in common." He looked satisfied and almost happy, which was the least appropriate reaction in this moment, at least to Chandra.

"What are you talking about?"

"Screwing up," he said, his satisfaction so clear that she wanted to smack him. "I always seem to be letting things slip in that last key minute, right when everyone's counting on me." He grinned at her. "It's reassuring, actually, that you're not completely perfect. Our firestorm has a chance."

She sensed that Thorolf was making a joke, that maybe he was trying to make her feel better, but she'd never feel good about being a failure.

How could he talk about the firestorm at a moment like this?

"This has never happened to me," she said, appalled by her own failure. "I've never failed..."

Then she fell silent, her gaze snared by the golden glimmer of the firestorm.

The *Pyr* thought the heat of the firestorm could burn away whatever was affecting Thorolf. If it could destroy magic, was it destroying her own powers?

Thorolf was right to talk about the firestorm. It was changing her as well as him.

She'd thought it was just lust, but there was more. She could still feel the heat the firestorm had awakened in her. In fact it was inescapable, a hum of energy that fed a simmering burn of desire whenever she was near Thorolf. That was a new sensation to her. She'd thought she could flirt with the spark of the firestorm, help Thorolf recover and it wouldn't cost her anything.

Instead, he kept drawing her into a sensual experience that she couldn't stop—and didn't really want to—and now her abilities were affected.

Badly.

She thought of her new impulsiveness and the passion his touch had awakened in her. She thought of the temptation Thorolf offered, an invitation to physical pleasures that had never tempted her before.

"This is your fault," she said, spinning to face him.

He didn't look troubled. In fact, his eyes were gleaming with an intent that might have made a lesser woman's knees turn to butter. Chandra was feeling a bit less steady on her feet than she should have been.

"I wish I could take all the credit," he said and smiled.

That dimple was trouble.

"You chose me. You came to me," he reminded her in a low and very sexy voice. Oh, he was confident, that was for sure. "You kissed me. A couple of times. Just a few minutes ago, in fact."

"It was supposed to help you."

"I feel much better, thanks." He smiled a slow smile that did dangerous things to her knees. "How about another?" His gaze turned assessing. "Or maybe even more than a kiss? We're in this together, Chandra."

"No! It's not like that."

"You told me you work alone," he continued with that infuriating confidence. "But the firestorm is changing that. We need to work together."

No. She'd never had a partner and she wouldn't have one now.

Chandra spun so that her back was toward Thorolf and furiously tried to change shapes. Nothing happened. She stretched out a hand, conjuring a flurry of snowflakes for a vision, but saw only the glimmer of the firestorm. The dark-haired *Pyr* they called the Apothecary watched her warily. She fired a look at him and he turned away.

Rafferty was drumming his fingers on his knee, as if the entire world wasn't coming to an end. "That's the beginning of the verse the Drake brought back to Erik."

Chandra was busy trying to conjure a vision. No luck.

Rafferty looked at the ceiling and recited the verse from memory, the one that Hera would have said in Chandra's vision if her powers hadn't completely failed.

"Across the centuries and the years,
You will wait and shed your tears,
Until the darkfire is freed again;
Your vengeance can cause Pyr *no pain.*
I close the portal, for once and all,
To see those I love out of your thrall.
When darkfire will burn once again,
Your sister's death can be avenged.
When daughters of all elements are mates
Then will the dragons face their fate."

"That was what I wanted to show you," Chandra muttered. She

couldn't summon so much as a snowflake.

This was bad.

This had to be why the mirror spell wasn't holding.

"Brandon's mate Liz is a Firedaughter," Rafferty continued. "We just need three more."

Niall shook his head. "No, Liz had to have been last. The terms of the prophecy must have been fulfilled."

Chandra nodded impatient agreement. "This mate who appeared out of nothing was an Airdaughter, a nymph under Hera's protection. The one in Hades was an Earthdaughter, and the mate of Alexander, who we didn't see, was a Waterdaughter. This Liz must be the last."

"But where's Tisiphone?" Rox asked.

"She has taken the form of a woman named Viv Jason," Chandra said. She wished she could have shown that to them. They were all shocked and she could feel Thorolf's disbelief.

"Is this why you were trying to kill her?" Thorolf asked.

Chandra had to wish that he wasn't quite so loyal. She turned to face him, her hands fisted at her sides. "Tisiphone is one of the Erinyes, given the right by Hades to avenge herself on the *Pyr*, as you just saw. The form she has taken in this realm is that of Viv Jason. They are one and the same."

Thorolf swore. "I don't believe it."

Chandra gritted her teeth. "My pledge to destroy her could have been completed today, but I was...*interrupted*." She fired another look at Thorolf, who now seemed embarrassed. "So, your kind remains in peril, thanks to Thorolf's efforts to *help*." Chandra softened her tone a bit. "Your loyalty is admirable but misguided."

"Okay, you're my mate. So, we're a team." His gaze hardened, his eyes becoming a steely blue that sent a thrill through her. "How do I fix this?"

"Guess." Chandra saw him struggle against the idea of injuring the woman who had been his lover and knew he wouldn't be able to do it.

Loyalty was a double-edged sword.

"She's never done anything to me," he protested and she turned her back on him. She'd never convince him, not without a visual display. She tried to conjure one again, but there was nothing.

"So how do you come into it?" the fair-haired *Pyr* asked her.

Chandra glanced toward him, then straightened. She might as well lay it all out for them. "I am Chandra, Freya, Selene, Artemis and Diana, the virgin goddess, the huntress, the daughter of the moon and the sister of the sun. I am the one who vowed to defend the *Pyr* against Tisiphone's vengeance."

"Not just any goddess," Thorolf said with such approval that she found herself blushing. "A major kick-ass deity. I like it."

To his credit, the blond *Pyr* didn't seem to be surprised. "But why you?"

"My brother asked it of me and I pledged my word to him that I would see it done."

"That still doesn't tell us why you'd care about defending the *Pyr*?" the Apothecary said.

Chandra cast a glance over her shoulder at Thorolf and her heart leapt at the admiration in his eyes. "I am the patroness of thieves, outcasts, wild animals and the wilderness. I guess that puts the *Pyr* in my jurisdiction."

Thorolf chuckled and that dimple, hmm.

"I accepted a challenge to eliminate a threat to the survival of the *Pyr*." She gave Thorolf a hard look. "It was supposed to be simple."

He gave her a look that should have melted every reservation she had. "Simple is boring," he said in a low voice that made her body thrum. He dropped his voice to a whisper. "Kind of like chastity." He winked and her heart skipped. "This is way better." He beckoned and Chandra found herself moving back toward him, lifting her face for his kiss, savoring both the sparks of the firestorm and the majestic power of her mate. She stretched to her toes, ready for that kiss, then someone spoke behind her.

"Maybe it's *Slayers* who are under your jurisdiction, not the *Pyr*." The husky voice came from within the room but not from any of the occupants. They all looked around in confusion, and Chandra caught her breath at the telltale blue shimmer. "After all, the *Pyr* consider them outcasts and that would explain your relationship with Thorolf."

A young Asian woman manifested right in front of Chandra, her long red nails painted exactly the same color as her fitted cheongsam dress. The woman smiled, the light in her eyes malicious, even as she snatched Chandra's wrist. Her grip was as cold as ice and sent a strange paralysis through Chandra's body. When she struggled, the woman's smile broadened. "The problem here is the firestorm and its interference in my spell," the woman hissed. "And the mate is always the weakest link."

"Chen!" the *Pyr* shouted in unison and leapt toward the two women. Thorolf roared and shifted shape. His bellow of pain echoed in Chandra's ears as the wind began to swirl around her.

"Just bring the sword!" she shouted to the *Pyr*, then held fast to the *Slayer* who planned to destroy her. A new resolve filled her even as she had to close her eyes against the rushing wind and the nausea in her gut.

If Chen thought the mate was the weak link, he could think again.

"What sword?" Niall asked just as Chandra and Chen disappeared. Thorolf knew which sword, but he also knew it was gone.

Just like Chandra.

It was easy to decide which was more important.

It was, in fact, time to stop screwing everything up.

"Not my mate!" Thorolf bellowed and the sound make the walls shudder. He couldn't wait for his fellow *Pyr* to change the permissions on their dragonsmoke. He had to follow Chandra!

He shifted back to dragon form in a brilliant shimmer of blue, then lunged through the dragonsmoke barrier. It burned his scales with ferocious power, stabbing into the skin at one spot on his chest, but he didn't stop and he didn't scream. He already felt flayed alive—a little more pain was no big deal. He endured it and emerged on the other side, his scales blackened and smoking.

Chandra might be infuriating. She might not tell him everything, and she might have chosen him initially because she wanted him to complete a task. She was persistent and determined to keep her word, and he admired that. The ghosts and the visions didn't lie. Best of all, she was his destined mate, chosen for him by the Great Wyvern.

Chen wasn't going to claim her as a sacrifice.

Thorolf seized Rafferty in one claw and held him aloft. He wished his friend wasn't so tired but he knew that Rafferty would push himself to the max for the sake of the firestorm. "We have to follow her!"

"Where?" Rafferty demanded in old-speak. He sparkled and became a salamander, coiling his tail around Thorolf's claw. *"Where did he take her?"*

Thorolf inhaled sharply and peered at the space where Chandra had been. He stretched out one talon and saw a single spark of the firestorm's golden light.

"Follow it!" Rafferty advised and Thorolf tried to pursue the elusive spark. He filled his mind with the firestorm's heat and the passion of its promise. He recalled Chandra's sweet kisses and the feel of her body against his own. He thought of the way the heat burned over his skin and through his veins, and the light brightened before his very eyes.

He believed he could succeed.

That was when he saw a trail of sparks, a line of fire, a path of light that had to lead directly to her. He leapt toward it, narrowing his eyes as the wind began to tear around them. He took flight and flew after the spark, beating his wings hard as he chased it through time and space.

"Focus," Rafferty whispered in old-speak, his words resonating in Thorolf's mind. *"Keep her bright in your thoughts."*

Thorolf focused. Thorolf let his admiration for Chandra fill his mind. He thought of her various forms, the way she shifted shape beneath his kiss, the way she responded to his touch, the way she challenged him and surprised him. He thought of how valiant she was, how she'd nearly kicked his ass, how resolved and stubborn and beautiful she was. He thought of the way she blushed, and how she'd already learned to kiss him back. He thought about tutoring her in the delights of the flesh.

Rafferty murmured encouragement, words that Thorolf felt more than heard. He kept his focus tight upon Chandra. He saw the light shed sparks, like a sparkler lit on the Fourth of July, like a firecracker shooting into the air over a park, like a comet racing across the sky.

He raced after the spark as it grew into a flame, then smiled as it became a bonfire in the distance. He flew harder, straining himself to get to her side in time. He seemed to fly right into the blaze and be surrounded by it. He flew enveloped in a sphere of light that steadily became both brighter and lighter, its radiance such that his eyes were narrowed to slits against it.

When the light burned white hot, he knew they were close.

So, he wasn't that surprised when they manifested high above a mountain range. There were snow on the peaks, a few clouds overhead, and the sunlight was piercingly bright. The mountains were sharp and rose steeply on every side.

And below him, on an angled face of sheared stone, Chandra was kickboxing with an opponent he knew had to be Chen.

Thorolf roared and turned, diving toward his mate with ferocious power.

This time, he wasn't going to fail or fall short. Thorolf had finally found something worth fighting for, and something worth dying for. The heat of the firestorm burned hotter with every beat of his wings, filling him with joy and power, as well as the sense of being a hero with a plan. He found himself smiling in anticipation of thumping Chen for once and for all, and then his smile broadened as he imagined how he and Chandra would celebrate.

It would be the perfect time to satisfy the firestorm.

And he'd make sure she never regretted it.

Chapter Eleven

Chandra was caught in a now-familiar maelstrom, but this one was filled with burning coals of debris. Chen's was a dirty wind, one that seemed to have swept up all the ashes and filth of the world. She felt sick, as she had when Rafferty had moved them through time and space, but the dirt in the air made it worse. She was surrounded by soot and covered by it, polluted by it and disgusted by it. Chen in his female form held so tightly to her wrist that those long nails dug into Chandra's skin. The wind kept them apart, although Chandra wanted to pound her opponent to oblivion.

Suddenly the wind stopped and she was slammed so hard into rock that the breath was driven out of her. She saw stars, but felt Chen's grip loosen on her wrist. Chandra rolled to her feet, ready to fight, only to be faced with a shimmer of pale blue light. When it faded, she faced a young and agile Asian man in a leather jacket and jeans. The line of his mouth was mean and she saw the knife shoved into his boot.

He wouldn't fight fair.

But then, he was Chen.

It was a shame really. That tightly fitted cheongsam and the high heels would have hampered his female form's ability to fight. Chandra had been looking forward to the advantage. She reminded herself that Chen had many forms, just as she did, and was determined not to be disconcerted by any sudden changes.

That trick should work only on amateurs.

They circled each other, watchful and ready for the first move. They were on a small plateau notched out of the side of a mountain. There was a snowy peak far overhead, as well as an endless blue sky, and the drops were sheer on every side. Whether they were in Myth or the remote mountains of Tibet didn't matter: death was possible in either place. One misstep would send the loser plummeting into the abyss below.

The trick was that Chandra couldn't shift shape into a dragon. If she tossed Chen over the side, he'd shift and survive. If he pushed her over the edge, she was a goner.

He smiled at her and she knew he'd guessed her thoughts. Maybe he could read them. Maybe he'd heard the skip of her heart or the accelerated pace of her breathing. Chandra was determined to school her reactions to hide her intent from him.

She was going to kick his butt, for Thorolf and the *Pyr*.

"Yes, you will die here," he said, his voice so low and melodic that he might have been trying to convince her. There were flames dancing in his eyes, orange flames that couldn't possibly be there. Chandra was tempted to look more closely at them. "After all these centuries, aren't you weary?" he murmured and it seemed like a tempting prospect. "Don't you long to surrender the battle and finally rest?"

Chandra abruptly remembered about the *Pyr*'s ability to beguile. If the *Pyr* could do it, and *Slayers* were *Pyr* turned bad, it made sense not only that *Slayers* could beguile but that they'd use it for their own purposes. Beguiling was a kind of hypnosis, an ability to direct the thoughts of humans. The *Pyr* used it to convince humans that they hadn't really seen a dragon overhead, or a man shifting to a dragon. Beguiling worked best if the dragon shifter in question found a secret urge in the victim that could be exploited. Most humans didn't want to believe dragons lived among them.

Chen, however, was trying to give Chandra a death wish, maybe to make this an easy triumph.

She *was* tired.

But she wasn't done yet.

She sighed, as if his argument made sense, and let her shoulders relax. "It's so hard," she murmured. She looked over the top of his head instead of into his eyes, and hoped they were far enough apart that he would be fooled. "The same fights, the same issues; nothing ever changes."

"But you grow more weary all the time. It seems so futile. It has to seem that mortals can never learn."

"They repeat their errors over and over again," she agreed, with another heartfelt sigh.

"They don't deserve you. They shouldn't have your help. The *Pyr*, too, want only what you can do for them. It must be so very tedious."

Chandra exhaled and dipped her head, apparently in resignation, but she was ready. "It's all true," she whispered.

Before she even finished speaking, Chen spun and aimed a kick at her head. He was fast, faster than she'd expected.

Maybe Chandra was faster than *he* expected. She ducked, then leapt up and seized his ankle when his leg passed over her head. She might not have her powers, but she was still strong and a good fighter. She twisted his leg, continuing the movement, and tossed him bodily over her shoulder. She flipped him quickly and gave him a shove, making the most of having surprise on her side. She divested him of the knife in his boot, tossing it into the abyss.

He howled with fury as he landed on his back, at least until he thunked his head hard on the stone. His hands scrabbled at the smooth stone and he managed to stop himself when his head was over the lip of the precipice.

Chandra felt his shock that she had fought back with any success.

Then she felt his determination to make her pay.

It was now or never. Chandra loaded her crossbow with lightning speed. She didn't even take an instant to check the rune. It was always right. She fired, hoping to finish him off before he recovered.

But Chen wasn't an old dragon for nothing. He roared and rolled, shimmered blue, and shifted shape even as the arrow whistled past him and buried itself in the stone. "Lying bitch!" he roared. "What else can be expected from the patroness of thieves and outcasts, liars and criminals?"

"Just your type, I would have thought," she countered even as she jumped. There was no target in the shimmering blue, and she didn't dare wait. Chandra leapt upon him while he was still shifting.

Chen was an old man when Chandra fell on his back, but his form didn't make her hesitate. It was an illusion and no indication of his true power. If he was hoping to make her pause, he'd hoped wrong. She decked him, but he elbowed her and fought with a ferocious strength uncommon in old men. She grabbed him by the beard and slammed his head against the stone.

They struggled together, fighting for supremacy, back and forth across the small platform of stone. They came precariously close to the lip of the stone, close enough that Chandra had more than one glimpse of the dizzying drop. Chen moved suddenly, twisting around, seizing her and flipping her to her belly.

Chandra caught her breath that she was looking down into the abyss. She couldn't even see the bottom. Far far below, there was mist gathered in a valley, but the river that must be at the bottom was hidden from view.

Chandra closed her eyes and pretended to faint. She tried to slow her heartbeat.

"You won't fool me this time," Chen muttered as he shoved her forward. Chandra let him push her until the lip of stone was beneath her shoulders. She waited one beat more, until he'd be sure that her weight would inevitably carry her over the edge.

He eased his grip, just a little, confident that he'd won.

Chandra kicked up and back as hard as she could and Chen yowled in pain. When he staggered backward, she bounced to her feet and spun around. She swept his feet out from beneath him with one good kick. He spun to catch his balance and snatched at her throat. His hands changed to dragon claws, his eyes to dragon eyes. He snatched her crossbow and flung it over the chasm. She snatched after it impulsively but he laughed that she couldn't do anything but watch it fall.

He grinned at her as he hovered between forms, his talons tightening around her neck with savage force. Chandra couldn't breathe, she couldn't break free of his grip, and she knew that he really would kill her.

Then who would save the *Pyr* from Tisiphone?

She couldn't fail.

She *never* failed.

Chandra roared with new strength. She kicked and scratched, and managed to get one hand beneath his claw. His talon tore at her skin as she ripped free of his grip and she felt the warm flow of her own blood.

Blood? How could that be? She was never wounded, not really. She certainly didn't bleed. She looked and discovered that she was bleeding now. There was no time to think about it, not when she was battling Chen.

Chen shimmered blue even as they fell, locked in a battle for supremacy, and this time, when he landed on top of her, they were facing each other.

And he had completely shifted shape to a lacquer red dragon. He smiled, letting her see the sharp array of his dragon teeth, and she knew he had to feel her panic. She couldn't control it, not when she was going to lose, not when she was going to die, not when she was going to fail to keep a vow for the first time in her long life. Not when the *Pyr* would be lost. Not when Thorolf would be turned *Slayer*.

Not when she was going to be either flown over the cliff and dropped, or fried alive. Chen took a deep breath, his eyes glittering, a move that revealed his plan.

Fried alive, it would be.

He reared back, presumably to awe her with his majestic form. He probably assumed she couldn't escape because there was nowhere to run. He took flight, hovering over her, his dark wings spread wide, and inhaled even more. His chest swelled and his eyes shone with malicious intent.

The underside of his belly was only six feet above the stone platform.

And he'd forgotten her quiver.

She could injure him, at least. That might help Thorolf.

Chandra pulled an arrow from her quiver just before Chen exhaled. She ran her thumb over the arrow head, satisfied with the rune etched on it. *Eihwaz*, the death rune, would do very well. She hoped this arrow would be as toxic to Chen as the yew that the rune was named after.

She ran beneath him suddenly and jabbed the hard point of the arrow up, forcing it between his scales. She moved quickly and shoved hard, guessing this might be the last deed she ever did. Black blood spurted from the wound, the foul smell of it making her stagger backward as she gagged.

Chen bellowed in pain, even as his blood sizzled on impact with the stone. To Chandra's horror, it seemed to be dissolving the stone, because big fissures opened in the surface. The stone platform cracked and crumbled, beginning to fall away. Chen flapped his wings, flying high above her as he roared in anguish.

The platform was cracking beneath Chandra's feet and she leapt from one part to the next, trying to land on a stable piece of rock. One collapsed just as she landed on it, the pieces tumbling into the valley far below. She caught her breath after jumping to one that seemed stable and looked up. Chen pulled the arrow from the wound and snapped the shaft in half, before he breathed fire at it.

When he turned his furious gaze on Chandra, she knew it was over.

Given the choice of Chen or the drop, it might be better to jump.

She had no chance to decide.

Chen snatched Chandra up and flung her off the side of the mountain. The wind rushed around her as she tumbled through the air, powerless to affect her course. It could have been a thousand miles down to the river at the root of the mountains. She looked up, even as she fell, and saw Chen bearing down on her. His eyes blazed with fury. He bared his teeth and she saw that he intended to fry her to cinders before she hit the ground.

She also realized that his focus on her was so great that he hadn't realized they weren't alone anymore. High in the sky, silhouetted against the sun, was a second dragon, and he was headed directly toward them. His wings beat the air with powerful strokes, his intent so absolute that he might have been hunting them. Chandra wouldn't have recognized the charred and blackened dragon if she hadn't felt the tingle of the firestorm deep inside.

Thorolf!

She had to make sure the firestorm didn't give him away.

"Dragonfire," she scoffed at Chen. "What makes you imagine yours is hot enough to hurt me? I'm a *goddess*!" And she spat at him to ensure she enraged him.

"Yes, I can see your invincibility," he retorted.

Chandra laughed. "I'm immortal, you fool. You can't kill me." That had never been entirely true, and she doubted it was true at all now, but her declaration startled him.

"Let's find out," Chen purred. He closed his eyes, then loosed a stream of dragonfire so wide and so hot that Chandra's confidence faltered. She'd miscalculated, because Thorolf was still too far away to reach her in time. Once again, the firestorm had messed with her tendency to plan carefully, making her impulsive...

Before she could blame herself too much for her mistake, Thorolf appeared before her. He grinned and even though he didn't have a dimple in his dragon form, there was a recklessness about his expression that made her heart sing. He snatched her out of the air and passed her toward his back. He turned gracefully, but not quite quickly enough to avoid all of Chen's dragonsmoke. Chandra winced when she saw it strike his tail and gagged at the smell of burning scales.

He looked terrible, she noted with horror. He should look glorious and jeweled, but his scales were blackened and dull. They were more than tarnished: they looked stained.

Tattooed.

"Hold Rafferty," Thorolf said and she saw the opal and gold salamander on his extended claw. The other *Pyr* looked pale and his eyes were closed. If he'd used his ability to spontaneously manifest elsewhere to get himself and Thorolf here, he had to be worn out completely. He'd been doing that too much for his own health.

Chandra doubted she could say anything to change his choices, given Rafferty's devotion to the firestorm. She cupped Rafferty carefully against her heart, glad he'd helped Thorolf. She climbed between Thorolf's wings, wrapping her legs around the joints where they grew from his back. His wings sheltered her a bit, beating high above her.

Rafferty's tail wound around her wrist, just like the dragon tattoo on Thorolf's wrist, and he sighed with relief. She leaned against Thorolf, sheltering Rafferty between the two of them, and the golden glow of the firestorm seemed to surround him. She heard the rumble of thunder, but didn't know what it was.

"He said there's nothing like a firestorm," Thorolf murmured to her. "Hang tight." Chandra had time to nod, then there was a clash of dragon against dragon. The mountains seemed to shake with the impact as Chen and Thorolf locked claws. They spun in the air, then fell together, tumbling end over end. She heard the rumble of thunder, although the sky was still clear.

"Taunts," Rafferty said weakly. "In old-speak. It's tradition."

Chandra stifled a smile. Of course. It was common in many cultures for warriors to exchange insults when they first met in battle, a way of establishing emotional supremacy before the fight began. She knew she shouldn't have been surprised that dragons, of all creatures, would sustain that tradition.

The pair thrashed and snarled at each other, breathing fire as they continued to fall toward the earth. Chandra supposed that was tradition, too, like a game of chicken.

When she adjusted her grip, Chandra realized that where she'd touched Thorolf, his scales looked more moonstone and silver. The taint was being purified by the heat of the firestorm.

How could quickly could she run her hands all over him?

She caressed Thorolf's hide, running her hands over him as much as she could, given that she had to hang on. She was excited to see the golden touch of the firestorm returning the brilliance to his scales.

"You're distracting me," Thorolf complained.

"She's saving you," Rafferty corrected. He moved weakly up her arm, freeing her hand from holding him, and gave her a quick look. "Only the firestorm can save him," he whispered.

Chandra stroked her favorite *Pyr* as far and as wide as she could. It took many passes of her touch and the firestorm's heat to even begin clear the scales, although she was sure she saw the incremental difference each time. She tried not to think about how long it would take to heal him completely, but tried to work steadily. She felt almost as if she were polishing him, as a medieval squire would polish his knight's chain mail.

Meanwhile, the dragons fought. Chandra felt the heat of dragonfire and felt each blow they exchanged. A plume of dragonfire shot over Thorolf's shoulder, singing the tip of his wing. He howled in pain, then struck Chen with his tail so hard that the red lacquer dragon lost the rhythm of flight. Thorolf released his opponent, flinging him against the side of a mountain. The impact launched an avalanche of snow and ice that plummeted down the side of the rock face and obscured Chen.

Chandra had a moment to hope that he was injured, but then he came raging out of the falling snow and ice. He roared dragonfire and leapt toward Thorolf. Thorolf spun and flew hard toward the mountain peaks again. Chandra couldn't help but look back at the dragon giving chase. Chen chuckled then seized Thorolf's tail in two claws, slowing his flight. Thorolf turned to fight, but Chen bit down hard on his tail, nearly severing the end of it. Thorolf bellowed and thrashed, then twisted to strike Chen in the face. His blow broke one of Chen's small golden horns and black blood began to flow from it.

There was a rumble of thunder again and Thorolf stilled even as Chen smiled. He rubbed his head on Thorolf's tail in an unexpected move. Chandra didn't understand until she saw his black *Slayer* blood run into the gaping wound on Thorolf's tail. To Chandra's horror, the blood dripping from Thorolf's wound began to darken.

Worse, the scales she'd polished to moonstone and silver blackened all over again, as if she'd never touched him.

Thorolf faltered and struggled, as if he wasn't sure what to do. He spun to confront Chen but didn't seem able to strike a blow. His one claw rose as if he'd grab Rafferty, but Chandra leaned closer to him, trying to encourage the firestorm to burn hotter.

He was snared in indecision, caught between two states of being.

Then Chen began to breathe slowly, exhaling so steadily that Chandra knew he had to be breathing dragonsmoke. Thorolf jumped as if he'd put his claw into an electrical socket and Rafferty swore softly.

"The missing scale," he said, which made no sense to Chandra. She was aware that Rafferty's breathing had been very shallow and feared that he'd done too much. She didn't know much about salamanders, but he looked paler than he'd been before. His eyes were closed, too.

"Once more," he whispered, then flicked her a quick bright look. "Once more for the firestorm."

Chandra watched in horror as Chen reached for Thorolf, his

eyes shining with triumph. She felt the wind as his claw snatched on empty air. She heard his shout of frustration.

But they were caught in that tornado again, surrounding by the spinning power of wind. Chandra buried her face in Thorolf's back, even as that pale blue light shone. He shifted to human form, then back to dragon form, cycling between his forms with increasing speed.

She held tightly to him and to Rafferty, and hoped Thorolf's involuntary shifting wasn't a bad thing.

Even though she knew it was a sign of a *Pyr* having a fatal or near fatal injury.

When the wind stopped and they were dropped against the ground, she was surprised that Rafferty disappeared. Thorolf was in human form and the firestorm was burning with a faint silver light.

Rafferty had brought them back to her sanctuary, back to Myth. He instinctively understood that Thorolf was safe here, and that Chen's spell lost its hold over Thorolf here.

Chandra understood that the other *Pyr* was trusting her to heal Thorolf.

She hoped with all her heart that she could.

Then she rolled him over, hating how motionless he was. She brushed her fingertips beneath his nose and was relieved to find him still breathing. As she angled herself over him, the firestorm burned a little brighter, its silvery light encouraging her as nothing else could have done. She surveyed him, thinking of how well he had fought, admiring how much he'd given of himself to try to save her, and knew in her heart that she'd chosen the right *Pyr* all those centuries before.

Now she had to give as much as was necessary to save him.

Liz Barrett felt her husband Brandon leave their bed. His quick movement awakened her immediately. She saw the shimmer of blue light that announced his pending shift, and knew he'd sensed a threat.

The weird thing was that she felt one, too. A flame had

flickered to life somewhere in their vicinity, but it wasn't a natural flame.

She was out of bed, following Brandon before she realized what it was.

Darkfire. The blue-green spark of unpredictability that was associated with the *Pyr*.

And it was in the boys' bedroom.

Brandon was right ahead of her, his sense leading him to the same place. He blocked the doorway, keeping her from their sons, his posture so protective that she knew he'd seen something. "Marco!" he said in sudden relief. "You gave us a shock."

Liz slipped past her partner, smiling to find the Sleeper of the *Pyr* in the rocking chair in the boys' room. Marco had dark hair and dark eyes and tended to be quiet. He was rocking quietly as the boys slept, Christopher in his big boy bed and baby Andrew in his cradle.

"Brothers," he murmured, looking between the two boys.

Liz and Brandon exchanged a glance. Of course their sons were brothers, but Marco said the word as if it had unexpected meaning.

The darkfire crystal that Marco had given to Liz during her firestorm with Brandon was still on the dresser. The spark of darkfire snared within the quartz crystal had been so faint in the past two years that it had been easier to sense than to see. Now it flickered brightly, dancing within the stone and casting its blue-green flickering light over the room. That was the spark Liz had sensed.

"I'll guess you came for a reason," Brandon said, checking on first one boy and then the other. To Liz's surprise, both continued to sleep deeply. Maybe Marco had that effect on small children. "Is it because of the firestorm?"

"Thorolf's firestorm," Marco supplied. When Brandon nodded, Liz realized he'd known that. "Which is complicating Chen's quest for a sacrificial dragon with an affinity for the element of air."

Brandon had an affinity with air. That was why he'd been targeted by Chen, too.

"Not the boys," Liz said, stepping further into the room.

Marco shook his head. "The affinity of *Pyr* sons isn't clear until the shift comes upon them, until puberty." He smiled serenely at her. "They are usually safe until then."

He put a slight emphasis on the word 'usually' and Liz seemed to remember that he had been targeted himself as an infant.

"I'll guess you didn't come to admire them," Brandon said, his tone light.

Marco shook his head and pointed to the crystal.

"You could have just taken it," Brandon said. "You got through my dragonsmoke, after all." Liz could see that he was unsettled by this, since Marco wasn't the only dragon shifter who could manifest spontaneously inside a dragonsmoke barrier.

"I believe in courtesy," Marco said softly. "I gave the stone to the Firedaughter." He looked at Liz, his expression inscrutable.

"I'm happy to give it back to you," Liz said. "Especially if it can be used to defeat Chen forever."

Marco smiled and she knew she'd said exactly what he wanted to hear. He didn't move, so she crossed the stone and picked it up. The darkfire flared more brightly when she held the crystal, and she felt the strange prickle of its energy. It was electric and felt unpredictable. The truth was that the stone made her uncomfortable, but she'd believed it had been given to her for a reason. She'd used it to defend herself against Chen, so had left it in this room with the boys, in case it might protect them, too. Dragon magic was different from her own, and Marco didn't seem inclined to explain much about darkfire.

She'd be glad for it to be elsewhere. She turned and offered it to Marco.

"That's not the only reason I came," Marco admitted, his gaze flitting to Brandon.

"Do I need to help with the firestorm?" Brandon asked.

"We need five *Pyr*, each with an affinity to air, to defeat the spell Chen cast to snare Thorolf."

"I'm in," Brandon said immediately. He reached over and took Liz's hand. She felt a bit of worry, but she knew that the *Pyr* would ensure that she and their sons were defended. "Tell me what to do."

"Wait and listen," Marco murmured, his gaze darting to Liz. "Watch for the darkfire." She nodded, because she could feel it. "All will soon become clear." His smile turned sweeter as he accepted the stone and its light brightened to blinding intensity.

It faded suddenly, making Liz blink. The rocking chair was still rocking gently, but Marco was gone.

"I wonder what he meant about brothers," Brandon said quietly, taking Liz's hand.

"Do you have one?"

He shook his head. "Somebody does, though. Somehow it matters."

Melissa could have wept with relief when Rafferty appeared in the suite again. He looked pale and was unsteady, even in his salamander form. He managed to shift shape, then collapsed on the couch in his human form.

"What happened?" Sloane demanded, but Melissa waved him off.

"He needs water and food, maybe a good glass of wine," she said. She knew her *Pyr* well enough to recognize when he'd done too much. "Call room service, please."

"I'll go get him something," Niall said. "It'll be faster."

"Maybe not," Rox argued. "This is a pretty swish place."

"We'll do both and he can eat whatever's here first," Niall suggested.

Melissa was relieved when they busied themselves with arranging the food, leaving her to concentrate on Rafferty. He was in bad shape and she feared the consequences. She wished it was their firestorm again, because its heat could have revived him.

She had to make do with her touch. Melissa caressed his cheek and kissed him gently, feeling his mouth curve beneath hers. His hand nestled in the back of her waist, pulling her closer, and his eyes opened ever so slightly. She could see the gleam of his eyes, which relieved her as little else could have done.

"You push yourself too hard," she whispered quietly, then kissed him again before he could argue with her.

"The firestorm is the greatest cause," he replied, just as she'd known he would. His fingers eased into her hair and he rolled, so that she was wedged between his muscular chest and the back of the couch. It suited her just fine. He kissed her then, showing his usual vigor, then whispered in her ear. "Because it's a gift that continues to give," he murmured, making her smile. "Maybe food isn't all I need."

"You're going to have to tell us what happened first."

He lifted his head, his gaze warm. "Thorolf's firestorm is strong. His mate is stronger. They've chosen each other, and I've given them the opportunity to save him from Chen's spell."

Melissa smiled. "You think they'll satisfy the firestorm now?"

"I know it," he replied with complete confidence. "He's lost a scale. She was prepared to sacrifice herself to Chen to ensure his survival. He went through dragonsmoke to save her." Rafferty nodded approval. "This is an epic passion, and it can only bode well for the *Pyr*."

"But Chen?"

Rafferty paused and laid back, his eyes closed. She saw again that he was pretending to feel better than he did. "I believe our task is to find the sword she mentioned."

He kissed Melissa again, then helped her to sit up beside him. He still looked weary, but at least there was purpose in his gaze. The others, who had been pretending to be oblivious, turned to him with open curiosity. Rafferty smiled, and Melissa guessed he wouldn't pretend that they hadn't overheard everything he'd told her. "Did you find out anything about that sword?" he prompted.

"It must be the one Erik has," Sloane said. "He sent a message asking for ideas for getting it through airport security. He doesn't want to check it and he said he'll be too tired if he flies all this way himself."

"He never was one for long distance flights," Rafferty mused, his quick sidelong glance making Melissa remember a long flight to England in Rafferty's dragon embrace. She put her hand on his thigh and he covered her hand with his own, an indication that he was remembering the same night.

Then Melissa realized something. "But if Erik intends to leave Chicago, what about Isabelle?"

"Donovan and Quinn have gone to Chicago to defend Erik's lair," Sloane supplied. "Delaney is coming with Erik."

"I thought commercial flights were being canceled," Rox said, sitting on the end of the coffee table.

"You're not spontaneously manifesting again," Melissa said to Rafferty, anticipating him. "You've never done it so many times in a row so quickly before. You need to rest!"

"But we must have the sword," Rafferty argued, just as she'd known he would.

"I agree with Melissa," Sloane said to Melissa's relief. "You aren't going anywhere until you get some sleep." He turned to the others. "We could maybe fly the sword in stages, taking turns with it."

"How will you get it to Thorolf?" Rox asked. "And why does he need it?"

"I'll have to take it to her sanctuary," Rafferty said. "None of you can argue with that."

"Unless they show up here again to get it themselves," Rox said.

"Let's plan that route," Melissa said, booting up her laptop. The further she got the *Pyr* to bring the sword before Rafferty felt obliged to intervene, the better. She took one look at him, noting his pallor, and feared he would make too much of a sacrifice to the firestorm.

She had to solve this another way.

"It's in Chicago," she said. "Erik to Los Angeles."

"Delaney to Hawaii," Sloane said, perching on the end of the couch beside her. It was far, but Delaney would do it, for the firestorm.

"Brandon to Australia." Melissa said, because Brandon was on Hawaii.

"He won't leave Liz and the boys," Rox said, biting her lip.

"Brandt is on the northwest coast," Rafferty contributed, referring to Brandon's dad in Australia. "Liz and the boys can stay with grandma."

"Brandon can bring it to Bangkok," Sloane said. "Or I can head down there to pick it up, if he's too tired. We'll figure it out."

"Talk to Erik," Rafferty said tiredly, and Melissa wondered whether it was indicative of his exhaustion that he didn't want to contact Erik himself, or the way the two *Pyr* had parted.

To her thinking, they could sort it out once Thorolf's firestorm was resolved.

To her relief, Sloane took the job of contacting Erik, just as

Niall came in the door with chicken curry and rice. Rafferty was falling asleep, but she'd feed him herself to get some sustenance into him.

Because she just didn't trust him to leave the retrieval of the sword to the others.

She knew her *Pyr* too well to guess that he would feel compelled to aid the firestorm.

CHAPTER TWELVE

Thorolf awakened in a familiar state. He felt like crap. He had a headache, which could have been the result of over-indulgence of one kind or another. He was sore all over, as if he'd lost more than one fight he didn't particularly remember.

He hoped, as usual, that he didn't have any new tattoos.

His skin burned though, burned with the fury of that new and extensive ink. That had been one upside of being Rox's "project": he'd had a guardian angel with a tattoo gun, one who never over-indulged and who fiercely protected the art on his body.

Thorolf sighed, wishing for the old days when he'd hung out with the *Pyr*. His one glimpse of Rox had been of her chewing him out for this tattoo, but even that had been welcome.

The good news was that there was a woman lying on top of him, a woman whose long hair touched his face and whose breasts were crushed against his chest. Even better, the spark of the firestorm heated him right through when she touched her lips tentatively to his.

Chandra.

Seemed like she was coming around to the idea of fulfilling the firestorm.

Bonus.

He opened his eyes to see Chandra in her ebony-haired huntress form, almost nose-to-nose with him. She was gorgeous enough to steal his breath away, and smart enough that she should have worried him. She was studying him, her expression one of uncharacteristic uncertainty. She looked almost as if she'd just kissed him. He liked when her lips were swollen a little and he could get used to her watching him so closely.

"Hey." Thorolf ran his hands over Chandra and smiled slowly, making sure she could read his amorous thoughts. He liked how she caught her breath and blushed a little. It was fun to disconcert a goddess. "I'm hoping it's not an accident that you're on top of me like this."

"I was afraid you would die," she admitted quickly and sounded as if she thought that was a bad thing. She averted her gaze and caught her breath as he cupped his hands around her butt and squeezed slightly.

He wasn't nearly dead yet.

He liked how her eyes widened with the reminder of his vitality.

She didn't pull away, though, much less thump him.

Something good was going down.

Finally.

"I thought you'd be relieved to be rid of me," he countered, sliding his hands up her back, then pushing his fingers into her long hair. It was thick and soft, luxuriantly wavy and incredibly feminine. The firestorm shimmered and shone with silver light, heating him to his core and making him *want*. "We're back in Myth, then?"

Chandra nodded and eased a little closer, brushing her lips across his with aching sweetness. That light caress stole Thorolf's breath away. The heat surged through him, making him feel a little more alive than just moments before.

He sighed. "So, I guess you'll want me to pick a skull."

"Not just yet." To his surprise, her fingers framed his face, her touch both cool and electrifying. She looked into his eyes, then her mouth locked over his, her kiss more demanding than it had been yet.

Thorolf decided it would be rude not to show enthusiasm for the change.

He could count on her calling a halt to this sooner than he'd like. He might as well make the most of her moment of weakness. He pulled her closer and deepened their kiss, astonished on some level that she met him touch for touch.

But not ready to complain about it. The firestorm's heat slid through him like molten lava. He felt it push back some toxin in his body, and purge his mind of doubt. He knew exactly what he had to do and why. When Chandra's tongue touched his, he nearly exploded with desire. When she slid her hands into his hair, holding him captive to her ravenous kiss, he was sure he had died and gone to heaven. When she straddled him, her thighs tight around his waist and that sweet softness of her pressed against his erection, he didn't care how many layers of cloth were between them.

Except that he wanted to get rid of them all.

He rolled over, pinning Chandra beneath him and settling himself between her thighs. He halfway thought she'd smite him, but she locked her legs even tighter around his waist and pulled him down for a very satisfying kiss. She smelled sweet and hot, and felt even better. He wanted to take it slow, but wasn't sure he could.

"No skulls," she whispered moments later. "Not this time."

He opened the front of her shirt with one hand, bracing his weight over her as he bared her skin to his view. "What else is there to do in this place?" he murmured, then eased the cloth aside. Of course, she wore no bra. She was a goddess. She was muscled and lean, her breast ripe enough to fill his hand. Her nipple was tightly beaded, inviting his touch, and Thorolf wasn't inclined to refuse. He bent and suckled her gently, smiling against her skin when she gasped and gripped his hair tightly.

She didn't pull away, though, and didn't stop him.

It was finally his lucky day.

She ran her hands over his bare skin, her light caress making his skin feel so much better. It was better even than Rox's aloe gel. When her fingers dove beneath the waistband of his jeans and she squeezed his butt, Thorolf raised his head to look at her.

"Who are you and what have you done with my mate?" he asked, not having to work that hard to feign astonishment.

Chandra laughed. "Get naked already. I might regret this, and you don't want to give me time to change my mind."

Thorolf didn't need to be invited twice.

He had to make sure Chandra didn't regret her decision.

"Just for the sake of interest," he said as he peeled off his boots and flung them aside. "Why?" His jeans were next, his Jockeys gone in record time. He turned back to Chandra to find that she'd chucked her own clothes just as quickly and was nude beside him.

"I like dragons," she said.

"All dragons," he teased and she blushed.

She tapped a finger on his chest. "This dragon." She rose to her knees before him and he caught his breath at her beauty. "Besides, it might be my last chance to find out."

"No pressure then," he said with a grin.

She laughed. "Intimidated?"

"Not a chance." Thorolf smiled down at her, then spared a quick glance around. They were on a bed of dense vegetation in the jungle. It could have been moss for all he knew, but it was as soft as a bed and dry enough. A stream ran near them, but he couldn't sense any predators, and a night sky arched high over them.

There could be snakes, though. He shuddered despite himself.

"I guess we don't have to worry about privacy here," he said and she laughed at him.

"Don't tell me you're shy," she teased, her eyes dancing.

"Surprised," he said, taking her in his arms and pulling her into his lap. He kissed her on the mouth. "Amazed, even." He kissed her again and took his time about it. "Lucky," he murmured, then kissed beneath her ear. She tipped her head back and sighed contentment. "But not shy. I missed the line where they were giving that out."

Chandra laughed and pushed him down to his back. "You were too busy in the other lines," she said before she kissed him slowly. Her hair fell around them, curtaining them from the world.

If there were snakes, he wouldn't see them coming.

He was surprisingly good with that. This was worth it.

"What other lines?" he asked when she lifted her head.

"The one for loyalty." She kissed his jaw, then the hollow of his throat. Thorolf sighed as the firestorm surged through him. "You had to be right at the front of that one." She kissed his shoulder, then ran a line of kisses toward his nipple. Silver sparks danced over his flesh, burning too much to tickle.

This firestorm just might kill Thorolf, but it would be so worth it.

"The one for valor," she murmured, then suckled his nipple the same way he'd kissed hers. Thorolf caught his breath at the sensation and wanted to roar with pleasure.

"You like that?" she whispered against his skin.

"Oh, yeah."

"So that's why you taught me to do it," she replied, then closed her mouth over his other nipple. She used her tongue and her teeth, teasing him so he thought he'd lose his mind. Her other hand worked his other nipple, her fingers as distracting as her mouth.

"The one for a strong moral code," Chandra whispered, then dragged the tip of her tongue down toward his navel. Thorolf had forgotten what the heck she was talking about. "You were early in that line, too."

Right.

Lines.

A strong moral code?

He felt obliged to argue with her. "You've got me confused with someone else," he protested. "But don't let me mess with your illusions."

She laughed and he looked down at her, his heart aching at the glow in her blue eyes. "No," she said with a quiet confidence that made his heart thump. "You pretend to be a party animal who takes nothing seriously, but you're the most valiant, loyal and moral man I've ever known. You stick with your friends through thick and thin, you never forget your alliances, and you give everything you've got when you fight." Her hands were on his thighs, her feather-light touch making it impossible for Thorolf to think straight. As he watched, she closed one hand around his erection. The heat of the firestorm raced through him from that point and he thought he might lose it completely.

Chandra was smiling at him, all mischief and sparkling eyes.

"I'm guessing that works for you," he managed to say.

"*You* work for me," she replied, her conviction making his heart nearly burst with pride. She then kissed the tip of his erection, flicking her tongue across him in a way that nearly made the rest of him burst.

The spark that erupted at that point could have stopped Thorolf's heart, but that was nothing compared to the power of Chandra's touch when her mouth closed over him. He felt the silvery light of the firestorm flood through him, banishing the shadows and darkness like the light of the full moon. Quicksilver might have been running through his veins, filling him with light and power and strength. His heart thundered with new vigor, as the firestorm healed him from his marrow out.

He felt celebratory, as only dragons could. He hadn't eliminated Chen, but that would come. For the moment, there was this magnificent moment with his mate. He wanted to make love to Chandra for the rest of his life, every day and every night. He was hard and hot and ready for her, his blood pumping and his body filled with demand.

But not like this.

Not the first time.

Her pleasure had to be first.

He pulled her into his embrace, lifting her mouth to his. He was surprised when he opened his eyes to find that the firestorm had brightened to a sphere of brilliant white light. He rolled Chandra to her back, smiling at her surprise.

"That wasn't right?" she asked with an uncertainty that charmed him.

"It was awesome," he admitted, then kissed her sweetly. "But the firestorm is about mutual pleasure." He looked her in the eye. "And the mate should be pleased first."

"Gallant," she whispered. "I should have figured you'd hit that line, too."

Thorolf held her gaze, waiting until she blushed with understanding of what he intended to do. Her lips parted in a little gasp of surprise, which was just about the most delicious thing he'd ever seen.

He kissed her with satisfaction, then slid down the length of her. He ran his hands over her, smiling at the sparks that lit beneath his hands and his mouth, illuminating every point he touched her. He kissed her nipples again, teasing them to tight peaks, loving how she moaned with delight. He eased lower, taking his time, savoring the scent of her arousal and smiled when she parted her thighs in anticipation.

He kissed her there slowly and thoroughly, letting her become accustomed to the intimate embrace, loving when she began to squirm with pleasure. His mouth was filled with the fiery heat of the firestorm and the sweet taste of Chandra, and he knew he'd never get enough of her. She would be just as enticing without the firestorm's spark—and he was determined to ensure that she felt the same way about him.

Once again, he felt his heart match its pace to hers. He knew his breathing had synchronized with hers as well, when he felt that wonderful sense of union.

This was the gift of the firestorm.

This was the future he would claim.

Thorolf pleasured Chandra deliberately, ensuring that he was slow about it, that he prolonged her arousal as long as possible. He used his lips and his tongue, loving how she responded to his touch, feeling the rise of her passion. She was breathing quickly and flushed scarlet, her hands knotted in his hair. He loved the sound of her moans and the way she writhed beneath his touch, and he savored when she began to beg for release.

He teased her and tormented her, making the pleasure last as long as he could. He wanted her first time to be amazing. Chandra was incoherent in her arousal, flushed and so far from her usual commanding self that Thorolf was entranced.

He chose his moment with care, then pressed his thumb hard against her to launch the explosion. Silver sparks flew in every direction as Chandra cried out in delight. Thorolf watched her climax with pride, his eyes widening in wonder as she once again rotated through a thousand forms. He watched, fascinated by all that his mate was and had been.

The show must be linked to pleasure. She'd done this shifting the first time he'd kissed her, he recalled, that first hot sweet kiss.

Maybe being overwhelmed made it impossible for her to hide this truth. Thorolf didn't much care. He watched in wonder as she shifted and knew he'd lost his heart completely.

Her hair was dark, fair, chestnut, red and every shade in between. It was long, short, straight, wavy; her eyes were blue, grey, brown and green, her lips were full or thin, her face changed shapes, her breasts were larger or smaller, but it was Chandra each and every time, Chandra in all the glory of what she had been and would be.

Until she took a familiar shape.

Ulrike?

Thorolf blinked as Chandra continued to shift, but then she again assumed the guise of Astrid's closest friend. She cried out as she came, then fell back, flushed and exhausted, her breath coming quickly.

What was that about?

Whatever it was, the sight was enough to trash the mood.

Thorolf had forgotten all about Ulrike, but now he remembered how she'd always seemed to appear at the most inconvenient times, to nearly catch him and Astrid in intimacy. He'd wondered then how much his beloved's friend had known about the two of them.

About his true nature.

He hadn't worried about it too much. But if Chandra was Ulrike, it couldn't have been unimportant. Something twisted in his gut, an uncertainty he could have lived without. He distrusted this revelation, just as he had instinctively distrusted Ulrike then.

Goddesses didn't take mortal guise and walk among humans for nothing.

"Now it's your turn?" Chandra murmured. She braced herself on her elbows to look down at him and smiled, clearly unaware of his reaction. She was the blond Viking again, her hair having worked loose from her braid to flow over her shoulders. Her eyes twinkled with a satisfaction that should have pleased him. It was as if Thorolf had imagined what he'd seen.

But he hadn't.

Thorolf eased away, letting the firestorm dim so he could think.

She'd tried to have oral sex, which wouldn't satisfy the firestorm. She'd allowed him to please her the same way, but no one conceived a son like that.

Maybe she hadn't yet decided to surrender to the firestorm.

Maybe she just wanted to take the edge off.

Maybe she had some other plan.

"Is something wrong?" Chandra reached after him, her fingers landing on his shoulder. The silver heat of the firestorm burned there, a simmering spark that challenged what Thorolf had just seen. Was the firestorm right about his mate or not?

"I'm not sure," he said, needing to be honest no matter what she'd done. He looked around them and saw the temple where she'd first taken him, the temple filled with skulls.

The ghosts had shown him Chandra's truth before. Maybe they

would again.

There were three skulls hanging from the Valkyrie's discarded belt, perched on their tangled clothing. Before he could think too much about the wisdom of his choice, Thorolf seized one of them.

"Show me Ulrike!" he said, hoping to command the ghosts.

"No!" Chandra cried in obvious dismay, but the snow had surrounded them again. Lightning cracked across the sky, taking the firestorm to a white heat, then icy rain pounded down. Thorolf gripped the skull tightly, refusing to let go despite the onslaught.

The rain stopped.

He smelled a wood fire burning.

And he heard Astrid's whisper in his ear. The sound of her voice brought a tear to his eye, one he blinked away before he opened his eyes to look.

Chandra couldn't stop the vision. Even knowing that didn't stop her from trying. It was the worst possible moment for Thorolf to learn what she'd done, and she knew he'd see it as a betrayal.

The irony was that now she'd see it the same way. Then, she'd had no idea how it felt to be mortal and at the whim of gods. She'd given no consideration to the limits of a single short life, to the loss of hopes and dreams. She'd never imagined that Thorolf could have loved this mere mortal woman so deeply.

She knew it now. She regretted her choice. But she feared it was too late to make amends.

When the swirling snow disappeared, they were in the village again, that hideous primitive village. Chandra was Ulrike, a human guise she'd created with care. She'd pretended to have been from a nearby village that had been burned to ash by the dragon shifters they'd ultimately come to call *Slayers*. She'd pretended to be a sole survivor, a widow and a bereaved mother. The villagers had taken her in, feeling compassion for her plight.

In truth, there had been no survivors of the attack, but that meant there had been no one to challenge Ulrike's story.

Except the dragon shifters who had hunted and destroyed every soul in that village.

In those days, in that valley, the humans knew only of dragons. They didn't know the truth of the *Pyr* and their shifting abilities, much less that of *Slayers*. They had no real understanding of the battle being waged, the debate as to whether they were themselves treasures of the earth to be defended or a scourge to be removed. They certainly hadn't guessed that dragons could walk among them, disguised as mortal men.

They knew only that dragons periodically attacked their villages, seized their maidens, devoured their livestock and burned their homes. The dragons came out of the mountains without warning, as majestic and beautiful as they were cruel and bent on destruction. The villagers feared the dragons, reasonably enough, and sought ways to win their favor.

Knowing that Astrid had to be removed, Chandra as Ulrike had suggested a way.

She felt sickened now by what she had done.

The village had always looked the same, at least until its final destruction. The mountains had framed the valley the same way, and the villagers had followed their routines the same way. It could have been any day that they arrived, but Chandra could have named the precise moment. She knew what the ghosts would show Thorolf.

She as Ulrike was in the forest, creeping closer to a hidden lover's nest. Thorolf and his lover Astrid were nestled in a hollow in the forest that was thick with furs, whispering together after their lovemaking. The trees were in spring leaf, arching high over them, and the sunlight was golden yellow.

Astrid's father pretended to oblivious to the encounters, but the truth was that he admired Thorolf. He would have welcomed him into his household and his family—because he didn't know the full truth of Thorolf's nature. He thought him a warrior and a good one. He had no idea Thorolf was *Pyr*. He had advised his wife to let their daughter conceive a child. He was sure that a man like Thorolf would be responsible.

Chandra as Ulrike had hidden behind a large tree, close enough to eavesdrop on the lovers. She endured the sounds of robust lovemaking and the nonsense of lovers' whispers, hoping that this would be the day that Astrid took the bait so carefully presented.

"My friend says that you are uncommonly strong," Astrid whispered and Thorolf chuckled. Ulrike straightened with hope.

"I thought you liked that," he whispered, cupping her breast in his hand and kissing her nipple. Chandra recalled all too well how good that felt. She couldn't see his eyes from this angle, but she guessed that they were vividly blue and filled with humor.

"I do," Astrid sighs. "But she wonders if you are more than a man."

Thorolf stilled. "What is this?"

"She says they had a story in their village. The seer insisted that there was a man in this valley who was dragon, as well. He said the man could change his form, and choose to be either dragon or man."

Thorolf, Chandra saw, was motionless, his attention fixed upon his lover. Little did he realize how that very stillness and focus revealed the truth of his nature.

Astrid smiled up at him. "Their seer said that this man is the only one who can stop the dragons from destroying villages. She said that if you were that man, we would be so lucky."

"And you hoped I might be."

"I love you, just the way you are." Astrid kissed him sweetly. "But you are stronger than most and taller than most, and it wouldn't surprise me if you were that man."

"It wouldn't frighten you?"

"I love you. I know you would never hurt me, no matter what you can do."

Thorolf studied her for a long moment and Ulrike held her breath in the shadows. When she saw the pale blue shimmer of light, Ulrike smiled, knowing that he would step into the trap she had set.

But Chandra's gut churned with guilt.

"Let me show you something," Thorolf whispered. He kissed Astrid's eyelids one after the other, even as her fingers lifted toward the blue light. "Close your eyes until I bid you open them, and then you will see all of my truth."

"Oh, Thorolf," Astrid whispered, her delight clear.

Thorolf stepped from the bed, his nude body magnificent. The blue shimmer grew brighter as he threw his head back, then he shifted shape in a brilliant glow of light. A large and muscular dragon took his place, a dragon with scales of moonstone and silver. He gleamed in the sunlight, his scales like a coat of polished mail, or one made of moonlight, and Chandra blinked at how much he had changed. "Look," he whispered to his lover.

"I knew it!" Astrid cried and leapt upon him, planting a thousand kisses on his chest. "I knew that if there were such a man, he would be you." Thorolf lifted her in his claws, his touch protective and careful, even as Ulrike leaned back against the tree to keep herself hidden. She felt his attention sharpen. She heard him inhale, and feared she would be discovered.

The village wasn't far.

She decided to risk it.

She broke and ran, darting toward the meadow that could be seen from the village. She heard Thorolf roar and Astrid beg him to let whoever it was flee. She raced through the forest, holding her hood over her head and ducking low. To her delight, there were boys in the meadow with their goats. She ran into the sunlight, knowing she looked distraught.

"What is it?"

"What is the matter?"

"Are you well?"

The boys surrounded her immediately, their concern providing her the perfect opportunity to close the trap. She easily feigned horror and dismay. "I saw...I saw...Astrid making love with a dragon!"

And then it was done. The story took on a power of its own with startling speed. The boys told other boys, who told fathers and brothers and mothers and sisters, and by the time Astrid came back to the village, smiling with contentment and pleasure, her fate had been sealed.

She was allied with the dragons.

She would be the human offering made to them, in the hope that she would be enough to sate them.

When she protested, she was over-ruled.

When she fought, she was bound to a rock outside the village.

When she begged for mercy, her father called her a whore before he threw the first stone.

Chandra turned away, just as Ulrike had done, looking up in time to see the first of the marauding dragons appear in the sky overhead. The difference was that this time, she regretted what she had done.

If only she could turn back time and never become Ulrike.

If only she could give Thorolf back the lover who had claimed his heart. She watched him relive the pain of that last parting and felt her own tears fall. She had believed not that long ago that the firestorm was a purely biological act of survival. Against all odds, she'd fallen in love with the passionate and troublesome *Pyr* who was her mate. She wanted him to be happy, no matter what the expense to herself.

She owed him a debt for stealing his true love away.

And she was going to have to find a way to pay that balance.

No matter what it took.

The snow swirled around them, even as Thorolf's thoughts churned.

Chandra was the woman who had betrayed Astrid.

She'd done the dirty work of disposing of his "distraction".

The snow faded away, leaving them facing each other in Myth again. The firestorm's light burned silver between them, tempting Thorolf's body to fulfill its promise, but he felt only disgust. He wanted Chandra to deny what she'd done, but saw the look in her eyes and knew she wouldn't.

It was true.

This firestorm was tearing him apart. It was messing with him now, its heat and light turning his thoughts in a very earthy direction. He was well aware of Chandra's appeal, that she was his destined mate, that he had an obligation to his kind to seduce her.

And that undermined the fury of betrayal with frightening speed.

"I'm sorry," she said, lifting a hand toward him. "I had no idea in those days. I didn't understand."

It would have been easier to believe her if he hadn't seen her nearly shoot Viv in the head.

"Then why are you doing the same thing to Viv?" he demanded, his voice as raw as the wound on his heart. "Aren't you eliminating a woman who is my lover? Isn't she just another *distraction*?"

"No! I told you. She's Tisiphone..."

"A story that only you know," Thorolf challenged. At some level, he acknowledged how good it was not to have to hold back with Chandra. He could say what he thought, he could dish out hard truths and he knew she could take it. She'd probably send some harder truths right back at him, and he admired that. "Let's face it, it's an awfully convenient story." He stepped back, seizing his jeans and tugging them on. "You're the one who has this big mission for me. You're the one who chose me at birth to complete some quest for you."

She bowed her head in silent acknowledgement instead of fighting.

That made him feel that he might be wrong, which stole a lot of the steam from his indignation. "You're the one who eliminates every distraction, every pleasure that could keep me from doing what you want," he charged.

Chandra shook her head emphatically. "No, it's not like that." She looked at the ground and frowned, and he waited, knowing she was mustering her argument. He was surprised to realize how much he wanted her to justify this to him. "Removing Astrid was your father's idea. He thought you weren't sufficiently focused on your training. I trusted his judgment." She shrugged. "He was *Pyr*. I'm not."

"You could have *asked*! You could have made a suggestion instead of sacrificing her!"

"He said you'd fought about it already."

Thorolf exhaled, knowing that was true. "She didn't have to die. Not like that."

"I know I was wrong." Chandra put a hand on his arm and the firestorm's sizzle unsettled him even more, softening his anger. "I said I'm sorry."

"Thank you for that." He meant the words to sound sarcastic, but they didn't quite.

Still, Chandra understood. She folded her arms across her chest, a determined gleam lighting her eyes. "I can't bring her back, no matter how sorry I am."

Thorolf blinked, not having considered that possibility, then pushed her a bit more. "Maybe that's even true."

"What's done is done. You have to believe me."

"I don't have to believe anything."

She visibly gritted her teeth. "Then at least *listen* to me."

"I've heard plenty, thanks." He spoke so firmly that she fell silent. He wondered if she realized he was trying to convince himself to hold his position. "I'm not going to be your go-to dragon. I do what I choose to do, not what others choose for me to do. It's a matter of principle."

"Don't you want to learn more about the plan? It might actually have been a good idea." Her voice hardened. "It might be important."

It made Thorolf even angrier to realize that he was being persuaded. "It's *principle*," he said with force. "If you'd asked me, if you'd been straight with me, or if you'd convinced me to volunteer—that would be one thing. Instead, you've tricked me, lied to me, deceived me, and stolen from me." He flicked a glance over her, only to find her lips set with a stubborn resolve he recognized.

Maybe they had that in common, too.

"So you'll die," she said quietly, her gaze rising to his. "And that would be awful."

"Because you'll have to find another victim to finish your plan?"

"No! That's not why." Chandra took a deep breath. "I don't want there to be a world without the *Pyr*," she said, her voice passionate. "And I really don't want there to be a world without you." Her heart was in her eyes, and her words echoed with honesty.

Thorolf wanted to believe her.

But he was afraid that would be the stupidest thing he'd ever done.

Which would be saying something.

He had to get away from the firestorm's influence to sort out his reaction. He couldn't make a reasonable decision with Chandra right in front of him and the firestorm's glow distracting him so much.

He wanted to believe in the firestorm.

He wanted to believe in her.

But he needed to be sure.

Had he ever met a woman who could piss him off so much? Had he ever met one who turned him inside out like this, and forced him to reconsider everything he'd believed to be true? He was sure he hadn't and knew he'd think about that later. And the firestorm was relentless. He frowned at the light. "I don't know what you did to make there be a firestorm between us, but whatever it is, you can stop this trick."

Chandra's expression was mutinous. "No, I can't. It's not faked."

"The only thing I ever wanted in all my life, the one thing I was living for, was my firestorm. Thanks for trashing that, too."

"I didn't trash it!"

"Explain this to me then," he invited. "I'm supposed to conceive a child with a goddess who manipulates me? The firestorm is supposed to be with a mortal woman, one who can conceive the *Pyr*'s son. It supposed to be with someone who will bear and nurture that son, as well as be a partner to the *Pyr* in question."

She glared at him and he tried to ignore the tears glimmering in her eyes. "Who says I'm not that person?"

Thorolf flung out his hands. "It's obvious! You're not mortal and you're leaving!"

She took a step closer, her gaze locked on his. "I'd argue that we *are* good partners. I think we fight well together, and our weaknesses balance each other's strengths."

"Except for the part about you not telling me details that might help me to survive."

She blushed but didn't blink. "I'm getting over that. You're teaching me how."

"Except for the part about you refusing to satisfy the firestorm."

Her lashes fluttered and she seemed at a loss for words. She swallowed, then looked at him, so soft and feminine that his guts knotted. "Maybe I'm getting over that, too," she whispered.

Thorolf's anger abandoned him then, but he refused to let her see that just yet. She was good at defending his back, but he needed more. "You said you'd never satisfy the firestorm. That you work alone."

She looked pointedly back at the place on the mossy bank where he'd pleasured her. "Did that seem as if I was fighting the firestorm?"

"Oral sex isn't good enough."

She lifted a brow. "Then why did you stop?"

It did seem as if that had been a bad idea. "You're not mortal."

Her lips tightened and she averted her gaze. She swallowed and Thorolf saw that he'd upset her, even though he'd simply told the truth. Why had she softened now? Why wasn't she striking back?

He had to think. "Just don't follow me."

"But the firestorm...."

"Will keep burning. I need to think without it or you messing with my mind. There: we have something in common after all." He gestured to the jungle around them. "This is supposed to be a sanctuary, right? So, how much trouble can I get into alone?"

She watched him in silence, looking so hurt that he felt like he'd kicked a puppy.

But she'd betrayed Astrid. And she admitted it. She might as well have killed Astrid with her own hands.

Could a goddess change?

Thorolf didn't know. It made no sense. But so long as he was with Chandra and the firestorm was tempting him to satisfy its sexual promise, he couldn't reason anything through. He wanted to be sure of the nature of the mother of his son before he conceived that child. He marched into the jungle, reminding himself not to even think about snakes, and hoped he made sense of it all soon.

He refused to regret that Chandra did as he asked and didn't follow him. He'd never wanted anything to do with deities and quests and duties assigned to him before he'd spoken his first word. All he'd ever wanted was for someone to love him as he was, for what he was, and the one woman who had done that had been stolen from him. That Chandra was responsible for Astrid's death was the worst news possible.

Everything he'd always believed was wrong.

And frankly, if the firestorm was a lie, Thorolf no longer saw the point of being *Pyr*.

CHAPTER THIRTEEN

That night in Bangkok, Niall tried to dreamwalk again.

Rox sat beside him, her hand folded tightly around his own. She was right about Thorolf's strange new tattoo. It was odd how it became steadily darker, then faded before the firestorm.

It had to be *Slayer* blood, and it had to be from a *Slayer* who had drunk the Elixir. The way Thorolf fought them reminded Niall all too well of his brother's state when Phelan had been turned into a shadow dragon, never mind the way he didn't seem to feel pain then.

If they knew how the tattoo had been applied, maybe they could figure out how to remove it. It was a long shot, but Niall was more than ready to try.

He let himself slide into a meditative state. He thought of Thorolf and tried to follow the other *Pyr*'s consciousness. He lost the trail quickly, unable to pursue Thorolf wherever he had gone. Maybe he was too far away.

"He's in Myth," someone murmured, and Niall recognized the dreamy voice of Marco, the Sleeper. He felt the prickle of darkfire pass over his body, like a wave of electricity that left his hair standing on end. "You can't follow him there," Marco continued serenely. "But the darkfire beckons."

Niall found himself in a cavern, lit with flaming torches that were mounted on the walls. He immediately saw Thorolf in his dragon form, motionless in the middle of a large spiral that seemed to be burned into the cavern floor.

"This is the past," Marco continued softly, much as Chandra had spoken when she conjured that vision. "It has shaped the present."

Was this where Thorolf had been for so long? He looked thinner and his scales were dull.

They were also tattooed. Niall heard a bubbling sound and turned to see a large arrangement of glass and tubes. A fire burned under a large sphere of glass, the heat fogging the interior. He could see a dragon trapped inside the bubble of glass, though, an emaciated dragon who had apparently passed out.

He might even be dead.

His yellow topaz scales were edged with silver and looked familiar, but not as familiar as Chen's spiraling brand on his neck. This was JP, albeit a much less healthy version of him than when Niall had last fought the *Slayer*. JP had drunk the Dragon's Blood Elixir, which should have given him immortality, except that the supply had been destroyed. And evidently, being simmered slowly while trapped in glass didn't allow for the usual regeneration.

The sphere had a spout, a tiny spout that dripped black liquid into a simmering beaker.

Niall realized in a flash that this was a still, and it was being used to extract a liquid from JP's body.

There was only one liquid it could be.

Niall remembered Cinnabar, the dragon trapped by Magnus and used to create the Dragon's Blood Elixir. That substance had been addictive, and he was glad that the source had been destroyed during Delaney's firestorm.

But those who had drunk the Elixir needed more. Niall remembered Jorge devouring the corpse of Magnus, the *Slayer* who had ingested the Dragon's Blood Elixir for the longest period of time, just to get another hit. Jorge had sucked the marrow from Magnus' bones in his desperation for the Elixir.

"He returns," Marco whispered and Niall took a quick scan of Chen's lair. He saw the needles that the *Slayer* was using to tattoo Thorolf's scales. He saw that each scale was tattooed with a swirl, one just like the ones on the floor, just like JP's brand, and guessed that they were part of Chen's spell.

He caught a glimpse of a strange rock on the far side of the lair, one that looked like a massive egg but was wrinkled all over its surface.

Then the darkfire glimmered. He felt Rox's grip on his hand

and opened his eyes to find himself back in the hotel room again. He knew what was turning Thorolf *Slayer*.

The Elixir had to be working through Thorolf's scales, passing through his skin and entering his bloodstream.

But Niall had no idea what they could do to stop the toxin's progress.

Tisiphone had pulled the shards of the mirror together, using all of her sorcery and considerable force of will. She'd just managed the feat, and that only because she was in Myth.

In the realm of mortals, it would have been impossible. Their collective skepticism and doubt in magic shaped the possibilities in their sphere. At its very basic level, magic only happened because of belief, because of faith in possibilities, because of a conviction that the world could be reshaped to suit the sorceror's will. As mortals became less persuaded that anything existed beyond the material, the power of magic had steadily faded.

No wonder it was time for the gods to leave their realm.

What would happen to Myth? Tisiphone didn't think it was an accident that Myth was so empty. Maybe even the ghosts were forgetting how to reach this place. Maybe the old lessons learned here weren't of any relevance. But when the last portal closed, she wasn't going to be left behind. She would be with her sisters, wherever they were.

She had to get out of the mirror.

That was a challenge, given that some sorry soul had to look into the mirror to free her from its depths. In a realm devoid of occupants, there weren't exactly a lot of takers.

All Tisiphone had was her belief that it could be done, that it must be done, that it would be done. She closed her eyes and believed. She envisioned someone—anyone!—coming through the jungle and stumbling upon the large mirror that held her captive. She imagined that person being surprised and intrigued. She thought of how that person would look into the mirror, quickly the first time, uncertain how a mirror could be in this place. Then he or she would look again, more lingeringly, curious. He or she would note details in the reflection, that hair was a bit too long over the forehead, or that there was mud on the cheek, or even that the lips that curved into a smile were particularly inviting. Mortals all had a sliver of Narcissus deep inside, and once her liberator had glanced and looked again, he or she would lean in to study the reflection.

One good long stare would be all it took. Tisiphone would be free, once more, even if her savior never looked in a mirror again.

Every action had consequences, after all. Every mortal had his or her purpose. Tisiphone was less interested in the price paid or the balance struck than in her own survival. She'd suck the mortal dry who freed her from the mirror, taking every last crumb of his or her strength to fuel her own.

She could see it all so clearly, and she believed in the possibility of it happening with all her might. She knew that she could shape at least part of her reality and she turned what was left of her power upon making that dream come true.

She smiled when she heard the tread of a foot in the jungle.

She willed the person to come closer.

She straightened when the footsteps became louder, when the jungle leaves were brushed aside, when the person froze in wonder.

Tisiphone opened her eyes and looked out of her prison, astonished to find Thorolf staring back at her. "Viv!" he cried, then raced to the mirror. He ran his hands over the glass, his glance running around its perimeter. He was broad and strong, a warrior who always persisted. What a sexy beast he was. He looked to have been tested, though, and in rough shape as a result, his skin burned and his hair disheveled. She felt a pang of guilt for having had any part in his injuries.

The worst part was that she knew she'd have to do it all over again.

It was her or him, and that choice was easy to make.

She swallowed and stood, wishing it didn't have to be this way. "Thorolf!" she whispered, filling her voice with an affection she didn't have to feign. A smile touched his mouth at her tone and he glanced at her face. She spread her hands in appeal, knowing his weakness when it came to women. "Just look at me."

She conjured a tear, letting it slide down her cheek, and knew her vision would come true.

Thorolf couldn't stand it when women cried.

To see Viv crying in frustration just about ripped his guts out. She was always so strong and resilient, always razzing *him* about being emotional.

That single tear killed him.

Chandra had bewitched her and trapped her, once again removing a woman he cared about from his life. It didn't matter that Viv wasn't his destined mate. He cared about her. She deserved better than this. They could talk and part ways. She didn't have to die.

And he couldn't believe all that crap about Tisiphone's vengeance upon the *Pyr*, not when he saw Viv cry. He and Viv had been pretty good together. If she'd wanted to finish him off, she'd had plenty of chances to do so. There had been lots of nights that he'd slept deeply by her side. She'd had a thousand opportunities.

That she'd never taken one told him that Chandra was wrong.

He stared at Viv in the mirror. "You've lost some weight," he said.

She smiled sadly. "No woman can ever lose enough."

"We'll get out of this and go for dinner," he offered. Even if his only accomplishment was to get Viv to stop crying, he'd be doing something right. Besides, he *was* starving. "We were always going to check out that Japanese place a block over."

She raised her eyebrows to look him over. "But you have to turn it on a bit to go there. No flip-flops or sneakers."

She'd stopped crying anyway. He could work with that.

He winked and gave her his best smile. "Hey, you think I can't turn it on?"

She laughed and leaned her forehead against the glass barrier. "I know you can." She took a deep breath and raised her hand to the other side of the mirror, spreading her fingers flat. "I've missed you," she murmured, her voice breaking slightly.

Thorolf hesitated only a moment before he matched his own hand to hers on his side of the glass. He felt a twinge of guilt because he hadn't really missed her that much. She'd been fun, but not his mate. He had to admit that she wasn't nearly as attractive as Chandra, never mind as intriguing. He'd been marking time.

He'd been messing around with Viv instead of stalking Chen.

He tried not to think of Viv as a distraction.

But she'd been one. There was no escaping that fact. If he'd done as he'd planned when he came to Bangkok, he would have hunted Chen down and finished him off. He would have done right by the *Pyr*, and Erik wouldn't have banished him. He could have achieved something and made a difference.

Sex with Viv hadn't been nearly good enough to give up all of that.

Thorolf hated that he could see the point of his father's argument. He still didn't agree, and he didn't think that what had happened had been right, but there was nothing like a firestorm.

And he'd walked away from his. Thorolf felt like a failure, no matter how he looked at it.

He also had the definite sense that Viv wanted something from him, like she was trying to manipulate him. Maybe Chandra *was* right.

Maybe he should go back and talk to her.

But Viv looked like she'd start to cry again.

"I've missed you, too," he said with a resolve he didn't feel, then looked deeply into her eyes to reassure her. Darkness flickered in their depths, and he shivered in dread.

That made no sense. This was Viv. His lover, friend, room mate and fellow partier. He knew Viv. He trusted Viv.

He really wished she'd stop crying.

Even if he wasn't so sure anymore that he should have trusted her.

Was the firestorm right?

He kept looking, didn't even blink, and he felt the mirror ripple under his hand. He stared more determinedly and Viv stared back, neither of them breathing, as the mirror began to tremble. Viv's eyes brightened and she looked as if she might crack a smile. Thorolf held her gaze, willing her to abandon the tears. The mirror vibrated as if it would shatter at any moment, but he didn't look away.

If he'd been better at beguiling, he might have summoned

flames in his eyes and convinced her to smile. Thorolf stunk at beguiling, though. He'd practiced when he was with the *Pyr*, but he hadn't bothered while hanging out with Viv. Never mind those twenty-two months that were missing out of his life.

He wished, perhaps for the first time, that he'd learned to better use his innate abilities.

He wished he could shake the new idea that Viv had been a distraction.

But now it seemed he couldn't avert his gaze from hers. He felt snared.

When he saw the tear of blood form in the corner of Viv's eye, he didn't believe his own eyes. The mirror began to shake violently. It seemed to be rippling, like the surface of the ocean.

A tear of blood formed in the corner of the other eye, and he fought the power of her gaze. He was mesmerized, though, unable to look away, unable to avoid seeing her transform right in front of him. The mirror's surface bucked under his hand, and he heard the first crack.

Then to his horror, Viv wept tears of blood.

Thorolf seen tears of blood only once before.

In that vision.

The one in which Viv was one of the Erinyes, hunting the *Pyr*.

Chandra was right.

"No!" he shouted, but it was too late. The mirror shattered into a thousand pieces, shards flying everywhere as Viv erupted from its imprisonment.

En route, Viv shifted shape to one of those old women with bat wings. The blood ran down her face onto her sagging breasts and her hair turned to a nest of writhing black snakes. Thorolf stumbled backward over the shards of mirror as she burst forth. He was shocked when she laughed and bared her fangs.

"They do say no good deed goes unpunished," she said, then changed shape to a green serpent that rose from its coiled tail, poised to strike.

It was a huge snake, one that Thorolf had seen before. It hissed and its eyes glittered. Its fangs were enormous and dripping with venom.

Snakes!

He turned to run but the serpent launched itself at him, its substantial weight landing on his back. They fell together, the serpent's tail winding quickly around his legs to trap him. Thorolf struggled as he panicked. He caught the viper's head in his hand and tried to crush its skull. It thrashed in his grip as venom dripped from its sharp fangs. The drop of venom hissed and burned where it landed on his skin. It sent a frisson of heat through his whole body, both electrifying him and paralyzing him.

It *was* happening again.

Thorolf saw the apartment he'd shared with Viv. This was the serpent that had bitten him twenty-two months before.

The serpent that was really Viv.

Chandra hadn't lied to him.

And he'd been too stubborn to believe in the firestorm.

Thorolf rolled and slammed the serpent's head into the ground, just as he had once before. The viper hissed and writhed, more slippery and powerful than he'd expected. Its tail jabbed into his jeans, driving into his genitals so hard that he loosed his grip. It wriggled free, then rose over him. It seemed to laugh, and Thorolf saw a ghost of a gleeful Viv above him.

Then the serpent dove for his throat, fangs bared.

Thorolf recalled the same viper diving for him in the apartment. He knew exactly where it would strike, because he felt the old wound from the fangs burn on his arm.

The instant lasted forever, stretching out to feel longer than it really was, as if the serpent would taunt him with his powerlessness. Thorolf was reminded of a car accident he'd been in once, the whole incident happening in slow motion, inevitable and inescapable. He couldn't do anything, couldn't escape, couldn't shift shape, couldn't save himself. That first drop of venom had immobilized him on contact.

He heard Chandra shout, but her voice could have come from a thousand miles away. "She's mine!" she cried, and he had no doubt she was in her Valkyrie form.

Then the serpent fell on him, crushing him beneath its weight. The fangs sank into the same two wounds on his arm and the wounds burned as the venom poured into his body. Thorolf closed his eyes and would have screamed, but he couldn't make a sound.

This definitely would be his last mistake.

Chandra feared she was too late.

She saw Thorolf fall backward and the serpent poise to strike. She wished for her crossbow, but it was gone forever, thanks to Chen. Instead she had only the knife jammed in her belt. She flung it at the serpent, cursing herself for letting Thorolf be alone for even a moment.

If anyone could find trouble in Myth, it had to be the dragon shifter chosen to save the *Pyr*.

"She's mine!" she shouted, hoping her presence would give Thorolf more encouragement to fight.

He didn't move.

Her knife flashed as it spun end over end. She kept running toward him, determined to wrestle down the serpent and smash its head if necessary. Her shot was sure and the blade sliced the viper's head cleanly from its body. Its body continued to twitch, even as blood spurted from the wound. The serpent became Tisiphone, then Viv, then the snake again. All versions of Viv were decapitated. Only when the body stilled and the shifting stopped did Chandra heave a sigh of relief.

Her quest was completed.

She'd saved the *Pyr* from Tisiphone's vengeance.

She could leave Myth and the mortal realm, get another assignment.

She was shaking when she turned to Thorolf, expecting him to give her a hard time about how long she took. She was ready to give him a hard time for getting into trouble, even in Myth, probably for the last time ever, but the words froze on her lips.

He was out cold.

No, he'd been bitten.

She *had* arrived too late.

Those two holes in his arm were brilliantly red, burning red, swollen and angry. She could see the glisten of venom on the wound and knew it was inside his body as well. She fell to her knees beside him and closed her mouth over the wound. She sucked then spat out venom, repeating the move over and over and over again.

Snow cried out three times in rapid succession, and Chandra recognized her brother's sign. It might be time to leave Myth and this realm, to return to Asgard, but she ignored the bird. She had to help Thorolf. She tried to surround the wound with her hands, keeping the venom from spreading, but she could see that she was failing.

She worked, aware that he was becoming colder with every passing instant. His breathing became more shallow and his heartbeat both slowed and became fainter. She heard Snow make a different cry, but didn't have time to attend the falcon. She put her hand on Thorolf's chest and the silvery radiance of the firestorm sputtered to mere sparks.

She pulled the last arrow from her quiver, worked the point free and discarded the shaft. *Berkana* was the rune carved on this one. She felt it beneath her thumb. A rune sacred to her, a rune symbolic of regeneration and new beginnings. Once again, it was perfect for her purposes. She put it in Thorolf's mouth and held his jaw closed, willing him to take power from the stone.

Was it her imagination that the firestorm flickered with new life?

It must have been because a heartbeat later, Thorolf began to shift shape, rotating between his human and dragon form. Chandra knew that was a sign of distress, but it was better than him being dead. She placed both of her hands on his chest, desperate to revive him. The sparks of the firestorm sputtered and faded to mere embers.

"No! You can't die!"

"But he *will* die," a woman said from beside Chandra. She jumped in shock, then looked up to find Chen beside her in his female guise. The woman in the cheongsam with the red fingernails held Snow's tethers in one hand, while the bird flapped in a futile effort to escape. Chen seemed amused by the falcon's efforts, then turned that cold smile on Chandra. "Even better, he'll die slowly."

"How did you get here?"

"Either you left the door open, or the *Pyr* are a step closer to becoming myths themselves." Chen didn't seem troubled by that possibility.

"Won't that doom you, too?"

The woman laughed lightly. Her eyes were hard, though. "Don't worry about my survival. I have everything I need now."

To Chandra's horror, Thorolf stopped shifting. He remained unconscious and in human form, looking so pale that she feared he really was dead. The tattooed spirals covered his torso and his arms, darkening and thickening of their own accord. Chandra was alarmed to see that his skin would be completely black with the tattoo soon. What skin was still visible became paler and paler. The two marks on his arm from the serpent's bite glowed red, pulsing in a way that was just not right. He looked sepulchral, as far from his usual vital self as possible.

"I've been close enough to taste immortality before. Now I have the last piece of the puzzle." Chen flung Snow into the air, then shifted shape in brilliant blaze of blue.

He was in his dragon form again. His broken horn had healed, and had healed so well that it might never have been injured. He watched her look, then bared his dragon teeth to make a hungry smile. He swept her aside with his tail, then bent and picked up Thorolf, cradling him with the care one would show to an infant. "I doubt we'll meet again," he said and inclined his head to Chandra with a formality that grated on her nerves.

As if she didn't count.

As if she couldn't touch him. Chandra desperately wanted to prove him wrong.

Snow screamed, then circled back toward them with talons extended. It was time for Chandra to go to Asgard before the portal closed.

But Chandra wasn't returning to Asgard. Not this time.

She was going with Thorolf.

She ducked the bird and evaded its grasp. Snow cried and circled around again, swooping low with a gleam in her eye that meant she wouldn't miss this time. Apollo must have instructed the bird to ensure that Chandra wasn't left behind.

When Chen shimmered blue, Chandra guessed that he was going to disappear and spontaneously manifest elsewhere.

He wasn't taking Thorolf without taking her. She leapt toward Chen and locked her arms and legs around Thorolf. Chen screamed but he'd already started to shift through space and time. He wasn't going to forsake his prize, not anymore than Chandra was going to be abandoned. He cuffed her and she kicked him. She held fast to Thorolf though, hoping it wasn't her imagination that she felt his heart skip a beat.

She felt Snow's claws slide through her hair, then the whirlwind caught her up in its dark circuit again. Chandra hung on tightly, certain that if this was the last time she endured this journey, it would be plenty.

She felt suddenly free.

She'd been a hostage in Asgard for so long. She'd been dutiful for so long. She'd done what she was told and pursued what she should. She'd been a mission machine, but now, she was choosing with her heart.

And she was glad.

That was when Chandra realized the full import of her situation. She'd declined Snow's collection of her, which might mean she could never return to Asgard. She might never see those of her kind again. She was surprised by how little it mattered to her. In fact, she felt relieved.

Maybe it was time for a new adventure.

One as the mate of a dragon shape shifter.

Provided she could help him to survive.

One thing was for sure: she was off the map, and there were definitely dragons here.

Spontaneous manifestation wasn't gentle, that was for sure.

They landed hard in a dark cavern, slammed into a stone floor so hard that Chandra knew she'd be bruised from head to toe. The impact didn't awaken Thorolf, which couldn't be a good thing. The flames in the wall torches simultaneously leapt high on all sides, as if welcoming their hero.

Chen. It had to be his lair.

Chen was still in dragon form, his scales shining in the firelight. He snatched Chandra up, then flung her into a cage at the farthest point of the cavern. The firestorm's spark died, and she knew she didn't imagine that he smiled.

"I'll let you watch," he said to her, his eyes shining in

anticipation. "Either my magic will triumph and he'll turn *Slayer*, or he'll die."

Chandra bit her tongue, as much as she wanted to antagonize the old *Slayer*. She managed to look fearful, hoping to feed his confidence that he was winning. She could see the broken arrow lodged between his scales, though. He'd pulled out the shaft and broken it off at some point after their fight, but his scales looked disrupted there. Chandra believed there was even a shard of the arrow head left in his skin.

If there was, she could work with it. Chen wasn't the only one with ancient magic on his side.

He settled back on his haunches, his gaze flicking between her and Thorolf with satisfaction. His golden eyes shone like gems in the night as he breathed slowly, and Chandra knew that he was completely surrounding Thorolf with a dragonsmoke barrier. She crouched in her cage and took stock of the situation.

They were in a cave, clearly, and one that she sensed was far beneath the earth. She had no idea whether it was in Myth or in the realm of mortals, but it didn't matter. It was filled with old magic, dark magic, magic evil enough to make everything inside her clench. It was snatching magic, selfish magic, magic that changed the world and didn't care about the consequences. She preferred more earthy magic, magic that accepted the rhythms of life but encouraged them in chosen directions.

Chen was mortal. He might have longevity, thanks to his nature and to the Elixir, but ultimately, he had to die. It was the rhythm of life.

She would encourage that death to happen sooner.

Chandra didn't like that Thorolf was in the middle of a spiral burned onto the stone floor. It gave her a bad feeling.

That might have been because there was another spiral burned into the floor of the cavern. There was a dragon in the center of it, but he was certainly dead. He looked to be a shell of his former self, a faded husk sucked dry. She wondered who he'd been, and why he'd been sacrificed.

Thorolf still looked dead, and she suspected he was supposed to share the first dragon's fate.

Even given their dire situation, even knowing that she could have left and returned to the other gods, she knew she was in exactly the right place.

The firestorm was right, and she was going to prove it to Thorolf.

She spared a glance to his still figure and hoped she had the chance.

She sat down, with her palms together and the soles of her boots pressed together. She breathed slowly and evenly, conjuring the magic she knew best. She envisioned the rune *Berkana*, carved into the arrow head she'd left in Thorolf's mouth. She envisioned the rune *Eihwaz*, carved into the arrow head she'd jammed beneath Chen's scales. She breathed power into both of them, slowly and deeply, calling to the runes to answer her.

Chandra smiled when Chen winced and his breathing faltered.

There was a strange flicker of light on the far side of the lair, a blue-green light that licked a large oval stone from the underside. Chandra hadn't noticed the stone before, but the light drew her attention to it.

It was shaped like a large egg, but the texture of the stone made it look like it had a wrinkled shell. The light flicked once, quickly, then faded.

Chen surveyed the lair, his suspicion clear. Had he sensed the light? Had he seen it? Was it important somehow? Chandra had to think it was a sign of some kind. It's blue-green color was unusual, and she wondered about darkfire.

She had to concentrate on the magic she knew, though. Chandra called to the rune hidden in Thorolf's mouth once more, putting all her will into the summons.

Thorolf shifted back to dragon form, making the old *Slayer* turn to stare at him.

The blue-green light licked the surface of that egg-shaped stone again, illuminating it like a flash of lightning. For a second, it seemed to be lit from within and Chandra thought she saw a dragon trapped inside the stone.

Then it looked like a rock again.

Chen's head swiveled toward the egg, his concern clear. It had to be darkfire, then, the force of unpredictability. Chandra chose to be encouraged by its presence.

She called to the rune beneath Chen's scales. Chen winced again, then shuddered. He scrabbled with one claw as if to scratch his underside, but Chandra willed the arrow head to move deeper into his body. There was no mistaking his grimace then, but she hid her pleasure.

Chen looked around the lair once more, then put down his chin. His eyes glowed through the slits of his half-closed lids as he began to breathe slowly and regularly.

He was probably breathing dragonsmoke.

He was probably buttressing a spell.

He wasn't the only one. Chandra hadn't lost all of her powers yet, and she'd willingly use them up to see her favorite *Pyr* free of this place.

Thorolf dreamed.

He was crashed on his back, hurting from head to toe, struggling to catch his breath. His skin burned painfully but he could feel the heat of the firestorm. He was glad and not just because its caress drove back the pain. Its silvery radiance, visible even through his eyelids, meant he wasn't alone.

And that they were back in Myth.

"One of these times, you will kill me," he muttered, complaining but not really. He was getting used to having Chandra around.

She leaned over him, her hair falling on his chest. He opened his eyes again to find her smiling down at him. "Don't tempt me."

Her hair was chestnut this time, wavy and falling just past her shoulders. She was wearing a crimson dress that laced across the bodice and a white blouse beneath it, but similar tall boots. He could feel them through the cloth, and guessed that she was always ready to fight. The idea that she'd never really be a damsel in distress made him smile.

He eyed her, then asked what he wanted most to know. "Why *did* you choose me?"

She sighed and laid down beside him on her back, frowning at the star-studded sky. Thorolf impulsively reached over and took her hand, entwining his fingers with hers. The firestorm's heat pulsed through him, drawing them into that beguiling union when their breathing and heartbeats matched. Thorolf closed his eyes, intoxicated with the sensation.

There was something so good about being with her, something so right. Thorolf had to make this work.

He had to undertake her mission.

"It seemed like a good idea at the time," Chandra admitted and Thorolf chuckled at the humor in her voice.

"Why?" When she looked at him, he held her gaze. "Seriously."

She sat up again, bracing herself on her elbow and leaning over him. Thorolf didn't let go of her hand. He wanted to be connected to her like this forever. "In every culture, there are myths," she said. "And every culture creates myths that echo the reality that surrounds them."

"To explain it."

She nodded. "So, while the myths are specific to a place and a people, they have common elements. Maybe we could call them human concerns."

"There are always gods," Thorolf guessed.

Chandra nodded. "There is always something or someone greater than humans, something or someone with the power to be unseen or to influence events. These divinities may have control over life and death, or they might influence wherever it is that people's souls go when the physical body dies. Death, and what happens after it, is always a concern, maybe *the* human concern." She fell silent, drumming her fingers on his chest. Her touch sent a staccato of desire through him, each tap making him want her more.

Thorolf waited while she chose her words.

She met his gaze and he noted that her eyes were brown this time, brown with a circle of gold around the iris. "In every culture, there is a concept of evil, of some wicked force against humans. In the west, it's often presented as a dragon. As a result, in every culture, there is an archetypal hero." She smiled. "A dragon slayer, to defend humans and defeat evil so that peace and justice can reign."

"And that's where I come into it?"

"If you're going to pick a dragon slayer, I think it makes sense to pick one who can fight fire with fire," she said, her eyes glowing. Her fingertips slid down his chest, creating a burning line of desire. Thorolf guessed her destination when her fingers passed his waist. "I think you should pick the strongest and most resilient of all the candidates, the one who comes from a lineage of noble and principled warriors, the one who carries all the traits of a hero in his heart, mind and body."

"But I had just been born when you chose me."

Chandra shook her head. "No, I chose you long before that."

"How could you know?"

"There was a time when I could see past, present and some of the future. There was a time when I saw the man you would become, even when you were just a gleam in your father's eye. In the spark of his firestorm, I saw his son, and I knew that you were the one."

Thorolf winced. "I wish you wouldn't say that."

"But it's true. You are the one. You are the only one who can do this."

"And if I refuse?"

"Then the *Pyr* and the world won't be saved."

"And if I fail?"

She shrugged, her gaze holding his steadily. "I don't think you'll fail. I chose you, after all."

He thought of what she'd said and wondered why he'd fought this for so long. It was just a task. If he'd been chosen, it must be one that he could do. And the fact was that loving Chandra made him want to accomplish more with his life.

He wanted her to have a good reason to choose to be with him.

"You said there was a time," he said, recalling her words. "Does that mean you can't do it anymore?"

She nodded, a sadness touching her features.

"Why not?"

"It's time for the gods to leave the mortal world behind forever."

"But you're Vanir," he protested, hating the idea of losing her.

Chandra shook her head. "Not any more." She smiled. "I decided not to go."

He stared at her, awed that she would make this choice.

For him.

For the firestorm.

"All eras end, Thorolf." Chandra tapped a finger on his chest again, the firestorm's sparks nearly stopping his heart. "Like it or not, it's up to you to make sure this one ends right."

And there it was: the responsibility he wouldn't deny any longer, and the reward of the firestorm. Thorolf knew then, right to his heart and soul, what he had to do.

His father and Chandra had been right all along.

All he had to do was believe in the firestorm and himself.

CHAPTER FOURTEEN

Nobody said that succeeding at this challenge would be easy, though. Thorolf exhaled as he thought of all the forms Chen could take. Then there was Jorge, whatever had happened to him, and a host of other candidates for the source of all wickedness in the world. Now that he'd decided to take on the task, he needed a plan.

He could learn from her, planning ahead instead of charging it and dealing with whatever resulted.

He closed his hand over hers. "Which exactly is the monster I'm supposed to slay?"

"All evil draws from one source," Chandra said. "Strike at the heart and stop it where it begins."

"I'm going to guess that's not too easy."

She smiled. "No challenge worth winning is easy."

Their gazes locked and held for an electric moment. Did she think he was a challenge worth the fight? Thorolf hoped so.

"We're in the right place. That's a good start." Chandra touched her lips to his, making him groan with desire.

He tried to roll her to her back and deepen the kiss, but she slipped from beneath him. "We could just draw some power from the firestorm," he suggested.

"No time," she said and got to her feet. She offered him a hand. "The hunt is already on."

"Any hints? How will I recognize the root of all evil?"

Chandra bit her lip, drawing his gaze to its ripeness. "I'll guess that we'll be working in the myths of your heritage."

"Ragnorak?"

"It's already started to snow heavily in much of the world."

"Fimbulvetr," Thorolf muttered. "The mighty winter."

"The moon has devoured the sun."

"The total eclipse." Thorolf got to his feet, his determination growing as he recognized the signs.

"Nidhug, the dragon chewing beneath the world tree Yggdrasil, will finally bite through its roots and sever the connection between the natural world and its people."

"That would be Chen, I'll guess."

"There have been tidal waves and earthquakes, which are supposed to foretell the end times."

"Because Jormungand has been roused from the bottom of the ocean for the battle at the end of the world. He's thrashing in the seas, making the tidal waves and earthquakes." Thorolf pushed his hand through his hair as he recalled the rest of the story. He remembered these stories of the end times all too well.

Then he thought about the implications of Chandra's choice. "Will this make you mortal?" He paused then asked what he really wanted to know. "Does this mean you'll be able to have my son?"

Chandra's quick smile making his heart leap. "I know of one good way to find out." Her eyes sparkled as she considered him. "You've convinced me that I've kept this vow of chastity long enough."

Thorolf caught her up in his arms and kissed her thoroughly, loving how she gripped his hair in her hands and kissed him back. The firestorm surged through him, driving Chen's poison from his body and filling him with a silvery fire of purpose.

Chandra broke their kiss but smiled down at him, a sensual promise in her eyes. "Maybe fighting for the chance to satisfy your firestorm is the cause you always needed."

"No doubt about it," Thorolf agreed, then he grimaced. "The Midgard Serpent is at the bottom of the sea, right?"

Chandra nodded. "So?"

"This is probably a bad time to admit that I can't swim."

She rapped him on the end of the nose with a playful fingertip. "But an excellent time to learn."

Before he could protest that it wasn't that simple, she broke from his embrace and marched away with purpose. "You'll need your sword!" she called over her shoulder.

Thorolf grimaced. "That's the thing. It's gone forever."

Chandra's backward glance was scornful. "Nothing so powerful is ever gone forever."

"I don't need a sword..."

She spun to face him, her expression resolute. "Trust me on this. You do not want to bite this viper, even in dragon form. He's toxic, through and through. This is *Myth*. This is my turf and I know the rules better than you. Trust me."

"Okay. I do," Thorolf said, and meant it.

Chandra folded her arms across her chest and they faced each other toe-to-toe. Even faced with the challenge ahead, Thorolf felt jubilant. They were going to make an incredible team.

"We need the sword," she reiterated.

"Then let's find it," he replied with resolve and seized her hand. "Come on, let's do this thing already."

Marco was late.

He knew it because the darkfire was crackling with new vigor within the quartz crystal, as if impatient for him to finish what had been started. He surrendered his will to the power trapped in the stone, letting it do with him as it would.

There was no fighting darkfire.

It flashed brilliantly, so bright that he closed his eyes against the light. When he opened them, he was in a cavern, one lit by flaming torches that sent dark smoke against the high ceiling. He glimpsed the back of a dragon that could only be Chen, and not that far away. He felt the icy burn of dragonsmoke and knew he couldn't linger in this place. He was hidden behind a large oval stone, one that seemed to him to have power.

The stone throbbed in his hand, and he understood that it wanted to be broken. He knew the darkfire desired release, and he hesitated only for a second before complying.

This was the destiny of the third crystal.

He cracked the stone in half.

The darkfire leapt toward the oval rock, its blue-green light illuminating its wrinkled surface.

Chen caught his breath and turned just as the light faded away.

But Marco felt a pulse begin within the stone. Maybe it had been there all along, too faint to be discerned, but now it grew in power with every beat. He smelled *Pyr*, as well, a faint scent that he was sure was coming from inside the rock. He had time to run his hands over the stone in awe then the darkfire glittered again and flung him on his way.

He opened his eyes warily to find himself in a bustling market, surrounded by humans. He'd appeared in the shadows of a deserted stall and only a parrot in a cage had taken notice of his arrival.

He'd wait here for whatever happened next.

"Neither rain nor snow nor dark of night," Delaney muttered, as he flew through an apparently endless storm with Brandon. The wind was fierce and the seas tossed violently beneath them. The skies were filled with dark clouds, and lightning shot between them at intervals. They'd flown higher to avoid rain and lower to avoid the wind. They'd flown over the ocean and over islands, the lights of human habitation far beneath them.

The good thing was that in this weather, there would be no one to beguile into believing they hadn't seen dragons overhead. The *Pyr* regularly passed the weight of the sword between them, each taking a break from the burden. It hadn't seemed heavy at the start, but with each mile, its burden seemed to grow.

The journey had improved after they'd left Brandt's lair in Australia as then they'd only had the sword to carry. Liz and the boys had remained with Brandt and Kay by previous arrangement. Erik had been clearly exhausted, that it hadn't taken much to convince him to remain in Australia as another *Pyr* to defend Brandt's lair.

It had been tougher for Delaney to convince Ginger to remain there, because she didn't want to miss anything. He and Brandon were making much better time, even though it had to be the foulest weather Delaney had ever seen.

And it kept getting worse.

Delaney wasn't going to think about Chen calling out the

elements to keep the blade from ever reaching Thorolf.

"We're not exactly the post," Brandon replied.

"Couriers, then."

"Special delivery."

"*Very* special delivery," Delaney replied and they chuckled together. It helped when they joked back and forth a bit. The conversation took Delaney's mind off his aching wings.

And his fear that they'd be too late. He scanned the churning seas below, wishing he recognized some island beneath them. Brandon flew confidently, certain of his direction.

"We have to be getting close," Delaney said.

"Borneo, coming up," Brandon said. "Pretty much halfway."

"Finally!"

"Look at the bright side. At least we haven't had to fight in this weather." As if Brandon's words had conjured an opponent, the silhouette of another dragon appeared against the clouds ahead of them.

Delaney caught his breath and inhaled the scent of the approaching *Pyr*. "Sloane," he said with relief, seeing then the lightning touch the Apothecary's tourmaline scales.

"And Rafferty," Brandon agreed. "I can't see him though."

"He must be in his salamander form."

"Excellent." Brandon grinned. "Something tells me this sword is on its way to wherever Thorolf is."

Thorolf's eyelids fluttered and his skin burned. He grimaced as he opened his eyes, hating that the firestorm was the barest flicker of heat. It was golden, though, as golden as a sunrise, and not completely extinguished.

He'd take encouragement where he could.

He was in a cavern, one that looked familiar. He was in the midst of a spiral burned into the cavern floor and he wasn't alone. He saw the dead dragon in the spiral alongside him, just as he had been when last Thorolf had been in this place.

JP. It was JP.

And it wasn't all bad for there to be one less *Slayer* in the world.

The sight of JP brought it all back. He remembered the serpent biting him. He remembered being collected by Chen and being powerless to do anything about it. He remembered being trapped in this spiral, drugged and pricked, over and over again. He remembered the chill of the Elixir sliding into his body, filling his mind with shadows, even as his hatred of the *Pyr* and his father was fed to new fury. He remembered Chen's smile when the old *Slayer* chose to release him, as well as the conviction that he wasn't going to survive long.

But he had.

Because of the firestorm.

He and Chandra were going to get out of this.

Chen was dozing in front of him in his dragon form, breathing dragonsmoke steadily as his eyes glittered. The torches on the walls of the cave had burned low, their flames mere embers of light. Thorolf remembered that their flames were indicative of Chen's mood, so he guessed the old *Slayer* was partly asleep.

He didn't move, not wanting to awaken Chen before he fully assessed the situation. There was a cage on the far side of the cave, one with a woman sitting in it. She had her head bowed, her hands and her feet pressed together, and was the source of the firestorm's light.

Chandra.

Relief flooded through Thorolf that she wasn't dead.

There was something in his mouth and he surreptitiously had a look. It was the head of one of her arrows, and he guessed that she'd given it to him for a reason. In his dragon form, it was easy enough to swallow it.

When he did so, she glanced up and smiled, her look of approval sending a surge of heat through him.

"She can watch your final transformation," Chen said, and Thorolf turned to find that the old *Slayer* was in his female form. Thorolf thought this was Chen's creepiest form, and not just because he'd tried to seduce Thorolf once in it. She was wearing those incredibly high heels again and that tight Chinese dress that made her look curvy and hot. Her lips were red, her hair twisted up, and her gaze unblinking. She carried a hypodermic syringe and was walking toward him, carefully stepping over the lines of the spiral burned into the ground.

"It was almost done," Chen said. "So very close. But then you carelessly lost a scale, leaving a gap in the new armor I'd so carefully made for you."

Thorolf's hand rose to his chest and he felt a gap in his dragon scales.

"We'll just fill that in," Chen said. "And finish the job for once and for all."

Chandra got to her feet. It wasn't her nature to shout for Chen to stop, but she was watching avidly and poised to fight. Thorolf wished he could have broken her out of that cage.

He thought of the dream he'd just had and wondered if she'd given him that.

Was Chen the source of all evil? He was certainly a good candidate. Thorolf eased back, tentatively trying to shift shape.

He couldn't do it.

He couldn't breathe fire and he hurt from head to talon. He couldn't breathe dragonsmoke either. Chen smiled, clearly aware of his efforts, and Thorolf knew he'd been incapacitated.

"Some fight," he scoffed, resorting to taunts. "You can only defeat me when you've taken away all of my powers."

"Not true," Chen said. "I'm far stronger than you know."

Thorolf laughed. "I can tell." He lowered his head, dropping his chin to the ground in front of Chen's female form. "Is that what the spiral does? Take away my powers?"

"I don't have to explain anything to you."

"Why not?" Thorolf taunted. "Afraid that if you explain how clever you are I'll be able to defeat you?" He mocked the *Slayer*, knowing it would annoy him. "That's confidence. It must be easier to escape this than I'd realized." He looked around, caught Chandra's smile and winked at her.

"You don't have a chance," Chen insisted. "Everything is prepared. Everything is perfect. I will conquer you and possess the element of air, and become the last and final of the legendary dragon kings."

There was a shimmer of blue light. Thorolf caught a glimpse of a yellow salamander, which disappeared as quickly as it had manifested.

Jorge.

He had vanished already.

But to Thorolf's astonishment, Lorenzo stood between him and Chen in his human form. The flames in the torches around the perimeter of the cavern leapt high, just as he'd heard they did during Lorenzo's stage show, and Chen glanced around in surprise.

"But you have just a little bit of doubt," Lorenzo said, his voice pitched low enough to beguile. His back was to Thorolf, but Thorolf recognized the melodic cadence of his words.

"How did you get here?" Chen demanded, scanning the lair with concern. The woman took a deep breath, and even Thorolf could sense that Chen wasn't doing well with this interruption.

Could Lorenzo beguile Chen? Thorolf hadn't imagined it could be done, but if it was possible, Lorenzo was the *Pyr* to call. He stood in front of Thorolf, his stance completely confident.

"Thorolf has escaped you before, after all," Lorenzo said in that same beguiling voice, then strolled toward Chen. "Don't tell me you've forgotten Niall's firestorm? I wasn't there, but I heard all about it..."

Rage lit Chen's eyes and Thorolf knew the fight was on.

Lorenzo felt Chen's disgust and his dismay.

He saw the old *Slayer* hesitate.

Lorenzo didn't trust Jorge, but he trusted Chen less.

The trick was to get this done and then—somehow—get out of here alive. He was hoping that Thorolf's mate would help with that, but now that Jorge had abandoned him here, he had to wonder if a double *Pyr* sacrifice had been Jorge's plan all along.

Either way, he wouldn't let the *Pyr* down.

He wouldn't prove Erik's doubts right.

He wouldn't abandon Cassie.

Lorenzo walked toward the old *Slayer*, deliberately keeping his heart rate steady and slow. He felt as if his entire career had been training for this moment and knew that if Chen caught one whiff of his uncertainty, that doubt would be used against him.

Just as he intended to use Chen's against him.

"Thorolf always escapes you," he said, letting the flames burn bright in his eyes. Chen took a step back, his wariness considerable. "Thorolf always gets away."

"Thorolf has been evasive," Chen admitted, clearly fighting the lure of the spell.

Lorenzo worked the flames harder and deliberately used Chen's own words. "Thorolf has been evasive," he said. Chen caught his breath, looked left and right, then glanced at Lorenzo's eyes. For a heartbeat, he thought he had him snared, then Chen tore his gaze away.

He took another step back in those heels.

The syringe dropped to his side.

Lorenzo followed, keeping the distance between them to about six feet.

"Thorolf has been evasive," he repeated.

"Thorolf has been evasive," Chen said quietly. "Because he's defiant!"

"Because he's a champion," Lorenzo suggested. Chen inhaled sharply and he knew he had it right. "That's why you want him, isn't it? Because he's the key to the puzzle."

"Key," Chen whispered.

"Or the key to the spell?"

The old *Slayer*'s gaze flicked.

"He's the element of air," Lorenzo said and Chen hissed. "He holds an affinity to the last element you need."

"The last element," Chen agreed, his manner hostile.

"But he keeps getting away," Lorenzo said, struggling to hold the attention of the old Slayer. "He evades you. He escapes you."

"He escapes me."

"Maybe he's not meant to be captured," Lorenzo suggested softly. "Maybe you're not meant to win."

Chen shifted shape with a roar, becoming a massive red dragon. Lorenzo shifted in the same moment, taking his own golden dragon form. They both leapt into the air and leapt for each other, locking talons in the traditional manner. Lorenzo bared his teeth to breathe fire, but Chen spun hard. He swung Lorenzo through a dragonsmoke barrier that must have taken centuries to create and the pain nearly finished Lorenzo.

Then it made him mad.

He roared and spewed dragonfire across the floor of the

cavern. To his pleasure, what looked like an impetuous response burned away half of the spiral that was holding Thorolf captive. He could almost feel the other *Pyr* recover his strength.

Before Chen could notice and interfere, Lorenzo spun, turning the flames in his eyes to infernos, and seized the *Slayer* fast. He slammed Chen hard into the roof of the cave and held him captive to his gaze. "You old serpent," he said in his best beguiling voice. "You'll never triumph."

"Never triumph," Chen echoed, some of the fight slipping from his body.

Lorenzo didn't trust him one bit. "Thorolf will never be conquered," he said, wondering all the while if it were true. The other *Pyr* looked terrible.

He had one measure of doubt, and it was all Chen needed. The old *Slayer* came to sudden life in his claws, seizing Lorenzo and slamming him into the cavern walls. They fought hard and fast, holding nothing back, until Chen bit Lorenzo's shoulder. He felt the blood flow and made the mistake of glancing up. He saw the flames in Chen's eyes and tried to look away, but didn't do it fast enough.

"He's all mine," Chen whispered, his own beguiling voice no slouch. "And you're next."

"Next," Lorenzo echoed, then Chen chucked him down into the spiral occupied by the dead dragon. It was JP, Lorenzo noted dully as his body hit the floor. He didn't move but laid there as if finished, not wanting Chen to guess that the fight was far from over.

Lorenzo just needed another plan.

He caught a glimmer of darkfire from the corner of his eye and bit back his smile.

Chandra watched Chen shift shape again, once more becoming the young man she'd fought on the mountain. He picked up the syringe he'd dropped, his gesture savage, then marched toward Thorolf with purpose.

Thorolf looked weak, his scales dark and his movements

sluggish. He moaned quietly, as if he was nearly finished. She'd had hopes with the arrival of the other *Pyr*, but he looked as if he were down for good, as well.

To her dismay, she watched Chen push Thorolf backward. Even in his dragon form, Thorolf fell bonelessly, like a puppy nudged to his back for a tummy rub. She saw the glimmer of blue between his eyelids, though, and dared to hope he wasn't really out cold. Chen surveyed Thorolf's chest, clearly spotted the empty space where a scale was missing, and raised the syringe.

"A hundred little injections," he said with satisfaction. "The last bit of *Slayer* blood to make you mine."

Slayer blood. Chandra understood then why the other dragon had been sacrificed.

Then she remembered why the *Pyr* lost their scales. They became vulnerable when they fell in love. Thorolf had lost his scale after meeting her, which made her heart flutter in a very strange way.

She pressed her palms together, summoning every last increment of her magic, and commanded that sliver of arrow head to move. She envisioned it diving into Chen's gut, severing veins, sliding into organs, becoming septic and killing him slowly. She imagined it actively moving, and when Chen cried out in pain, she knew her powers as a goddess weren't gone yet.

She'd use every last bit of them for her *Pyr*, and not regret the loss.

"You!" Chen cried, pivoting to face her.

"Me," Chandra agreed, getting to her feet. "I'll finish you yet."

"Too late," Chen declared with a smile. "I'll claim him first and be invincible." He turned back to Thorolf, the syringe held high.

But Thorolf wasn't waiting passively to be injected anymore. He was on his feet, his eyes blazing as he bared his teeth to breathe fire. Chen shimmered on the cusp of shifting, but Thorolf smacked him hard with his tail. The blow sent Chen flying to the ground.

The syringe jumped from his grasp, fell to the cavern floor with a rattle, and rolled to a halt. Chen sprang after it in his dragon form, but Thorolf was there first. He smashed the syringe and the dark contents disappeared into the rock by the time he turned to fight Chen.

They didn't bother to lock claws but fought immediately. Chandra watched Thorolf bite into Chen's wing and swing the *Slayer* around. His black blood fell sizzling to the cavern floor, even as the flames leapt higher in sympathy.

Chen roared and fell on Thorolf, tearing into his shoulder. To Chandra's relief, Thorolf's blood was burgundy not black. She'd done that by caressing him. Thorolf rammed Chen into the wall hard enough to make the roof of the cavern crack.

At the same time, that strange egg-shaped stone began to rock on its end. Chen was immediately distracted by its movement, which gave Thorolf a chance to strike him and tear one of his horns. There was a glimmer of blue-green light, again coming from beneath the stone, then it cracked like an egg.

"No!" Chen cried and threw himself toward the stone.

The rock split in half vertically, the two pieces of stone falling away to reveal a pale and weakened dragon trapped within it. He looked up with dazed eyes and shook at the sight of Chen's approach. He was faintly gold, as if his color had faded, and he looked so insubstantial that he might have been a ghost.

Without moving the rest of his body, he reached down behind himself to grab something with one claw from beneath the stone. Chandra realized that Chen couldn't see the move, and she wondered what the dragon had taken. He looked just as vulnerable as before, even fearful as Chen launched himself at the weaker dragon.

"I should have killed you centuries ago," he spat, and lifted a claw to slash at the smaller dragon. "I shouldn't have been sentimental."

The other dragon quaked and cowered, as Chen moved to strike.

But the smaller dragon's hidden claw plunged suddenly upward, driving something deep into Chen's gut so hard that black blood spurted all over the pale dragon. A thirst for vengeance shone in his eyes, and he didn't stop until Chen staggered backward.

A blue-green light pulsed from beneath Chen's scales then.

"The last darkfire crystal," he whispered, his disbelief clear.

"Half of it," the smaller dragon said, driving a second missile into Chen's eye.

Chen fell back with a scream of pain, his black blood spewing from both wounds.

The released dragon spread his wings and from his joyous expression, Chandra was sure it was the first time he'd been able to do so in a long while. He looked bigger then, and more powerful, the color already returning to his scales.

"You could never bear that Father chose his younger son over you," he said, his voice louder than she'd expected. "Your pride blinded you to the fact that he knew you weren't worthy."

"That's a lie!" Chen cried. He reached for the dragon who was evidently his brother, but the pale dragon vanished in a glimmer of blue-green light.

"No!" Chen shouted, but even Chandra could taste his despair.

There was a rumble and the crack overhead widened dangerously, chunks of rock beginning to fall into the cavern. Just how far beneath the mountains were they? Chandra shook the bars of her prison, fearing they wouldn't survive. The floor opened into a massive fissure where Chen's blood had fallen, as if the mountain had disintegrated beneath it. The crevasse gaped wide, even as *Pyr* and *Slayer* filled the space with fire and smoke.

Chandra fell off her feet when Thorolf's tail swept her cage from the floor and cast it into the spiral with Lorenzo. Lorenzo might not have all of his *Pyr* powers but he was still a strong dragon. The other *Pyr* ripped open the bars so that she could escape, then cast her through the air. Thorolf caught her with a grin and she saw his scales brighten at the contact. He passed her to his back, and once again, she held on between his wings.

Chen breathed fire, fighting to the last. Thorolf ducked the flames, then drove his head into the *Slayer*'s belly. They fell to the ground in a tangle of talons and tails, then Thorolf bit Chen in the chest. The *Slayer* moaned and writhed, even as Thorolf spit out the chunk. He ripped the *Slayer* open, but Chen continued to fight even as his black blood ran. Thorolf decked him, then locked his claws around Chen's neck, choking the life out of him. Chen struggled, then he flailed.

"You lose," Thorolf said, his voice pitched low to beguile. "You lose."

"You lose," Lorenzo agreed, from his captivity inside Chen's spiral. "Thorolf always escapes."

Chen cried out in anguish. He fought the pair, but his struggles became weaker. He tried to snatch at Thorolf, but his claws simply slid over the *Pyr*'s hide. He tried to smear his blood into the gap in Thorolf's armor, but he never managed it. He struggled to breathe dragonsmoke, but he didn't have enough air left to do it. He weakened and faded, looking less vital with every passing second.

"Thorolf always escapes," he managed to whisper, and Chandra realized the other *Pyr*'s beguiling had found a conviction to exploit.

There was a shimmer of blue light, one that set the falling stone alight, then a topaz yellow dragon appeared in the space. Unless there were two who were very similar, it was the *Slayer* who'd appeared outside the Garden of the Hesperides.

Chen gasped at the sight of him.

The yellow dragon smiled. "Well done," he said to Lorenzo. "Not exactly as planned, but effective enough." He landed beside Chen and dipped a talon into the *Slayer*'s guts. He sucked the black blood from it with satisfaction. "They say revenge is a dish best served cold, but I like mine still warm."

"No!" Chen moaned, but it was too late to change his fate.

Jorge bent and bit into Chen's guts with satisfaction, his move making Chen groan in pain.

"We made a deal," the golden *Pyr* said with a certain edge.

The yellow *Slayer* laughed, looking up with black blood dripping from his teeth. "Your mistake," he said, then there was an ominous rumble of stone moving.

The three of them looked up as the ceiling of Chen's cavern cracked and chunks of stone fell all around them. The fissure in the floor yawned wide and Chandra feared the worst.

In the city of Bangkok, near the antiquities market, an Asian man suddenly appeared amidst the market stalls. A parrot in a cage squawked in surprise, but no one else seemed to notice. The man's clothing was unusual, in that it was in the fashion of centuries past. He was pale and looked weak, as if he'd suffered from a long illness. His hair was even white, although his face was unlined. He shook a little as he straightened, but he stood on his feet. There was determination in his eyes.

His gaze dropped to the ground and he bent to carefully pick up a dragon scale. It was the color of moonstone and silver, with a black spiral of a tattoo on it.

"He'll need this," he said to no one in particular.

A dark-haired Caucasian man came to stand beside him, his smile so serene that the new arrival found himself smiling back.

After all, they were both *Pyr*.

"Yes, Lee, he will," that man agreed quietly. He put out his hand. "Let me take you to meet the others."

Thorolf burned the spiral surrounding Lorenzo with dragonfire, freeing the other *Pyr* exactly the same way he'd been freed. They exchanged a nod and took flight.

"I'm guessing that wasn't your plan," Thorolf said in old-speak. He was wondering what kind of idiot Lorenzo was to trust Jorge, but the other *Pyr* laughed.

"It was exactly what I knew would happen," Lorenzo said. He lifted a talon, even as chunks of stone bounced off his shoulder. "A perfectly choreographed performance accommodates every eventuality."

"I'm ready for Plan B anytime," Thorolf said, sparing a glance at the falling rock. How were they going to fly out of this place?

There was another of those flickering lights, then an opal salamander gleamed in the dust. He was sitting on the hilt of a sword, his front claw on the Helm of Awe in its pommel.

Thorolf gave a hoot of joy and claimed the sword. Lorenzo snatched at Rafferty as he leapt from the hilt and clutched Thorolf's claw. The blue shimmer enveloped them as Thorolf told Chandra to hang on.

They were immediately flung through space and time once more.

Thorolf landed with a splash in water that was knee-deep. He could feel the heat of the firestorm behind him. He glanced down at the Avenger of the Aesir in his hand, then back at his mate in her Valkyrie form. She grinned at him as he tested the weight of the sword in his hand.

He remembered the balance of it well and recognized how right it felt in his grip.

There was no sign of Lorenzo and Rafferty, much less of human civilization. They were on a beach somewhere cold, a beach rimmed with snow and ice, a cold blue sky arching overhead.

Thorolf locked hands with Chandra, holding the blade high. He'd been made for this, and he was going to do it right. They exchanged a look, then strode into the water together.

The firestorm lit the surface of the water with golden radiance and filled Thorolf with a welcome heat. He was glad to have Chandra by his side. He hoped she remembered that he couldn't swim.

The water stretched endlessly in every direction and they were steadily walking in deeper. It wasn't exactly Thorolf's idea of fun, but he supposed responsibilities were like that. The seas were far from calm, though, the water churning in the distance.

No, it wasn't the water churning.

It was the Midgard Serpent approaching. It swam toward them with such purpose that they could have had a date.

Or maybe a destiny.

It was one big snake.

Thorolf was tempted to shift shape, but then, this sword was supposed to be the key to triumph. He couldn't wield the blade in his dragon form, he wouldn't even be able to hold it properly.

Human form it would be, even if he felt too small and weak. He flicked a glance toward Chandra and she nodded. He told himself that wasn't fear in her eyes. She led the Valkyries, after all.

At least she used to.

He had to hope no one would be collecting his corpse anytime soon.

He thought there were probably a few thousand things he should tell her, just in case.

But Jormungand reached them all too soon. The serpent rode the tide toward them, rearing up high overhead. It was covered in silvery blue scales, twice as thick as he was tall, and too long to see completely. Thorolf remembered that it was supposed to wrap all the way around the middle of the earth, holding its tail in its mouth to make a circle. It had clearly given up that job, just to come and trash his butt.

Its mouth had to be fifty feet wide. Even in dragon form, he would have been puny compared to it, and the sword seemed ridiculously small against such a foe. The incoming wave smashed over them and Thorolf only kept his footing with an effort. He refused to freak when he was surrounded by the ocean water, although losing touch with Chandra didn't help. He struggled upright, dripping wet, and had time to see that Chandra was safely on her feet.

The serpent was focused on him. Jormungand flicked a fin, twisting so that the water swirled around Thorolf and the next wave did pull him off his feet. He heard Chandra shout, but forced his eyes open in the water. He could see the scaled side of the monster and struggled toward it, still holding to the sword.

Why hadn't he ever learned to swim?

The beast heaved, and Thorolf thought it would slam him into the bottom of the ocean. That might have been its plan. He managed to get out of the way, broke the surface and took a gulp of air. It roared and turned on him, but he deliberately dove into the water.

He had to be nuts. He kicked his feet, heading straight for the bottom. He kept his eyes open even in the murky water. Jormungand has stirred up the sand, making him feel that he was lost in a cup of mud. He saw the flash of scales and these ones were paler.

Could he be so lucky that it was Jormungand's belly?

Maybe it was softer.

His lungs were screaming for air, his chest aching, but Thorolf was getting used to pain. He kicked again, was right up against the monster's side, and took his chance.

Thorolf drove the blade into Jormungand. He buried it as deeply as he could, pushing it so that even the hilt was jamming into the flesh.

Jormungand screamed and thrashed. The monster reared back out of the water, carrying Thorolf into the air as he hung on to the sword desperately. He took a deep breath of air, before he was slammed back into the water again. Jormungand fought, like a fish on a line, but Thorolf twisted the blade. He worked the blade in the beast's side, opening the wound and shoved the sword in farther. Could it go deep enough to kill this beast? His entire arm was inside the monster when he was hauled out of the water again, his skin burning.

This time, Jormungand flopped onto the water, blood running from his wound. It was deep crimson this blood, redder than any Thorolf had ever seen before. It was thicker, too, and ran more like honey than blood. Jormungand thrashed again, twisting so hard that Thorolf's arm were expelled from the wound in a rush of blood.

He tried to grab for the blade, but it was out of the question. The monster rolled, Thorolf's hands sliding over his scaled flesh, now covered with blood.

The sword was lost.

Thorolf was flung down so hard that he was left dizzy. To his relief, when the wave receded, he was on his hands and knees in shallow water. Chandra wasn't far away, judging by the firestorm's light. He took a couple of quick breaths, then turned, hoping the monster was dead.

Jormungand was covered in blood but still alive. The monster screamed then snatched at Chandra. Thorolf roared and shifted shape, leaping at the serpent in his dragon form. He breathed fire at the beast, then tore at it with his talons. He kicked the beast in the mouth until it spat out Chandra. He snatched her up, then breathed fire again.

Jormungand roared at Thorolf, the might of his breath and the stench of it sending Thorolf tumbling to the beach. He shoved Chandra behind himself as the monster bore down on him. He'd expected to be bitten, but Jormungand spewed venom at him.

It was vile. The venom was green and so acidic that it burned. It sprayed all over Thorolf, drenching him, and putting him in agonies of pain. That new tattoo could have been sucking it up, drawing it into his body. He shook, trying to get it off his hide, but it eased beneath the scales to his skin.

Then it burned even more. He bit back a scream, determined to defend Chandra to the last. He stumbled and fell to one knee, his wings dropping. Chandra came to him, wiping the venom away with her hands. He stopped her, seeing how red it turned her skin.

To his relief, spewing the venom was the beast's last act. Jormungand fell to the ocean with a splash, then moved no more. That crimson blood stained the water, spreading in every direction, even as the waves lapped at the fallen body.

Thorolf had a heartbeat to feel relief, then the venom reached the spot where he'd lost his scale. The pain was so intense that he thought he was being cooked to death. He thought of Astrid's last moments, hoped he'd set the balance right, then knew no more.

CHAPTER FIFTEEN

It couldn't be.

Chandra couldn't lose Thorolf, not now.

But it was just as the old story foretold. Chandra saw the venom wash over Thorolf. She felt his pain when it slid over his scales. When she saw the bare flesh where he was missing a scale, she feared the worst. She tried to cup her hand over the spot, but the venom burned so badly that it could have been dissolving her flesh.

She'd never felt such pain.

She'd never felt such nausea.

And then the toxin was beneath her hands, running into the chink in his armor, driving straight to the heart of him. Thorolf could have been dipped in tar, he turned so black, then the blackness was running out of his pores like viscous ink. It poured from his body, so much more venom than she realized had even washed over him.

Was it the *Slayer* blood?

Whatever it was, she couldn't stop it. When the flow slowed to a trickle, Thorolf was as pale as ice.

And just as still.

Chandra wasn't sure what had happened. His scales looked brilliant and clear, cut from ice or diamonds. She could hardly look straight at the bright splendor of him. There were no spirals on his scales, and nothing resembling a tattoo. The holes in his forearm from the serpent's bite were still ringed with red, but looked dry. They weren't pulsing anymore. Had the serpent's venom undone Chen's spell?

Chandra might have hoped, but she felt the firestorm fade and feared the worst. Thorolf began to shift between forms without regaining consciousness, shifting from man to dragon and back again with convulsive speed. They were engulfed in a shimmer of pale blue, but even that light was fading steadily.

"No!" Chandra roared. Her protest made no difference.

She tried to summon magic, but felt that there was no response to her appeal.

There was only the dim golden glimmer of the firestorm, but it was diminishing fast. She had to do something, but there weren't many choices.

The firestorm! On impulse, Chandra kissed Thorolf, sealing her mouth to his. She coaxed his reaction, echoing every caress he'd ever given her, feeling the inadequacy of her amorous experience. To her relief, the firestorm's light brightened.

She felt his heartbeat quicken.

She stripped him naked, running her hands over the muscled strength of his body, her lips following her fingers as she caressed him from head to toe.

"Come on, firestorm," she whispered, willing it to grow in power.

Moments later, she saw its silvery gleam flicker between her palms and his body, lighting to a bolder radiance. She repeated her caress, sliding her hands over every inch of him, slowly coaxing the firestorm. His skin warmed. His color improved. His breathing became deeper and more regular, and his heart beat with greater strength. She felt her own body respond, a sexy heat unfurling in her belly, a desire that made her survey him with pleasure. She caressed him ceaselessly and whispered to him, unable to imagine her world without him.

"I love you," she admitted.

Thorolf sighed and turned his head, his hand landing on her shoulder.

He had to have heard her.

Chandra ran her hands across his chest once again, then quickly cast off her own clothes. Even losing that contact for a moment made her worry that she'd lose the progress she'd made, but Thorolf looked to be asleep. His breathing remained the same. She ran her hands over him once more, making sure she guided the firestorm over all of his skin.

He murmured something, a word under his breath. Chandra leaned over him, her hand on his chest, and kissed him again.

The firestorm heated to a silvery blaze, encouraging her as nothing else could have done.

Thorolf's eyes opened the barest slit, but enough that she could see their vivid blue hue. "Firestorm," he murmured, his voice a little louder this time. His hand fell on her shoulder, the weight of his palm sliding up her neck to cup her nape. There was satisfaction in his slow smile, and something about his expression that left her very aware of his dragon nature. His quick downward glance prompted his smile to widen even more and lit a sensual gleam in his eye.

He liked that she was naked.

Chandra liked that they were both naked.

"We did it," he said, a bit of a question in his tone.

"*You* did it," Chandra corrected, bending to brush her lips across his. The firestorm launched a volley of tantalizing sparks, leaving her dizzy.

Thorolf caught his breath. "Surprised?"

"Not at all." Chandra braced herself on his chest. He closed his eyes, clearly savoring the way her hair trailed across his lips. "I always pick champions."

Thorolf grinned, prompting that dimple to make an appearance. Chandra felt her heart thump, even before his hands locked around her waist in a possessive way. "And what do you do with your champions after they've proven themselves?"

Chandra felt herself blush, because she knew exactly what he wanted to do. "Historically, I've given them some token and moved on." She bent and kissed him again, unable to resist the allure of that dimple. She heard him catch his breath and ran her hands over his shoulders, then kissed his earlobe. He practically purred.

"Then you've taken another quest," he guessed and she nodded.

"Always." She kissed him again. "But not anymore."

Thorolf pulled back to look her in the eye. "You're not just messing with me?" he asked, his teasing tone telling her that he knew she wasn't.

Chandra smiled. "Is it so hard to believe that you changed my mind? You can be pretty persuasive."

"You're no slouch there, either." His eyes narrowed as he thought. "Your quest was done when you killed Tisiphone, but you're still here."

"I couldn't leave the firestorm unsatisfied, could I? I have it on very good authority that that's a bad idea."

His eyes twinkled and she loved that he teased her. "How many *Pyr* give you advice?"

"Just one." Chandra took a breath and looked into his eyes. "My destined mate. If I can't trust him, who should I trust?"

He smiled, then sobered, looking at her with wonder. "Did I dream that you said that?" he whispered, his intensity telling her just what he meant.

Chandra felt herself blush. "I think I chose you because I loved you, even then."

Thorolf grinned, the sight of that dimple making her heart skip all over again. "Good thing it's mutual, then," he whispered, running a finger down her cheek. "I love you, Chandra."

She nestled against him, savoring the heat of the firestorm. "Want to do something about it?" she invited, running her toe down his leg. By the speed of his response, she had to be learning a bit more about the art of seduction.

Thorolf gave a hoot of delight and rolled her to her back, his eyes shining as his hand swept down the length of her. "The firestorm," he murmured, his voice low and hot. "It's always right."

Then his mouth locked over hers, his kiss sending fire through her veins. Chandra arched to meet him, knowing that even when the firestorm was satisfied, her need to have this dragon in her life would continue to burn bright.

Thorolf couldn't believe his luck.

Chandra was his mate, chosen for him by the firestorm and the Great Wyvern. She'd decided to remain in his realm just to heal him, even surrendering immortality to be his destined mate.

They'd fought together as a team. They'd triumphed over Chen and fulfilled the quest she'd entrusted to him at his birth. He could return to the *Pyr* proudly and serve with them, Chandra's hand held tightly in his own.

The firestorm had delivered on its promise.

He wanted to be tender with her and take it slow, because he knew that this intimacy was new to her and because he wanted to make it last. She was in her Valkyrie form, her long fair braid hanging over her shoulder, and it was a keen reminder of her identity.

Despite his yearning to go slowly, the firestorm was burning furiously hot, making him want as he never had before. Chandra seemed to feel the same fire, because she returned his kisses with an exciting hunger. He was amazed that she gave him this gift, using the firestorm to make him whole. With every stroke, he felt stronger and healthier, more invincible. The venom seemed to be incinerated within him, destroyed by the healing power of the firestorm.

He unfastened her braid, running his fingers through the golden splendor of her hair. He wanted to remember this moment forever. He teased her nipples again, loving the fullness of her breasts and how perfectly each nestled into his palm. The scent of her arousal was as intoxicating as the most potent drink he'd ever had. He remembered the sweetness of mead and its heady influence, then remembered that honey was sacred to Freya. He fitted his hands around her waist and would have pleasured her with his mouth again, but she stopped him with a touch.

"There has to be more," she whispered, need in her tone. Her hair was strewn beneath her in a blond tangle and her eyes were steely blue. He smiled that she looked both disheveled and ready for battle. He slid up the lean length of her, settling himself between her thighs as he did so. He pushed his fingers into her hair, awed that she had chosen to do this.

Then he wondered.

"Will we even make a son?" he asked.

She smiled. "Isn't that the point of the firestorm?"

"But you're a goddess..."

Chandra shook her head. "Not any more. I'm mortal now."

Her choice still blew Thorolf away. It was epic. "You

shouldn't have done that. You shouldn't have given up your powers."

Chandra smiled. "The alternative wasn't acceptable."

He stared at her, amazed and honored. "No one ever gave up anything that big for me before."

"Maybe they made the mistake of underestimating you," she said with a smile.

"You didn't have to save me."

"Maybe you saved me." Chandra rolled so that she was facing him, and punctuated her words with taps of her fingertip on his chest. Each touch launched a spark, and each spark made his desire heat even more. "You said that you were tired of people saying they loved you because they wanted something from you, that love shouldn't be an exchange. You said you wanted someone to love you for your own self, and that the firestorm was supposed to bring that person to you."

"I did. So?"

She met his gaze. "I understood exactly what you meant. No one ever loves a goddess for her own self. It's all about what that goddess can do for you. It had never occurred to me that things could be different."

"I do love you for your own self," Thorolf admitted.

Chandra flushed a little again, his innocent seductress. "I know."

He ran one hand over her hip, savoring the insistent burn of the firestorm and trying to think straight. "Does that mean you can't shift shape anymore?"

She pursed her lips, considering. "Maybe one last time." She smiled at him. "Do you have a preference?"

Thorolf claimed her lips in a thorough kiss, one that left them both breathing quickly. "I love you," he said, his mouth the merest increment from hers. "And that doesn't change, no matter what you look like. Whatever you choose is good with me."

Her smile was blinding in its brilliance, and her hands locked around his neck to pull him closer. This kiss was hungry and passionate, a kiss that fed the core heat of the firestorm and took it to a fever pitch. When Thorolf opened his eyes, Chandra was the ebony-haired huntress, her blue eyes filled with sparkles. "Your fave?" he asked against her throat.

"It was how we met," she answered, her breath teasing his ear. She parted her thighs and wrapped her legs around his waist. Thorolf sank into the sweet heat of her, dizzy at the feel of her softness closing around him. The firestorm burned like an inferno in his veins, and his body matched its rhythms to hers in that amazing way. He stared into her eyes as they moved together, then she kissed him, drawing him deeper into her embrace, making their union complete. The pleasure consumed him, even as the firestorm burned hotter and hotter, driving him on to heights he'd never reached before. Chandra was right with him, her wonder and pleasure encouraging him to make it last.

He'd been right before: she just might kill him.

But Thorolf couldn't think of a better way to go.

Chandra awakened in Thorolf's embrace. He was wrapped around her from behind, his arms around her waist and his legs entangled with hers. His breath was warm on the back of her neck. She felt surrounded and protected, and she smiled with pleasure.

They were in a bed in a hotel room, perhaps the same one where the *Pyr* had gathered earlier. She rolled over and surveyed Thorolf, very pleased that Chen's tattoo had faded to nothing.

She wasn't really surprised that they were no longer in Myth.

She doubted she'd ever be there again.

She heard the rumble of conversation from the adjoining room, and guessed that the *Pyr* were there. She couldn't discern their words and wondered if they were using old-speak. There was a television turned on, from the sound of it, and she guessed they were watching the news.

She already knew that the mortal world had survived Ragnorak, and that the link between mortal and divine had been severed. She ran a hand over her stomach, liking the thought of Thorolf's son being the first of a new line of *Pyr* for a new world.

She slipped out of Thorolf's embrace and went to the washroom, noticing something in the mirror that tempted her to look closer. Her hair was long and ebony, just as it had been for centuries in this guise, but on her left temple, there was a single silver hair.

That was all the proof she needed. She *was* mortal, just like Thorolf, and she knew from her study of the *Pyr* that his body would match its aging process to hers. The *Pyr* and their mates often passed from the world together, after a long and contented life together.

Chandra was good with that.

She heard the cry of a bird when she returned to the bedroom and was startled to see a silver falcon hovering outside the sliding glass door to the balcony. Chandra knew that peregrine falcons often nested in the towers of skyscrapers, but this wasn't just any falcon.

It was Snow.

She knew because the falcon was carrying a skull.

She hurried to open the door, but Snow had already put the skull down on the balcony. The falcon landed on the railing, then turned to regard her steadily. The noise of the city rose from the streets far below.

Chandra had a sudden fear for her companion. "Can you get back there? Or did my choice compel you to stay, too?"

The bird cried and took flight again, circling once as if to say farewell before she flew straight toward the sun. Chandra watched and she saw her brother in his chariot, framed in its brilliant light, driving the sun across the sky. He lifted a hand and the falcon flew directly to him, landing on his hand.

He'd said he would be last.

Chandra lifted her hand to wave farewell.

She bent and picked up the skull Snow had left, a memory unfolding in her mind with remarkable speed. Centuries before she'd argued with her brother about her vow. She heard him again say that a vow of chastity was unnatural. She smiled at her own reply that he'd certainly never try it. They'd dared each other, as competitive as ever.

"Find me a man who's worth the trouble," she heard herself taunt once again.

She saw her brother's smug grin, then turned to survey Thorolf. He was sitting on the edge of the bed, looking tousled and sleepy. When he smiled, that dimple appeared and her mouth went dry.

Incredibly enough, Apollo had done just that.

"What's up?" he asked, coming to her. His arms encircled her waist and he kissed the side of her neck. Chandra smiled, avoiding the obvious answer.

She gestured to the skull. "A last gift. I thought it was for you but now I'm not sure."

"Why?"

"Because I thought you were the only one with unfinished business."

Thorolf winced. "Not my father."

"I'll guess so."

"I have to tell him he was right?"

"Maybe he wants to say something to you."

"Give me another job probably," Thorolf said with a grimace. He tugged on his jeans and reached for the skull. "You coming?"

"I'm not sure."

Then his hand closed over the skull and she knew the answer. He shimmered before her eyes, the sight of him rippling like the surface of a lake in the wind.

Thorolf was suddenly gone.

Something fell from the skull to the concrete patio. Chandra saw that it was an arrow head. It looked like one of hers. She picked it up, turning it in her hand, and smiled in recognition of the rune etched into it.

Berkana. New beginnings and regeneration.

It was the one she'd put in Thorolf's mouth. She looked up at the sun, knowing her brother had sent it back to her.

She blew the sun a kiss. It seemed to become brighter and she had to close her eyes against it.

And then it was just the sun.

She suspected it always would be now.

Thorolf could have done without a visit to his father, but he supposed there wasn't any way to duck it. He was feeling good about things, about Chandra, his firestorm and his partnership with the *Pyr*. He was feeling as if the future held promise in a new and exciting way, and he didn't want to listen to his father explain that he was wrong.

Much less a disappointing loser of a son.

Thorolf figured he might as well get it over with.

Maybe that was the change Chandra had made in him. He couldn't see the point of avoiding the inevitable anymore. It made more sense to just shoulder through a challenge and get it behind him.

Thorolf supposed he should have anticipated that the skull would take him back to Astrid's village, but it shocked him to be deposited there. He was flying down the valley in his dragon form, but there was no scent of Astrid. There was no fire or ash either, no smell of burning timber.

Although he knew where he was, he had no idea when he was.

Maybe it didn't matter.

He found the spot without even trying. The massive boulder was still there, but the grass was green all around it. The smaller stones were gone and there was no sign of the village. He landed there and shifted shape, his mind full of that last parting.

He jumped at the weight of a hand on his shoulder. He didn't need to turn to know who it was. He took a breath of his father's scent, wood smoke, *Pyr* and virility all mingled into one.

"I'm sorry," his father said gruffly. Of course, he spoke the old language, but it was the first one Thorolf had ever learned.

He turned slightly, halfway expecting the old man to deny his words.

Instead, Thorvald looked as if he doubted his son's response. "I was wrong," he said, his words thick. "She was a treasure, even though she wasn't your mate."

"My mate is the gem in my hoard," Thorolf said.

His father smiled. "It's impossible to know the difference until you feel it. I'm sorry, too, that you had to wait so long for your firestorm."

"I'm sorry you were alone again so quickly after you had yours." The words came quickly, impulsively, without thought, but they were exactly right.

Thorvald's eyes brightened suspiciously, then he offered his hand. "I hope you will tell your son about me," he said, a strange uncertainty in his tone.

That his father could doubt the merit of his legacy was humbling. This was a breach Thorolf had to mend and a mistake he had to fix. He'd been too stubborn for too long.

Thorolf took his father's hand, shook it, then pulled his father into an embrace. He found his own eyes pricking with tears as he held the old man tight. It had been so long.

"I'll teach him everything," he promised, his voice husky. "Just as you taught me."

"I'm so proud of you," Thorvald whispered with heat. "I always told them all that my son would be the one to change the world. And then she picked you to do it." He pulled back and smiled at Thorolf. "I never thought you'd do it so well, though."

They grinned at each other, and all too soon, the scene faded to mist.

Thorolf took a shaking breath, then smiled. He should have listened to Chandra. She'd been totally right, and he couldn't wait to tell her so. He strode into the mist, confident that he'd soon arrive in a familiar place.

He was going to miss Myth and the ghosts.

The bonus was that he had Chandra.

And a son on the way.

It was enough to make a *Pyr* want to celebrate.

Repeatedly and with enthusiasm.

He was pretty sure he knew what Chandra would say about that and quickened his pace. When the fog cleared, he was standing just inside the balcony of the room and the shower was running.

It was a perfect place to start.

He'd no sooner stepped into the steam that filled the bathroom than there was a loud growl from the shower stall. Thorolf could see Chandra standing under the shower spray, poking at her stomach with a fingertip.

"What was that?" Chandra demanded, looking from her body to him in confusion.

Thorolf laughed as he kicked off his clothes. He stepped into the shower, closing the door and drawing her into his arms. "Kismet," he said firmly. "I didn't know it had a sound until just now, but it does."

She laughed with him, but he could see that she didn't entirely understand.

"You're hungry. I'm starving." He kissed her quickly. "It's perfect."

And their union was, but for many more reasons than that.

The *Pyr* gathered at Angkor at the new moon.

Rox couldn't have chosen a better site for a scale repair ceremony.

Thorolf and Chandra were already there, having spent a week exploring the ruins—and the local cuisine—on their own. The *Pyr* who were on the right side of the world flew in from Bangkok in their dragon forms, carrying mates and children over the mountains and jungles.

Rox was sure it was the most romantic dragon flight of her life, and she'd had more than a few. Niall carried her and the boys, and she rubbernecked something fierce, looking ahead at Rafferty and back to Sloane, Erik, and Delaney behind them.

She took careful note of the details, knowing that she'd paint this scene when she got home. She loved these rituals of the *Pyr*. They always felt sacred and powerful to her, and she was honored to be allowed to witness them. Kyle and Nolan, her twin sons from her firestorm with Niall, would be three years old in a week. Although they'd attended scale repairs before, she hugged them tightly and hoped they might remember this one.

It promised to be magical. There was no mist over the mountains, which were covered in thick and dark vegetation, because at this time of year, the days were very hot. The earth seemed to radiate heat even now, long after the sun had set, and the ground looked dry and dusty.

Rox might leave that bit out.

The wind was warm and caressed her skin, blowing through her hair as Niall carried her and the boys to the temple. No one talked, not even in old-speak, making her wonder if everyone else felt this moment was as special as she did.

Rafferty led the way with Melissa in his careful grasp, his opal and gold scales glinting in the darkness. Niall was next—in Rox's biased opinion his hide was the most magnificent, his scales the color of amethyst and silver. Sloane's scales were the hue of tourmalines edged with gold in his dragon form, and his coat shaded over his length from green to purple then gold. Rox could never look at the Apothecary without thinking of the tattoo she'd done for him, of two dragons wrapped around a staff, a twist so to speak on a the caduceus favored by humans.

Delaney was next, carrying Ginger. Delaney's scales were emerald with copper. Rox was glad he'd returned to Australia to get Ginger, but she knew it hadn't been easy for Ginger to leave their boys at Erik's lair in Chicago. Liam was five and becoming independent, but Sean wasn't quite two.

She doubted she'd be ready any time soon to leave her boys behind when she and Niall came to a firestorm, even for their own safety. Rox thought young *Pyr* were safest with their fathers.

Behind Delaney was Brandt, carrying his mate Kay, flying beside his son Brandon. Kay carried her newest grandson, while Brandon's mate Liz carried the older boy, who was the result of their firestorm. Brandt's scales were amber, golden amber lit by the sun, and Brandon's were dark as jet, with fiery edges. His scales always made Rox think of lava simmering beneath a dark crust.

Erik, who flew alone, was last, his scales an onyx as dark as the night sky with pewter edges. The *Pyr* flew silently, circling the ancient site before landing in order.

Rox heard a rumble of old-speak before Kyle pointed to the couple standing on the lip of a large rectangular reflecting pool. It was Thorolf and Chandra, waiting hand in hand. Rox smiled at the sight, knowing that T was finally happy and grounded.

Because of his firestorm, of course. As much as she adored dragons and as fond as she was of T, a firestorm was one thing she couldn't have given him.

The two of them looked like characters from an old saga, both tall and muscular, both majestic and beautiful. They wouldn't just stand taller than most in the crowd, they'd draw the attention of everyone in the vicinity. There was an energy between them, too, a force of attraction that hadn't been extinguished with the firestorm's spark.

She watched Thorolf kiss Chandra's hand and decided that

love was good for her old friend. Thorolf then cast out his hands and a shimmering blue light surrounded him. He shifted shape, taking his dragon form, and his scales were more brilliant than the moonlight. She'd always thought his scales looked like moonstones set in silver, but now they shone like diamonds lit from within. He looked bigger and stronger now, too, although he'd always been magnificent.

He looked like a dragon bred of a long line of champions.

The *Pyr* landed one at a time, flanking the new couple, folding back their wings and remaining in their dragon forms.

"First," Rafferty said solemnly. "A small matter of business."

Only Erik appeared to be confused about this, which gave Rox a clue as to what was going on. Rafferty bowed deeply, then took flight over the pool, pausing before Erik.

"We took that vote," he said and Erik remained watchful but impassive. "You won the leadership again."

"You don't have to do this," Erik protested.

"We do," Thorolf insisted. "Because it's right."

Rafferty and Erik eyed each other for a moment, then embraced, opal scales against ebony ones. Rox blinked back tears, the sight reminding her of Rafferty's ring, then the pair parted and Rafferty took his place with Melissa again.

Erik took a low turn over the still reflecting pond, his wings stirring a ripple on its surface. Rox thought he'd done a triumphant lap, but after the ripple on the surface, the reflections weren't what she expected to see.

She saw Quinn, the Smith of the *Pyr*, where Thorolf's reflection should have been. His scales were sapphire and steel, and his mate, Sara, the Seer of the *Pyr*, stood beside him. Their sons were with her, Garrett who had just turned six, Ewan at three and the baby, Thierry, in Sara's arms.

"It worked," Quinn said in his usual thoughtful manner, his deep voice as audible as if he were standing there.

Erik chuckled as he landed alongside the others. "There's magic in the air tonight," he acknowledged. "The scrying is particularly good." He gestured to his own reflection, or to the place where his reflection should have been. Rox saw his mate Eileen in the dark mirror of the pond, her hands on the shoulders of their daughter Zöe. Zöe would be six this year, as well, taking her dark hair and maybe her intensity from her father. Rox refused to think about the only female *Pyr* having lost all indicating signs that she might be the new Wyvern.

Rox looked down the reflecting pool and saw Donovan opposite Delaney, his lapis lazuli and silver scales shining almost as brightly as the pearl in his own repaired scale. His mate, Alex, was with him, along with Nick, who would be six within a few weeks, and Darcy who was also three.

Rafferty's adopted daughter Isabelle, the oldest of all the children by a few months, was mirrored opposite Rafferty and Melissa. Melissa fell to her knees and reached out her hand, smiling as their daughter raised her own hand to match. Some of the *Pyr*—including Rafferty—believed that the soul of Sophie, the lost Wyvern, had taken the form of this little girl, and every time Rox saw Isabelle, she hoped it was true.

Lorenzo appeared in the lake, opposite Sloane, his scales gleaming in shades of tri-color gold and cabuchon gems. His mate, Cassie was pregnant again, their toddler in Lorenzo's arms. Lorenzo had returned to Venice after his battle with Chen to ensure her safety. Rox knew they had to be in Italy and guessed from the protective look in Lorenzo's eyes that even the Dragon Legion in his lair hadn't been enough to convince him to stay for Thorolf's scale repair.

A blue green light flickered across the surface of the water and Marco, the Sleeper, appeared opposite Brandt, his figure more shadowy than usual, as if he were hidden in the depths of the dark water.

Finally, Drake appeared opposite Niall, as dark and inscrutable as ever. He looked with approval at Thorolf though and inclined his head at the other *Pyr* in respect. Rox guessed that he felt responsible for Tisiphone's quest for vengeance, since it had been one of his men who had assaulted her centuries before.

She realized that there were seven *Pyr* standing alongside the reflecting pool, which had to be a magical number. The water rippled again and the ranks of the Dragon Legion filled the pond, that remarkable surge in the population of the *Pyr* that were the result of Drake's adventures with the darkfire crystal. Rox knew she didn't imagine that he caught his breath as he looked over them, his eyes narrowed slightly with pride.

There was a murmur of old-speak that sounded like a single pulse of thunder to Rox. The *Pyr* looked up as one as another dragon flew closer. He glittered gold, red on his scales and his talons, with pale feathers streaming behind him. Lee still had color and strength to regain, but he was beautiful and exotic.

He hovered before Thorolf and presented that *Pyr*'s missing scale with a bow.

Thorolf accepted it with an answering bow. "Thank you, Lee."

The newest member of the *Pyr* backed up, remaining in flight over the still water. Rox had a lump in her throat, given what he'd endured because of Chen's jealousy.

"We gather to heal one of our own," Quinn said and the other *Pyr* raised their wings high. He breathed dragonfire into a small jeweler's forge. The flames shone in the depths of the pool, but also rose as if the fire sat on the surface. Rox caught her breath as its golden light touched the scales of the gathered *Pyr*, making them look like the jeweled treasures she knew them to be. They were virtually motionless and she ran a hand over Niall to reassure herself that she wasn't dreaming.

He caught her hand gently in his claw, gave her fingers a squeeze, and lifted her hand to his chest. She felt his own repaired scale, along with the gift she'd given him to see it done. She also felt the beat of his heart beneath her palm.

Quinn breathed more dragonfire on his forge, the flame heating to silver in its brilliance. He reached up with one claw and to Rox's surprise, his talon passed through the water, as if the surface was a portal to another world. Thorolf surrendered the loose scale to him, and Rox caught her breath as Quinn took it to his side of the barrier. He heated it, that spiral glowing with dark malice.

Would it make T sick again?

Chandra leaned forward to address Quinn. "You need a gift from me," she said softly. "Let me give it to you."

She offered an arrow head with the rune carved in it to Quinn, holding it out in her bare hands to the flame Quinn had conjured. Rox had heard all about Chandra's past and her runes. Still she wasn't sure what to expect, but Quinn coaxed the fire to burn hotter. White flames erupted from the surface of the water to lick the stone in Chandra's hands. The arrow head heated to white.

Chandra caught her breath in pain and Rox saw three tears fall to the water.

They were gold, though, instead of clear.

Quinn laughed with delight as he caught them, and his claws came through the surface of the water.

Thorolf caught his breath in awe. "Tears of amber," he whispered.

Chandra flashed him a smile. "Probably the last ones," she said. "I'm fresh out of magic."

"You won't regret surrendering it for me," Thorolf said with a vehemence that made Rox shiver. She'd always known that if he came to care for anything, his love would be potent stuff.

Quinn worked the teardrops of amber into the surface of the scale with his usual dexterity and Rox could see how proud he was of his work. Thorolf took flight, then hovered low over the surface of the water, the brightness of his reflection making Rox narrow her eyes.

"Fire!" Quinn declared and pressed the arrow head into the gap in Thorolf's armor. Rox knew that fire was one of Thorolf's affinities. Thorolf tipped his head back, grimacing at the pain, then blew a plume of dragonfire over the pool.

"Air!" the *Pyr* cried in unison, for this was Thorolf's other affinity. Chandra blew on the repaired scale.

"Water!" Quinn said, running a talon over the amber tears that Chandra had shed.

Thorolf scooped up his mate, his manner triumphant. "And earth," Chandra concluded, her voice both practical and sultry. She folded her hands over the repaired scale, obscuring it from view. She then kissed his face before lifting her hands away. The scale shone on his chest, the amber tears like jewels on its surface.

And the dark swirl completely gone.

"The final gift of the firestorm," Niall murmured, and Rox knew it was true.

Thorolf shimmered blue once again, landing in his human form to kiss Chandra soundly. The other *Pyr* shifted shape right after him, and Rox wasn't the only mate to receive a celebratory kiss after Thorolf's healing. She might not be the only one thinking about celebrating a little bit more, dragon style.

Niall winked at her when he broke their kiss, and Rox knew

she wasn't.

"Another son," she whispered to him. "Tonight's the night." Niall's answering grin made her heart skip a beat, and Rox knew that was one thing that would never ever change.

THE PYR: THE NEXT GENERATION

A number of firestorms (never mind a lot of *Pyr* committing to their mates for the long term) means a growing list of sons born to our favorite dragon shape shifters. Here's a list of the next generation so far.

This list is also included on my website and will be updated with new firestorms. There's also a new page there about eclipses and the Dragon's Tail.

Kiss of Fire
Quinn Tyrrell and Sara Keegan
Firestorm sparked March 3, 2007 (but Quinn and Sara didn't meet until the following July)
Garrett—April 16, 2008
Ewan—February 21, 2011
Thierry—June 11, 2012
*(Sara pregnant again in **Serpent's Kiss**.)*

Kiss of Fury
Donovan Shea and Alexandra Madison
Firestorm sparked August 28, 2007
Nick—May 10, 2008
Darcy—August 4, 2011

Kiss of Fate
Erik Sorensson and Eileen Grosvenor
Firestorm sparked Feb 21, 2008
Zöe—November 16, 2008
(Zöe's coming of age as the new Wyvern of the Pyr *is recounted in the paranormal young adult trilogy, **The Dragon Diaries**. Nick Shea, Liam Shea and Garrett Tyrrell also feature in this series.)*

Winter Kiss
Delaney Shea and Ginger Sinclair

Firestorm sparked February 9, 2009
Liam—November 23, 2009
Sean—May 14, 2012

Whisper Kiss
Niall Talbot and Rox Kincaid
Firestorm sparked June 26, 2010
Kyle and Nolan—April 28, 2011

Darkfire Kiss
Rafferty Powell and Melissa Smith
Firestorm sparked December 21, 2010
Isabelle—March 5, 2008 is their adopted daughter

Flashfire
Lorenzo de Fiore and Cassie Redmond
Firestorm sparked June 15, 2011
Antonio—March 27, 2012
Bartholomew due May 2014

Ember's Kiss
Brandon Merrick and Liz Barrett
Firestorm sparked December 10, 2011
Christopher—September 16, 2012
Andrew—January 7, 2014

And more to come...

Ready for more Dragonfire?

Read on for an excerpt from

FIRESTORM FOREVER

The Final Dragonfire Novel

October 8, 2014—California

Sloane Forbes, the Apothecary of the *Pyr*, was frustrated.

He was exhausted by his efforts to find a cure for the plague ravaging the Pacific Northwest and knew he'd spent more hours in his lab than were healthy. He was discouraged, though, because he'd made so little progress. Every time he thought he had a good lead, it came to a dead end, and he had to start over again.

Yet another one was in the petri dish in front of him. This vaccine had showed promise, killing the virus as he watched through the microscope. Within minutes, though, the tables had turned and the ridiculously efficient virus was encircling and destroying the antidote that should have finished it.

Sloane grimaced and shut down the lights. He sealed up the lab, ensuring that the virus was contained. He had a smaller version of a lab designed for working with Level 4 biohazards, buried into the hill under his house. He followed all the CDC protocol in locking up and cleansing himself, then wearily climbed the stairs to the basement of his house. He was nude, but it didn't matter. The house was sealed from human eyes, and the dragonsmoke barriers were piled thick against curious dragon shifters.

The fact was that while Sloane searched ineffectively for a cure, people were dying. That knowledge burned. It was the responsibility of the *Pyr* to defend the treasures of the earth, which included humans, so he felt like a failure. That this malady had been brought from the ancient world by one of his own—well, by

Jorge, a *Slayer* but still a dragon shifter—only multiplied his sense of duty.

The weather didn't help. It had been hot and dry since spring, as it seldom had been in this part of California before. Reservoirs were drying up and the land was parched. Heat made Sloane irritable and he missed the breezes that used to slip down from the hills here. He'd chosen this location because of its temperate weather and didn't like finding that he was living in a virtual desert.

He reached the kitchen and opened a beer. The sight of his swimming pool sparkling in the moonlight sent another pang of guilt through him. Denying the local kids their usual access to his pool in summer—because of his secret possession of the virus that spread the plague from Seattle—only made him more annoyed. He was trying to be cautious and responsible, but knew that everyone in the valley thought he was a selfish prick, given the weather.

He put the barely tasted beer down on the counter and strode into the yard. He dove into the pool and began to swim laps, working his body furiously.

If nothing else, he'd make sure he slept.

The worst of the worst was that there would be another full moon on this night, and another lunar eclipse. That meant there probably would be another firestorm, and another *Pyr* would feel the spark light that identified his destined mate. Sloane had always been patient about the firestorm, trusting that his time would come, but his patience was disappearing fast. He realized that he'd always assumed he'd have his firestorm before the end of the Dragon's Tail cycle of eclipses.

Once it had seemed as if the Great Wyvern were steadily working her way through the ranks of the remaining *Pyr*, and that his own firestorm had to be soon. Now, there were dozens of new Pyr, thanks to the darkfire crystal and Drake's adventures in the past. The odds were skewed decidedly against any of them.

Thorolf had had his firestorm in April. There would be an eclipse tonight, another in April 2015 and the final eclipse of the cycle next September. Only three left, before the fate of the *Pyr* was decided forever.

Sloane was beginning to feel as if he were being punished for his failure to solve the riddle of the plague.

The presence of his new neighbor made him resent the fact that he couldn't choose his own mate. He turned underwater and roared through another pair of laps. Samantha was exactly the kind of woman he'd have chosen for himself. She was blonde and delicately built, but clever and sensitive. She was feminine but pragmatic, too, which had to be the most enticing combination.

He'd met her when she'd come to buy herbs from his greenhouse. She was a tarot card reader who sometimes cast spells with herbs for her clients. She had a secret, though—Sloane could smell it on her—and a vulnerability that got him right where he lived. The thing was that until he had his firestorm, he couldn't promise anything more than a short fling to any woman. He sensed that Sam needed more than that, and plowed through another half dozen laps disliking that he didn't have more to offer.

The moon moved, the first shadow of the eclipse touching its radiant glow.

Sloane swam harder.

He closed his eyes as a firestorm sparked, his heart sinking with the realization that it wasn't his. He reached the end of the pool with a growl, pulled himself up out of the water, then caught a whiff of roses and lavender.

Sam's perfume.

She was standing at the gate, watching him with care.

Sloane froze, braced on the side of the pool, and stared, transfixed. It was as if he had conjured her out of nothing, willing her to appear. He halfway thought she was a vision, but he could smell her hesitation and her uncertainty. He saw her swallow and wanted to reassure her.

No, he wanted to protect her forever from whatever she feared.

And he wanted to spend the night making love to her first.

Sam evidently took his silence as agreement, because she opened the gate and stepped into the paved yard. She slipped out of her flip-flops and eased the linen shirt from her shoulders. She was wearing a bikini so small that Sloane's mouth went dry. She flicked a glance at him, then smiled as she unfastened the clasp in the middle of the top. She bared her breasts to the moonlight, then slipped out of the bikini bottom. Sloane could have been turned to stone.

She walked toward him and he told himself he had to be

dreaming. The moonlight made her skin look silver and her eyes luminous. She sat down on the lip of the pool beside him and put her feet into the water. She smiled, licked her lips, then touched his shoulder.

"I was so hot," she whispered, her gaze clinging to his. He didn't dare survey her again, because he didn't want to spook her, but he could see the patina of perspiration on her upper lip. He wanted to kiss it off. "It made me think of you," she admitted, and her words astonished him.

She wasn't lying.

So, he wasn't going to.

"I was just thinking of you," Sloane admitted and she smiled with pleasure.

"But you're too much of a gentleman to have done anything about it," she charged, then shook her head.

Sloane might defended himself, but she was right. He wouldn't have gone knocking at her door on a moonlit night, no matter how much he wanted to do so.

"Is that why you were swimming laps so hard?"

Sloane dipped his head and grinned that she'd guessed at least part of the reason for his frustration. "Caught," he murmured, daring to look into her eyes once more.

She was pleased by that and her eyes started to sparkle. She looked good enough to eat, but whatever happened had to be her choice. Sloane was keenly aware of that vulnerability, an indication of an emotional wound, and wanted to heal her more than anything in the world. He sensed she was trying to make a change, to move past something, and he wanted to help.

Which meant he had to wait.

He wasn't sure how long they stared into each other's eyes before Sam reached out and touched his mouth with her fingertip. "I'm hoping you're not too much of a gentleman to do something about this," she whispered, then bent closer and replaced her fingertip with her mouth.

Her lips were soft and sweet, her kiss gentle, her scent beguiling him as little else could have done. Her mix of boldness and vulnerability kicked all of Sloane's desires into overdrive. Before he could think twice—much less be cautious and responsible—she was in his arms and he was slanting his mouth over hers, deepening his kiss.

A firestorm sparked somewhere, sending a spark of fire through Sloane's veins.

It wasn't his firestorm. It might have been a thousand miles away.

And the funny thing was, Sloane no longer cared.

Watch for

FIRESTORM FOREVER

The Final Dragonfire Novel

Coming Soon!

Deborah Cooke sold her first book in 1992, a medieval romance called *The Romance of the Rose* published under her pseudonym Claire Delacroix. Since then, she has published over fifty novels in a wide variety of sub-genres, including historical romance, contemporary romance, paranormal romance, fantasy romance, time travel romance, women's fiction, paranormal young adult and fantasy with romantic elements. She has published under the names Claire Delacroix, Claire Cross and Deborah Cooke. *The Beauty*, part of her successful Bride Quest series of historical romances, was her first title to land on the New York Times List of Bestselling Books. Her books routinely appear on other bestseller lists and have won numerous awards. In 2009, she was the writer-in-residence at the Toronto Public Library, the first time the library has hosted a residency focused on the romance genre. In 2012, she was honored to receive the Romance Writers of America's Mentor of the Year Award.

Currently, she writes the Dragonfire series of paranormal romances featuring dragon shape shifter heroes under the name Deborah Cooke. She also is writing the True Love Brides series of medieval romances as Claire Delacroix, which continues the story of the family introduced in her popular title *The Beauty Bride*. Deborah lives in Canada with her husband and family, as well as far too many unfinished knitting projects.

SUBSCRIBE TO DEBORAH'S MONTHLY READER NEWSLETTER:
http://eepurl.com/reIuD

VISIT DEBORAH'S WEBSITES:
www.deborahcooke.com
www.delacroix.net

LIKE DEBORAH'S FACEBOOK PAGES:
www.facebook.com/AuthorDeborahCookeFanPage
www.facebook.com/AuthorClaireDelacroix

Made in the USA
San Bernardino, CA
07 September 2014